AMERICAN HOMEMAKER

JOHN KAINE

Published by John Kaine
ISBN: 9781916488410

Book design by Guido Henkel

For Charmaine

ONE

KIM LOOMIS SCANNED THE FACES OF THE ASSEMBLED members of the fledgling Homemakers Association of Vermont (HAV): Brooke Draper, Paige Gardner, and Megan Hawkins. Kim was the association's founder and self-appointed president, and had made a promise to all three women that elections for the post would be held as membership—by invitation only—increased. And she was waiting for an answer to her question: What was the best method for cleaning a dirty microwave? She stood, hands on her hips. The silence in the great room of Loomis Hall grew as the homemakers pondered the answer.

The women were gathered at the head of a long table, their steaming peppermint tea forgotten. An oil-on-canvas gilt-framed portrait of Martha Stewart watched from her perch above the fireplace. The great room was paneled in dark wood from floor to ceiling, and the lights recessed in the walls burned even during the day. The hammerbeam trusses were crafted from Douglas fir, and Megan recalled Kim explaining with obvious relish how the frames were constructed with mortise and tenon joints, secured with hardwood pegs. Megan didn't know what mortise and tenon joints were, and didn't care. She just wished she'd thought to have them installed in her own home first.

Megan had accepted the invitation to join HAV out of simple curiosity. The homemaking skills they were discussing, and supposedly mastering, were performed by her domestic help. She employed two cleaners, a gardener, and a housekeeper, information she felt no pressing need to share with anyone, least of all the Loomis woman. Who did she think she was, anyway? And why was she dressed in a red Chanel mini dress with crew neckline? And Christian Louboutin nude Pigalle heels? What kind of homemaker dressed in such godless fashion? Kim was a mortician and should wear clothes befitting one. It was undignified, strutting around in whore heels and sullying her profession with her big-brand slutty short dress. What must her husband, Norman, think when she left the house looking like a Rodeo Drive bimbo? Did Kim think she was superior because she had a job and earned her own money? Megan supported her husband with his business ventures, and surely that was worth paying for. Was that the main reason she disliked the Loomis woman? The way she flaunted her success was...unseemly. Yes, that was the word she was looking for. *Unseemly*. Kim Loomis had the confidence of the self-made woman, and Megan Hawkins didn't like it.

She *had* been curious about the Loomis woman's little club, but Megan hadn't expected to become firm friends with Brooke and Paige. Brooke was twenty-five and Paige was a year older. They were both sincere in their efforts to become better homemakers. The Loomis woman on the other hand...she hadn't figured out who Kim was yet.

"Okay," Kim said, "let me explain how I do it. The best method for cleaning a dirty microwave is to fill a bowl halfway with water, add a tablespoon or two of white vinegar, turn the microwave on for six minutes, then use paper towels to wipe down the inside. Wash the glass turntable either in the sink or dishwasher. And there you have it—a tried-and-true method for cleaning your microwave."

Paige and Brooke applauded. Megan sniffed hard and folded her arms across her chest. She shifted in the chair and glanced around the great room. Again, she was struck by the idea that all of this was owned by the young confident woman presiding over them. It had hurt her in ways she couldn't articulate when Brooke and Paige had applauded. Did her friends aspire to emulate Kim? Perhaps. And why wouldn't they? Miss Chanel mini dress worked *and* she was a homemaker. Megan couldn't accept that Kim could take the vocation of homemaking seriously *and* work. To do anything well you had to commit yourself fully to the task.

"I use lemons," Megan said, and a hush fell in the great room. "I cut the lemon in half, place the two halves face down in a little water on a plate. A tablespoon should be enough. Turn the microwave on for a minute to get the lemon hot, and a little steam will build up. Clean the inside with kitchen paper and wash the turntable in the sink. I find that washing by hand gives you the assurance you've cleaned it properly. Also, lemon smells better than vinegar." Megan settled into the chair, hands intertwined on her midriff, satisfied, like a lioness after a successful hunt.

The silence was broken by spontaneous applause from Brooke and Paige. Kim stared at her, a weak smile gathering strength on her mouth. Then she began to applaud, too. Megan was stunned.

"Very good, Meg," Kim said. "We're so grateful to have the benefit of your experience."

What does she mean? Megan thought. *Is she saying I'm old?*

"Whatever suits you guys," Kim said. "Or whatever agrees with your olfactory senses, go with it. In honor of our senior member, let's have some banana cake."

She's doing it on purpose. Megan was furious. *She just called me old right to my face…Bitch.*

7

TWO

MELODY MORGAN DRAGGED THE BODY ACROSS THE PALE marble floor. The heels of the dead man's shoes squeaked in a rapidly spreading pool of blood, leaving twin tracks in his wake.

She dug her heels into the slippery marble and leaned her weight backward to move the hedge-fund manager she'd shot seconds earlier. She wished she hadn't worn the blue velvet Manolo Blahnik high heels on this job. Now the stilettos would have to be burned. A fine spray of blood dotted the crystal-embellished buckles on both shoes. She considered going barefoot—it would be easier to haul the corpse to the utility room—but was afraid she'd leave her DNA behind even after she cleaned up. There was always a chance she'd miss a spot.

If there'd been curtains on the large bay window she wouldn't have bothered moving the body. But anyone passing in a truck on Meadow Lane could see over the tall hedges that bordered the property. What kind of people didn't have drapes? The kind who wanted to display the enormous chandelier that hung from the living-room ceiling...what the hedge-fund manager and his ilk would no doubt call a *drawing* room. Whatever the case, the house was unusual in that it wasn't set far back from the road like the others along the five-mile stretch of billionaires' row.

Sweating, legs apart, black dress riding high on her thighs, Melody gripped his wrists and pulled. She reminded herself that she'd trained for such a contingency. All those hours in the gym had been worth it. If things went wrong, manual labor could put them right again. Moving dead bodies was hard work. Charles Shaker must weigh two hundred and fifty pounds. At least. Her neck and back muscles strained, and Shaker's suit whispered on the polished marble.

In the foyer, an ornate staircase meandered high up toward the upper floors. She concentrated, sensing she was nearing the utility room. Progress was slow, and Shaker seemed to have gained thirty pounds since she'd started dragging him.

Earlier

Melody parked the white Chevrolet Express cargo van outside the Shaker residence, despite the NO PARKING signs spread at intervals on the grass verge; most of the mansions on Meadow Lane had them. The road wasn't busy. She'd sat there for twenty minutes and not a single vehicle passed her in either direction. Of course, that didn't mean a car wouldn't drive by while she was inside. She couldn't see the house; she was parked right next to the tall, full hedges, collecting her thoughts. Even after twenty-six successfully executed contracts, she wasn't immune to nerves. It was a positive sign. If she wasn't nervous, she was getting complacent, which would increase her chances of making a mistake. In her line of work, mistakes sent people to prison for life.

She unlatched the glove compartment and removed the keys and a fob for the gate that her client had given her. She started the engine and rolled slowly up to the white gates, then pressed a button on the fob. The short driveway led her past boxwood shrubs in large terracotta pots. The white shingled façade of the residence gleamed in the early-morning July sun. The windows were sandwiched between black shutters, and as she took in the details of the mansion, Sammy nuzzled her hand.

She patted the pug on the head and caressed his dark face. "Okay, Sam, I have to work. I won't be long so be a good boy while Mommy keeps us in fine dog treats. Understand?" Sammy tilted his head. "Sure you do. Be good and I'll take you for a walk later."

Sammy's ears twitched at the promise and his wet tongue flapped with excitement.

She opened the driver's and passenger windows halfway and went to the rear of the van, slid two rolls of thick-gauge polyethylene plastic sheeting from underneath the sanitary bulk-handling truck, and dropped a roll of duct tape and some scissors into the wide pocket on the front of her yellow-and-black cleaning smock. The decal above her breast, SPIC N SPAN CLEANING, matched the one on both sides of the van. Melody thought it was as good a ruse as any. Who noticed the cleaner?

She stretched a blue hairnet over her head, the kind worn by surgeons, tucked the blonde strands under the elastic folds, and went inside.

She hurried through the foyer and power walked further into the house. After she'd found the utility room behind the kitchen, she unrolled the plastic sheeting and looked up at the ceiling. It was higher than usual.

She returned to the van to retrieve a stepladder. As high as the ceiling was, Melody knew from previous experience that blood spatter could find its way into the most unlikely places.

THREE

IT TOOK HER LESS THAN FORTY MINUTES TO COVER ALL FOUR walls, ceiling and floor in polyethylene sheets. When she'd first started in the business, the job had required two hours or more. But with repetition, she'd become faster. Now the work was easier and her muscles didn't hurt as much.

Shaker was due home in twenty minutes, according to her client. She moved the gun from the waistband of her dress and placed it in her smock pocket. She examined her work one last time, proud of the neat lines where she'd razored the sheeting to fit snugly in the corners, blunting the shape of the washer-dryer, its dials and buttons opaque beneath the heavy plastic.

She waited in the living room, sitting on one of the armchairs slipcovered in a white Perennials fabric, glanced at the Restoration Hardware cocktail table and the blackened steel floor-to-ceiling fireplace surround, and wondered if people thought this kind of décor and furniture were cozy. There was too much white in the rooms. Perhaps it did brighten the interior, but Melody hated the combination of pale walls and black tables and fireplaces, and realized she could never feel comfortable here.

She didn't envy the Shakers. She visualized her house on Sleepy Hollow Road in Westchester. Brick fireplace, wood-paneled walls, oak floors, a *home* that radiated warmth.

There was something antiseptic about the Shaker mansion, probably a reflection of her client's personality, Mrs. Shaker, who had paid her one million dollars to kill her husband and make his remains disappear.

Mrs. Shaker—she of the high tits, too much mascara and sunbed-toasted skin. Melody had disliked her from the second she'd laid eyes on her. She was nothing more than a gold-digger, but the reason she had given (despite Melody's not asking for one) for wanting her husband dead was that he was cheating on her. Melody hadn't bought it. Mrs. Shaker was all about the money. And she wanted it all for herself.

Melody wasn't interested in the reasons why her clients wanted their spouses, business partners, or siblings murdered, because the reasons weren't *interesting*. The reasons were usually petty, and often involved an insurance policy on the husband's or wife's life and other forms of greed. Without exception, her clients were selfish killers who lacked basic humanity.

Melody wasn't complaining, though. She'd gotten rich from accepting contracts from these lower life forms masquerading as people. The only surprising aspect of her job was that there was no shortage of those willing to pay to have others killed. The numbers were startling. In the past thirty days, she'd been contacted by over four thousand prospective clients in forty-eight states. But she could afford to be selective. She turned down most of them. There were a small number of contracts worth the risk. And Charles Shaker was an acceptable risk.

Melody was a psychopath. Not in the Norman Bates or Ted Bundy mold—she didn't derive any pleasure from killing. Her attitude to murder was neutral. The ghosts of the dead didn't haunt her dreams or her waking hours. Psychopathy was a useful aid, nothing more. Without it, she couldn't do her job. There were many psychopaths roaming the world, and most didn't become killers. They became financiers, Wall Street hotshots and CEOs of multi-billion-dollar companies. But Melody liked to work alone. She had no one looking over her shoulder. And the work itself wasn't demanding.

In the beginning it had been, until she'd figured out how to become more efficient. She'd led all her victims to their deaths with the help of a little theater. She chose the smallest room in the house, usually the utility room; it was easier to forensic-proof than a larger space. She'd inform the victim there was a dead cat behind the washer-dryer. It was a ludicrous, reckless lie, but in every case the person she would shoot in the back of the head was curious enough to go and look. She hoped Shaker was the curious type.

She touched the knurled handgrip of the revolver and checked her watch. Mr. Shaker would be home in ten minutes. Melody fidgeted with the barrel of the gun, squeezing it between thumb and forefinger. It was a familiar nervousness. Psychopath or not, she was still human and not exempt from worry. It stemmed from the notion that things could go wrong; it skirted the edge of her consciousness like a predator sniffing for weakness. She'd probably take on two or three more jobs before she retired at the age of thirty. She smiled at the prospect, but it died on her lips when she heard a car pull into the driveway. Less than a minute later, a key rattled in the door.

FOUR

MELODY HURRIED INTO THE ENTRANCE HALL, PAST A SUN-
burst mirror and yet another black glossy table framed
against those same anonymous white walls, heels clacking on
the marble.

Soulless, she thought. Nothing about the house said the
Shakers lived here. It could have belonged to anyone.

Charles Shaker was in his early forties, cropped black
hair miraculously untouched by hair dye. His forty-plus years
told on his face, but not in an unpleasant or unattractive way.
He stood just under six feet, and she guessed his build could
be described as athletic, which was how some of the more
deluded men on dating websites described their physiques.
But it wasn't always a deal-breaker for Melody. As long as
they were non-crazy, had something interesting to say, she
gave them a chance. Although lately, that area of her
personal life had been somewhat dormant ever since she'd
ended things with Landon Forbes.

Shaker's suit was creaseless, its blue pinstripes almost
matching the color of his bright-blue eyes. She liked him
and didn't know why. There was *something* …

Don't make it harder than it has to be.

Shaker lingered in the doorway, sizing her up, his gaze
hesitating on her shoes.

Should've taken them off. Why the hell didn't I?

Had she forgotten? Melody made a note in her mental ledger, recording the mistake and swearing she would *not* make it again.

"I'm Melody. The cleaner. Your wife hired me."

Shaker continued to stare at her shoes.

The goddamn shoes.

At last, he looked at her. "Charles Shaker. Pleased to meet you, Melody." He shook her hand, and Melody was grateful he hadn't crushed it with one of those masculine grips designed to convey his superior confidence and general manliness.

That's how some of them think. Amazing.

"There's a slight problem, Mr. Shaker. There's a dead cat in your utility room."

"I'm sure you can take care of it," Shaker said, and he went into the living room, briefcase in hand, eyes on the floor, not giving her another look.

It hadn't occurred to her that he might have other matters on his mind. It had never failed. A dead cat in the utility room was cause for curiosity, for questions, especially since her client had said they didn't own a cat.

She softened toward Shaker. She'd make it easy for him, do it fast. He wouldn't even know it was her. She would fix an image of Mrs. Shaker in her mind and imagine she was killing the sunbed junkie who was perhaps only a few horizontal sessions short of skin cancer.

Melody followed him to the living room. He was sitting on one of the featureless sofas, briefcase open, perusing some documents, engrossed in the intricacies of managing other people's money, no doubt.

Too much time has passed already. *I have to do it. I'm starting to like the sonofabitch, and for no good reason.*

Her fingertips touched the gun in her pocket.

Shaker must have sensed her behind him because he said, "My wife didn't mention she'd hired a cleaner."

She was surprised to feel her hand drift away from the gun. Did Shaker know she was here to kill him?

The shoes. The goddamn shoes.

"A dead cat?" he said, as though speaking to himself. "We don't have a cat."

"It got in somehow," Melody said.

"Where are you from?" he asked.

"Vinegar Hill."

He turned his head, then continued to examine the documents in his lap.

"What do you think of the house?" he asked.

"It's, um, okay," she said.

"Yeah, I don't like it either."

She was dismayed that she was weakening.

Shaker straightened, as though a horrible realization had just dropped out of the clear blue sky. "There is no dead cat," he said, his voice a concoction of terror and disbelief.

Melody stepped toward him, her resolve snapping into place. She pointed the gun at the back of his head and squeezed the trigger. The explosion seemed amplified by the marble floor.

In the aftermath of the report, the silence took on an almost physical presence, hanging thick and heavy in the air. Shaker fell forward. Melody stared into the black hole in his skull as he tumbled to the floor.

She knelt beside him. His eyes stared into eternity. Melody held one of his hands. It was warm with the residual memory of life. "I'm sorry, Charles," she said. "I should've done it before you realized." She caressed his cheek.

I'm doing my job.

But she was worried. She'd had a lapse. Her usual professionalism had cracked briefly, and she scolded herself for allowing it to happen. *Goddammit, you have to do it* before *they know.*

She had enough money. Two or three more jobs and she was out.

She made herself a promise that she wouldn't let the next job slide into difficult territory. She would be quick. No more talking.

Everyone had a bad day.

And today was that day. The house was no longer forensic-proof. There was blood on her hands and it was spreading into a darkly gleaming puddle. Droplets had spattered far and wide, and there was no way she'd be able to find and remove it all.

I have to burn it.

She had no choice.

And she'd have to change the dead-cat story.

FIVE

THE POLYETHYLENE CRACKLED UNDER HER FEET AS SHE heaved Shaker's corpse into the utility room, staring at the bloody wake the leaking body had left in the foyer. Her shoulders sagged. *Yes, it's my mess and I have to clean it. So do it.* She grabbed handfuls of plastic sheeting and ripped them loose, draping Shaker's remains and rolling him in it like a burrito filling.

She went out and checked on Sammy, who regarded her with open-mouthed patience, then removed the bulk-handling truck from the rear of the van, tossed in a can of lighter fluid and a book of matches, and lowered it to the ground on the custom-installed hydraulic lift. She wheeled the truck into the house, its casters squeaking, and made a mental note to oil them.

She parked it in the utility-room doorway, put the lighter fluid and matches in her pocket, and locked the wheels in place by stepping on the lever brakes. It was the kind of truck used in hotels and hospitals to transport laundry. Melody had customized it to accommodate a door in the side—a zipped canvas flap.

Okay, Mel, today's toil is your punishment for being sloppy.

Grunting, her face engorged with hot blood, she wrestled the body into the truck, relieved the rubber wheels had kept it from sliding.

I'm going to sleep well tonight.

Outside, as the lift raised her and the truck level with the floor of the van, she spotted a pair of tennis shoes behind the driver's side seat.

Should've worn them. Just another of the many mistakes I made.

She stooped over, retrieved the shoes, and sat cross-legged on the van's floor while she put them on. *No need to continue making mistakes.*

Then she circled to the front of the truck and pushed it into the van.

She returned to the house and sprayed the lighter fluid everywhere she could see Shaker's blood, giving the utility room a generous dose.

She struck a match and stared at the flames, and an image of a bronze-seared Mrs. Shaker appeared in her mind.

I earned my money today, bitch.

SIX

MELODY'S ANXIETY HAD LOST ITS INTENSITY ONCE SHE'D gotten off the Long Island Expressway. Transporting a body was a worrisome business, no matter how often you did it. The tension leached out of her muscles as she passed the sign for Sleepy Hollow Village, and the one next to it informing her that the speed limit was thirty, which she observed. She would never forgive herself if she was pulled over by a cop for speeding. She had driven more than a hundred miles with a dead billionaire in her van, and was experiencing the first caress of exhaustion. But her work wasn't done. She couldn't rest until Shaker was planted deep in the ground.

The houses on Sleepy Hollow Road were spread far apart. The area was closely wooded and everyone minded their own business. It was the main reason Melody had chosen to buy a second home here. For added privacy, she'd had a high fence and entrance gates installed; they enclosed the front of the large colonial house. The three-car garage was at the rear. Anyone standing outside would see nothing but the roof of the property. There were no gaps in the gates, which were steel but painted with a wood-effect veneer.

She opened the gates with her fob and waited for them to close before following the asphalt path to the back of the house. She parked in the garage and went into the expansive garden. She passed the JCB mini excavator and stopped at the lip of a wide, seven-foot hole. She'd added the extra foot for luck, even though she didn't believe in it. She didn't examine the paradox too closely because it wasn't important. What mattered now was making Shaker one with the soil, and quick. He'd start leaking even more fluids if she didn't hurry.

In the fading twilight, she scanned the garden. The vegetable patches sat in a neat row close to the treeline. Each rectangular patch produced a different flower or vegetable. There were cabbages and lettuces, leeks, onions, peppers, roses and sunflowers. She had forgotten most of the names of those buried under each one, but they were all businessmen, company directors, financiers, and Wall Street tycoons. Melody had nothing particular against them; their spouses and business associates had simply paid her well to dispose of them.

As she returned to the garage, her thoughts turned to Landon Forbes, a man who had traveled to Sunset Park in Brooklyn—deliberately—to pay *eighteen* dollars for a cup of coffee, and believed it was reasonable. A man who constantly wore flannel and denim, and an enormous hanging bush of facial hair, and listened to obscure music, and took Polaroids of whatever landscape he was hiking in at the time, including photographs of his feet (but never his face, because Landon was an uncommon individual who was *authentic*). Landon, who had a fetish for wood—wooden phone and laptop covers, and distressed wooden furniture. Landon, who had carried around a cracked leather backpack for no discernible reason. And his constant use of the word *authentic*, and his fulsome denials that he was a hipster. And the fact he was unwilling to accept that he was part of a consumer sub-culture where everyone wore the same uniform of beards, and the same lumberjack garb, and thought they were different, even though it was a lie.

Melody could have forgiven all of it—except Landon Forbes hated dogs. *Hated* them. She still had difficulty accepting that a *human* could hate dogs. And she had broken up with him the instant his mask had slipped. She'd overheard the unique—*the authentic*—Landon Forbes swearing at Sammy while she was in the shower. She had confronted him, asked him to be honest, and he'd admitted he had hated dogs all his life. She'd asked him to leave.

That had been two days ago, and she wondered if she was distracted because she had ended a perfectly fine two-year relationship. She'd had no intention of marrying Landon. She couldn't commit to a man who tried to be like everyone else instead of just being himself. But it hadn't been terrible, either. They'd had good times. Melody wouldn't have stayed with him if it had been all bad.

Was Landon the reason she had made so many mistakes? Why had she worn those goddamn heels on the job if she wasn't distracted?

The West Village was full of Landon Forbeses. There were slight variations but, essentially, they shared the same homogenous cultural views. She would get over Landon, forget about him completely. Melody began to worry about Joe Bernstein instead, her neighbor on Bleecker Street. She hoped he had enough food left.

She was pushing the bulk-handling truck toward the hole she'd dug the previous day when her cell phone buzzed in her pocket. It was Mrs. Shaker.

"You burned my fucking house down."

"Hello, Jennifer," Melody said. "I had an unexpected complication. It happens."

"My house—you *weasel!*"

Weasel?

"Okay, take it easy. You have insurance."

"How do you know I have insurance?"

"Lucky guess, Jennifer. You'll make the transfer tomorrow?"

Mrs. Shaker paused. Melody sensed her fury. "As agreed. Tomorrow. What did you do with…him?"

"I took care of it. Are you satisfied with the work I did?"

"The whole downstairs was burned. It's only thanks to the neighbors that the whole house didn't go up in flames."

"Apart from fire damage, are you satisfied with the work?"

Jennifer Shaker hesitated again, then said, "Yes. Yes, I'm satisfied."

"Nine a.m., Mrs. Shaker. You won't forget to make the transfer, will you?"

"The money will be there."

"The phone you're calling me on—"

"Yeah, yeah, I know. I'll destroy it like you said. Don't worry."

"Oh, Mrs. Shaker, I'm not worried at all." Melody hung up and unzipped the canvas flap. Then she hauled Shaker's body free and tumbled him into the grave.

Too bad you didn't take out a contract on your wife, Charles. I liked you. But a deal is a deal.

Melody wasn't in the habit of murdering her clients. It was bad for business. But Jennifer Shaker had made a fatal mistake: she had thought Melody was stupid, that she hadn't noticed the woman following her the first time they'd met. And now she knew where Melody lived, her client would have to pay for her snooping…just as soon as Melody figured out how to get rid of the newly minted widow.

SEVEN

NORMAN LOOMIS WATCHED HIS WIFE WATCHING HIM FROM the head of the table as he poked the peas on his plate with his fork. He couldn't decipher her facial expression; not because the long dining table created distance between them, nor because of the low light. He just couldn't work out whether she was regarding him with warmth, worry or the cool calculation of a predator.

With his free hand, he kept touching his face and pulling on his lower lip. Hard. He was oblivious to it. He was a teeth-grinder, too, but there was nothing he could do about it since it happened while he was asleep. Kim would nudge him awake with her elbow on nights when his bruxism was at its worst. But Norman was awake now, and far beyond simple agitation. His aching jaws and violent headaches were all the evidence he needed: Norman Loomis was afraid. He shouldn't have listened to Kim, but he had agreed to it nonetheless and it was the source of his mounting disquiet.

"Norman, you have to eat," Kim said. He glanced at her, and at her dinner plate, which was almost empty. The food in front of him was cold. His appetite was gone. He stared at the night through one of the tall windows. The dark reflected his mood.

"Norman," Kim said, her voice louder, and Norman detected a hint of exasperation. "What's wrong? You're pushing your dinner around like a five-year-old child."

Norman was pushing his food around because he was considering divorcing his wife—that's what was wrong. The notion was terrifying. He believed hell existed, and that one day he'd probably become a permanent resident as a consequence of the things he had done. But the idea of being alone at forty-six was worse than any biblical torture chamber. He hadn't told anyone he had been alone all his life before he'd met Kim in South Burlington. They had both been taking a course in mortuary science. Kim had shown interest in him and Norman had experienced the first giddy thrill of what he'd come to identify as happiness. The memories of being in foster care, of having adoptive parents who had taken him into their home, a place where he had become invisible once the state had begun sending checks to his new family, had faded, until the knowledge that he'd been discarded by his biological mother and father had become unimportant. For the first time in his life, someone had *noticed* Norman Loomis.

Kim was still watching him. Her left shoulder was tilted forward—a signal that she expected him to answer her.

"Nothing's wrong. I'm sorry, I was in dreamland. How was your meeting with your friends today?"

"My *friends?* Well, it was enjoyable…People don't take homemaking seriously, Norman. People in general, I mean. Telling someone you're a homemaker reduces you in the eyes of the person asking the question *What do you do?* It's a question you can bet on when you meet new people: What do you do? I am a homemaker first, Norman, and a mortician second. Think how some women must feel—they don't have a paying job and they get asked that horrible question. I'm hoping to change attitudes. Homemaking is a vocation; it's nothing to be ashamed of. I am proud to say I'm a homemaker, who also happens to get paid for doing her other job. It doesn't make me better or worse than anyone else. I work hard at both jobs."

Norman didn't need to be convinced. The homemaker was not just important but vital. He understood this, since his own homemaking skills were rudimentary at best, and for most of his life had involved the operation of a microwave oven and washing a solitary plate and fork. He accepted homemaking and the homemaker as essential for a household to function, so why was she trying to convince him of its merits all over again?

"Remember our Christmas party last year?" Kim continued, and Norman nodded. "We invited a select number of people, and one of them was Nora Sanderson. The tech tycoon's wife. You know what she said to me when I told her I was a homemaker? *Oh, that's nice.* That's what she said. Like she was talking about the hors d'oeuvres. *Oh, that's nice.*"

Norman cleared his throat. "What does Nora Sanderson know? She's privileged. She has a horde of cleaners and housekeepers to do her dirty work."

"Exactly! Sanderson hasn't cleaned a toilet in her life. She's never known the ache in her knees from crouching to clean around the bowl."

"She's snooty," Norman said. "You can't expect a person like her to understand the organization required for effective homemaking."

Kim's face softened. "Norman, you always know the right thing to say."

Because I'm scared of my dark collection. I'm scared of you.

"I'm meeting the broker tomorrow, Norman," Kim said. "We can't keep up with demand. We have to increase our productivity."

He felt sick. The dinner plate grated on the uneven wood grain of the table as he pushed it away.

No one had forced him to do anything. He'd done it fully aware and couldn't blame her for everything. He didn't have to agree to it.

"Kimberly," he said, and she became watchful. He only called her Kimberly when he intended to be disagreeable. She straightened, and Norman bore the full weight of her stare. He looked at his hands; they clenched and unclenched. He willed himself to stop. In wonder and dismay, he found he couldn't. He stared as his hands balled into fists, the pulsating purple-green veins standing prominently against the sallowness of his skin. When was the last time he had eaten properly? He couldn't remember.

"I'm waiting, Norman," she said, her tone spun from the finest silk.

But Norman wasn't fooled.

"We have to stop what we're doing," he said, sweat beading on his brow. "Kimberly, please. What we've done is wrong. It's…it's criminal."

She slid out from behind the table, brushing against it with a soft whisper of fabric on wood. She walked toward him, the hollow clack of her heels on the floorboards echoing in the great room. She hoisted herself onto the table, sitting in the same spot his poked and prodded dinner had sat moments before. She placed the tip of her forefinger under his chin and tilted his head toward her. His eyes were moist and rimmed with the redness of insomnia. He looked up at her and wondered if he'd wilt, if he would give in to her grisly demands. He knew she wouldn't stop their dark collection easily. If he could find the strength—

"Norman, I worry about you. You don't sleep well; you don't eat. Can you see why I worry?"

Norman nodded. Her fingertip remained fastened to a patch of stubble beneath his chin. "And I worry about your lack of concern for our business. *Our* business, Norman. We have a mansion, on Main Street, in one of the finest capital cities in the world, and it all has to be paid for. Fresh air doesn't pay the bills. People are not dying fast enough to sustain *our* business. We have to take the initiative. If you can't give me what I want, I will get it myself."

"What do you mean?"

"What I mean, Norman, is simple. Conscience *cannot* be allowed to stand in the way of free enterprise. The violent-crime rate here is low, and as a result we lack victims of stabbings and shootings. We must adapt."

"But it's wrong…"

She pressed her finger to his lips. "Shh, Norman. I love you. You are my husband and we'll figure out the way forward *together*."

Kim leaned into him and her lips touched his. She raked her fingers through his hair, and Norman Loomis's thoughts of divorce were lost in her scent, choked by the softness of her irresistible embrace.

EIGHT

NORMAN LOOMIS SHOULD HAVE BEEN HAPPY. THE SKY WAS cloudless and the sun warmed his neck. And he only had to walk twenty yards to Loomis Memorial. But a casual observer would have wondered why the gaunt man in the black suit seemed to be measuring each step. Why a man who dressed for business was so intent on his shoes, which were gleaming from their daily polish.

He passed the redbrick structure of Main Street Middle School. Its lawns and the trees lining both sides of the wide entrance the kind of vivid green you see only in dreams. His pace slowed, and he looked up, blinking. He was standing at the foot of the path that led to the door of Loomis Memorial. He blinked again, as though he might remove a dirty vision if only he kept opening and closing his eyes. But Loomis Memorial was still there, a dignified colonial-style building—white siding, black window shutters that were never used, discreet sign on the front lawn informing the public of the services available within. It was wholesome, respectable, and innocent.

Who am I kidding?

He took a half-step forward, and his leg twitched and pulled back, as though he was about to walk across a sinkhole. It hadn't collapsed yet, but it would. *It would.*

Norman took a deep breath and held it. A car drove by behind him on Main Street, and he got moving. The last thing he wanted was the local gossipmongers spreading the word that the Loomis man was standing in the street, staring at his shoes. For a man in his position, perception was important. People had to trust you with the remains of their loved ones.

He opened the door into the reception area. Except for the embalming room, the carpet throughout was maroon. Norman had chosen it, believing it would somehow impart warmth and professionalism. Now he wanted to rip it up; it resembled blood in the early stages of drying. He was glad he'd kept the white walls. He passed the chairs and looked toward the curved black walnut reception desk. He and Kim took turns consulting with the relatives of the deceased. Kim hated dealing with the bereaved, Norman knew; her contrivance of anything remotely like empathy was awkward to witness. Consequently, he spent most of his time reassuring and comforting those who were often experiencing the worst period in their lives.

He walked left into the doorway of the casket room where coffins of varying price points were on display, and saw no one. He moved further along the hall, into the viewing room, and looked past the rows of seats. A coffin sat atop a metal casket gurney. No one. He strode to the two doors at the rear of the building; this was off-limits to the general public. The embalming room. He paused, listened, his hand hesitating on the handle. The only sound was the hum of the air-extraction system.

A wave of heaviness descended on him. Ray Porter, the broker, was standing at the end of the room near the metal cabinets, sinks and countertops, keeping his distance from the embalming table in the middle where Mrs. Angelique Gibson reposed, draped in a white sheet. Norman had made sure to cover her face. He felt sick with shame whenever he looked at Mrs. Gibson…the things he'd taken from her.

Porter eyed him with open suspicion. Ray was nothing more than a common criminal wrapped in a three-piece suit. How had he ever gotten mixed up with him?

He was alerted to the answer by a noise: Kim was sliding a large box from the refrigerator, a longer and deeper version of a lunch cooler. Norman knew what was inside; he'd packed it himself. A part of him wanted to help his wife but another would have happily watched her struggle if she hadn't glanced up and seen him.

"Help me with this goddamn box."

He snapped into action, hauling it onto a stainless countertop, like a ten-year-old again, unable to understand why the adults were shouting at him.

Kim was breathing hard, but a smile began to stretch her flushed cheeks.

She couldn't be enjoying this.

Porter removed a large brown package from a pocket inside his jacket. Kim reached for it and Porter held it to his chest. "We have further business to discuss," he said.

"And we will discuss it. Now hand it over."

Porter gave it to her. She looked at Norman. "Do me a favor, Norman," she said. "Bring the box outside and put it in Mr. Porter's trunk."

Ray handed Norman the car keys, his lips thinning into a grimace.

***

They watched Norman leave, leaning to one side under the weight of the box.

"Okay," Porter said, "I won't waste anymore of your day. Skin and bone allografts are always in demand and the pay is good. But we need organs—hearts, livers, kidneys, lungs."

"We don't have the equipment yet to meet your order."

"I can help with the hardware, Kim. A heart can fetch a hundred grand, minimum. We're talking serious figures here."

"One hundred thousand for a heart?"

"At least…Norman isn't going to be a problem, is he?"

"What makes you think he'll be a problem?"

"You see the way he looks at me. I get the feeling Norman isn't fully on board."

"Don't worry about my husband. Norman gets a little twitchy sometimes, that's all."

"If you say so. Anyway—hearts, Kim. I need four. Preferably two from young women aged between eighteen and forty-five. And two from boys aged ten to fifteen. Hearts are in constant demand. If you manage to locate an extra heart or two, I'll take them immediately."

"Where am I going to *locate* these hearts? Have you forgotten where you are? We're in Montpelier, Ray. Violent and accidental deaths here are rare for young people."

"I'm just telling you what I need," he said. Porter unsnapped his briefcase on a bent knee. He gave her a thick sheaf of papers encased in a plastic folder. "You'll have to read and understand what's in it. By the way, the heart donors have to be *living* donors."

"What?"

"The hearts have to be taken from a living body."

"How—?"

He held up a hand and said, "It's none of my business how you retrieve the organs. None. It's not my problem. This order, like any other, is strictly voluntary. Understand that I am not asking you to do anything illegal."

"You can pretend we're not breaking the law if you want."

"Kim, I like doing business with you. I know what I'm going to get. I am not trying to persuade you to do anything. It's up to you."

"I want two hundred grand for each heart."

Porter's expression was pained. "Jesus Christ, you make my job a misery."

"What you're asking for could ruin me. The risk involved has to be worth the reward."

"A hundred and fifty," Ray said, sticking out his hand for her to shake.

Kim folded her arms across her chest. "I'll give you what you want, but for the right price. Take it or leave it."

He wasn't going to win. Instead of prolonging the agony, he agreed and they shook on it.

NINE

THE STOREFRONT OF SPIC N SPAN CLEANING ON BLEECKER Street was the same color as the company's logo: yellow trim and black letters. Melody saw Rosa Mendes through the plate-glass window, standing behind the counter, tapping at her iPhone.

She entered the store, Sammy leading the way but not straining against the leash clipped to her belt. The paper bag of groceries crackled as she shifted it from her left arm to her right.

"You watching the Kardashians again?" Melody said, and Rosa's face lit up. She went around the counter and embraced Melody, kissing her on the cheek.

"The Kardashians and RuPaul," Rosa said. "It's so good to see you, Mel. Let me help you." Rosa took the grocery bag and hefted it onto the counter.

"How's business?" Melody asked.

"It's been good. In fact, it's been crazy busy. Today, a little slow. Hey, cutie." Rosa crouched and patted Sammy's head. The pug licked her hand.

They'd met in Washington Square Park. Rosa had been sitting on a bench, weeping in silence, and Melody had done something most New Yorkers wouldn't dream of—she'd talked to Rosa, asked her if she was okay. Through hitching sobs, Melody learned that Rosa had ended up in a relationship with an abusive man, the kind of man who believed he could somehow compensate for his cowardice by beating a woman to the point of fracturing her ribs. Rosa had left him, finally, but had nowhere to go. And she was flat broke. Melody had just opened Spic N Span. That was four years ago. It was a risk to hire a total stranger, but Melody's instincts were sharp, and Rosa didn't do drugs or alcohol. Melody had asked her directly if she had a substance-abuse problem, something that would have given her pause and possibly changed the course of events. Rosa had said she wasn't an addict and Melody had believed her, because as they'd talked for hours in the park Rosa had proven herself a terrible liar. Mel had tested her theory by asking if Rosa still loved her ex. Rosa had said no, and Mel knew it wasn't true. That was all right. She would have lied, too.

Rosa had recovered. She had thanked Melody for "rescuing" her—giving her a job and taking her into her own apartment for a year. She'd bought Melody gifts that Melody had told her to take back to whatever store she'd got them from and ask for a refund. Rosa had gotten her confidence back, and that was all the payment Melody needed.

"How's Joe?"

"He's fine, Mel. I go up to see him almost every day but he wants to see you."

"I'm going to see him now."

"Your business trip went well?"

"Could've been better, but it wasn't a total loss, Rosa. See you soon."

Melody's apartment building was adjacent to Spic N Span. She climbed all six stories of the walk-up and knocked on Joe Bernstein's door. He hugged her hard, squashing the groceries between them. Sammy yelped, excited, his short legs shuffling in a jittery dance.

"Jesus, Joe, you're going to break the eggs."

He released her. "Oh, sorry. For me?"

"Yes, sir."

"I told you not to call me sir. As if I need reminding I'm old."

"You're not old, you're just wiser than the rest of us."

"Uh-huh…Are you gonna stand out there all day or are you coming in?"

"You old charmer! I believe I'll come in, sir."

Joe rolled his eyes and joined Melody in the kitchen as she put the food in the fridge. Mel unclipped the leash from Sammy's neck; he farted obligingly, waddled to a corner by the stove, walked in a circle, and lay down to sleep.

"Your dog's getting fat, Mel."

"He's a pug, Joe. A pug. They're naturally chubby."

"True, but not *that* chubby."

Melody looked over at Sammy, sound asleep in the corner, and wondered if the pug was a little on the heavy side. Maybe she'd put him on a diet. "Okay," she said, "I see what you mean."

"That dog's been living like a lord."

"I got you a small tub of butter, Joe. Use it sparingly. You should probably watch your cholesterol."

"If cholesterol was gonna kill me it would've done so already. Come on in the living room. Take a load off."

Melody followed him to the couch, noticing he was clean-shaven, wearing a freshly laundered shirt, and pressed brown corduroy trousers. His shoes shone like black mirrors.

"Who is she?" Melody asked.

"Huh?"

"Don't *huh* me. You didn't get dolled up for me, Casanova, so who's the lucky lady?"

"Christ, you don't miss much."

"You bet. Now, spill it."

"Her name is Anna."

Melody squealed with happiness and lunged across the couch, squeezing the air out of Joe.

"Okay, okay," Joe said, laughing. "These old bones aren't as strong as they used to be."

Melody let go of him but she was still leaning close, eyes bright. "Where did you and Anna meet?"

"Café Espanol down the street. I dropped my wallet and she picked it up."

"I bet you dropped your wallet deliberately, you old dog. How old is she?"

"Seventy-seven, a year older than me."

"Dear me, so you managed to bag yourself a grandma. I'm so proud of you."

"It's early days, you know?"

"I do. But you like her, I can see it."

"Yeah, you really don't miss a thing."

"Why do I get the feeling all isn't as it seems, Joe?"

She caught him glancing at the photograph on top of the TV. A woman in her sixties beamed at them. It was Tania, Joe's first and only wife.

Mel clasped his hand in hers. "Oh Joe, I see. It's been ten years since she passed. She'd be so happy for you."

Joe's gaze remained fixed on the photograph. His cheeks reddened as his eyes began to fill.

"It's guilt, that's all," he said, clearing his throat and taking a deep breath. "We were loyal to each other for four decades. I know it's not so, but I can't help feeling I'm cheating on Tania."

"Hey now, Tania wouldn't see it like that, Joe. She'd be as delighted for you as I am. You deserve it, you *need* it. This is good news…Give it time, Joe. The guilt will pass."

"Will it?"

"Yes, because happiness will overwhelm it."

He looked at her. "What would I do without you?"

"Well, you'd probably start a red-hot romance with a pensioner called Anna, for starters."

He laughed and coughed at the same time and Melody slapped him on the back. "It's okay, I'm not choking," he said. "Agh, I meant to offer you something to drink but I completely forgot."

"Joe, I'm fine. I'm going to take off. I have some business I need to take care of. If you need anything—"

"I'll take the fifteen steps to your door and knock."

"You got it."

TEN

MELODY CROSSED THE HALL TO HER OWN APARTMENT AND
counted the steps.

Fifteen. He was right.

Sammy headed to his dog bed next to the bathroom
door and lay on the memory-foam mattress, and Melody
resolved to feed him smaller portions at dinnertime. She
showered, still on a high from Joe's good news. Joe had
promised her she would meet Anna soon, and Melody
looked forward to it. She'd been Joe's friend for five years.
They had met when she bought the apartment. He'd helped
her move in, cursing at the weight of each box he'd stacked
in her living room. Melody saw right through his grumpy
demeanor; there was something in Joe that made her want to
protect him, but she couldn't have said what it was.

An exposed brick wall separated the living room from
the bedroom. Spanning almost half of it was an aerial
photograph of Vinegar Hill in Brooklyn. Melody didn't need
a reminder of where she'd been raised; the blown-up photo
was simply a marker of her progress. She had lived on
Hudson Avenue, so close to the Con Edison power plant
that she could throw a stone from her front door and hit the
high chain-link fence that surrounded it.

The yuppies and hipsters who'd moved in no doubt
found the Belgian block streets, nineteenth-century

wood-frame houses, and brick row houses on Front Street charming. Or in the parlance of one Landon Forbes, *authentic*. But Melody knew better. She'd lived in poverty in Vinegar Hill long before she'd developed an understanding of fashion and the trends that motivated people.

Her parents, both drug addicts, had left when she was ten years old, telling her they were going out to buy her cake. Melody had suspected something was wrong. Her parents *never* bought her cake, or any other treats. She'd waited and waited. By midnight, she'd known they weren't coming back. She had been scared, in the house all by herself, but glad, too. Relieved. She had no respect for her parents. They didn't deserve any. They'd put their own needs before hers. And she hated them for it. Her parents had called her Aunt Joan, who'd lived around the corner on Water Street, and told her they were breaking free to start a new life. Those were the words Aunt Joan had used— breaking free. Aunt Joan had moved Melody into her home, into the same unending poverty, which Joan viewed as an acceptable burden. If poverty could be endured by the saints, then there was no reason they couldn't follow in their footsteps. But Melody wasn't applying for sainthood; she couldn't understand why anyone would take pride in being poor, as though living in poverty somehow made you superior. *We don't have much, but we're happy*, Aunt Joan was fond of saying.

Melody thought Aunt Joan was crazy. Melody's stomach burbled and groaned almost constantly. She was weak from hunger, in need of another piece of bread that she seldom got, often running her fingers over her prominent ribs and wondering if she'd survive another month. Aunt Joan never complained about being hungry, and didn't hesitate to remind Melody what she'd done for her—fed her as often as she could, put a roof over her head—and that she should be grateful.

On her eleventh birthday, Melody had exposed her ribs and the scant flesh that covered them, and asked Aunt Joan to show Melody *her* ribs. It was the one time Aunt Joan had struck her, slapping her with such force that she'd fallen sideways into the locked refrigerator. The kitchen cabinets also had locks. Aunt Joan insisted they served a vital purpose—to ensure that the rations were distributed fairly. Melody, stung from the slap, had considered asking Aunt Joan why *her* stomach never growled, why her cheeks were full, and why the flesh on her bones was plump and well-nourished, but she'd stopped herself. Aunt Joan had been furious. Her eyes shone with a dangerous blackness. Melody had retreated and made a decision. If she were going to survive, she'd have to steal.

Flatbush Avenue became her regular shoplifting beat. She learned to navigate her way through the streets, memorizing landmarks. She'd had no choice. She knew she'd be in danger if she couldn't find her way home. Honing this skill had been her first real experience of self-discipline.

She had carried around her empty book bag like a suitcase, taking only food. Melody didn't believe in miracles. The closest thing to a miracle she'd experienced was never to have been caught stealing. She didn't believe God was looking out for her, protecting her, because God didn't know she existed. It was just an extraordinary piece of luck that had saved her life.

She picked up the iPad on the couch beside her and folded her bathrobe tight, tying a knot in the belt. She connected to a VPN and checked her bank account in the Cayman Islands. Jennifer Shaker had paid Valerie Price, one of Melody's aliases, in full. Melody even had a passport and Social Security number in Valerie Price's name.

She logged in to her email account. There were hundreds of messages. The dark web was a busy place, and it had made her rich. The worst thing about making so much money was that you wanted to make more. Melody recognized the problem. It was powerful, addictive, and like an addict, she promised to teach herself to *just say no.*

She read some of the emails, all from people desperate to have someone murdered. She nodded stiffly at reasons given. As though they mattered. They were petty and reeked of greed. Killing someone for the insurance money was by far the most popular excuse for having an individual shot. But Melody's decision always came down to the money. There was no way she was killing somebody for twenty-five thousand dollars.

She signed out of her account, typed adultfriends.com into the search bar of her browser, and swiped through a gallery of semi-naked men. She paused at a man calling himself Bill Steel, probably a fake name, and Melody placed her order.

Thirty-five minutes later, Bill Steel appeared at her door. She welcomed him in. He was tall, with a slight paunch that was nothing more than a gentle slope, blue eyes, dark hair, angular jawline, and he was smiling. Melody enjoyed it more when they liked their job.

"How do you want it?" Bill Steel said.

Melody went to the window and looked down on Bleecker Street. She undid the robe, shrugged, let it slide to the floor, and placed both palms on the sill. She bent over, legs apart, and said, "Fuck me. Hard and deep. And no talking."

ELEVEN

Montpelier, Vermont

COREY BAYLISS WOKE UP ON HIS TWELFTH BIRTHDAY TO HIS ringing cell phone. It was an old LG his mother had purchased for him. He'd wanted an iPhone. His mom, Lillian, had said that when he got an education, then a job, he could buy his own iPhone. She had kissed him on the forehead and told him to be grateful that he *had* a smartphone, that there were children in Africa who not only didn't have a phone, but also had to contend with famine. Corey wasn't sure what she meant, or why he'd felt guilty, but he'd stopped complaining.

"Hello?" he said, his voice thick with sleep.

"Morning, asshole. Happy birthday." It was Evan Fairbanks, his best friend. His mother had promised him that Evan would end up in jail or dead if he didn't mend his ways and smarten up. He was always getting into scrapes and spent a lot of time in detention. Corey thought all of Evans's horsing around was a bid for attention and nothing more. There were plenty of other kids in the running for class clown and they probably wouldn't end up dead or in jail either. Evan wasn't bad. He was, to borrow one of mom's words, misguided.

"Jeez, Evan, you know what time it is? It's ten after nine, why are you calling so early?"

"It's not early. To me, 9 a.m. is like the afternoon. You get anything good for your birthday?"

"I don't know yet. I asked my mom for a Netflix subscription. She worries about me spending too long on the internet, so we'll see. That's what she said—*We'll see*."

"It'd be cool if you could get it. Anyway, you're twelve, so do you feel like a man?"

It would have been an odd question if it had been asked by anyone other than Evan, who believed—for reasons known only to Evan—that when you turned twelve you were a man. Corey wasn't sure what a man should feel like, only that he felt no different than he had yesterday.

"Yeah, Evan, I feel like a man." He rolled his eyes.

"Awesome, man. I was going to bike up to Hubbard Park, hang out a while. Wanna come with?"

"Sure. I just have to get up. I'll call Rachel and Luke. We'll have a race, loser buys ice-cream. What do you say?"

"Corey, maybe you could ask Kaylee if she wants to come. You know, it'd be better with five people. A better race, I mean."

"Sure, I'll call her and ask. Evan, do you have a romantic interest in Kaylee?" *Romantic interest* was another phrase he'd overheard his mother using, twice, as she was talking on the phone with Mrs. Weston.

"What? Fuck you. I don't do romance!"

"Okay, Evan. Calm down. What's wrong with you?"

"I'm sorry, man. *Sorry*, all right? You won't tell anyone I like her."

"Of course not. Who do you think I am?"

"I know, dude. Sorry."

"I'll call you soon."

"It's fine. I'll come over."

Corey got dressed and went downstairs, worried that his friend might not be all right. Evan's outburst was unusual.

Corey had seen it once before, a day after Evan's uncle Dan had died and Mr. Hamer had reprimanded Evan for running in the hall. And Evan had responded with a shrill scream: *Go to hell, Hamer!* Evan shouted when he felt strongly about something, and Corey wondered if he'd react in the same way if Kaylee wasn't interested in him.

Corey's father, Jim, was sitting at the kitchen table, reading the *Times Argus*, dressed for work in gray slacks, white shirt, and tie, even though he was on vacation. He was chief of finance and administration for the Vermont Judiciary, whatever that was. Corey had the impression that his father handled money all day. Dad had explained what he did, but Corey had discovered that if he wasn't interested in something, he stopped hearing it. So all he really knew was that his father worked hard, and Corey thought he had the best dad in the world.

Mom was eating toast and reading a magazine, the glossy kind, her head craned downward at an angle that dad said would give her a *bad neck*. She had insisted it wouldn't, her neck was just fine, and Dad had eventually stopped worrying. She saw him, sprang from her chair, and hugged him, then kissed the top of his head. "Happy birthday, Corey."

"Thanks, Mom," he said, his voice muffled against her shoulder as she squeezed the breath out of him.

"Yeah, happy birthday, son," dad said. "Don't get too drunk tonight."

"Jim Bayliss!" mom said, "don't be joking about alcohol with your son."

"Oh, relax. We've got a smart one. What are you doing for the rest of the day, son?"

"Probably take a ride to Hubbard Park with Evan and the guys."

"Be home for lunch, Corey," she said. "I don't want you wandering the streets with the Fairbanks kid."

"Mom, he's not a felon, he's just…uh, misguided. Evan's my friend."

"All right," she said. "I trust you, Corey. Don't give me any reason not to." She fished a small piece of paper out of her blouse pocket and handed it to him. "Happy birthday, Corey. Your dad and I discussed it, and we both agree you've earned it."

Corey studied the square strip of paper and his eyes widened.

"Mom, is this what—"

"Yes, Cor, it's your Netflix username and password."

He ran to his mother and kissed her on the forehead, then shook his father's hand.

Dad seemed surprised by the gesture. "See?" he said. "We've definitely got a smart one, Lillian."

Corey sat at the table and poured himself a bowl of Cheerios. The magnitude of his happiness was such that he thought he might be experiencing something closer to awe. He ate breakfast in a hurry and drank his orange juice.

The doorbell chimed. It was Evan.

TWELVE

THEY PEDALED UP MAIN STREET, THE WARM WIND RIPPLING their tee-shirts, Evan leading a race that existed only in his mind. But the fear of losing, of being *behind*, was real. Corey seemed content to cruise.

The sun warmed their faces as they passed houses with picture-perfect mansard and gambrel-style roofs, some red, others light gray, and still others white, taking on a high gleam in the intense sunlight.

Evan braked at the middle school, but he ignored the building. He was looking across the road at a house painted the same shade of green as oxidized copper. It had black window frames and a sloping mansard.

"What's going on?" Corey asked.

"You know who the crib belongs to?"

Corey shrugged. "No."

"The funeral director. I've seen him around. Tall, wears a real black undertaker's suit. Skinny guy."

"Evan, what are you talking about?"

"I bet they store the bodies round back."

"I bet they don't. Come on, let's go."

Evan wasn't listening and made no attempt to move.

"What if they have bodies back there? You're not even a little curious?"

"No. Why would I be?"

"I am. I'm going to check the place out sometime. Have a look-see."

"Evan, seriously, don't do it. You'll get in trouble."

Evan took a last, long look at the house and then shook himself free of his daydream.

"What's gotten into you, Evan?" Corey said from behind, but he didn't respond.

They resumed their journey, mounting the sidewalk as they got closer to a rotary. They turned right and walked their bikes past the redbrick Central Vermont Medical Center, its pitched roof facing the road, its lawns tinged brown under the sweltering sun. Then they were onto Spring Street, crossing the bridge over the Winooski River. Mounds of wooded hills rose in the north and northwest, bright green against the clear blue sky.

The boys got on their bikes, riding single file this time, Evan in the lead. They were beside Hubbard Park, the trees thick on one side, sporadic on the other, the greenery broken at intervals by large houses. Parkway Avenue was one lane of blacktop. Evan rode the bike harder and faster, glancing over his shoulder, checking if there were any cars tailing them. It was dangerous, especially if some drunk tourist speed-freak came around a bend…They walked their bikes up the last incline toward the twin stone pillars of Hubbard Park, sweating and panting.

"That was awesome," Evan said, smiling and gasping.

"Yeah, don't know if I have any gas left for a race."

"Course you do. We'll take a rest." Corey touched Evan's shoulder and they leaned on the handlebars of their bikes. "Evan, I wanted to talk to you for a minute."

"Okay, douche, spill it."

"You won't get mad and blank me all day?"

"Dude, no! You can tell me anything."

Corey used his tee-shirt to wipe the sweat off his forehead, and straightened. "Don't take it personally if Kaylee isn't interested, okay? You know how girls are."

"Maybe you know how they are, but I don't. I hear you, Cor; I get what you're saying. I changed my mind, anyway. I'm not gonna ask her on a date. I'm not even sure where I'd take her." Evan punched Corey lightly on the shoulder. "Besides," he said, "there are far more interesting things than girls. Am I right?"

"Totally right. Hey, let's take Parkway Street. The guys said they'd meet us at the Old Shelter parking lot. Then we'll go down Tower Loop to Corse Street. It's a good straightaway; we can get up a lot of speed, too."

"You know I'm gonna win, Cor. Hope you brought money for ice-cream."

"You have the advantage, Ev. Your legs are shorter, so you can pedal faster."

"Yep, it's true. God blessed me with short pins because he wanted me to win."

Corey laughed.

They emerged from the trees into sunshine and the Old Shelter Pavilion on a grassy hill. There were people sitting at picnic tables and cars in the lot. They spotted Kaylee and Rachel throwing a Frisbee and waved. Luke was sitting on top of a picnic table, both thumbs tapping on the screen of his smartphone. He looked up, saw them, and said, "Are we gonna race or what?"

"Can't wait to get beat?" Evan said, and all five of them headed back to the road, winding their way down Tower Loop. At the top of Corse Road, they lined up side by side, the girls' expressions set hard with determination, the boys determined not to lose.

"On your marks, get set, *GO!*" Evan yelled.

They took off, slowly at first but picking up speed, Rachel in the lead. Evan followed close, his butt high off the saddle, standing, pedaling with the fury of an Olympic athlete on the scent of victory. Kaylee, who Evan had avoided eye contact with at the Shelter, was in third, Luke fourth by a hair, and Corey last.

The trees were a blur on both sides of the road, and Evan had the strange sense that someone was running through the woods, trying to keep up.

"Giddy up, old horse," Evan shouted. "Come on, *giddy*—"

His front wheel struck something in the road and bent sideways. The bicycle came to a standstill but Evan kept going. His hands left the handlebars and he somersaulted through the air, landing on the asphalt with a bone-crunching thud.

Corey veered left to avoid a crash. Rachel, in the lead, didn't notice anything until she'd reached the finish line, a granite boulder on the roadside. Luke pushed himself off his bike while it was in motion; it continued, riderless, into the trees. He rolled to the ground and was on his feet almost immediately. Kaylee was lucky; she pulled hard on the rear brake, narrowly avoiding a collision. As she stopped, the rear wheel lifted briefly off the road. She ran to Evan, who was lying on his side, moaning.

Corey kneeled beside Evan and asked if he was all right. Evan sat up and examined his pants. They were torn at both knees and blood oozed from the scraped skin. A pebble was lodged in one of the cuts. He blinked, plucked it loose, and threw it on the road, where it bounced and disappeared into the trees. His hands were bloody and Kaylee wiped them with a tissue from her knapsack.

"It has aloe vera," she said. "It might ease the stinging."

Evan realized she was helping him. He needed to appear brave. Wounded but brave. He forced himself not to wince as she pressed the tissue into his bleeding hands and knees, tried to plaster an impassive expression on his face and not the look of a child in pain.

Rachel joined them, walking with her bicycle from the winning post. "Good race, Rachel," Evan said. "Well done. First time I've been beaten by anyone."

"You would've won if someone hadn't left a stupid rock in the road."

"No, fair is fair. You won."

Kaylee and Rachel helped him to his feet.

"Dude, that was insane," Luke said. "I swear to God you were actually flying there for a second."

"Ice-cream is on me," Corey said.

Everyone cheered.

***

Corey was glad to see his friends smiling again. Evan was injured but he seemed fine. A sudden wave of exhaustion hit him then, something he'd later recognize as overwhelming relief. Evan could have died.

"Cor," Rachel said, "will you get me chocolate-chip vanilla?"

Corey smiled. A genuine, warm smile. "Sure," he said.

"Do you really want to do that?" Evan said.

Everyone looked at him.

"What do you mean?" Rachel asked.

"I'm just saying, maybe you should consider a diet. You're not exactly wasting away, if you know what I mean."

Shocked silence fell among them. Evan's smile faltered, as though he couldn't understand the change in the atmosphere. Rachel picked her bike up and left. Kaylee and Luke followed her.

"What?" Evan said. "What'd I say?"

***

They were on Spring Street. Evan didn't speak on the long walk home and neither did Corey until they were back on Main Street, near the middle school.

"Why did you say that?" Corey said.

"What?"

"Don't play dumb, Evan. You called Rachel fat."

"No, I did *not*."

"What's happening to you? You didn't used to be like this, so what's the problem?"

"There's no problem."

"Apologize to Rachel. I mean it. We all meet tomorrow at the stone benches at 10 a.m. outside the middle school. You tell Rachel you're sorry, with Kaylee and Luke there, too."

"No way."

"If you don't apologize, *sincerely* apologize, we're no longer friends."

"Are you serious?"

Corey moved toward him in one lightning-fast step. "You were an asshole, a fucking asshole, and if you don't apologize I don't want to see you ever again. Am I serious? Goddamn right I am."

Corey left him standing there as twilight darkened to night.

It was the last time he saw Evan Fairbanks.

THIRTEEN

THEY SAT WAITING FOR EVAN ON THE STONE SLABS THAT
served as benches at the entrance to Main Street Middle
School. Corey had asked Luke and Kaylee to be here, too.
Not only had Evan insulted Rachel; he'd done so in front of
an *audience*, and in Corey's mind, that added a level of
viciousness to the incident that he hadn't believed Evan was
capable of.

He had spent ten minutes the previous night trying to
convince Rachel to let Evan say he was sorry, and with the
same audience. She'd agreed, eventually, and it occurred to
him now that Rachel was only doing it to please him. This
augmented his anger toward Evan.

"You're really not going to be his friend anymore if he
doesn't show up?" Luke asked.

Corey nodded. "Yeah."

Rachel was staring at the ground and Kaylee was tapping
her foot on the concrete. What had Rachel ever done to
Evan except be nice to him? Corey shook his head, reaching
for answers, but none of them made any sense. The idea
that his mother was right about Evan was horrifying. His
mother actually *knew* things. He wished he had the same
kind of insight into other people's characters.

It was 10 a.m. An occasional vehicle passed on the road,
but there was no Evan. Corey figured that if his best friend

wouldn't apologize to save their friendship then it probably had no value to Evan anyway.

"He's not gonna show, Cor," Luke said.

"We'll give him five minutes."

"Sure, no problem."

Corey noticed the bandage on Luke's forefinger. "What happened?"

"Oh, this?" Luke held up the injured finger with visible pride. "I got fat finger from hammering a nail into a cabinet I'm making. I'm gonna be a carpenter, like my dad."

"That's great, Luke. Just make sure you don't cut a finger or toe off with one of those electric saws."

"My dad won't let me use his saws. Says I'm too young."

"Did it hurt?" Kaylee said.

"Yeah, but only for a minute. It swole up big and purple, but my mom brought me to the emergency room and they said there was nothing broken. I can take off the bandage and show you guys."

"No! Ugh, gross," Kaylee said.

"No, thanks, Luke. I just ate breakfast," said Rachel.

Corey laughed. "Yeah, Luke, keep your fat finger to yourself."

Luke looked at his watch. "We can wait some more, Cor, if you want."

"What time is it?"

"Ten after ten."

"No. He's not gonna show. Sorry, Rachel."

"It's all right, Corey. Like I told you last night, it's not important to me. I'd rather not speak to him again."

"Yeah," Corey said, "me too. I'm gonna head home. Catch up with you guys later."

"I could come by in the afternoon to see you, Cor?" Kaylee said.

"No," Luke said. "Come by my house and help me finish my cabinet. I've got too much stuff in my room and my mother said I have to start storing it someplace other than the floor. She said my room sends her into anaphylactic shock."

"What's that mean?" Rachel asked.

"It means boys are dirty," Kaylee said.

"OHHHH," Luke and Corey shouted, holding their chests as though wounded.

"You guys can make fun," Luke said, "but if you need a new cabinet when you grow up you'll be calling me, Luke Greene, master carpenter, to fix all your furniture needs."

"Nice sales pitch," Corey said.

"I thought so, too." Luke waved at them as he crossed the road.

Rachel and Kaylee left. Corey waited until ten forty, then gave up and went home.

Guess we're not friends anymore, Evan.

He walked along Main Street, feeling sick with sadness and confusion, experiencing for the first time the loss of a friendship. An unnecessary loss. It was so stupid, he thought, his mind finding it difficult to process. Was his former friend willing to sacrifice their friendship over an apology? Yes, he was. The brutal truth was hard to accept. Corey wondered how many more hard truths life had up its sleeve.

Mom was talking to someone on the phone in the kitchen when he got home. He detected disapproval in her tone, and paused in the hallway.

"No, I haven't seen him, Mrs. Fairbanks," she said. "It's five after eleven. You should know where he is… Mrs. Fairbanks, have you been drinking?" There was a moment of silence, then she said, "You're slurring your words, Mrs. Fairbanks. No, I have to go. Evan should be around somewhere."

He went into the kitchen. "Mom, who was that?"

"Mrs. Fairbanks, looking for Evan. Wasn't he with you yesterday?"

"He was."

"When did you see him last?"

"Outside the middle school."

She looked at him closely, reading his face. "Did you guys have a fight?"

"Kind of. He said a mean thing to Rachel, and I didn't want to talk to him."

"Do you know where he is? Where he might have gone?"

"No, Mom. I thought he was at home. Where's Dad?"

"In the bathroom." She caressed the back of his neck and said, "Wait here. I'm going to talk to your father." She ran upstairs.

Corey listened as there was a muffled discussion between them.

Then he heard his mother say two words that chilled his blood. "Hello, police."

FOURTEEN

NORMAN WATCHED THE ACTION FROM THE DRAWING ROOM, which Kim had insisted was its proper designation, since it was far too grand and regal to be described as a mere living room—the wallpaper a circular gold filigree against a backdrop of black; handstitched, ornately designed sofas; a marble fireplace; a brilliant chandelier; and ambient wall-mounted lighting. The round rosewood table he was sitting behind had cost thousands of dollars. Norman couldn't coax a precise figure from Kim. She seemed to think it was distasteful to divulge the amount she had paid.

At first, it had caused Norman serious anxiety. All that money, and for what? Appearances? To show everyone how well she'd done? But he had learned to stop worrying when Kim started spending. She was never short of a perfectly constructed reason for a new purchase, and she had a gift for making those reasons sound logical. Somehow, he always felt foolish for questioning her. She seemed confident, like she knew what she was doing.

Norman looked on through the open heavy oak door, and into the hall and the great room beyond. Kim was handling the reporter from the local TV station, WCAZ, with the same self-assurance. She was telling the reporter, Diane Battle, that homemaking was a vocation, and that the key ingredient to becoming a great American homemaker was in the name: homemaker, making a house a home. Sure, Kim said, you could clean your house, do the laundry and all the other things necessary to the efficient running of a home, but you had to inject warmth, a sense of belonging, a place your husband wanted to spend a lot of his time.

A producer at WCAZ had contacted Kim, asking her if she'd be interested in participating in a special report on homemaking. The producer, Arthur Dunhill, had seen her YouTube channel, American Homemaker, its hundreds of thousands of subscribers, and her massive fan base on Pinterest. Arthur Dunhill recognized a ratings draw when he saw one.

Norman hadn't been aware of her YouTube channel. Not that he was interested. The internet had passed him by, and Norman felt vaguely grateful that he didn't have a Twitter or Facebook account. He didn't hate the internet. Kim had told him it could be useful—for promoting their business and creating new opportunities—but it was also a breeding ground for malcontents, or, to use Kim's term, The Entitled; those who sought offense, those who were *entitled* to be offended, morally outraged, poorly adjusted individuals who'd turned the web into a sewer. Norman was glad he was old enough to have missed it.

The sound of approaching sirens prompted him to look out the window. Three state police cruisers sped up Main Street.

In the great room, Brooke Draper, Paige Gardner and Megan Hawkins rose from their seats by the wall to see what the commotion was. It was unusual to see one speeding police cruiser, siren wailing, but three was positively rare. Diane Battle was wrapping the interview. The cameraman and boom operator began to pack away their equipment. The lighting technician turned off the lights. Diane Battle had sniffed a story elsewhere.

Norman sipped his peppermint tea as he watched the TV crew leave, get into their van, and drive off in the direction of the police cars.

Kim paused in the hall, looking at him, a faint smile on her lips.

"How'd it go?" he asked.

"It was perfect, Norman. It was perfect." Her eyes were filled with dreamy possibility, and her smile broadened. Norman shifted in the rosewood chair, searching for something to say.

"Sounds as though you made an impression, Kim," he said. "You did a good job."

"The homemaker's job is never done, Norman. The girls and I are going into closed session, to discuss how we can improve as homemakers. You don't mind, do you?"

"Of course not," he said.

She turned toward the great room, elegant in a short lime-green dress and red pumps. She was still smiling as she closed the door.

FIFTEEN

COREY WONDERED IF IT WERE POSSIBLE TO BE TRAPPED IN a dream while you were wide awake. A glacial calm had settled in his stomach. His limbs were heavy, his mouth dry. The two state police officers didn't seem real. They were leaning forward on the sofa, elbows on their knees, notepads open. He couldn't see what they were writing. They gave no indication of whether they thought he was a suspect. He couldn't shake the idea that he was guilty of something. They were asking him the same questions over and over, and Corey repeated the same answers. He'd seen enough TV cop shows to know they were probably trying to catch him out, to poke holes in his account of events. That was their goal: to wait for him to change his story. Then they would pounce.

His parents sat either side of him, his mother's arm around his shoulders. The older officer did the talking, his voice low, although Corey was sure he could shout if he needed to. He'd introduced himself as detective Maher. The other cop, the younger one, watched him, probably in an attempt to make him nervous. But Corey was determined not to crumble under that hard stare. Corey couldn't remember his name. He wouldn't stutter and stumble as he gave his account of what had happened, which was nothing at all. He hadn't done anything wrong. Had he?

"You say you had an altercation with Evan," Maher said.

"What's an alter—"

"An argument, Corey."

Why didn't you just say argument then? he thought, alarmed at the anger steadily breaking through the calm in his gut. Was his anger directed at himself or the police? He didn't know, and his frustration grew.

"Yes," he said, "we had an argument."

"What about?"

"He called one of my friends fat. He was being mean for no reason. I left him at the middle school and that's the last time I saw him."

"Was he mean a lot lately?"

"Yeah. I don't know why but he was. Usually he was okay. I don't understand why he had to be cruel to Rachel." His mother's arm tightened a notch on his shoulders.

"Corey, did Evan ever talk about running away?"

"No," he said. "Evan would *never* run away. He didn't say anything to me. Something's wrong. I know he wouldn't be gone this long if everything was all right."

"Did he ever talk about his mother, Corey?"

"No."

Lillian removed her arm from his shoulders and her body became rigid. "That woman is a drunk," she said. Corey was shocked by how loud her voice was. "A no-good drunk. Maybe you should charge her with neglect. She was most likely drinking all night and didn't take the trouble to look for her son."

"Please, Mrs. Bayliss," Maher said, holding his palms toward his mother as though trying to quell any further outbursts.

"Someone took him, didn't they?" Corey said.

"We can't comment on our investigation, son."

"So what *are* you doing to find him?" Lillian said.

Maher sighed, looked at the floor, then at Lillian. "We've issued an Amber Alert, Mrs. Bayliss. We're doing everything possible to locate Evan Fairbanks, I promise."

"In the meantime," she said, "our children are not safe outside until you find Evan alive and well or you apprehend the person responsible for kidnapping him?"

Maher dropped his head, examining the floor again. The word *kidnapping* struck terror right through Corey's center; it meant Evan might be dead. He'd watched enough cop shows…His throat constricted, and he bounced his legs up and down restlessly.

"We have a few more questions, Corey," Maher said, "then we'll leave you in peace."

Corey didn't believe he'd ever feel peace again if the police found Evan dead. He should have gone with him to his house and then left. Evan wouldn't be missing if he'd just stayed with him. His eyes began to burn.

"Did you notice anyone, any vehicles in Hubbard Park that seemed out of place, anyone acting strangely?"

"No," Corey said. "No! I told you everything! *Why are you here instead of looking for him?*" Tears stood out in his eyes.

"It's okay," Lillian said, putting her arm around his shoulders again.

He shook it off, stood up fast, the tears streaming freely now, his voice cracked and pleading. "Bring Evan back. I promise I won't be mad at him anymore. Please bring him back. We can be friends. I promise I won't leave him again."

His parents went to him, embracing him as he sobbed, his body shuddering between them.

SIXTEEN

KIM WAS BEAMING WITH THE AFTERGLOW OF HER DEBUT TV appearance. Could they see it? Could they see the residual radiance that orbited her, a bright golden aura? It was validation. Diane Battle had spoken to her as though she was an authority on homemaking, and she had performed like a professional. These women knew it, too. Paige Gardner and Brooke Draper were smiling at her. It didn't matter if Megan Hawkins was staring at her as if she'd failed to pay back a loan. Megan's hatred fed her, spurred her on, made her crave even more success. She was a YouTube star, and now quite possibly a TV pundit, too. She would guide the homemakers of Vermont through their daily chores and make them feel good about their vocation. Diane Battle had been impressed, and Diane herself had been impressive. Her blonde hair perfect, full, not a split end to be had on that flawless mane. And still, faultless, as though it had been molded in a factory and carefully lowered onto her head by a crane and a group of highly skilled workmen. Makeup that would be the envy of a Hollywood actress. And an immaculate cream suit complemented with businesslike heels. And that smile! Warm, caring, a smile the public trusted. Diane Battle. Kim's mind was in a whirl. Nothing could ruin her day, not even the sour presence of Megan Hawkins.

She drew in a deep breath to stifle the excitement in her chest, and said, "Okay, ladies. It's back to business as usual —"

"I'm sorry to interrupt, Kim," Brooke said, "but I must say it again. You did an excellent job."

"Yeah," Paige said, "we couldn't have hoped for a better advocate."

"Thank you both. My God, you two are going to have me blushing. But really, thank you." Kim's attention shifted to Megan. She wondered why the older woman was here. They were never going to be friends; Megan clearly hated her. Kim guessed that she was simply a masochist. Or perhaps she had nothing better to do than come to her home and stink up the place with her bad vibes. Kim had invited her only because Megan was rich. She had influence in the business community; she might be useful when it came to funding some media projects she had in mind. But her efforts at befriending this woman had been met with an immovable stoniness that was testing her patience.

What do you want?

"We're going to tackle the bathroom today. We're not just a talking shop. We need to discuss practical steps. It's not my favorite place to start. Sometimes we have to face the unpalatable in order to appreciate the things we enjoy. I begin by dealing with hard-water stains on the faucet. Step one: Soak a rag, or whatever cloth you have handy, in white vinegar and wrap it around the faucet. You can leave it for an hour. I tend to give it two because I can do other things while the vinegar does its job. You'll be amazed by the results. Now onto the shower curtain, and a problem I know some of you are familiar with—black mold. Throw it in the washing machine and add some bleach. Black mold is nothing to be ashamed of, but it can be serious, even more so if anyone in the household has asthma. I'm afraid in most cases Clorox is the only answer to black mold. It can grow on the grout between your tiles. Attack it with bleach, ladies.

I haven't found anything that works better. All right, before I get sidetracked, we're focusing on the bathtub. Mold on your caulking is no laughing matter. Take a pan, one you're not going to eat out of but use exclusively for cleaning, and pour in some bleach. Soak a whole bunch of cotton pads and line them up along the full length of the caulking. Don't be afraid to get your fingers sore. Push those cotton pads hard into the edges and crevices. It's up to you how long you leave them in place. Personally, I'm fine leaving them to soak overnight, but make sure you give it a few hours, at least. If you're not amazed by the results, then my name isn't Kim."

Paige and Brooke laughed. Megan merely watched her, as though she'd discovered a strange and exotic creature and was studying its ways.

***

Megan was stunned. She glanced at Paige and Brooke; they were taking notes, writing furiously, jotting down the precious words of Kim Loomis, words of such value they deserved to be memorialized in ink. Megan stared at them, eyes narrow, squinting, as though convinced she was seeing a mirage.

"Cleaning the bathtub is essential," Kim continued, "and not always straightforward. If you have a cast-iron tub, and it's enameled with porcelain, forget the acidic cleaners, scouring pads and powders, which can dull and damage the surface. Baking soda, ladies. It is *the* true American homemaker's friend. Humble baking soda and ammonia with a dash of lemon does wonders for your tub. Mix those three in a bucket and simply scrub with a soft sponge. Honestly, the quickest and most labor-saving way of removing the scum from your tub is bleach. But we want to do things right. We want our bathtub to last, so we treat it properly. For regular enameled tubs, it's fine to use Comet or Ajax, but don't use too much. For stubborn stains, make a paste from the Ajax powder, cover the stain, and let it sit for thirty to thirty-five minutes. If you want to avoid complicating matters, you can always just use hydrogen peroxide. It won't break the bank, that's for sure. Finally, for acrylic tubs, Mrs. Meyer's Clean Day is all you need. It's a cream cleanser and the final word in dealing with greasy scum. And now, to the part I dislike the most—cleaning the commode. The simplest way to clean the toilet bowl is with any household disinfectant and a disposable rag or kitchen roll. On the other hand, if you want to keep things minty fresh, you can whip up some toilet fizzies. To make, throw a cup and a half of baking soda into a mixing bowl and whisk, then pour in a half cup of citric acid, one tablespoon of vinegar and hydrogen peroxide. Use a separate bowl for this and add slowly or you'll be mopping it off the floor. Then add twenty-five drops of peppermint essential oil. Mix it all together and spoon the mixture into an ice-cube tray. Let it dry overnight and then put the cubes in a jar, or whatever's available. You'll get roughly fifty fizzies, ready whenever you need them."

Megan had been trying to pinpoint what was troubling her about Kim, the one thing that had caused her resentment and dislike to fester. She thought she'd stumbled on the answer. The absence of any reference to God in her lectures, and how important He was to the true American homemaker, to use one of Kim's terms, disturbed her. Was the woman a heathen? She must be, Megan thought, otherwise she would've mentioned Him. A Christless homemaker was not to be trusted.

SEVENTEEN

COREY'S TEARS HAD DRIED TO A STIFF CRUST ON HIS CHEEKS. He lay on his bed, staring at the ceiling, listening to the quick, murmured conversation between his parents somewhere below. He didn't want to know what they were talking about. He wasn't eavesdropping; he just wanted to drown out the voice in his head, low and irresistible, almost casual, telling him it was all his fault. If he hadn't left Evan, he'd still be here. What if Evan's bad behavior was because his mother was a drunk? It made sense to Corey and would explain why Evan wouldn't invite him over. Was Mrs. Fairbanks abusing Evan? There was no way to be sure, but what if she beat him? What if she shouted at him? Wouldn't that explain Evans's worsening attitude?

He sat up fast, startled. Someone was knocking on the front door. And yelling at the top of her lungs. A woman. He went to the window and pressed his face to it, flattening his nose. There was a commotion downstairs and the sound of the door being unlocked.

"*Where's my son?*" A female voice, high, distressed.

"What are you doing here, Mrs. Fairbanks?" mom asked.

Then Corey saw her, backing away.

"WHERE'S MY SON?" Mrs. Fairbanks bent into the scream, spilling clear liquor from the bottle jouncing by her side. She swayed as though she were onboard a ship in heavy seas.

"Go home, Lena. We don't know where he is." A sudden stillness descended on Mrs. Fairbanks. She wasn't swaying anymore. She hauled back, like a pitcher getting ready to throw. The liquor bottle went flying. Corey's mouth fell open. His mother yelped in surprise and the door slammed shut. The explosion of breaking glass was enormous in the windless night.

"Hello, police? Hello?" It was his father. Corey held a hand to his stomach. It felt loose, unmoored somehow.

Mrs. Fairbanks saw him. Their eyes met and Corey's breath stopped.

"What did you do to him? WHAT DID YOU DO?"

His legs weakened and he slid to the floor, resting against the side of his bed. He hugged his knees close to his chin and rocked gently. Mrs. Fairbanks kept shouting the same question at him, the same accusation. Then her voice broke and she began to sob in great wracking moans of despair.

I didn't do anything. I didn't do anything. I didn't do anything.

The sirens grew louder. He couldn't hear Mrs. Fairbanks now, or the thought repeating itself in his mind, *I didn't do anything.* It sounded less true with each utterance.

EIGHTEEN

New Haven, Connecticut

RICARDO TORRES STOOD AT HIS UPSTAIRS OFFICE WINDOW, hands loosely clasped behind his back. He wasn't panicking yet. But it beckoned. The knot in his stomach tightened a little more. He distracted himself by tracing the humpbacked three-hundred-foot backbone of Ingalls Rink, its ventral grooves similar to those found on a whale's jaw, the reason it was commonly known as the Yale Whale. The ice-hockey rink was part of Yale University, his alma mater. Beyond the curved spine of the arena was the School of Forestry and Environmental Studies, Kroon Hall. Most of its barn-shaped roof was covered in an array of solar panels.

As he stared, his vision blurred. He missed being a student. There was no downside to it, at least not for him. Everything had been paid for by his parents. Money smoothed the rough edges of life. And he was determined to make a lot of it. Spending money on designer goods and mansions didn't appeal to him. The promise of the freedom it held was far more enticing. Just knowing he had enormous wealth was enough to make him feel comfortable.

Known to the less civilized of his white friends as the White Mexican, a consequence of his fair complexion,

Torres boasted a full head of silver hair swept back on his head. He had cultivated a professorial air. The spectacles riding low on his nose reinforced his persona, as did his agile, intelligent eyes. He wore suits. Nothing too fancy. His car was a mid-range urban sedan devoid of ostentation. Low-key and friendly, anyone meeting Torres for the first time would struggle to believe he was the leader of the Los Mochis cartel, named after the coastal city in northern Sinaloa, Mexico, his father's birthplace. Torres himself had never been across the border. There was no need to. Modern communications technology had made such a trip unnecessary. Not that he would have gone to Sinaloa, anyway. He had no desire to get involved in infighting, messy politics, and violence. He wasn't averse to violence but it was to be employed only under very special circumstances. Now circumstance demanded he take action.

He watched the SUV pull in to his driveway. Two men got out. They approached his front door, and a bell rang somewhere in the downstairs hall. Torres went to his desk and pushed a button beside his landline. He didn't use cell phones, or DEA listening devices as he preferred to think of them. He sat at his desk, relaxing in the chair. The office had once been a bedroom. After Gabriela had divorced him, it had made sense to have a home office rather than paying rent in the central business district downtown. Gabriela had persuaded him that a business address in a shiny new block gave him an added layer of respectability. Torres knew it was just something for Gabriela to brag about to her friends at the New Haven Country Club.

He rose from the chair to greet the two men, embracing them both. Juan Sanchez was twenty-eight, hair cropped close, always dressed in a plain black long-sleeve tee-shirt and a pair of fashionable denim jeans he had heard kids refer to as "skinny." Juan was a hothead. That was all right with Torres. Hotheads had their place and purpose, too. The other man, the taller one, was Miguel Cabrera. He had a fearsome reputation for getting the job done. Miguel was precise. Reliable. A strategic thinker, he helped run Los Mochis with a calm calculation that had impressed Torres. He was also a highly effective sicario. A naturalized American citizen, Cabrera was his emissary south of the border. It was for these reasons Torres had made him a partner. They had something in common, too. Neither Torres nor Cabrera *had* to become narco-traffickers. Cabrera had a bachelor of science degree in materials science from MIT. Torres's was in biomedical engineering. Torres wondered why Cabrera had chosen the path he was on. He'd ask him some day, when he managed to successfully answer the question for himself. The fact that Torres's father was also a trafficker didn't explain why he had become involved in the business. He'd had options and chosen the most perilous one. Why? He didn't know. There was no satisfactory explanation.

Cabrera and Juan sat. Torres remained standing, his back to them, looking down at Mansfield Street.

"We have a problem."

"Don Ricardo, what happened?" Cabrera asked.

Torres turned and sat at his desk. "I'm going to speak directly. We have to move fast. Charles Shaker is missing, possibly dead. I want you to locate him, or his body."

Cabrera gripped the armrests. It took a moment for the scale of the problem to sink in: Shaker was their launderer, the only man with access to hundreds of millions of dollars of *their* money.

"How much?" Cabrera said, his voice low, almost a whisper.

"Five hundred and three million."

Juan dropped his eyes and fidgeted with the sleeve of his tee-shirt.

The atmosphere in the room grew weightier by the second. They all felt it. Cabrera ran the knuckles of his hand back and forth across the stubble on his jawline. The rasping sound made the silence seem longer. Juan's eyes were fixed on the floor. He didn't dare glance at his boss sitting next to him. His body loosened with visible relief when Cabrera finally spoke.

"Do we have a solution to the problem?"

That was another reason Torres respected his partner. Cabrera was forever in search of solutions to problems.

Torres passed a small square of paper to Cabrera.

"What's this?"

"An address," Torres said. "There you'll find Jennifer Shaker. Commit it to memory. Then destroy it."

"The wife," Cabrera said, licking his lips as though the words had a promising flavor. "You think she knows something?"

"It's the best place to start. Who is the main suspect when a spouse or partner goes missing?"

Cabrera didn't say anything. He didn't need to.

"Let me be clear," Torres said, "I want you to question Mrs. Shaker. Thoroughly. When she lies to you, remove one of her fingers. If she tells you ten lies, she'll have no fingers left."

Juan had perked up. He was looking at Torres with interest, his eyes shining.

Cabrera nodded. "Is there anything else we should know?"

"I don't know if it matters, but there was a fire in the Shaker residence. It was contained in time. Charles might be alive but I don't know. He's definitely missing."

"Could it have been a competitor?" Cabrera said.

"No. If it was a cartel, they'd want us to know he's dead. The wife, Miguel. She had something to do with it. Nothing was stolen from the house. Maybe Shaker was having an affair. Hell hath no fury…"

NINETEEN

HE WAS IN THE DARK. THERE WAS NO SOUND EXCEPT HIS breathless whimpering. Evan focused on the bottomless black. White dots swam in the abyss. His hands were bound. Thin rope bit into his wrists. There was a cloth stuffed in his mouth. His nostrils flared as he sucked in air. He was blindfolded. He screamed. The muffled sound scared him. He stopped.

Where am I?

His back was against a wall. He tilted his body sideways and fell to the floor. He tried to straighten his legs. The rope around his feet pulled on the one that secured his hands. Hog tied.

Oh my God help me.

His face was slick. Damp, itchy wetness prickled his scalp. The urge to scratch, powerful and useless, drove another scream into the cloth choking off his voice. Deep, maddening. It itched and itched, a taunt that rippled under his skin.

A sound. Thudding, rhythmic. He listened. It was his heart. Beating as fast as that of the injured sparrow he had once held in his hand. The bird had survived and flown again. Evan sensed death in the darkness. Adrenaline flooded his muscles. He kicked and strained and begged for help, but no one answered, not even God. If He hadn't helped his mom quit drinking, He wasn't going to help him. The idea that God had abandoned him caused a speckle of gooseflesh on his arms. His skin seemed to tighten, shrink. The rag covering his eyes was damp with tears and sweat. A heavier fluid was leaking from his head. It trickled down his face. Some of it had hardened on his cheek.

I'll be good I promise I'll be good.

He wriggled and twisted. His face touched the cold ground, catching grit like flypaper. He thrashed from side to side. The rag remained stuffed in his mouth, the blindfold didn't budge, his hands remained tied, and the fear became unbearable.

I promise I'll be nice to Rachel I won't be mean to her please I'll say I'm sorry I don't know why I was mean to her please...

He didn't know if it was day or night. Time had ceased to exist. Had a minute passed since he'd woken up or an hour? He counted seconds off in his head and thought he was doing it wrong. No one knew where he was. He felt he was far from home. The sensation of total isolation built and built. Frantic and alone, in an airless void, he struggled harder. Trying to loosen the rope. Alone. The word only kicked his desperation up a notch. Air whistled through his nose. There wasn't enough of it. Blood rushed to his head. His heart stammered high in his chest, the loudest sound in the world.

Then a memory surfaced, and he was still. He saw himself climbing through a basement window, in search of corpses. In search of adventure. He watched *The Walking Dead*. He was a big fan. His mother had said he shouldn't watch it. He was too young. It was off-limits. She'd said it with such a lack of conviction that he had completely ignored her. But he had believed the tall, creepy undertaker stored the dead in his basement. In his twelve-year-old brain, it had been plausible. It was foolish; he knew that now. There had been no bodies in the basement. Just expensive-looking medical equipment. And a steel table attached to special hoses of some kind. He couldn't remember much after that, other than a blinding white light, then nothing at all.

He noticed how quiet it was. No noise penetrated from the outside. He was in a room. He had been leaning against a wall. It *must* be a room. *What if it's not?* he thought. What if it was a tomb?

His lower lip trembled. Something moved across the room. He *felt* it.

A shuffling sound. His body was electrified with terror. His skin seemed to crackle with it. It shocked his eyes wide behind the blindfold. He froze. Something moaned. Something was in here with him.

TWENTY

THE NEWS CAME ON. KIM INCREASED THE VOLUME TO AN earsplitting level. She aimed the remote from her position on an extravagant, gold-embroidered armchair, feet tucked beneath her. Norman didn't complain about the indecent volume. It was a daily ritual. They turned on the news every evening at six. He watched the anchor deliver the headlines. And he watched Kim from the corner of his eye. She was peeling an apple with a knife so large it looked ludicrous. Norman could set his watch by her. She carved the skin off an apple at six on the dot every single day. Even on Sundays.

Norman's attention was drawn to the TV screen. He saw the middle school, a picture of a boy said to be missing. And the exact spot where he'd last been seen. The camera panned wide enough to take in his own front lawn. Uneasiness percolated in his gut. A detective appeared, and standing next to him, an FBI agent. Norman heard the words *no leads at this time* and the volume dropped. He glanced at Kim. Her forefinger hovered over the volume button, as though she was wrestling with a decision. In the end, she pressed Mute. Norman continued looking at the screen and sensed Kim's gaze on him. He was in her sights.

"It's a horrible world, Norman," she said in her best isn't-it-awful voice. "Kids can't even play outside without some pedophile snatching them. On our own doorstep."

Norman's mind was working too hard. His thoughts came in a flurry, all at once. One thought floated above all the others, like a dumped body buoyed to the surface of a lake by its own fetid gases. He refused to examine it, to consider it. Kim was many things, but she wasn't…

She came toward him. Apple in one hand, knife in the other. Sat in his lap, the arm holding the apple around his neck. The knife flashed with reflected light.

"Norman, you have no idea how worried I am for you." There was no mistaking the concern in her expression. Her forehead was tight with it. To Norman, it looked genuine. "You can't continue to be stressed to the extent you are. You work hard, so hard, Norman. At some point you have to depressurize. I don't want you stroking out on me because you won't deal with your stress. We have a stressful job, as you know. None of this is easy. When I was a little girl, I didn't want to be a mortician. It has no glamor. It's dirty and it can be hazardous. I wanted to be a fashion designer, but I'm not an artist. I wanted to run an animal shelter, but I wasn't good at taking care of animals. All the dogs and cats I had, died. I did my best to give them a good home. And my best wasn't good enough, Norman honey. I suffered badly from stress in those years. I worried about myself, Norman, just like I'm worried about you now. So I have a suggestion."

As she talked, Kim waved the knife in front of his face, as though she was using it to emphasize a point. Whatever the case, Norman was tense. He couldn't take his eyes off the long, broad blade.

She reached into a hip pocket of her polka-dot dress and extracted a bottle of pills, holding the cap between thumb and middle finger, in the same hand as the knife. "These, honey, are high-strength Xanax. I know you're not keen on exercise as a means of dealing with stress, and I would hate to force you to do something you don't want to do. I want you to take one, Norman. For me. To take the edge off the stress. I want you to take at least one every day."

At first, he hadn't noticed. Now he couldn't help but see it: the knife was getting closer to his face. Kim didn't seem to be aware of it. She took a bite from the half-eaten apple and chewed, arm still around his neck, pulling his head toward hers.

"What do you say, Norman honey?"

Norman cleared his throat. "I…uh…I mean I…"

"It's okay, it's okay. Shh. Let me help you." She handed him the apple. It was turning brown in places. She used her free hand to twist off the cap. She shook one pink pill into her palm. Then pinched it between thumb and forefinger.

"Open wide, Norman honey." She moved the pill to his mouth and Norman felt his head backing away from it. The pill paused mid-journey. Kim's concern turned to disappointment.

"Norman. I'm trying. To. Do. What's. Best. For. You." The knife was so close to his eyes that Norman flinched as she shook it in his face after each word. "If your own wife hasn't got your wellbeing at heart, who has?"

The tip of the blade touched his lower lip. She moved it back and forth over the soft flesh. Then she pressed down with the knife. His lip sprang forward, revealing his teeth.

"Just one little tablet, Norman. Open wide."

Norman opened wide. The pill, still hanging in mid-flight, continued to its final destination.

She watched him dry swallow and said, "Open wide for me. Big and wide. Lift your tongue."

Norman did as he was told.

"Good. See? It wasn't so difficult."

Norman was relieved when she stood up. Glad the knife wasn't so close to him anymore. He looked at the apple in his hand. It was now completely brown.

TWENTY-ONE

East Hampton, Long Island, New York

IT WAS HOT AS HELL IN THE VAN, EVEN WITH THE WINDOWS open. Miguel looked through the Bushnell binoculars again and saw gravestones. They were parked in Methodist Lane, next to North End Cemetery. The gray hexagonal shape of Old Hook Windmill loomed in the optics beyond the boneyard, raised on a landscaped hump, its broad sails framed against a perfect blue sky. He made an adjustment and picked out the front entrance to the Windmill House Hotel on North Main Street. According to Torres's contact, Jennifer Shaker had checked in. With a male companion. This information was not promising. The cops would be looking at her closely. How much did she know? And had she killed her husband?

Miguel doubted Charles Shaker would have boasted about his connection to the cartel. Torres had chosen him carefully. At first, he hadn't trusted him; he'd had him followed and watched twenty-four hours a day for months. But Shaker had never disappointed them. And Torres gave up looking for mistakes. Shaker wasn't going to run.

Miguel had liked Charles, respected him. He'd done his job well. He had taken his cut and not tried to squeeze them for more. Low-key, reliable. Someone you could do business with and not lie awake at night worrying he was stripping you of your assets and sailing away on the high seas with your loot. Charles had actually purchased a yacht, rapidly lost interest in it, and it was still moored in Sag Harbor, unused and gathering barnacles. But, Miguel was beginning to suspect that Charles's judgment had been seriously lacking. He had no idea what had attracted Charles to Jennifer Colson, apart from the superficial obvious. And then he'd gone and *married* her. Miguel couldn't understand it. Of all the women in the world, Charles had chosen to spend his life with a woman clearly only interested in his money. Had she had information that had compromised him? Had she threatened him? Miguel was baffled and appalled by the extent to which people allowed themselves to be taken advantage of, especially those who were rich, and therefore powerful. She'd probably killed him, he decided, or had him killed. Either way, Miguel was confident she would answer him honestly when he asked her. He looked forward to *asking* her.

In the seat next to him, Juan sighed. He was bored. He missed Mexico, his parents and siblings. In Mexico excitement could be had in large doses. And Juan craved excitement, among other things.

Yet here they were, sitting in a stifling van with Manhattan Plumbing Supplies decaled on its sides, a legitimate business that Miguel ran with his wife and sister. A map was open on the dash. If a cop came along, Miguel had a story prepared—they were lost, looking for a customer on Further Lane. They *did* know someone at that address, but there was nothing wrong with his plumbing.

Miguel glanced at him. Juan's legs were pumping up and down as though he needed the toilet. "What's wrong with you? Restless-leg syndrome?"

"No, *patron*, it's hot."

"It's not as hot as Mexico."

"The heat in Mexico is different."

Miguel shifted his body, turned toward him. "Are you saying the same sun heats Mexico differently than America?"

"Yes, *patron*, it's not so uncomfortable."

Miguel nodded, as though Juan had provided a perfectly reasonable explanation.

Miguel's cell phone vibrated and he answered it, listened. "How deep is the hole?" A pause, then: "It's not deep enough. Twelve feet. And make it fast. It better be finished when I get there. You understand me, Antonio? Good."

He hung up and tossed the burner phone into the glove compartment. He changed his number every week. Torres demanded it of everyone in Los Mochis. Those who broke the rule were fined one million dollars for a first offense. Second time around, they had their legs broken. A third lapse was a death sentence. No excuses. Miguel agreed with it. If there was a breach in security, they were all vulnerable.

"Relax," Miguel said. "You'll get to play soon."

Juan nodded, and his eyes brightened. Miguel checked his mirrors. There was no one on Methodist Lane. It was a quiet area. To their left, there was a green open space, mowed, dotted with trees. The old church building up ahead looked deserted. He lifted the binoculars, looked through them for a few seconds. Then he froze. Juan seemed to sense the change and looked at him. Miguel watched a man emerge from the hotel. He stood for a moment, nonchalant, waiting. A woman joined him. Miguel started the engine. Pulled away from the grassy verge toward Pantigo Road.

"You know what to do?" he asked.

Juan said, "Yes, *patron*."

Miguel thought the strategy was risky. Snatching two people from the street in broad daylight was fraught with danger. But he'd met Jennifer Shaker once. She knew his face. If he checked into the hotel and forced them to leave quietly under threat of violence, there was risk in that, too. Jennifer could spot him, call the police. She'd at least be smart enough to understand he hadn't booked into the same hotel for a holiday. He just didn't know what she'd do.

He observed the speed limit, not wanting to hand a cop a readymade excuse to stop him. He swung a U-turn onto North Main, stopped the van, hazard lights blinking. Juan jumped out, landed on the sidewalk and broke into a fast walk, hand under his black shirt. Jennifer Shaker was walking directly toward him. There was almost a foot of empty space between them when Juan showed Shaker the gun. They came to an abrupt stop, eyes wide. Mouths gaping.

Juan spoke quickly. "If you scream, you die. If you run, you die. If you don't act normal, like you know me, you die. Get in front of me. Move it, assholes."

Juan fell in behind them. The door on the side of the van slid open. The man was hauled inside by his shirt collar. He groaned in protest. Miguel struck him on the forehead with his gun. The van rocked as he collapsed into a loose pile of flesh and bones. Juan pushed Jennifer Shaker in after him with such force that her shoes came off. He picked them up off the sidewalk and threw them into the van. Miguel handcuffed Jennifer. Juan secured the man's hands behind his back.

Jennifer Shaker moaned. "What—?" She fell back as Miguel slapped her. Blood sprayed from her mouth and her head snapped sideways. Then she retched.

"Don't say a word," Miguel said. He climbed into the driver's seat.

It was hot as hell, still. Hotter, since Miguel had closed the windows. But it was good to be back in action.

TWENTY-TWO

NORMAN HAD SWALLOWED HIS SECOND XANAX WITHOUT protest. It was easier to avoid confrontation. He accepted he wasn't strong enough. Kim was though. Kim had no problem with confrontation. She seemed happier now that he was taking his medicine. More pleasant to be around. Norman tried to locate the point in history when Kim had become decidedly unpleasant. There was no doubt in his mind—filled with cotton wool as it was—that things had changed with the arrival of Ray Porter. The broker had planted a seed, dangled a carrot in front of her. Once she understood how much money could be made, there had been no stopping her illegal extraction of human tissue. And Norman had abetted her, helped her bring in the dark harvest.

These thoughts came to Norman not in words but in images. Processing words was too difficult. But all those images had lost their power. He no longer felt despair. Guilt had no meaning. What they had done didn't seem to matter. His lifelong anxiety had loosened its grip. Now he was in awe. Maybe Kim did know what was best for him, really was trying to help him. Maybe she was genuinely worried about him.

He sat at the head of the table in the great room, watching Kim on her hands and knees, scrubbing the floors.

The back and forth of the huge yellow sponge was hypnotic. He could stare at the movement all day. All week.

She had already cleaned the bathroom and the kitchen. She'd vacuumed the bedrooms, the halls. She didn't use a duster anymore because, she insisted, it only spread the dust around. Instead, she used a small attachment on the vacuum cleaner. Earlier, she had even vacuumed Norman, passing the nozzle over his suit, his hands, his cheeks. How they had both laughed. With the pills, Norman had felt something close to happiness. More importantly, it had made Kim happy. He hadn't heard her laugh in a long time. He wanted her to laugh more. He wanted *them* to laugh more.

Norman was proud of Kim. She'd had a tough early life. He didn't believe her confinement to the psychiatric hospital in Berlin had been entirely her fault. If she'd posed a threat to society, they wouldn't have released her. Her sister, on the other hand, was still locked up because *she* was dangerous. Norman believed everyone deserved a second chance, even a third. Kim had demonstrated that she was well. She was making progress. She had mapped out the road to success. And she had friends. The organ-transplant business was an anomaly, an aberration. It wasn't Kim's fault. It was her personality—when she latched onto an idea, she saw it through to the end. She couldn't let it go. Kim couldn't cope with the suspicion, however unfounded, that she'd missed a spot while cleaning. It was the reason she sometimes cleaned the bathroom twice, or mopped the kitchen floor four, five times. Maybe it was the same as taking organs from the dead. She needed to do it several times before she realized everything was okay…Norman's thoughts melted, evaporated to nothing. The images were gone. Despite his almost supernatural calm, he felt the need to wander. He left the great room.

He walked down the wide, wood-paneled hall. Although his anxiety had lost its intensity, it hadn't dulled his curiosity. He paused at the basement door, wondering why a new lock had been fitted. He pressed on the handle. It didn't move. It was locked. Norman thought it was strange he hadn't noticed it; he walked by the basement dozens of times a day. Kim had asked him not to go down there. It was her hobby room. It was where she sewed. It was fine if his wife wanted a private space to herself, but why would she lock him out? He hadn't gone into the basement since she'd asked him not to.

Norman saw Kim from the corner of his eye. He would have jumped if his startle reflex hadn't been dimmed to the point of extinction.

"What are you doing, Norman sweetie?"

"Oh," he said, "I was…was the mechanism broken?"

"You know I like my privacy, Norman. I don't think I'm asking for too much, do you?"

"Oh no, no, of course not," he said, the words coming fast. "I didn't mean…I was just curious."

"You know what happened to the cat when curiosity got the upper hand, Norman? He met a sad end. A sad, sad end, Norman."

"I wasn't prying," he said. His voice had dropped to a whisper.

"Of course not, sweetie. I mean, that would be awful. Beneath you. It would also be wrong, Norman."

"Yes, it would be wrong."

"Come on," she said. "I'll make you some peppermint tea and we can forget this."

She took his hand and led him to the kitchen. Norman looked over his shoulder at the shiny new basement-door lock.

TWENTY-THREE

"Wake up, bitch." The unconscious man didn't respond to Juan's voice. Juan slapped him.

Jennifer Shaker whimpered and closed her eyes.

They were on Further Lane. The van slowed, turned left. Antonio Martinez had already opened the gates. He was standing between the fluted Victorian columns of his mansion, his considerable gut spilling before him.

Miguel exited the van and waved Martinez over. Juan threw the van door back on its rails and hauled Jennifer onto the driveway, tearing her blouse.

Miguel saw the way the younger man was staring at the woman. He didn't like it. He helped Jennifer to her feet and said, "Are you okay?" She nodded. "The man you are with, what's his name?"

"Paul," she said. "Paul Reed."

He looked at Juan. "Take her inside. Sit her down. And that's all you do, understand? Antonio and I are going to carry Reed. Stay in front of us, where I can see you."

"Patron," Martinez said, "you want me to carry him?" Martinez didn't seem to relish the prospect of transporting a dead weight the short distance to the gymnasium attached to the rear of his house. Miguel soon discovered why. Martinez grabbed Paul Reed's legs, and Miguel hooked his arms around his armpits. As they carried him across the driveway, into the house, sweat streamed down the big man's face, soaking his blue shirt, turning it dark navy in places. Martinez huffed and puffed. Great gusts of air wheezed from his overburdened lungs. Miguel wanted to get this job done fast. His logistical manager's complexion had flushed a worrying shade of red. His lips flapped as air was propelled from his slack mouth. Spittle flew in strings.

At last, they reached the gymnasium. Three chairs stood empty in the middle of the floor, one chair facing the other two.

The gym was packed with thousands of dollars' worth of equipment. It had been moved against the walls to give them room. There were barbells, dumbbells, kettlebells, a bench press, dipping bars, preacher bench, pull-up bars, a pec deck, Smith machine, squat rack, cables and pulleys, treadmills...and all of it was covered in a delicate skin of dust.

They managed to get Reed sitting in the chair. Breathless, Martinez handed Miguel a roll of duct tape. He secured Reed's ankles to the chair legs, then his hands, and wound it loosely around his neck and the chair's high backrest.

"Patron, you want me to tape her up?" Juan asked, pointing at Jennifer, who was trembling, insensible with terror.

"No," Miguel said, "I'll do it." He kneeled in front of Jennifer and said, "If you kick me, I'll hurt you. I'm going to take off your shoes. We understand each other?" Her head jerked up and down. She glanced over Miguel's shoulder at Juan. There was fear in her eyes. "Look at me," Miguel said in a whisper and she turned to meet his eyes. "Nothing like that is going to happen. I promise."

Miguel fixed her blouse, buttoning it all the way, careful not to touch her. Juan had pulled the buttons apart but they hadn't broken off.

When he was finished, he cut the tape with a box cutter, patted the strip into place. He sat and said, "Antonio, smelling salts for Mr. Reed. Hurry up."

Martinez fumbled in his damp shirt pocket, went to Reed, held a vial under his nose. He slapped him, not too hard, just enough to get his attention.

Reed's eyelids fluttered. He looked left and right, then up at the tape on his forehead.

Juan left the gym and returned moments later holding a towel-wrapped bundle. He put it on the floor beside Miguel, strolled toward the exercise equipment, and ran a hand over it.

"Hey, Martinez. Ever think about using this shit?"

Martinez was still sweating next to Miguel. He ignored Juan and said, "Patron, please don't make a mess."

Miguel raised his head, looked at him, said nothing. Martinez shrank from the room and closed the door.

Juan wandered back carrying something that resembled a wishbone encased in plastic pink foam.

"What is it?" Miguel asked.

"It's a ThighMaster 5000."

Reed was fully conscious now. His eyes flitted in their sockets as if looking for an escape route. Miguel watched Jennifer, arms folded on his chest.

"I can give you money," Reed said. "Let me go. I have money." Juan went to him. He swung the ThighMaster, a pink streak in the air. Reed's nose broke instantly. Blood spurted from the split skin. Bone poked through torn gristle. Jennifer yelped and bucked in the chair.

Juan stepped aside, the ThighMaster swinging gently in his hand.

"Can you give me five hundred and three million dollars?" Miguel asked.

Reed stared at him.

Miguel turned his attention to Jennifer. "Where is your husband?"

"I don't…uh…I don't…" Miguel nodded at Juan. The ThighMaster cut the air again, its hard joint breaking Reed's teeth and shredding his lips to oozing ribbons.

"Charles Shaker. Your husband. Where is he?"

"I…I…oh God…"

Miguel sighed. He reached for the towel on the floor and unwrapped it. A large meat cleaver gleamed in the harsh light. "Please don't make me do this, Jennifer," he said. Miguel waited for her to say something, but her mouth worked uselessly.

"One more chance, Jennifer," he said.

Still her mouth moved, trying to form words, but none came.

Miguel rose from the chair as though his body was weighed down. Juan backed away, an awed expression dawning on his face. Miguel stood by Reed's right hand, cleaver poised above it.

"Third and final chance."

Juan, rapt, glanced at Jennifer, then at Miguel.

"Please," Reed pleaded. "Tell them everything. Please, Jenny, tell them." Reed's entire body was shaking as though he'd suddenly developed a palsy.

"I…I don't…"

Miguel slammed down the heavy blade just short of the wrist. The severed hand dropped to the floor. Jennifer's scream echoed in the high ceiling, in the hollow bones of the building.

Miguel wrapped the cleaver in the towel and sat. He watched Jennifer in silence, feeling the blood spatter on his face. He'd get to it later. The job wasn't done yet.

After a while her voice hoarsened, cracked. She sobbed instead, her body shook with the force of her terror.

"You killed your husband," Miguel said. "You had him murdered."

She nodded. He knew. He wanted her to admit it though.

"Did you do it or have somebody do it for you?"

"Somebody…suh-somebody."

"Who is he?"

"I don't…I don't knuh…I…" Miguel looked at Juan, let his eyes drop. Juan pulled a gun from his waistband, pointed it at Reed's head and squeezed the trigger, showering Jennifer in blood, brain and bone. The blast was deafening.

Jennifer winced and squirmed against her restraints. Tried to scream again, but no sound came.

Miguel's ears were ringing. He let a few seconds tick by, enough time for the sound to fade. "Who is he?" he asked.

"Shuh…*she*."

Miguel frowned. "She?"

"Yes."

"It was a woman?" Female *sicarios* were rare. But not unheard of. Some cartels used them, not because they were equal-opportunity employers but because they were effective.

"Was she Mexican?"

"Nuh…no."

"Okay. Did she have brown skin?"

"Sh-she was white."

Miguel's frown deepened.

"Calm down. Take long breaths," he said. "Breathe. We're just talking now." He went to her, plucked a tissue from his pocket. "I'm going to clean your eyes up so you can see me better," he said, showing her the tissue. His hand didn't make contact with her skin as he wiped the tears and blood dry. He returned to his seat.

"Jennifer, what's this woman's name?"

"Valerie…Price."

"Where does she live?"

She paused, hitching in a breath. He waited.

"Bleecker Street. Greenwich Village. She has a business. Spic N Span Cleaning."

It was always the same, he thought. When they talked, they spilled everything.

"You mean she actually took you to her place of business?" It didn't ring true. A contract killer wasn't going to invite you into their home, or their business.

"I followed her."

"Why?"

"I didn't trust her. I wanted to be able to hurt her if she didn't come through for me."

"At least you're honest." He kept his tone gentle.

"I met her on Long Island, and I hired a rental car, and I had my own car parked next to it, and I followed her in the rental—"

"It's okay," he said. "Nice and slow. What does she look like? Can you describe her?"

"Tall, about five ten, slim, works out, short blonde hair done in a pixie. Green eyes."

"What was the name of the company she runs one more time?"

He had to be sure.

"Spic N Span Cleaning."

"Located on what street?"

"Bleecker."

"That's good, Jennifer. Thank you so much for your help." He stood, turned and walked toward the door, closed it behind him. Then he heard the shot. Muffled, but still as loud as thunder in the gymnasium.

TWENTY-FOUR

IT WAS A RAT. MOVING IN THE DARK, RUSTLING THINGS. He'd heard it squeak. His mind wouldn't make up something like that. It had made no sound since that first time. He began to doubt himself.

Evan was on the verge of exhaustion and afraid he wouldn't have the strength to fight the rat if it pounced on him, sank its teeth into his leg, his chest, his neck. At least his back was against the wall. The rat couldn't attack him from behind. He was convinced the rat was becoming brave. It crept closer...every hour? Every day? Time was meaningless. It knew he was trapped. It knew he was weak. Rats had a keen sense of smell. He'd read it somewhere. The rat shifted things as it walked. It must be enormous. It would get closer and closer until...

He had to look inward. The outside world was dark. He saw Corey in his mind. He wished with every last ounce of energy that Corey knew how sorry he was. Evan didn't have many friends, just people he saw most days. Corey was different. He was the kind of friend you believed in, trusted completely. He relied on Corey's friendship more than anything. His mom wasn't well; things were bad at home. But seeing Corey always seemed to make his situation less terrible. Seeing Corey somehow eased that sick feeling in his stomach when he arrived home to see his mother had been replaced by a person he didn't know. It was cruel how alcohol transformed your own mother into a total stranger. She had promised to get better. Sometimes Evan believed her.

It wasn't Corey's fault for leaving him that day. Evan wished he could take it all back. Wished Rachel would forgive him. Maybe there was something horrible and cruel in him and this was a just punishment. The dark made you think about the bad things you'd done. Maybe he deserved the dark. Deserved to be forced to look inward. To see his cruelty in the harshest mirror.

He was afraid to move. The sounds were louder. The scuffing of his sneakers in the grit was enough to make his heart leap high in his chest. He closed his eyes behind the blindfold. His hair felt matted and hard. The itch had passed. If it returned, he'd lose his mind. But had that itch even been real. Was the rat real? Had his mind invented these horrors? He didn't know. He only knew he could hear everything and see nothing. The slightest sound seemed to be amplified tenfold. His breathing had slowed until it was no more than little gulps of air. Sips. What if it was all a prank? No one would go this far, would they? Definitely not Corey. If Corey knew where he was, he'd rescue him. He'd find a way to get him out of here. Corey was smart and Evan was okay with that. It was good to have friends that were smarter than you. You always learned something new. Evan recalled the times they'd walked home from school together. Corey always had some interesting fact about science, animals, or movies. And Evan had listened. Corey had a gift for making the lamest stuff sound interesting.

He smiled and the gag tightened on his mouth. The itch had returned. His eyes burned; they had amassed a crust of sticky matter. He blinked and blinked. The blindfold was damp.

He made a promise to God again, vowed he'd be a better friend if He would heal his mom and make Corey and Rachel forgive him.

Something bit his sneaker. He screamed, hit his head on the wall. The world faded, became distant. In the void, he saw himself trying to catch his falling mind, a shapeless thing with no color, just out of reach.

TWENTY-FIVE

MELODY LUNGED, JABBED THE EVERLAST BAG, STINGING IT. Danced onto her other foot, snapped her fist back to her chin. Each jab was more relaxed than the last. As a result, she was getting faster. Satisfied her body had memorized the speed, she switched to the cross. Gloves at her chin, she let it go. Rotated her hips and threw her weight into it. The heavy leather bag barely moved on its chain. Franco "Two Picks" Beltran, owner of Right Hook Fitness, stepped out from behind the bag.

"Are you going to hit it or tickle it, Mel?" he said, shunting both toothpicks to the corner of his mouth. "This bastard had you co-sign for a loan on a car, wrecked it, left you holding the bill, and now your credit is ruined. Let him know how you feel."

Melody hit again, throwing combinations, sweat flying off her face and arms. Franco had to plant his weight into the ground. He was seventy, but he was tall and carried two hundred and fifty pounds.

"Okay," he said, "good. Now show me the hook."

She pivoted her feet clockwise, dropped the right heel and lifted the left. The leather rippled as she made impact. She was breathing harder. Her tank top was soaked. Her shorts stuck to her legs.

"Stop, stop," Franco said. "You lost your balance there a bit because you lost control. Don't lose your balance or you're in trouble. Stay in control. Start again."

Her arms were heavier, the muscles were as stiff as old rope.

"You're doing fine," Franco said. "Now the uppercut. Make me believe it."

She moved in closer. Her thighs and both flanks ached. Despite the pain singing in her body, Melody gave it everything she had.

"Use your shoulders and hips, for Christ's sake," Franco yelled.

For a moment, she had lost focus. Lost control. Franco brought her back.

"Okay," he said, "that's better. That's enough. Sit down." He pulled a stool under her and one for himself. He handed her a bottle of water and a towel.

Melody dried her face.

"Not bad," Franco said. "Not great either. You're a little rusty. You need a few more sessions before you can spar."

"I could take you in the ring any time, old man."

"I'm old but I could still go ten rounds with you."

"So you say." Melody looked over at the boxing ring, its floor bending under the weight of two men sparring.

"How long has it been?"

"A few months," Melody said.

"Enough time for you to lose your edge. To use a well-worn but true expression: use it or lose it."

"Yeah, I hear you."

"How's Joe?"

"He's doing fine. He met a lady."

"Ooh, a *lady*. Give him my best. I always liked the old geezer. A true New Yorker."

"Old geezer? Look who's talking."

"You're still running the cleaning business?"

"It's doing all right."

"I have to say, Mel, I was surprised you went into that. Seems a little tame for someone like you."

"You mean for an ex-military officer? What about you? Boxing instructor is not the same as training our nation's counterintelligence agents, is it?"

"No, it isn't. But I retired. You resigned."

"I work for myself, Franco. I don't answer to anyone. And I work alone. For the most part, anyway."

TWENTY-SIX

MEGAN HAWKINS BIT ANOTHER CHUNK OFF THE chocolate-chip cookie, homemade by her personal chef. Jeffrey was special, a real find. The cookies were delicious. She caught the crumbs in the Ziploc bag Jeffrey had packed them in.

She looked through the dusty windshield of her 1971 Plymouth Satellite station wagon. Her first car, one she couldn't bring herself to scrap. Jacob, her husband, had tried to get rid of it. He wanted the space for his luxury vehicles, his sports cars, and some outlandish contraption he called a dune buggy. There were no dunes in Vermont. Jacob wasn't content with one though. He'd bought *three* of the damn things. Megan hadn't even attempted to disentangle the logic behind that one. Wealth had bought Jacob a lot of nice things. It seemed to her that no amount of money could buy common sense. Still, Jacob had earned the right to make as many nonsensical purchases as he liked. He had worked hard for it. She had helped, of course. Even if she wasn't completely convinced at first, she'd encouraged him to build his agricultural business. It had started with dairy farming and expanded into crops and forestry. The more Jacob had, the more he wanted. But she was *not* going to junk the station wagon. She had pinched every penny for months to buy it. She'd worn her feet out as a waitress for it. Her customers hadn't been big tippers, but she had been grateful for any contribution to the car fund, a series of large mason jars lined up on the kitchen shelves, full of coins.

Megan knew where she'd gotten *her* money. What was less clear was where the Loomis woman was getting hers.

One of her few hobbies—if it qualified as such—was reading the local obituaries. Megan delighted in discovering she'd outlived someone she had known. Even more satisfying was learning you had dodged the reaper while an enemy hadn't been quite so lucky. That was the ultimate reward for living: knowing you'd outlasted the people you hated. Over the years, Megan had compiled a lengthy list of names in her mental Rolodex—people she couldn't wait to see appear in the obituaries. Satisfaction, of any kind, was what had kept her going. It had kept her *alive*. She was determined not to die before all the names on her list had met their maker. Only problem was, the Loomis woman was a new addition to her list. And *she* would probably live for decades after Megan was dead and buried.

She had noticed that not a lot of people made it onto the obituaries page each year. There were at least three other funeral homes she was aware of apart from Loomis Memorial in Montpelier. The Loomises had competition. Yet they had a huge mansion on the Main Street of Vermont's capital city. They had commissioned architects to make alterations to the interior of their home that must have run into tens of thousands of dollars. Their business was modest at best. Corpses weren't piling up in Montpelier and yet Kim was wearing Chanel dresses. Yes, she had subscribers to her YouTube channel. But not enough to rake in the kind of cash that had them living the lifestyle of the rich. The Loomises' primary source of income seemed to come from the funeral home. Megan knew they had prepared one body for burial in the past month. One body wasn't enough to have them living in luxury. Had they won the Powerball and told no one? No, it didn't seem likely. So where were they getting the money? It was the kind of question that made her blood itch and her heart feel lighter in her chest. She knew that something about Kim didn't add up. When she talked, Megan's neck hair bristled. It was as though every word she uttered was a lie.

Norman Loomis was on his way to work. Megan hunched forward, peered over the steering wheel. She was parked at the side of Main Street Middle School, a prime viewing spot and one she intended to use again. No one would recognize the station wagon. No one would believe she'd drive a vehicle so dirty and old. She thanked her good sense for holding onto it.

She didn't know Norman well. He seemed a little strange but essentially decent. Megan thought he would be better off ditching the undertaker's suit. He wore it every day, as though he was on duty all the time. She supposed he was. He could be called to pick up a body at 1 p.m. or 1 a.m. Yes, Norman was always on duty. He took his job seriously. The idea that Kim was a qualified mortician still surprised Megan. With her polished, stylish veneer she just didn't seem like the right fit for the job. Grudgingly, Megan had to admit the Loomis woman was attractive. Norman was tall, older, not exactly a catch. But not ugly either. They were mismatched. She couldn't see what Kim saw in him, though she could take a wild guess at what Norman saw in her. It was an odd pairing.

A car pulled into the Loomis driveway. A fat man got out. He was greeted at the door and invited inside by Kim. *Interesting*, Megan thought. Was Kim having an affair? She hadn't gotten a proper look at the man. He was fat, balding, but that was all she'd got.

And why was Kim staying at home? She ran the business together with Norman, so why did she get to stay at home? Did she send him out to do the dirty work while she swanned around the mansion, sipping wine or whatever it was she did when Norman wasn't looking? Who was the visitor? Binoculars. Should've brought binoculars. She vowed not to be caught short the next time.

And there would be a next time. Kim Loomis was up to something and Megan was going to find out what it was.

TWENTY-SEVEN

THE VIGIL OUTSIDE MAIN STREET MIDDLE SCHOOL WAS almost over. Candles in votive tea-light glasses and prayers hadn't brought Evan home. People who had never spoken to Evan were here tonight. Why? They hadn't talked to him when he *wasn't* missing. Rachel was somewhere in the crowd. He'd seen her earlier, just as it was getting dark. She had glanced at him and hurried along. Did she think he'd harmed Evan? Corey had prayed with everyone else. Except in his mind, he was begging Evan to forgive him. As he stood there in the crowd, his parents beside him, candle flickering in the gentle breeze, he had a keen sense of minutes, hours passing. Corey felt everyone's time would be better spent searching for his friend.

The state police and the FBI had carried out a statewide search for Evan with the help of volunteers and cadaver dogs. Evan had been missing for more than forty-eight hours. Corey saw the way his parents looked at each other every time the news came on. They hadn't said it outright, but his parents thought Evan was dead, Corey was sure of it. His father had stumbled over his explanation of why cadaver dogs were being used. Corey hadn't pressed the issue.

Mom and dad were under a lot of strain. It was obvious. They hugged each other more than usual. They had always been kind to each other, but more so now. He had overheard his mother sobbing yesterday morning. The only words he'd caught were: "I can't imagine it, Jim. I can't. How would you live? How would you cope with having a child missing?" Then Corey had felt guilty. He didn't want to be a snoop. He had gone back to his room, which he left only to eat. He was annoyed at himself for crying. It was such a baby thing to do. After all, he was twelve, not eleven. And it wasn't helping Evan. He needed a plan. Something that would prod people's memories. Cars drove along the street he was standing on nearly all day. Someone must have seen Evan.

A woman was winding her way through the crowd, handing out leaflets. Everyone accepted them. Even his parents. Mom and dad introduced themselves, shaking the woman's offered hand. Then she looked at Corey. *She's beautiful*, he thought. Her blue dress was stylish, different from all the other moms' clothes. Her long black hair was full, shiny. Her skin was milky white, and when she looked at you, she saw only *you*.

She gave him a leaflet. He thanked her, despite not having looked at the page. She held out her hand and he shook it.

"Hi," she said. "I'm Kim Loomis." He told her his name. "Well, Corey, aren't you the most handsome heartbreaker?" His parents laughed. Corey's cheeks burned. "Hope you can make it to our fundraiser, Corey." Kim Loomis waved to his parents and he watched her cross the road. Some of the other women were watching her, too. Corey noticed one woman pull her husband closer.

He looked at the sheet of paper. HOMEMAKERS ASSOCIATION OF VERMONT. FUNDRAISER FOR EVAN FAIRBANKS, it read at the top. He scanned the rest of it. Mrs. Loomis was having a dinner tomorrow to raise money for Evan's mom. He watched her go into her house.

She saw him, and gave him a seemingly furtive wave.

TWENTY-EIGHT

NORMAN WAS PREPARING DINNER WHEN KIM RETURNED from the vigil. He was a mediocre chef at best. But he tried. He was slow and careful. He didn't want to burn the food or overcook it. Kim was in the mood for simple fare. Mashed potato, gravy, pork chops, and peas. Norman was beginning to dislike peas. They fell off his fork and sometimes ended up on the floor.

He scooped a dollop of butter from the carton and added it to the potatoes. Sprinkled black pepper and salt. And mashed. His arm pumped the potato masher. Kim's arms encircled his waist.

"How was it?" he asked.

"It was beautiful, Norman. I hope they find the poor kid."

"He's been missing too long, Kim."

"I know the chances of finding him alive are…well, slim. But you never know."

Kim sat at the head of the table in the great room. Norman served her dinner, filling the gravy boat. She became silent and stared at him as if there wasn't enough gravy. He took his plate to the end of the table, a considerable distance. Sixteen chairs on both sides separated them. It was so long that the delivery men had assembled it in the room.

"How are you feeling, Norman?"

"I'm okay, Kim."

"Good. That's good. Are you ready for the fundraiser tomorrow?"

Norman paused, a sliver of pork at his lips. He lowered the fork and said, "Fundraiser?"

"Didn't I tell you we're having a fundraiser for Evan's mother tomorrow?"

Norman shook his head.

"Oh," she said. "It must've slipped my mind. You know how I am. Anyway, I thought it would be nice if we helped out. We should always think of others, Norman. Not just ourselves."

"Yes, Kim. We should always think of others."

She beamed at him. Norman did better than he'd expected by finishing half his dinner. Kim had cleared her plate. She pushed it aside, leaned her elbows on the table, fingers intertwined.

Norman produced a weak smile. The locked basement door was on his mind. Ever since he'd become aware of it, he could hardly think of anything else.

"Later, I'll give you your medication. But first, there are more important things to do."

She stood, walked toward him. Slowly. Very slowly. Norman, mesmerized, could only watch. Kim was like liquid given human form. Every movement was effortless. *Liquid.* She stood over him, a hint of a smile on her lips. She reached behind, unzipped her dress, let it fall to the floor.

Norman looked up and down her naked body.

Kim rested her hands on her hips. "It's time for bed, Norman."

TWENTY-NINE

FOLDING TABLES STOOD ON THE LAWN AND THE PATCH OF trimmed grass at the side of the house. A donation box had been placed in the great room. EVAN FAIRBANKS FUND was stenciled on the front in tall, glaring orange letters.

Corey had brought his allowance and pushed it through the slot cut into the box. His parents had also fed money into it. How much, he couldn't say. He watched Mr. Loomis attending to the diners; he was flushed and sweaty, making sure people were happy, walking hurriedly to bring food to the guests seated outside. Mrs. Loomis often whispered something in his ear and he'd try to smile. It seemed to be a struggle, though. Corey guessed Mr. Loomis was not a natural smiler.

It was a warm day. Perfect for al fresco dining. Corey and his parents had a seat at the main table in the great room, something his father seemed unreasonably pleased about. The sun was shining; the people outside were having a good time. They laughed louder, although Corey had to admit, the chatter in the great room had reached a deafening volume.

Mrs. Loomis had given Corey an idea. The leaflets she had handed to people had gotten quite a response. Corey believed he might get a response, too, if he printed a missing person's flyer with Evan's picture. He would need money to do it, though. He looked at his father and wondered how many times he'd have to mow the lawn or wash the car to get enough money to start his own campaign.

It could work, he thought. But right now there were more urgent matters to deal with. Corey had to pee. He tapped his father on the shoulder. "Dad," he said, "I'm busting."

"Yeah, I'm drawing water myself. Have a wander round, find where the bathroom is, then give me the coordinates." He winked at Corey and mussed his hair.

Corey decided he'd ask for money later. It was too noisy. He only hoped his father's good mood would hold until tonight.

He hadn't eaten any of the food. He scanned the smiling faces, wondering how these people could eat while Evan was still missing. Even though he was hungry, and the meal smelled good, he couldn't bring himself to tuck in.

He went into the hall. Maybe there was a toilet nearby. He tried to turn the handle on the first door he came to. It wouldn't budge. There was a new, gleaming lock on it. Maybe it was the basement. He knocked on the dark wood with his knuckles.

"Who's there?" Mrs. Loomis said.

Corey was startled and embarrassed. He'd flinched at the sound of her voice, as though he had been caught in the act of stealing. Or worse—snooping. Mrs. Loomis was smiling at him. She seemed almost concerned.

"I was just…um, where's the bathroom, ma'am?"

"Ma'am? My, a child with manners. Whatever next?"

"Um…"

"Upstairs," she said. "Third door on your left."

"Thank you." He went to the bottom of the stairs.

Kim followed him. "If you need anything let me know," she said. "I give extra dessert to young men who have manners."

"Yes, ma'am." He climbed the stairs and turned halfway up. Mrs. Loomis was still standing there. She waved, the same secret wave he'd seen the night before. The uneasiness in his stomach might have been due to him not eating all day. Or something else. Corey couldn't work it out. He figured he was probably traumatized but knew it was wrong to enjoy yourself when your friend was missing. He was betraying Evan again by being at a party.

Missing. There was some hope in that word. If someone was missing, they could be found. The news media used a different word. Abducted. A far more frightening word, in Corey's opinion. Everything about it was hopeless.

He went straight to the bathroom and locked the door. He leaned his back against it, overwhelmed by a sudden urge to cry. *No*, he thought, *don't do it. Don't be a baby.* He inhaled deeply. Held the air, released it, breath by breath. The lump in his throat had gone. The hot acid sensation in his eyes faded. *Keep it together.* He wished he could be more like his father. He was solid as a rock. He'd *never* seen him cry. Would his father be ashamed of him if he knew his son had almost cried like a baby?

Corey looked at his reflection in the mirror above the sink. He hardened his features. *I will be stronger*, he promised.

***

Megan was surprised the Loomis woman had invited her. She had to give Kim credit for maintaining the pretense, though: Kim hated Megan, and the feeling was mutual. The men sitting at the table gave Kim Loomis the side eye when they thought their wives weren't paying attention. Predictable, she thought. And look at her! Waltzing around the great room of her mansion in her handmade whore heels and short designer dress. No shame. That was what was lacking in that harlot—a healthy sense of shame. It was the shoes that caught her eye: custom made Christian

Louboutin royal blue pumps, a white star on the heel cap and four more on the tall heel, each one getting smaller as the spike tapered, the kind of stars you'd see on the American flag. Kim had delighted in telling her—even though she hadn't asked—that she had dealt with the Louboutin atelier herself on the 1st Arrondissement in Paris, as if to rub Megan's nose in the fact that even a peasant like Kim had access to exclusive products and the ability to travel.

It had cost a lot of money to throw this party, and Megan doubted that Kim would hand over all of the proceeds. She'd probably skim some for herself. To fund her Christless lifestyle.

Megan would keep a close watch on Kim. She was guilty of something. She was too good to be true. Too popular to be likeable.

***

Paige couldn't stop staring at Kim. She was a shining example of what a woman should be: hard working, compassionate, independent, stylish, and an excellent homemaker—a dictionary definition of a role model.

Paige wasn't the most organized person in the world, she accepted that. But she was improving. It was all because of Kim. She had set the bar very high. Paige marveled at how she'd organized the party on short notice, and so far it had been successful.

Kim made things happen. Before she'd met Kim, Paige had been prone to stress, easily flustered. All because she never knew where to start, whether cleaning the house, preparing dinner, or mapping out her day so that she had at least some hold on it. That was her main problem. But she wasn't alone. Paige had friends on Pinterest who experienced the same hot flush, the same frustration when the house was a mess and a starting point seemed to be out of reach. Then she had met Kim. *She* didn't get flustered. *She* was in control. *She* didn't wear the same sweatpants three days in a row because the laundry hamper was full and all her clothes were dirty and she'd run out of detergent and she couldn't go to the store because her husband was at work and the kids were screaming and she just wanted to curl up on the couch and drink wine and watch a movie and cancel the day.

The things we take for granted, she thought. In her former life, the one where she had been single and childless, she hadn't needed silence. Now she craved it, the sweet absence of sound. Kim had taught her to be kinder to herself. Paige really didn't know how she would have coped without Kim's guidance.

***

Megan saw Paige watching Kim. Saw the adoration, the respect, the trust she had in the Loomis woman and barely stopped herself from snapping to her feet and declaring Kim a fraud, a fake, a goddamn charlatan. Was she the only one who saw through the façade? Was it possible these people had been struck blind by her performance?

Where was she getting the Christing money from? Did anyone think to ask?

THIRTY

It was late evening and they were home from the fundraiser, at last. Corey approached his father, thinking he was drunk enough to be agreeable. He was sitting at the kitchen table, wiping the sweat off a bottle of beer. Mom's head rested on dad's shoulder. They were both drunk and happy. It was now or never.

"Dad," he said, "I have an idea."

"Yeah? What's that, champ?" For some reason, his father called him *champ* when he was drunk. It was another one of those peculiar things parents said on occasion.

"I want to print a missing person's flyer for Evan. But I need money for ink and paper. I can take care of the design myself."

His parents seemed suddenly sober. Had he said something wrong?

Mom sat up. "Oh, honey." Tears welled in her eyes, confusing Corey.

His father planted a heavy hand on his shoulder, squeezed. "It's going to be all right, son."

The sudden change in them baffled Corey. It had gone from happy to sad in an instant.

"How much do you need?" he asked.

"Is a hundred bucks okay? If there's change, I'll bring it back to you."

"Don't worry about the change." Jim was so full of beer and food he had to stand to extract his wallet from his jeans pocket. He counted out four twenties and two tens.

"Corey, wherever you plan on posting those flyers, you'll ask permission, won't you?"

"Sure, Dad," he said, taking the bills.

"You need my help, son, you talk to me. I mean, if you need help with anything, *anything at all*, you'll talk to me?"

"I will, Dad. I promise."

His mother wiped her eyes with her sleeve. Corey was alarmed to see his father fighting back tears.

"I'm proud of you, son." He squeezed Corey's shoulder again. "Your mom and I are here if you need us anytime. Okay?"

"Okay, Dad. Thanks."

***

Jim and Lillian watched their son leave the kitchen, listened as his footsteps faded on the stairs and his bedroom door closed.

"Lillian, we've really got a good one there. Don't know what we did to deserve him, but...he's our kid."

Lillian kissed her husband, caressed his face, and rested her head on his shoulder again. "Let's stay like this for a while," she said. "It's perfect, Jim."

THIRTY-ONE

MEGAN WAS NOT GOING TO BE CAUGHT SHORT TWICE IN one week. She adjusted the strap on the binoculars and hung them from her neck. This time, she was prepared. She had parked at the side of the school again, a place she had come to think of as her usual spot. There was a black Mercedes-Maybach S 560 in the Loomis driveway. Megan had seen it before but it was usually parked at the rear of the house, almost like they were keeping it out of sight.

The Loomis woman was brazen; Megan had to give her credit for that. She was flaunting her wealth, the source of which was a mystery. But if you watched someone often enough, they made a mistake. With the modest death rate in Montpelier, Megan knew the Loomises should be struggling to meet the funeral home's overheads; they should have been out of business by now. It would make her days a lot more interesting when she discovered what they were up to.

It had occurred to her that she might be wrong. Maybe Kim had savings. Maybe she came from money, as her mother used to say. And Norman didn't live an extravagant lifestyle. She had watched him yesterday. He'd looked like a drowning man—so far out of his depth he couldn't hide his discomfort. There was sadness in him. His eyes were moist with it. What had the harlot done to him? Norman had been careful as he set each place at the table. Kim had supervised him, scrutinizing his every move. It was as if Norman had been afraid of making a mistake. He had seemed younger, watching the world around him from the corner of his eye, expecting to be scolded at any moment.

Then Kim had done something that left Megan believing Kim was smarter than she had thought, and not to be underestimated. At the end of the evening, she'd emptied the donation box onto the table and counted the money in front of everyone, to the penny. Witnesses. The final tally was $6,453.86. There would be no rumors. No innuendo. She had announced she was going to deliver it personally to Mrs. Fairbanks. Her guests had applauded her. That one act of fake charity had boosted Kim's public profile more than any homemakers association. People would talk about her, invite her to events. She would become Someone in the community. Her little club, the Homemakers Association of Vermont, would attract new members, possibly force old ones out. Like her.

To make matters worse, WCAZ had broadcast Diane Battle's interview with Kim. Why hadn't Diane interviewed Megan? She was a businesswoman in good standing in Montpelier. Had been for decades. Why wasn't WCAZ interested in *her* story? It was all style over substance. Their target audience was millennials, whatever they were.

But Kim had done something wrong. Megan just had to prove it. What if she was wrong, though? Why was she convinced Kim was dirty? Was she becoming obsessed? Megan was fond of simple explanations. She kept returning to the money, and its unknown source. There was simply no way their small business could support their lifestyle. It really was that simple. *Isn't this a little sick?* she thought. *I'll stop if she comes up clean. I'll stop soon. I'm not obsessed.*

Norman was on his way to work. She didn't even bother using the binoculars. What did he do all day? She imagined him sitting at reception, waiting for customers that never showed up.

Less than five minutes later, a truck pulled in front of the Loomis house and lowered its hydraulic lift. Two men wheeled something up the path toward the door. Megan couldn't make out what it was, even with the binoculars. It was covered in a blanket.

The same fat, bald man she had seen the day before jumped from the driver's seat, the bill of his baseball cap pulled low over his face. He was carrying an envelope under his arm. Kim spoke to him and they headed into the house. The two men lifted the object up the steps. Kim closed the door when they were inside.

Megan waited. Fifteen minutes went by before the three men got back in the truck and left. Kim got into her fancy car and slid it into Main Street. Megan started the engine of her station wagon. It coughed and belched, but got going.

She followed, keeping a discreet distance, allowing a car to overtake her. The drive was a short one. Kim stopped further down Main Street, at a small house, its front porch leaning. She went up the steps, a brown envelope in her hand.

That's two brown envelopes I've seen today. Someone's getting paid under the table.

It was the Fairbanks house. Evan's mother, Lena, came to the door in her bathrobe. They exchanged words, and Kim followed her inside.

Megan couldn't stay parked on the sidewalk. It was risky. There was a good chance the Loomis woman would see her.

Tomorrow was another day.

And she'd been wrong once before. When Jacob had proposed the purchase of apple orchards all those years ago, she'd laughed, said it wouldn't take off. She had even apologized to her husband. She was big enough to admit he had made a sound business decision.

She wasn't wrong about Kim Loomis, though. There was badness in that woman. She could feel it in her hackles.

Same time again tomorrow, she thought, remembering how they had applauded. *You godless tramp.*

THIRTY-TWO

COREY AND JIM DROVE TO WATERBURY TO BUY INK. IT WAS unusual for his dad to offer him a ride. The standard response: He wasn't a taxi service; Corey had two perfectly healthy legs and could walk himself wherever he wanted to go. And if his son decided walking was an undue burden, he had a bicycle. He had walked three miles to and from school every day without complaint. But there was no speech today. Corey felt he was being treated differently and didn't understand why. He supposed it didn't matter, anyway. He had a new sense of purpose. He was trying to help Evan.

He purchased two reams of paper and four ink cartridges, just to be sure he had enough. Back at home, Corey paused, his hand on the car door.

"Dad, thanks for this," he said, holding up the heavy paper bag.

"You're welcome, son."

"I can mow the lawn whenever you want. I can even clean the car." He had wondered why his father hadn't asked him to do *some* chores. Maybe he'd forgotten. From an early age, his parents had drummed into him the idea that there was no such thing as money for nothing. You had to work for it. It didn't grow on trees.

"I'll wash the car, Corey. It wouldn't kill me to mow the lawn, either. You take care of your business." He pointed a finger at the bag. "You need any help, your old man might know some things you don't."

"I can take care of it, Dad."

"Didn't doubt it for a second, son."

Corey hugged him. Dad seemed surprised and responded with a pat on the back.

"When you go out, make sure your phone is fully charged. If you need me to pick you up, call me."

"Sure I will."

It took the Canon in his bedroom two hours to print a thousand sheets of paper. It was old and slow but it got the job done. He dumped his schoolbooks on the floor, glad he didn't have to study for the rest of the summer, then packed the reams into his book bag and cycled to State Street.

He leaned his bike against a bench, removed an armful of sheets from his bag, and stood with his back to the Winooski River, handing his homemade flyers out to passersby. Some threw him curious glances. Others simply folded the paper into four and shoved it in their pockets. A young couple, both wearing sunglasses, took two sheets from him. He watched them scrunch them up and toss them in a bin outside a restaurant. Corey hadn't anticipated some people's lack of interest in a missing boy. Some people didn't care. There was something awful about that.

His cell rang. Rachel's name appeared on the screen. "Hello," he said.

"I need to speak to you, Corey."

"Yeah, sure. Now?"

"Where are you?"

"State Street, by the Winooski, across the road from Subway."

"Give me five minutes." She hung up.

Corey didn't know why she had blanked him last night at the vigil. It was strange. He hadn't done anything wrong.

He looked at the sheet. The letters were black, the picture of Evan in color. He read it again: MISSING

PERSON, and below that, EVAN FAIRBANKS. LAST SEEN ON MAIN STREET. He had copied and pasted Evan's Facebook profile picture. The ink had wrinkled the page a bit, but it was still okay for his budget. Then he realized his mistake. He hadn't included the date of Evan's disappearance.

Shit. My brain's so scrambled I can't remember a simple thing like the date?

He sat on the bench. Rubbed his eyes with his free hand. He was tired. He looked around. Rachel was crossing the road. She sat beside him.

"How've you been?" she asked.

He showed her the poster. Corey regretted hurrying to get it done. It was amateurish.

"Not bad," she said.

"It could be better."

"Sure it could. It doesn't have the date. But the message is clear. Evan's photo is good; his name and the fact he's missing is in big letters. You gave the phone number of the Montpelier police."

"Are you trying to make me feel better or worse?"

"Corey, I'm sorry about last night."

"What's going on, Rachel?"

"Some of the guys think you're responsible for what happened to Evan. They said if I wanted to be friends with you then I couldn't be friends with them."

"Really? That's what people think? What do *you* think?"

"Well, I guess I can't be friends with them anymore."

Corey looked at her and smiled. She took a sheaf of paper from his bag and helped him hand them out to people on the sidewalk.

"Thanks for doing this," Corey said.

"I don't work for free, Corey Bayliss. You're buying lunch."

He smiled again. He'd rather have one real friend than ten who didn't care about him.

THIRTY-THREE

SAMMY WAS ASLEEP ON THE PASSENGER SEAT AS MELODY drove along Bowery, past Chinatown, headed toward the Manhattan Bridge. Sammy seemed to have more energy. Melody had finally put him on a diet. He wasn't allowed treats now. It broke her heart when he looked at her with his sad doggy eyes. Sammy missed his peanut-butter-flavored dog biscuits. She had taken him to Cooper Square in the East Village to have a veterinarian examine him. Yes, the vet had said, Sammy was a little overweight but he was healthy. He didn't see anything worrying. Maybe cut back on the treats. Melody wanted Sammy to be around for a long time. She caressed his soft coat. His hind legs twitched, but Sammy slept on.

Across the East River, the brick and pale concrete of the Con Edison buildings rose out of Hudson Avenue. The smokestack was still there. Had anything changed or was everything the same? She would find out soon enough. At least they were developing the Brooklyn Navy Shipyard right next to Vinegar Hill. To Melody, it all looked like an unchanged industrial wasteland.

Why am I being snippy? she wondered. Her mood had changed. There had been no slow roll up to it; it had turned in an instant. It was Vinegar fucking Hill. It was *square one*. It was one thing hanging a picture of the place on her wall as a monument to her escape, quite another to see it again in the flesh.

The van juddered over the cobblestones on Water Street. Sammy stirred, his teeth showing through his smile. Melody didn't know if he was angry or amused. She found a parking space on the sidewalk. No one was going to give her a ticket. Not here.

Water Street was more or less how she remembered it: graffiti, steel roller shutters, disused buildings. She rang the intercom on the brick apartment block. It was the nicest, cleanest-looking building on the street, a step up from the ramshackle house Aunt Joan had once called home.

She was buzzed in and knocked on apartment 3. Aunt Joan had her arms spread wide as if to embrace her. Melody held up a hand and walked past her into the small apartment. There were two armchairs by the window, a coffee table between them, chipped along its edges. Melody sat facing the door, out of habit. Aunt Joan had lowered her arms to her sides. Her eyes became quick. She bit her lower lip and wrung her hands together.

"Can I get you something to drink?"

Melody shook her head. She pulled a stack of twenty unwrinkled fifty-dollar bills from the inside pocket of her jacket and placed them on the thrift-store coffee table. A blue rubber band held the cash together in a neat pile.

"Oh, Mel," Aunt Joan said. "You've no idea how much you're helping me. I promise I'll pay you back."

Melody looked at the old woman. She was plump in face and body, hair gray but still full. Healthy. Well fed.

"How long has it been, Mel?"

Melody glanced at the watch on her wrist, then at Aunt Joan. "Sixteen years, two months, seven days, four hours and twelve minutes. Give or take."

Aunt Joan kneaded her hands as if she didn't know what to do with them.

"I'll pay you back, Mel. I promise."

As though Melody hadn't heard her the first time. She searched Aunt Joan's eyes, looking for signs of who she really was. It was hard to believe this chubby old lady was capable of evil. She looked like anyone's grandma. Easier to believe she baked pies and knitted cardigans. Outwardly she was wholesome, a harmless pensioner. It had taken Melody a long time to accept what Aunt Joan was. A monster. A monster disguised in the flesh of a human.

Melody knew what *she* was. She hadn't recoiled in horror like all the other kids while watching a slasher movie, or flinched as the killer's knife tore through the screaming jock and his bimbo when they left the cabin to investigate a noise outside. She hadn't enjoyed it either. But she had been curious. The library had provided her with answers. She'd read dozens of books on psychopathy. Even then she hadn't been sure. Her first contract killing had proved the books were right, though. And she now accepted she was a psychopath, but didn't think she was evil. She didn't revel in the suffering of others. Aunt Joan did.

"I don't want it back. It's not a loan. I'm buying something for my money."

Aunt Joan avoided direct eye contact.

Pretending to be ashamed, Melody thought. If Melody had been a different person, Aunt Joan would be sitting in a jail cell, not in subsidized housing, receiving public-assistance checks in the mail. It would be satisfying to see her behind bars. But Melody had understood the flaw in that right away. Satisfaction for her was temporary—there and gone in an instant. The risk of dealing with cops versus the reward of having Aunt Joan locked up wasn't worth it. Melody Morgan didn't want the police to know she even existed.

"Excuse me?" Aunt Joan said, her voice small.

"Two things. My money buys two things. A thousand dollars is more than the sum of your contribution to my life. You don't ask me for anything ever again. After today, we will never speak. Give me some sign you understand."

Aunt Joan nodded, looking at Melody from the corner of her eye. "What's the second thing?"

"You answer a question for me."

"I will if I can."

"No, you *will* answer or I put the cash in my pocket."

Aunt Joan nodded some more.

Melody had expected to feel anger, hate, rage, even regret. But there was nothing. Only a strange calmness. "Did it make you feel good?"

Aunt Joan frowned. "Sorry, I don't—"

"Being cruel to a child," Melody said, her tone casual. "Did it make you feel good when you were cruel to me?"

Aunt Joan looked at her with bald panic. Her face seemed to be in constant motion. It was incredible...*Did she think I'd grow up and suddenly forget what she'd done?*

"I...Mel, we were poor."

"Don't insult the poor by making excuses. I want an answer. Did it make you *feel* good by being cruel to a defenseless child?"

"No, no, it didn't. I'm sorry."

"You mean it made you feel bad? Did you get off on having power over a child?"

"How dare you?"

"I know who you are. Maybe you can hide your wickedness from your friends, but I see you clearly. A thousand dollars is worth the price to see you for who you really are. I don't want anything to do with you. Spend it wisely. You won't see another penny."

"You're successful, Mel. You made it. Please, I didn't mean for things to get out of control."

"But they did get out of control. Cruelty to a child is stepping way over the line. Have a miserable life, Joan. I'm glad I came here. I figure if you need a thousand bucks from me today you'll need money again tomorrow. Good luck with that."

THIRTY-FOUR

THE MOMENT KIM STEPPED INSIDE THE HOUSE, LENA
Fairbanks closed the door so fast the bottom corner of it
brushed the heel of Kim's foot, as though Lena was trying
to keep the fresh air out, or the bad air in. The house stank
of stale cigarette smoke and stagnant alcohol. Half-read
magazines and discarded clothes littered the floor. Liquor
bottles bristled on the glass-topped coffee table. An ashtray
smoldered somewhere in the mess. Kim prodded a pair of
jeans under the table with the toe of her shoe. They were
stiff. She went to the grimy window, looked through the
yellowed sheer drapes. It was hard to see anything through
the dirt. But Kim saw enough.

Lena wasn't in the best shape either. The bathrobe was
tinged a sickly yellow like the drapes, as though she wore it
constantly. And smoked while she was wearing it. Her dye
job was in need of some maintenance, too. Black roots
encroached on the colored strands, creeping steadily
upwards from her scalp. She hadn't brushed her hair in days.
Tufts of hair corkscrewed this way and that, like an
untended garden. Her complexion was the worst Kim had
seen. Norman was pale, but that was his natural color,
nothing to worry about. Lena was sporting a bleached-bone
look that was unsettling. She needed a doctor. She needed
help.

"Take a seat, Lena," Kim said. "Go on now. Easy does it. Take a seat."

Kim pushed aside clothes and newspapers on the couch, prospecting for a place to sit. She opened a magazine, placed it on the edge on the couch and lowered herself gingerly. Kim was less than a foot from Lena's shrine to booze. The alcohol fumes were stronger, eye-watering. There was nowhere to put her Hermes bag. The floor was filthy. The couch had its own self-contained atmosphere of foul odors. She settled for resting the bag on her knees.

Kim watched Lena sink into the La-Z-Boy recliner. Watched the way her head lolled on her neck. Her eyes glassy, unfocused. Lena was already drunk.

Lena bore no resemblance to the kid Kim had gone to Montpelier High School with. She had been popular, attractive, with her own exclusive clique of friends who were just as cruel as Lena was. Kim had seen them beat other kids. Lena herself had strangled a girl who'd had the audacity to walk by her without acknowledging her. Mary Purdue had had bruises on her neck for a week.

All the boys had gravitated toward Lena, including the most popular one, Billy Blasier.

The only kid they hadn't tormented was Kim Loomis. They had stayed away from her. She was the only loner they didn't bully. They ignored her, as if they had known even then that Kim was dangerous. That if Kim had strangled someone, she would have finished the job. That if they'd crossed her, it would have been the last thing they did.

It was funny, Kim thought, how the only thing she couldn't push around was the booze. *It* was in charge. *It* controlled her. *It* was killing her, one drink at a time. Kim guessed alcohol had made Lena its bitch after her very first sip. The woman had met her biggest, baddest bully yet. And it was winning.

Kim took the package from her Birkin and handed it to Lena. Lena removed the bundles of cash and the vague fear in her eyes disappeared. She returned the money to its large envelope.

"I topped up the donation," Kim said. "Including my own contribution. There's ten grand there."

"Thank you," Lena said. There were tears in her eyes.

It was time for Kim to leave. The stench was overpowering. She could deal with the dead and their odors, but there was something especially awful in the smells of the living.

"See a doctor, Lena." Kim stood.

"I really miss him. The police keep showing up."

"They're supposed to. They'll find him."

"What—? I wish I'd been kinder to him, you know? A better mother."

"Goodbye, Lena."

THIRTY-FIVE

EVAN CAME TO WITH NO MEMORY OF HITTING HIS HEAD and no memory of falling asleep. His mouth was dry and it hurt when he swallowed. His tongue was a dead thing. He willed it to move. It didn't. All the spit was gone. He had no energy, wanted to sleep again. It was all he wanted in the world—to go to a dreamless place where there was nothing scary.

How long had he been out? It could have been two minutes, two hours, two days. Two weeks? No, it couldn't be that long. If it had been two weeks he'd probably be dead.

His stomach grumbled, but his thirst was painful to the point of panic. He felt the rawness in his throat; it was from all the useless screaming he had done and now he regretted it. But he was thirsty. It was all he could think about. And the more he focused on it, the worse it got. Like someone had come in and dusted his mouth and sinuses with talcum powder while he slept.

There was no sensation in his hands. He considered moving his fingers but had lost the will even to try. His legs were numb, heavy lead slabs.

And the rat? It was here somewhere but Evan no longer cared. His fear was used up. There was nothing left.

He barely reacted to the shifting noises outside. People were talking. Things were being moved around. There was the sound of metal on metal. Something hummed and sucked.

His awareness heightened, tapped into his last reserves of energy.

People.

They could save him. Evan tried to call for help but it was useless. What emerged was the muffled moan of a cartoon ghost. He squeezed his eyes shut and gave it everything he had. The vibrations in his throat were loud in his ears. Enough surely to alert those outside his prison. And still the people talked. Someone even laughed. It was a woman. He demanded his body wriggle toward the noise. He tried to move, but rolled onto his back. A turtle turned on its shell. His hands were being crushed against his spine.

Evan felt nothing. He thought he might be crying, felt the heat in his eyes and the lump in his throat. But his eyes were dry. He had no tears left. He'd used them up.

Outside, no more than a few feet away, the woman laughed again. A man laughed with her.

THIRTY-SIX

MEGAN COULDN'T STOP HERSELF STARING AT THE LOOMIS woman. She itched, burned with curiosity. What was she up to?

She had gotten up earlier than usual that morning and was out the door promptly at 7 a.m. She'd parked the station wagon in her spot by the school. Nothing had happened for an hour. Norman had left for work as usual. Then the white truck had returned. The same men carried equipment covered in blankets into the house. Except this time, the three men hadn't come out for two hours. What had they been doing?

"Today," Kim said, "we're going to discuss cleaning floors. Brace yourself for methods and tips! Also, we need to go into more detail on how best to make a house a home for your children and your husband. We'll focus on your hubbies first. We don't want them to feel neglected. What can we do to make our husbands' lives easier?"

Great, Megan thought, summoning JFK and paraphrasing. *Ask not what your husband can do for you, but what* you *can do for your husband*. She shifted her eyes left. Brooke and Paige were rapt, actually *thinking* about answers to the question. The respect they had for Kim was disturbing. They were awed by her, would never question her, never doubt her.

But it was Kim who had her attention. Megan felt something close to mild shock. And outrage. Yes, that was it. She was outraged by the Loomis woman's dress. It was a yellow georgette Gucci number, Megan would have bet on it in a heartbeat. Floral bows—sweet honeysuckle pink, Megan thought—decorated the shoulder of its single sleeve, and the cinched waist. Ruffles ran the length of one calf. It was just after midday and Kim was standing here in her great room, in an evening dress, with one of her shoulders bare. Naked. Megan's internal organs squirmed at the sight. Then she laid eyes on the red stilettos and felt sick to her stomach. The only saving grace was the length of the dress: it almost brushed her ankles. At least it wasn't short. The bared shoulder though—that troubled Megan more than anything. That was the problem with the Kim Loomises of the world. They had no shame. No modesty. What kind of example was she setting for the two young women present? That it was okay to bare your flesh like you were on display at a meat counter? Why didn't she just go and stand in a butcher's window?

"Let's get to making our houses a home for our hubbies," Kim said.

Megan's stomach turned at the word *hubbies.*

"My Norman loves the smell of coffee. He doesn't drink it, of course; he prefers peppermint tea. But he enjoys the aroma of coffee. It's simple to do—put some vanilla wax and coffee beans in your wax burner and hey presto! I have his clothes laid out every evening, ready for the next morning. And I make him a packed lunch just before we go to bed so he won't have to spend good money on buying sandwiches. Every man wants to feel welcome in his own home. I greet my Norman at the door every time he arrives home from work. Ask him how his day was. These sound like small things but, trust me, they make your husband feel at home. I'm sure you all know by now that my Norman is not a talker. Don't be afraid to give your husband some quiet time. I give Norman space. I always try to have his dinner ready. When we're busy at the funeral home, we both share the work, and we prepare dinner together. This could be another opportunity to bond with your husband. After dinner, give him a massage. Help him relax."

Megan loved her husband dearly, but there was no way she was giving Jacob Hawkins a massage. He was perfectly capable of massaging himself, if he had a mind to.

"Men are simple creatures, as we know," Kim continued. "They don't require much maintenance. But we should put in the effort to make them feel needed. A gesture as insignificant as having them change a lightbulb is enough to give them the impression they're in charge. And necessary."

Megan could hardly believe what she was hearing. Jacob was an independent businessman and she was an independent businesswoman. They helped each other. They *needed* each other. There was no need to coddle Jacob. She didn't need coddling either. Why pretend to make him feel wanted? She and Jacob had always been equals, as directors of their businesses and in their personal lives. Sure, Jacob was a big spender and she didn't approve of it. But he'd earned the right to buy whatever he wanted as long as it didn't endanger their finances. *Men are simple creatures.* Did she mean they were stupid? Jacob was many things, but stupid didn't feature heavily.

Who is this tramp with the naked shoulder to call my husband a dummy? The blood rose to her face. She couldn't stand much more of this nonsense. Curiosity had brought her here and kept her coming back. And though she felt the urge to leave, she wouldn't without more information. How was she was doing it? Who, or what, was funding the heathen in the Gucci dress?

"Anyway," Kim said, "I'm getting off topic. We'll come back to the subject of spousal care in our next session. Floors. I'll put up a video on YouTube soon, going through each floor type. First, I want to admit to a mistake. When I was new to homemaking, I used a bleach-based product on my unsealed stone kitchen floor. And yes, you guessed it—it left white stains on the stone that wouldn't come out."

There was an audible gasp from Brooke and Paige. They clapped their hands over their mouths as though they'd witnessed a puppy being run over by a speeding drunk.

I'm going to get sick in my mouth, Megan thought.

"Luckily, only one of the tiles was affected. I had it replaced but it was mortifying. It taught me not to clean in haste. Take my time. Know how different chemicals can damage different types of floors. I use hot water and a Swiffer to clean the kitchen tiles when they need a light clean. You can also use a steam cleaner if you have one. If your stone is really icky, the best product for removing the *ick* is Naturally It's Clean. I have a confession to make, ladies: I use this on all my floors. Right there, that simple piece of information can save you all a lot of time searching for the right product."

Brooke and Paige clapped. Megan was startled and looked at the two women. They had *applauded* her. Kim seemed delighted, a big aw-shucks smile on her lips. Megan's blood pressure increased.

THIRTY-SEVEN

EVAN WOKE WITH ONE THOUGHT WINKING ON AND OFF IN his mind: escape or die. He had little energy left. Thirst had become his chief tormentor, almost a thing in its own right with its own physical form. His tongue was stuck to the roof of his mouth and his throat felt as if it had shriveled. The thought flashed in his mind, urgent—escape or die.

He used his legs to push himself into the wall. The effort left him breathless. Now he needed to push himself along the wall until he came to a door. His tee-shirt crackled against the brick. It got snagged and tore but he continued despite the bare brick grazing his back, scraping off the skin, drawing blood. His breath wheezed in and out. He blocked out the numbness in his hands and feet. Refused to dwell on it. The last dregs of adrenaline brought him to a corner. He was getting close. He focused on not falling onto his side; it would be too difficult to right himself. He inched his body along the brick, pushing up, sliding down, pushing up, sliding down. The stinging in his spine faded the further he went.

His head struck the corner of something. A doorframe? He twisted, feeling the object with his face. *Yes! Oh my God, yes! A door!*

He was making noises, but what they were didn't register. He might have been laughing or crying, even choking. But now there was something else. Excitement—this he recognized. He was so pleased he could identify a feeling that he forgot about the door for a moment. He pressed his cheek to the wood grain. He had a chance. Felt the warm blossom of hope.

He needed to get upright. Drew air into his lungs for the final big push. The plan was simple. Slide his body upward against the doorframe to stand straight. Shimmy from side to side using his heels and the balls of his feet. That would give him purchase on the door handle. He was worried about the lack of sensation in his hands but he had to try.

Every sinew, every tendon, was pulled tight as piano strings as he pushed down, bent his back into the frame, and slid upward. It was as though the doorframe was oiled. He stood, gasping for air, nostrils flaring. His heart slammed hard in his chest. Blood rushed in his ears. He was dizzy and waited for the vertigo to pass before rolling on his heels. His hands touched…

YES! Thank God! Thank you!

…the door handle. Even though his hands felt useless he managed to get his fingers around the handle and lower his body, using his weight as leverage to pull it down.

The door swung wide. He spilled Outside, a place that had become unreal to him, almost mythical, as if it had never existed, something he'd only dreamed of.

Someone touched him. Evan screamed.

"It's okay. It's the police. Stop struggling. It's okay. You're safe, Evan."

Evan stopped wriggling. They had found him.

"I'm going to take the gag out of your mouth," the female officer said. "Don't make a sound. The suspect is still in the house. Understand?"

Evan nodded.

The officer yanked the gag to his chin. Air, blessed air, rushed into his lungs. He smelled chemicals. Normally, he wouldn't have noticed or cared about that smell. But it felt new. It was the scent of Outside.

"Drink this," the officer said.

She held a bottle to his lips and Evan gulped. Some of the water spilled on his tee-shirt but the rest sluiced down his throat, drowning the pain, the rawness. He drank until there was nothing left.

"Good boy. You did good, Evan."

The gag was forced into his mouth again. Evan grunted. A drawer opened somewhere. He heard footsteps approaching. Someone was kneeling on the bottom of his spine, putting some kind of plaster on his back. He detected a strong odor of disinfectant. Then he was being pulled back into the closet. Away from the Outside.

THIRTY-EIGHT

THROUGH HIS BINOCULARS, MIGUEL WATCHED MELODY enter the apartment building. She was exactly how Jennifer Shaker had described her—tall, short blonde hair. Under other circumstances, he would have offered her a job. She'd be an improvement on his current partner. Juan had no patience.

They had been parked at a discreet distance on Water Street for five minutes, observing the woman who had cost the cartel half a billion dollars. Juan was restless, his leg bouncing in the footwell. Again. Yes, in another life, Miguel would have offered Valerie Price a job. Or anyone who wasn't Juan. That wasn't an option now. Killing this woman wouldn't help him recover his money. But there was no way he could allow her to live. That she might not have known she'd shot Los Mochis's most important financial handler didn't matter. She had to die. Her family had to be butchered first, though. In that respect, Los Mochis was no different from any other cartel.

Miguel made a decision. If Juan was using drugs, he was going to shoot him in the head. The young man was far too twitchy. Torres and Miguel had agreed two decades ago that there was no room for addicts in the organization. They were a liability. They made mistakes. The one aspect of running the cartel alongside Torres that Miguel disliked was hiring blunt instruments like the one sitting next to him. Thugs were a dime a dozen. Few had the intelligence and self-control to last long in the business. It was worrying, in a way. It was becoming increasingly difficult to hire good people. Miguel had no problem paying his staff a substantial wage but all the money in the world couldn't buy brains. The quality of the average criminal had declined as the years had passed. When had that happened? Was it something in the food? The water?

He shook his head, sighed, and lowered the binoculars.

"You okay, patron?" Juan said.

Miguel nodded.

"What do you think she's doing in there?"

That was another source of irritation: the inability of a goon like Juan to handle silence. This new breed of criminals talked too much. He didn't answer. Instead, he kept his eyes trained on the building.

And still, Juan's leg rocked up and down. His hands were in constant motion. Miguel took a deep breath. *This too shall pass*, he thought.

There was movement up ahead. Valerie Price was walking to her van. She hopped in and drove fast to the end of the street. An older woman had followed her out, and stood in the road until the van turned the corner. Miguel and Juan got out of their van and jogged toward the old woman. Miguel looked behind him. There was no one around. The folded newspaper was slipping in his hand. He gripped it tighter. The woman saw them too late to realize the danger she was in. Miguel opened the newspaper, showed her the gun.

"Don't say a word," he said. "I'll kill you in the street if I have to. Inside. Go." She led the way into her apartment. Juan locked the door.

"What's your name?" Miguel asked.

"Joan."

"Take a seat, Joan." She hesitated, and he pointed the gun at her. "Please, sit."

Joan fixed her gaze on the gun like she'd never seen one before. Juan took two steps, pushed her into the armchair.

"The woman you were talking to just now. What's her name?"

Joan surprised Miguel by giving it up right away. "Melody Morgan." Full name. Maybe this would be easier than his encounter with Jennifer Shaker. He'd suspected Valerie Price was an alias. A contract killer didn't give their real name to a client.

"Joan, we're going for a drive," Miguel said. "We'll have you home in time for dinner."

THIRTY-NINE

THEY ARRIVED AT THE WAREHOUSE UNDER THE Williamsburg Bridge as night fell. It was just off Kent Avenue, on South Fifth Street, an old brick building with a semi-disused air that no one noticed or cared about. The warehouse had been the cartel's distribution hub for New York City at one time, but they had moved their operation to another part of the state. It wasn't smart to stay in one place, especially in a major city. Los Mochis had changed their strategy. Distribution was better suited to rural environs. Fewer people, fewer questions. And if law enforcement were onto you, you could see them coming. Not in a big city. Here, they crept up on you. But warehouses by the river had other uses.

Juan had leant Joan against a load-bearing girder and wrapped her in duct tape from her feet to her neck. Cocooned her in it. Used almost an entire roll of duct tape. Another point of irritation for Miguel—unnecessary waste. He'd sealed her mouth, too. Neither of them had been able to listen to her beg any longer. The noise had driven them to distraction.

Miguel approached her. "Are you going to be quiet if I take the tape off?"

She nodded.

He peeled the tape away carefully. "There," he said. "It wasn't so bad."

She stared at him, eyes watery and wide. "Tell me how I can help you," she said.

"You didn't know she was a killer, did you?"

"Melody runs a cleaning business. I had no idea she was a criminal."

Joan had been helpful, that Miguel had to admit. She had given him Melody's apartment number on Bleecker. And the address of Joe Bernstein, Melody's friend. Joan had said she'd only ever visited once and had not been invited back.

"What's her problem with you?" Miguel asked.

"It's not her fault. She's weak. Thinks she had a hard childhood. I did my best."

"I don't doubt it, Joan."

"Are you going to let me go? You don't know me, but if you did, you'd know I wouldn't say anything about this."

"I'm sure," Miguel said. "Of course I'm going to release you. I promised you'd be home in time for dinner. I'm just going to put the tape on your mouth so you stay quiet. You'll be home soon."

Juan returned from the van with a black bag similar in shape to a guitar case. Hyundai was written on the side.

"What should I do, patron?"

"Chop her up. Weigh the parts down and throw them in the river."

Juan stripped to his underwear and unzipped the bag.

Joan screamed, the tape on her mouth puffing in and out.

Miguel went to the van. Finally, he had a chance to read the newspaper. He had almost finished scanning the front page when the chainsaw's engine roared to life.

FORTY

PAIGE GARDNER ADJUSTED HER KNEE PADS, PULLED ON latex gloves, got on all fours, and scrubbed. She was using Naturally It's Clean on the hardwood, the product recommended by Kim. As promised, Kim had uploaded a video to YouTube.

Paige had watched all of her videos. Ten times or more. She had stopped counting—or lost count—after the tenth viewing. If anyone had told Paige she had watched each of Kim's videos hundreds of times she wouldn't have believed them.

Juice stains were difficult to remove once they had dried. It wasn't always possible to clean up immediately when Will or Ernie spilled their OJ. Or when they flung their food at the wall or launched their mashed turnip from their spoons into the air; sometimes it was difficult to know where the airborne turnip had even landed. She was trying to get her boys to eat their vegetables. Climbing Mount Everest with a limp and limited oxygen would have been easier. But she was putting more effort into feeding her kids right. Whatever it took, she did it, including bribing them with treats. *Eat your veg, Ernie, and I'll give you some chocolate. Eat those carrots, Will, and I'll give you some marshmallow.* Every day it was a battle. Tantrums, tears, screaming, because her kids weren't interested in treats *after* they'd eaten their vegetables; they wanted them *now*.

Paige envied her husband on difficult days. Isaac got to go to work, safe from the bawling, the stress, and the loneliness. Envy made her feel guilty. She tried to block it out, but it was stubborn. It was a weakness she wasn't proud of. Her one outlet, the one thing she looked forward to, was going to see Kim. Paige's sister babysat. Without Emily, Paige really didn't know how she would cope.

Since she'd gotten to know Kim, Paige had felt herself getting stronger. She still had days when she thought she was going to crumble, to curl up and cry. But Kim had given her something special. Paige couldn't say what it was for sure. Maybe self-belief. Maybe Kim's *Just get on with it* attitude. Or perhaps it was because Paige really wanted to improve her skills as a homemaker and Kim had helped her do that. Her instructions were clear, easy to follow. She gave homemaking the respect it deserved. Having two children made a difference.

It was an ongoing fight to keep the house free of danger. At some point during the first few months of being a mother, Paige had become worried about MRSA. Worry had developed into fear, sometimes even panic. Germs. They were everywhere. Staphylococcus; it *sounded* malicious. She had become convinced that staph had colonized every surface in her house. She'd had to be a more effective homemaker to protect her family. What had started as a vague notion had solidified into hard certainty: if Isaac or her children contracted MRSA they were doomed. There was no cure. She was in charge of the house and the safety of her family. Good homemaking skills would thwart catastrophe.

Kim had taught her that a to-do list was the homemaker's friend and savior. Mornings were reserved for cleaning the bathroom. It was funny to look back at her early attempts at scrubbing the commode. How she had gagged! It was a horrible job. Kim had promised her it would get easier. And lo, it had. The more she cleaned the bathtub, tiles and toilet, the less disgusting it felt. The kitchen was next in line. She'd already sprayed the countertops, disinfected and wiped down the microwave, the toaster, the oven. A full load of laundry was in the machine, tumbling through its cycle. The hamper was empty. Paige was aware of how relieved she felt once she had washed her family's clothes, and that feeling wasn't embarrassing anymore. How could someone feel so good about something so ordinary? So utterly dull? It was another item off her list.

She still had to vacuum the bedrooms and Isaac's home office. She stood, groaned at the ache in her knees and the stiffness in her back. By area, the living room—Paige preferred *family* room—floor was the largest in the house, and now it was clean. She had finished the job and Will and Ernie hadn't woken up yet. Her luck was in today. She could feel it. Those days were rare, when progress came easily and the day felt readymade to be hers and hers only.

She stripped off the gloves, decided not to use the vacuum cleaner, afraid it would wake the children. Instead, she'd clean Isaac's office by hand. He had been in a hurry this morning. His desk was in disarray, paperwork scattered all over it. He'd even left the computer running. That was okay; she didn't resent him for it. He was busier these days, doing so well in his job that they might be able to hire someone to help with the kids soon. The idea was appealing and guilt-inducing at the same time.

She assessed what needed to be done. First, disinfect the floor. Then the keyboard. Wipe the screen and the desk. Put the paperwork into an orderly pile, ready for Isaac when he came home. She'd do it as soon as some feeling returned to her knees and the pain in her wrists faded.

Later, Paige thought that if it hadn't been for her aches, she wouldn't have done it. But now she was moving the mouse, guiding the cursor across the screen, clicking on History.

She gasped and fell to her knees, the pain forgotten, her mouth wide, eyes brimming with tears.

FORTY-ONE

THE WALK TO WORK WAS GETTING LONGER. THE ONLY benefit of the drop-off in trade was that he was alone. Mrs. Angelique Gibson had been his last client. He had embalmed her more than a week ago. It wasn't all doom and gloom though. If he had no clients, he couldn't steal their body parts. On the other hand, if things continued like this, Kim would remind him of the bills, and the way they had of dropping through the mail slot regardless of how slow business had become.

Norman thought his relationship with his wife had improved. Kim seemed happier. She wasn't constantly worrying about the state of their finances. She *was* pleased with his progress, even praising him for "managing" his stress. Norman had had no idea how stressed he'd been until Kim had given him those little pills. His wife had been right, after all. Norman now took his medicine without argument. Without resistance. In fact, he wanted more Xanax, but Kim had told him, no, she was rationing the pills so that he didn't take too many. She really had been worried for him.

He relied on death too much. He wouldn't have chosen the career of a mortician if he had been a younger man. But at forty-six, he was an old dog who didn't want to learn new tricks. He was stuck with embalming.

There was a solution to their long-term financial security: move to a more populated metropolitan area, where death was frequent enough to keep them solvent. He'd brought it up many times but the proposal was always met with cold silence. Kim was enjoying her little club; she had friends. She seemed excited, updating him on a regular basis about how well her YouTube channel was doing, how she was adding more subscribers every day. And she was getting fan mail. Her interview with Diane Battle was being talked about. Her email inbox was swamped with positive comments, and the occasional troll, whatever that was.

Norman guessed these were mostly good things. Kim seemed to think so, and that was all that mattered. It was an alien world to him, but if it was working for her, he hoped it lasted. No, Kim wasn't moving anywhere else. She was already home.

He wedged open the door to Loomis Memorial, letting in the warm morning air. His routine hadn't changed since he'd established the business. He vacuumed the viewing room, and dusted the chairs, the walls, the reception area.

The casket room was next. He took great care to make sure it was dust-free and Lysol-fresh. He polished the caskets with a rag and a can of Mr. Muscle, buffing them to a high shine.

The embalming room was spotless. The disinfectant smell of CaviCide was a reminder that he'd cleaned it yesterday. But Norman took pride in his work, in keeping his environment disease-free. Daily decontamination of the embalming room was necessary. As he sprayed the stainless-steel work surfaces, tables and sinks, he whistled. A moment passed before he checked himself—this was not the place to whistle a cheerful tune. The embalming room had a separate atmosphere, one that demanded respect. He closed his mouth.

How can I whistle after what I have done?

He finished his work in silence, then returned to the parlor, sat at the walnut reception desk and waited for someone, anyone, to come by. Cars passed on Main Street. A woman strolled past on the street, her dog straining at the leash. Being alone began to lose its appeal. He would have welcomed a stray cat. He hoped someone would die and for the family of the departed to use his services. It was horrible. He hated himself for it. He was supposed to be providing for his wife. Was that who he was? A man who couldn't give his wife the things she wanted? Kim had needed to harvest organs from the dead because he was inadequate as a husband, a poor provider. Norman blamed himself. To think he'd harbored thoughts of divorce. Thoughts that his wife was a monster for involving them with the Ray Porters of the world. He had hated her for climbing onto the embalming table and carving the precious in-demand tissue from the corpses that had been entrusted to them. And all this time he had been the problem. It wasn't Kim's fault for trying to keep them afloat. It was his. He was failing as a husband. It was surprising that Kim hadn't divorced *him*.

Norman wasn't managing his stress now. He wished he had one of those tiny pills. Just one.

FORTY-TWO

THE LOOMIS WOMAN WOULD MAKE A MISTAKE. SOONER OR later, Kim would reveal her true self. Megan intended to keep parking the station wagon beside the school and tailing her wherever she went until she did. The routine followed the same pattern. Norman walked to work, and nothing much happened. Sometimes Kim drove to the stores on State Street. Once she'd gone to the Walmart Supercenter in Berlin. Megan found it funny. The Loomis woman, with her upmarket pretensions, was just a peasant at heart.

She had expected to discover that Kim had a secret lover, a rich fool willing to fund her lifestyle, but it wasn't the case. That would have been the type of scandal Megan could work with. Easy to spread the word that Miss High Style Peasant was cheating on her mortician husband, a man who served his community, a respected individual who conveyed the dead to their final resting place with nothing less than eye-watering dignity.

She'd bought a camera, complete with zoom lens, to capture the moment when the harlot and Mr. Moneybags kissed, embraced, and ate at a fancy restaurant. Photographs she would have put on the internet for the world to see. No such luck. The camera was on the seat beside her, unused except for a few test shots she'd taken to understand how to use it.

Megan planned to tell Jacob about her suspicions. Megan imagined his reaction—complete lack of interest disguised by an obligatory frown an outsider might mistake for curiosity. Then he'd try to talk her out of following Kim. *What if he thinks I've lost my marbles?*

It was probably best not to trouble Jacob yet. At least not until she had evidence of wrongdoing. *I bet the truth is so juicy it'll make me squint.*

She jumped, startled. There was a knock on her window. The car rocked slightly as her weight shifted. She turned her head. Kim was looking directly at her, smiling. Megan rolled down the window. Her arm was heavy, numb, mechanical, as though it didn't belong to her.

"Hi, Meg," Kim said, still smiling. That smile never faltered.

It was too late to hide the camera on the seat. What was she going to tell her? Megan's thoughts came fast, became tangled as she scrambled for a convincing lie. Megan had gotten there at 7 a.m. How had the Loomis woman crept up on her? Had she been lying in wait? There was no other explanation. How long had she known?

"I went to the store to get some muffins," Kim was saying, "and I thought I recognized you."

Megan's ears were ringing. She had a moment of self-loathing as she noticed her heart was racing and her mouth had come loose at the hinges. *What am I going to say to her?*

"I was taking photographs of our native birds to post on Instagram," Megan said, stunned at the words tumbling from her mouth. She didn't have an Instagram account. Kim had mentioned Instagram several times during her lectures. The first thing she had to do when she got home was set up an Instagram account and post pictures of birds. It was stupid, Megan knew. She had been caught. She had I-am-spying-on-you written all over her face.

"I didn't know you were an amateur ornithologist," Kim said.

My oh my. What big words for such a lowly peasant.

"I love it," Megan said. "Birdwatching is more exciting than it sounds."

"Come have breakfast with me."

"I can't. I've achieved my goal for today. Must be going."

Why do I sound like someone else? Megan wondered.

"It would be unchristian of me not to invite you in for breakfast. I'll brew peppermint tea and heat these muffins."

Megan glanced at the brown paper bag in Kim's hand. She was dressed like a normal person this morning: white shorts, tennis shoes, and a yellow tee-shirt that didn't reveal her cleavage. At least she didn't look like a stripper today. She felt disarmed. *Unchristian.* The word had made her drop her guard. Kim was a Christian? Megan could hardly believe it, but she was curious. Maybe she'd learn more by accepting the invitation.

"Okay, I can spare a few minutes." Megan followed the still-smiling Kim across the road.

She was going to play along. They were both pretending Megan hadn't been staking out the Loomis residence. Megan had been caught but calm had taken the place of shock. *Fine, let's play this game.* There was no way Kim believed she had been birdwatching from a dirty old station wagon. Women of her caliber were clearly designed for finer, luxury vehicles. *She's a whore but she's not stupid. Or am I giving her too much credit.*

Then the possibility, dim and distant, surfaced. What if Kim did believe her? What if she'd bought her lame story?

Kim invited her to take a seat in the drawing room, then left. *How grand! Too grand for a woman with the heart of a stripper and the soul of a vulture.* A few minutes later, she returned, carrying a silver tray, which she placed on the table between them. Steaming chocolate-chip muffins, warmed, and two cups of peppermint tea.

"It's a lovely morning," Kim said.

"Uh-huh."

"Do you have children?"

Megan paused. "I had one."

"Had?"

"He died. Cancer."

"That's awful." Kim dropped her smile.

"My faith helps me cope…Are you a woman of faith?"

"Oh, of course. I keep it to myself. Don't see that it's anyone's business."

She's toying with me.

"Um…interesting."

"You know what else is interesting, Meg? It's an amazing piece of luck that I saw you. I meant to speak to you sooner. I've been getting requests from a lot of people who want to join the Homemakers Association of Vermont. I feel I need to take in younger people, coach them in their careers as new homemakers. I believe you have enough experience in these matters already, and there's therefore no need for you to continue attending our meetings."

Megan stared at her. "So I'm no longer a member?"

"I'm afraid that's the case. I'm really sorry to see you go."

No you're not. It's only a matter of time, you tramp. But I will take you down.

FORTY-THREE

KIM WASN'T EXPECTING VISITORS. SHE DIDN'T HURRY TO answer the ringing doorbell. Whoever it was, they were determined to see her, repeatedly pressing the bell and holding the button down.

Paige Gardner was standing on the doorstep. Tears had congealed on her pale face.

"Come in," Kim said, gathering her into the house and walking her to the kitchen, arm around her slumped shoulders. "What in God's name happened? Is everything all right?"

Paige sat at the table and Kim made peppermint tea. Paige attempted to explain but burst into tears. Kim said nothing, just rubbed Paige's back and waited.

"Isaac," Paige said. Another sob shook her.

"Isaac what? Is he okay? He's not sick, is he?"

Paige laughed. There was no humor in it.

"He is sick but not in the usual way."

Now Kim's internal curiosity meter was glowing bright red.

"It's okay," Kim said. "Take your time. There's no hurry."

They sat in silence for a few minutes, Kim gently rubbing her back. Paige's sobs died away and Kim used an aloe-vera infused tissue to pat her face dry.

Paige sniffled. "Thanks."

"There's no need to thank me. I consider you part of my family. This is what family is for."

Paige smiled. She squeezed Kim's hand. Kim returned the gesture.

"I hope it's not too bad, whatever it is."

Paige looked at her. "Isaac has been watching porn," she said.

Kim blinked. "Your husband? Isaac? I don't believe it."

"I saw it, Kim. There's so *much* of it."

"I hate to ask, but did you see anything illegal?"

"Oh no. I checked—I had to. What am I going to do? Is he a sex addict? I mean, am I not good enough for him?"

"He loves you, Paige. Could be just a phase he's going through, and it'll work itself out in time."

"I really thought I'd hit the jackpot when I married him, Kim. I mean, in terms of Isaac as a person."

"I know what you mean."

"How could he? *Porn?* I've been wondering why we haven't been…you know…lately. He's watching porn in his office all day and I thought he was doing paperwork."

"The good news is that this is a problem that has a solution like any other."

"What should I do, Kim?"

"It might be helpful to see what Dr. Phil has to say on the subject. I'm sure if you browse the internet you'll find tips on how to deal with Isaac's addiction." Kim was making a supreme effort not to laugh. She swallowed hard and bit her tongue and the inside of her cheek. The stinging pain sobered her. Everything was an addiction these days. Paige was young—she would learn that some issues were only problems when someone *made* it a problem.

"Is he cheating on you?" Kim asked.

"He's cheating on me by watching porn." *Oh dear Jesus above*, Kim thought. Maybe there was no hope for Paige. Kim recalled the time she had been stopped for speeding.

She hadn't complained about the police officer because he didn't hold her hand while he wrote out the ticket. She had paid the fine and moved on. Was Paige so delicate, so fragile that she couldn't look past her husband's viewing habits? Was she making it into a bigger problem because the talk shows she watched *said* it was a problem? What would *she* do if Norman watched porn? Nothing, she thought. As long as he didn't physically touch another woman, she'd do absolutely nothing.

Kim wanted to help Paige and Isaac, even if it meant lying to her friend. "You should talk to him," she said. "You have to keep in mind that your husband has a disease." Kim could hardly believe what she was saying. It wasn't a disease, but if it helped, why not?

"A disease?" Paige said.

Kim watched her turn the idea over in her mind and latch onto it.

"Yes," Kim said. "Maybe it's not his fault. Put it into perspective. Isaac isn't smoking crack cocaine or shooting heroin."

"Of course not."

"See? Gives you a new way of looking at it. His addiction isn't as bad as drug addiction, do we agree on that?"

"I suppose so."

"But he *does* have an addiction. And what do we do with addicts?"

"We help them."

"Exactly, Paige. That's good. You love your husband and you want him to recover from his addiction so you…"

"Help him?"

"And support him while he goes through withdrawal."

Paige nodded. Kim patted her hand.

"Once you think these things through, step by step, you often discover the answer to a question, a solution to a problem."

"I didn't realize sex addiction was such a big problem for men."

It isn't, Kim thought. It was made up, invented by celebrities to avoid taking responsibility for their actions.

"All problems can be fixed. If you remember that, you'll do just fine."

"Has Norman ever—?"

"God no! My Norman is as sweet as your Isaac. It's a bump in the road, Paige. That's all. Talk to him and you'll see."

"I felt like breaking things earlier. I had to call my sister to babysit the kids. I don't think I've ever felt rage before, until today. I mean real rage. There was violence in it."

"I'm glad you came by and chose to share with me."

"It's extraordinary."

"What?"

"How good I feel after talking to you."

Kim patted her hand again. "That's what I'm here for," she said.

Paige sipped the peppermint tea. Kim watched her, a quick light dancing in her eyes.

FORTY-FOUR

NORMAN'S THOUGHTS SHIFTED FROM LITTLE PINK PILLS TO the locked basement door. What was Kim hiding down there? The idea that his wife was hiding something had gained weight in his mind. Norman wasn't allowed into Kim's private space. It was *her* basement. Where did she keep the key? No doubt it was well hidden. If he broke the lock, what excuse would he have? None that Kim would believe or accept. And Norman didn't want to be on the receiving end of his wife's wrath, a force of nature in itself. He had seen her lose her temper. It was an assault on the senses, not to be forgotten. Simple curiosity had become an obsessive itch. He *was* going to look in the basement; he had decided that already. It was just a matter of when.

In the two hours he had been sitting at the reception desk, no one had died. Or if somebody had, the decedent's relatives hadn't called him.

The door was wedged open. The day outside was so bright it was almost white. Someone was walking up the path toward Loomis Memorial. He squinted. The approaching figure took the shape of a woman. Norman only recognized her when she was on the doorstep. It was Brooke Draper. One of Kim's friends. He frowned. Brooke was wearing a red-and-white polka-dot dress and black heels. The outfit of a sinner, his foster parents would have said.

But Norman didn't see sinners, just people. He had asked himself many times why a woman as attractive as his wife had married him. The answer he'd come to accept was that they were both orphans. The real sinners had been their foster parents. Norman believed that most people who fostered kids were good people. He only wished his luck had been better.

He stood, shuffled some brochures on the desk. He didn't want anyone to know he wasn't busy. There was something shameful about it. A lesson his check-hungry foster parents had made sure he learned and remembered.

Brooke smiled and Norman lifted the corners of his mouth in return.

"So this is where you work," she said.

Norman nodded. He watched her look around, fidgeted with his suit. Suddenly it seemed ill-fitting, as though he'd put it on wrong. He stuffed his hands into his pockets. Took them out. His fingers pulled at the buttons on his suit coat. None were undone. He straightened his tie. His hands shook; he had the urge to pull at his lip. The younger woman was looking into the casket room.

I should talk to her. Take her on a tour of the premises.

Norman sometimes forgot his manners. He never intended to insult anyone, but sometimes he neglected to smile and speak with clients in a friendly manner. It frustrated him, and he was trying to improve. Some mistook his shyness for snobbery. That was why he wanted Kim to take over from him. She should run Loomis Memorial. Simply put, Kim was far superior to the task than he was. He'd talk to her about it later. He was out of his depth, dealing with the public. Maybe he was surprised. No one ever came to visit him. Who wanted to look around a funeral home? Kim's friend, apparently.

Norman moved to walk toward her. He hesitated. Started again, stopped. Started toward her again, like a car stuck in the wrong gear.

"Ma'am," he said, "would you like me to show you round?"

Brooke turned to look at him. "Ma'am?" she said. "Brooke is fine, Mr. Loomis. Ma'am is my mother. Yes, I'd like that. After you."

Norman hoped she didn't see the heat in his face. Hoped he hadn't offended her.

He led the way down the hall to the viewing room. He considered giving her the sales pitch and decided against it. He hated the sales pitch. Norman would have made a very poor salesman—fired on day one. He often stumbled over his words or mangled his spiel entirely. Kim, though, was a master at selling. She didn't miss a beat. She injected excitement into the prospect of becoming a client of Loomis Memorial. He had seen her do it.

Brooke walked along the aisle. Her outstretched hand caressed the tops of the chairs.

"It's bigger than it looks from the outside."

He showed her the embalming room. Brooke puzzled him. She seemed genuinely interested in the machinery, the chemicals and the process. Most people weren't.

His smile was easier now, less strained.

"It's fascinating," Brooke said. She ran her fingers along the length of the embalming table.

That fascinated him. She wasn't afraid of picking up germs. Every surface was disinfected and disease-free. He knew it but how did *she*? Did she trust him to keep his workplace clean, to sanitize the table where he prepared the dead for burial? How *could* she know? Then he sniffed the answer: the strong chemical odor.

He didn't know her and she didn't know him. He had seen Brooke twice. At the fundraiser and when Diane Battle had interviewed Kim. He paused at the small kitchenette area.

"Would you like some coffee? Tea?"

"I'll have a cup of tea. If it's no trouble."

"No," Norman said, "it's no trouble."

"I'll help you." The kitchenette wasn't worthy of the name, merely an alcove with a counter he'd had built, atop which sat a microwave, a kettle, and a coffeemaker. There was a small refrigerator tucked underneath it. The space was tight, to say the least.

The kettle clicked. Norman poured the boiled water into two cups. Brooke's elbow brushed his. Norman felt a shiver run up his spine. It wasn't unpleasant. He handed her the milk carton. Her fingers touched his. The air between them seemed to crackle with static. She was looking at him; he saw it from the corner of his eye. He stirred his tea, making an effort not to turn his head and look at her.

He was relieved as they walked up the hallway toward the reception desk. His heart sounded too loud in his ears. He had carried a chair from the viewing room and invited Brooke to sit on his more comfortable swivel chair. They sipped their tea in silence. Norman stared ahead, out the door, at the white day.

"You did an excellent job at the fundraiser."

Norman turned to her. She was already looking at him.

"I did?" he said.

"Yes. You did. I noticed."

Her eyes were everywhere. On *his* eyes, his lips, his hair. Norman forgot himself. He looked openly at her lips, her neck, and lower…

He looked away, at the daylight, at someone passing by on the street. Usually he would have been uncomfortable sitting so close to someone. Brooke's knees were less than an inch away from his. But he didn't mind.

And that disturbed him. He wasn't uncomfortable. *He didn't mind.*

FORTY-FIVE

MEGAN HAWKINS WASN'T THE ONLY ONE WITH AN OLD CAR in storage. Kim had hosed the years of accumulated dust and cobwebs off her 2005 Ford F150 Lariat Supercab, which hadn't moved out of her garage in over ten years. And there it stood, drying in the blazing sunshine, its medium Wedgewood blue metallic paint looking as good as new. No one knew about the truck save for Norman. She fired up the engine. The battery still had juice. Kim looked after the things she owned. At least she washed her secret car, unlike Megan.

If she hurried, she would be back in time for the operation. But Megan had taken priority. She was dangerous...and a fool if she thought Kim hadn't noticed the dirty station wagon following her. *There's always one*, she thought. *One person in your job, in your life who's out to get you.*

She had made a mistake, and Kim didn't make many of those. She was disappointed in herself. Someone like Megan would never accept someone like Kim into their elite circle, she knew that now. There wasn't going to be any invitation to their ivory tower. Kim was building her own, anyway.

One thing was clear: Megan was determined to dig up something incriminating on her. But Megan didn't know what determination was. *When you've come this far*, she thought, *you go all the way*. Megan wasn't the only self-made businesswoman in town. Did she really believe she was one of the select few entitled to wealth? Probably. Kim was on her way up in the world, and Megan wanted to drag her down. But Megan didn't understand that *no one* dragged Kim Loomis anywhere she didn't want to go.

She put a full-body biohazard suit in the cab, a pickax and shovel in the bed of the truck underneath a blue tarp, and threw a Walmart bag containing a weighty instrument into the glove compartment.

She drove past the Fairbanks house, rounded the bend at the end of the straight stretch of Main Street, and turned right onto Towne Hill Road, headed toward East Montpelier. As the houses thinned to fields swaying with crops still to be harvested, Kim remembered the shocked expression on Megan's face when she'd knocked on her window. The camera on the passenger seat. She had been tailing Kim for days. It was the strength of Megan's distaste for her that she didn't understand. *How could she be jealous of me? She has everything. But everything's not enough for her. She has it out for me. She's going to ruin me. Well, she can try…*

The Hawkins farm lay up ahead. A massive red barn and tall grain silos resembling giant silver bullets stood further back from the house. Jacob Hawkins evidently took pride in maintaining the place. The silos looked as though they'd been painted recently, and the wooden barn belonged in a postcard.

Kim put on a pair of sunglasses and a baseball cap and parked on the grassy verge outside the house. Far enough from prying eyes. Even if Megan was watching from a window, binoculars poised, she wouldn't be able to see through Kim's disguise. She hoped not, anyway.

Can't wait to see the shock on your stupid face when you see how determined I am up close.

FORTY-SIX

THE PAIN IN HIS BACK WAS GONE. WHATEVER THE POLICE woman had plastered on it had helped. Evan didn't believe she was a cop. He wouldn't still be captive if that was the case.

He had trespassed and this was his punishment. So many times his mother had warned him he'd be punished for his bad behavior. That God sought revenge on little boys who didn't listen to their mothers. She had been right. God had sent the woman to make him pay for his small crimes.

His will to escape had wilted then vanished completely. All he wanted was to sleep. The woman had given him water. He felt grateful for it, which confused him. But his thirst had returned, an unending longing that was bigger than him. Bigger than his prison underneath the woman's house. The real police weren't coming to rescue him. The chance had come, and he'd failed. Hadn't been quick enough. But hadn't he tried? Yes, he'd put everything into the effort. Yet the result was his continued confinement in the abyss. Free-falling in a distant galaxy. Light years from safety. Life went on up there, above him. Day by day, the distance between him and the Outside increased. If he'd had any adrenaline left, he would have been shocked by his perception of that distance. It was incalculable. It had grown until it had no end. The rational part of him knew he must be mere feet from the Outside. But it didn't *feel* that way. And how he felt was what counted. His thoughts were fragmented anyway. Useless, rambling, senseless.

He visualized his mother, sober, searching for him. Going door to door, asking people if they had seen her boy. He held onto that image, clung to it. He saw his mother finding him, rescuing him. Imagined himself apologizing for his bad behavior, for his father leaving them. For his father, Travis Fairbanks, had left because of him. He hadn't wanted children, that much was obvious. So he'd walked out on them and never came back. Evan hadn't dared admit it to himself, but now there was no sense in lying. His mother had started drinking almost immediately. She hadn't been mean right away; the name-calling came later. The accusations, too. She had accused Evan of ruining her life, of bad behavior even when he had done nothing wrong. And since he had been accused of being bad then it made sense to be bad, because it made no difference. So he skipped school, was loud in class, flipped off their neighbors, talked back to his teachers, stole cell phones from his classmates. But not from Corey. He'd *never* steal from his friend.

He moaned somewhere deep in his chest. His arms were dead meat.

There was no blood in his hands. His feet tingled.

He thought he'd lost the capacity to cry. He hadn't. He wept.

Then he slept though he didn't dream.

And there were no more thoughts of escape.

FORTY-SEVEN

JIM BAYLISS HANDED HIS SON A STICK FROM THE TRUNK OF his car. It was sugar maple. He'd stripped it of its bark. Its dull bone color would be easy to spot if Corey dropped it once they got the search underway. He had told Corey the state police had already combed Hubbard Park for Evan. Corey had insisted they might have missed something. Jim didn't want to argue or tell Corey the truth. Neither did Lillian. They didn't have the heart to be honest with him, like in the past with the tooth fairy.

And the truth was that Evan was most likely dead. Jim didn't want to think about what had happened to the child *before* he was murdered. Every scenario that played out in his mind was horrifying. How could they explain such evil to Corey? Right now, Corey believed Evan was still alive, but he'd see the truth in his own time.

Jim was taking the easy route, he knew, but at least he was being honest with himself. He was saving himself from the heartbreak of stealing Corey's hope. Telling his son that Evan had probably been abducted by a pedophile and murdered—he couldn't do it. *Wouldn't* do it.

When did you let your children know what the world was really like? Or did you let them discover for themselves that the world was full of evil people capable of unspeakable crimes? Should he just tell Corey he was wasting his time? The state police had run cadaver dogs through every inch of the park. Hundreds of volunteers had participated in the search.

Jim decided not to mention anything. What good would it do? If his son had been an adult he would have had less of a problem sharing his views. But Corey was a child. Perhaps the boy could help himself by doing something.

Was Jim prolonging the agony by keeping his mouth shut? There was no manual on how to handle a situation as awful as this one. Corey seemed convinced that no one cared anymore, that everyone had forgotten Evan was missing. It wasn't true. The adults spoke about it in whispers, making sure their children didn't overhear their distressing conversations.

Some of those conversations had turned to Lena Fairbanks and her questionable parenting. If she had taken care of Evan properly and not filled her days with alcohol then maybe none of this would have happened.

Some had sympathy for her, but not many. Jim counted himself in the unsympathetic camp. Lena was a drunk, incapable of looking after a child. It was never discussed why no one had reported her to CPS. Jim was as guilty as anyone else in that respect. At the time, he had considered it none of his business. And he regretted that now. He'd only realized what Evan had put up with when Lena Fairbanks had come to his home, drunk and incoherent. News of that incident had gotten around fast. Montpelier was more like a small town than a state capital. Gossip traveled.

Who had kidnapped Evan? It was a question many had speculated about. Some said he had been taken by a drifter, a drug addict, an outsider. All that speculation had amounted to nothing. No one knew.

Parents kept a tight rein on their children now. There was no way Jim was letting his son go to the park by himself. He wasn't taking any chances.

The problem with searching Hubbard Park was its few open spaces. It was densely wooded. Jim looked around the Old Shelter parking lot. It was a sunny day, yet the place was deserted. Jim glanced at his watch. It was just after 2 p.m. He grunted.

"Evan used to come here," Corey said, "especially when he was in a bad mood. He could've come back here after… after I left him."

Jim put a hand on his son's shoulder and squeezed. He felt Corey's despair and felt angry and sad that his son had experienced such a terrible loss so young. He prayed the police found the sonofabitch responsible for the crime.

"Well, we'll see what we can see," Jim said. He looked at Corey from the corner of his eye. The boy was grieving; he just didn't know it yet.

They found a path through the trees. Jim took the lead, beating back heavy vegetation to clear the way. What if they did find a body? Jim thought it would be unlikely, but not impossible. He believed an opportunistic predator had snatched Evan from Main Street. The police hadn't found the bicycle; the perpetrator must have taken it along with the boy.

They spread out, poking the undergrowth with their sticks. Jim always kept Corey in his sights and checked his compass often, giving it nothing more than the quickest glance. But mostly he watched Corey, his heart broken for his son.

FORTY-EIGHT

THERE WERE SEVERAL CARS IN THE DRIVEWAY. KIM recognized the white Lexus Megan drove when she wasn't following her in a grimy old station wagon. The house was a sprawling old colonial-style mansion. Kim saw the problem immediately. To talk to Megan up close, she'd have to knock on her front door. But not today. There were too many cars on the property, and that meant people.

Kim sat for another two hours, a map open on the steering wheel. Then one of her suspicions was confirmed—Megan had help. Kim counted four maids. They even wore matching gray pinafores. Of course, the corn-fed country whore hadn't scrubbed a floor in decades. So why had Megan come to her house, sat in on meetings of the Homemakers Association of Vermont if she wasn't interested in housework?

Because she had been looking for clues. Anything to hang Kim by the ankles. Megan couldn't stand a woman like Kim rising above her natural station in life: obscurity, borderline poverty, keeping her little head bowed before rich farmers like the Megan Hawkinses of the world.

Blood warmed her face. Kim imagined Megan patting her on the head and feeding her from her hand as though she was an obedient dog. *Now back in your kennel!* Her heart rate increased and her fingernails pressed little crescent moons into her palms. Her pupils dilated. She blinked behind her sunglasses. She had work to do. She had waited long enough already.

Kim glanced at her watch, made a mental note of the time. After the maids had left, three cars remained in the driveway—the Lexus, a Mercedes, and the station wagon.

Where was the husband? The one she never talked about?

Kim needed to know who owned the Mercedes. The cab of the F150 was gathering heat. She cracked the window and waited. Her patience paid off. The door opened. A man kissed a woman Kim assumed was Megan, the fake homemaker, then exited the house and got into the Mercedes.

Kim noted the time on her watch. She started the engine and pulled into the road.

There were plenty of fields to choose from. Kim found one that had recently been plowed. She parked on an access road just off Towne Hill Road, then took the shovel and pickax from the truck bed and threw them over a gate. She trudged through the field, leaving footprints in the dry furrows that crumbled beneath her weight. She chose a spot that wasn't visible from the road and began to dig, grunting like a tennis player with each swing of the pickax.

It had to be deep. Deep enough to accommodate a corn-fed whore.

FORTY-NINE

JIM AND COREY WERE EXHAUSTED BY THE TIME THEY emerged from the woods into the parking lot. Sweaty and rumpled, they sat at a picnic table. Parents were ordering their children into their cars. One irate mother, voice raised, promised to give her son Ashton the back of her hand if he didn't hurry and quit pulling his sister's hair.

It would be dark in an hour, and the temperature wasn't as balmy as it had been earlier. Some people stared as Jim and Corey undid the foil on their sandwiches—corned beef garnished with sizeable dollops of ketchup. Father and son ate loudly, taking huge bites of bread and meat. Table manners were forgotten. Lillian wasn't there to remind them not to talk with their mouths full, or to offer the slow-down-anyone-would-think-I-was-starving-you look she reserved for when they shoveled down their dinner at speed. They were fast eaters, that was all.

"It's good," Corey said, spraying crumbs.

"Heaven, son. I swear it's delicious."

"Can't believe corned beef and ketchup tastes so good."

"I know, right?" Jim put the grim task of trying to locate the remains of Evan to the back of his mind. For a moment, anyway. Spending time with his son was more important.

He looked at Corey over the top of his sandwich. He knew so little about him, and the realization shocked him. Was this sudden interest in Corey sparked by Evan's disappearance? It shouldn't have been the case but Jim Bayliss was past lying to himself. He was often preoccupied, focused on work, on making sure his family had what they needed. Maybe Corey needed his old man to learn who he was. Jim hadn't known his own father, despite living in the same house for eighteen years. The elder Bayliss had barely spoken to him, engaged in a seemingly endless internal dialog, frowning and grunting at the conversation only he heard, often shaking his head if he disagreed with whoever was in his mind. Jim sometimes disappeared into his thoughts, too. He should be more alert to what was going on around him. More attentive to his wife and son.

Jim cracked open two Cokes. "Here son," he said, passing one to Corey.

"It's warm."

"Yup. Long as it's not warm beer. Now that *would* be a sin."

Corey laughed.

"It's really that bad?"

"Anything less than cold, sweating beer is bad, Cor. Don't tell your mother I told you so."

Corey pressed his lips together and made a zipping gesture.

He seems all right, Jim thought. Then a haunted look crept into Corey's eyes. Jim's frustration grew. He didn't know what to say. They had searched acres of Hubbard Park and turned up no trace of Evan.

"It's not your fault, Cor," Jim said.

"If I'd stayed with him, walked home with him, he wouldn't be missing."

Jim's throat tightened; his chest suddenly felt heavy.

"We don't know that."

"I do. I just wish I could apologize to him."

"We can look for him again tomorrow."

"I can't feel him here, Dad. He's gone."

Jim lowered his head, trawled his mind for words of comfort, but none came. The first starlight winked in the darkening sky. They walked back to the car in silence.

FIFTY

THERE WAS SOMEONE OUTSIDE. EVAN WAS SOMEWHERE between waking and sleeping when he sensed a disturbance in the air. At first, he thought the movement was inside his cell. Maybe the rat was still there. Had he imagined it? He hadn't detected its presence in days, it seemed. Maybe it had escaped.

The door opened, its hinges creaking. The sound grated on every nerve in his body. He became still, or thought he had—he was trembling all over. Who's there? he asked. But the question remained in his mind.

He gave voice to a muffled whimper, no more. That was what he wanted to say to the person he imagined was standing in the doorway most of all: no more. Please, no more.

"I'm sorry." It was a woman's voice. The same one who had pretended she was a police officer. What was she doing? She wasn't moving, just standing there, looking at him. Why had she put some kind of plaster on his back to ease his pain? If she was concerned about him and apologizing, then maybe she didn't mean to harm him. Maybe she would let him go.

Hope, faint, nothing more than a passing flicker, lit the darkness.

She's thinking about letting me go. She's sorry for keeping me here. She's just teaching me a lesson, not to trespass on her property, that's all.

Evan's stomach groaned, with hunger or excitement, he supposed it didn't matter.

For weeks, it seemed, he'd been desperate for signs of hope, of rescue. Like a child drowning in a swamp, scrabbling at weak tufts of grass to keep himself afloat, Evan had reached. For anything. For a path out of darkness. Was this woman his way back to the light? Evan wasn't so sure.

"I'm sorry," she whispered.

This time she was closer, right next to him. He hadn't heard her move. All thoughts of hope vanished, smothered by sudden terror. There was something underneath her apology, something that scared Evan more than the rat he had imagined had been trying to eat him alive.

Absence. That was it. An absence of feeling. There was *nothing* in the woman's voice.

A hand touched his shoulder. His body shrank. He whimpered again. A sound like crying seemed to come from far away. *I can't be*, he thought with wonder. *I don't have anything left.* And yet his face was wet.

Evan cried out.

The woman was gripping him, hard.

Pushing him into the floor.

A sharp thing pierced his arm.

He flinched, tried to break loose.

But she held him, putting all her weight into pinning him down.

He screamed.

The dots dancing across his obscured vision disappeared. The dark grew deeper and deeper. He plummeted toward sleep, even though he fought it.

And then, nothing.

***

He woke sometime later. How long had he been out? Time hadn't recovered any meaning. His stomach grumbled. How he wanted to eat. Even the tiniest morsel and he would be satisfied.

It took a moment for him to realize he could see. The lights overhead were blinding. He squinted against the glare. A machine chirped somewhere. He turned his head. Was he in the hospital? There was a monitor with jagged lines and a heart icon on its screen. It was too bright. He squinted harder, and more dots flooded his vision, which faded in and out. Panic stole over him. Was he going blind? Was he imagining this while still blindfolded?

He smelled chemicals. Rolled his eyes downward and saw his chest was covered in a dark-red substance. At first, he thought it was blood. But the skin was intact underneath the liquid. There was a needle in his arm and a tube. His back was cold. What was he lying on? He turned his head sideways. A steel table? He *must* be in the hospital.

A doctor appeared at his side, thumb poised on the plunger of a syringe. Terror made his eyes bulge as he recognized the woman behind the clear face shield. It was *her*.

She pressed the plunger and Evan struggled against sleep he didn't want.

Above him, a voice whispered, "You have no idea how many people you'll be helping, Evan."

FIFTY-ONE

IT WAS FULL DARK AND ISAAC STILL WASN'T HOME. WAS HE at the office? Who was he with?

Paige sat in front of her husband's computer, holding a printout of his sordid internet history in one hand and cupping the mouse with the other, moving the cursor around the screen, opening several windows at once and typing in keywords and phrases like *sex addiction*, *therapy for the sex addict*, and *is there a cure for porn addiction*? She got tired and confused while reading about the action she should take to save Isaac, to extract him from the morass of depravity into which he'd sunk. Instead, she checked for updates from Kim on Facebook, Instagram, Pinterest, Twitter and YouTube. Searching for new information, on any topic, afraid she was missing out on something important.

A video of Kim discussing how a homemaker could transform her house into a home played in the background as she came up empty on social media sites. There were no tweets from Kim. Radio silence for now. She'd check again in a minute. But at least Kim's voice was comforting. In her time of need, all she had to do was press Play.

Paige had followed Kim's advice, but Isaac didn't seem to appreciate how she had made their house a home. The reality was stark, nauseating—she had a smut-addicted husband, despite her best efforts to be a good wife.

She *had* been a good wife. She had put all her energy into making life easy for Isaac. He didn't have to lift a finger. She took care of everything, including their two children, who were too young to understand their father's disease, thank God.

Then a thought struck her like a bolt between the eyes: What if porn addiction was a genetic disease? What if her sons grew up to be like their father?

She opened a new window and asked Google if porn addiction had a genetic element.

Her heart was racing. She had to calm down. She was on the verge of information overload. She checked again for any new posts on social media from Kim. None. She stood, backed away from the computer, sat again, checked her email, promised herself she'd only login to Facebook but ended up checking all her accounts.

She left her husband's office feeling oddly deflated, somehow disappointed.

She went to the living-room window, peered through the drapes, tightening her grip on the printout. The indictment. *Where are you?*

Paige hoped her boys didn't wake up. Her sister had babysat. She knew how to handle them, had no problem getting them to sleep. *If only I was that good,* she thought, scanning the road, waiting for Isaac's headlights to sweep up the driveway.

Was it her fault? Was she the cause of Isaac's problem? The idea revolted her. No, she wasn't to blame. How could she even think that?

Maybe she was in shock. She had been convinced she'd won the lottery by marrying Isaac. He was ambitious, kind, didn't shout at her. *So I should be glad he doesn't shout at me?* She was furious. How was it possible for her mind to manufacture such nonsense? Fury gave way to sadness. The illusion of being married to the perfect man had been shattered. The notion that she *knew* Isaac had fallen apart, suddenly and without warning. And underneath the sadness and anger, another thought: I'm not good enough for him. It was that which troubled her more than any other.

Twin beams lit the driveway. Isaac was home. He revved the engine twice and switched it off. Why did men do that? She wasn't interested in solving that mystery tonight. She had questions for her husband.

His key slotted into the lock. Isaac had one foot on the threshold and the other on the doorstep when he came to a sudden stop. She glared at him.

"Where were you?"

Slowly, he inserted himself into the house, closed the door.

"At work," he said, a puzzled frown creasing his forehead.

"Do you know what time it is?" Am I being too harsh? She decided she wasn't. *Just don't use the eff word. Don't stoop to his level.*

He saw the paper in her hand.

"What's that?" he asked.

She shoved it into his chest.

Isaac straightened the crumpled sheet, eyes growing bigger, showing too much of the whites.

"Your internet search history," she said, momentarily baffled and disgusted by the pride in her voice.

"You spied on me?"

Paige shifted from one foot to the other. She didn't know what to do with her hands. She almost apologized, and hated herself for it. If he mounted a counterattack, she just might use the eff word, after all.

Her confidence returned. *She* was the one who had discovered evidence of wrongdoing. *She* was the one with the sex-pervert husband. *She* would stand her ground.

"So you're denying you watched this filth?" she asked, pointing at the sheet.

"No," he said. The weariness in his voice startled her, threw her off guard. Isaac dropped his briefcase on the couch and sat, leaning forward, hands clasped together.

"I'm sorry," he said. "It's all my fault."

For a moment, Paige hesitated, uncertain. Then she sat beside him, remembered what Kim had said. It was a disease.

"Is it something to do with me?" she asked. "Is that the reason you...um..."

"No," he said.

"Look at me."

Isaac turned to her.

"You have a disease, Isaac," she said. Isaac looked like a man whose hand had happened upon a life buoy after his ship had sunk. "You can go to rehab—"

"Yes," he said quickly, "rehab. Sounds like a plan."

"I thought this type of addiction only affected celebrities. We're regular people, Isaac. Why us?"

He shook his head. Maybe he didn't know. Maybe they would survive this setback.

"We'll get through it together," he said.

Paige didn't know if they would or not. Her upset was fresh. Her rage lingered. And she was exhausted. But she hadn't resorted to the eff word. A bright spark in an otherwise dark day.

FIFTY-TWO

WHY NOT ME?

The thought looped in Brooke Draper's mind as she updated her website, *True American Homemaker*, a phrase she had borrowed from Kim. Kim's site was *American Homemaker*. And she had thousands of followers. Brooke's fans were in the mere hundreds, but she would increase that number. She was learning from Kim, who had shown her (without Kim being aware of it, of course) how to make money from the internet. Kim also had subscribers to her YouTube channel. Tens of thousands of them. She was reaping the monetary rewards, so why not Brooke?

It was funny, she thought, how Kim Loomis called herself an American homemaker but didn't buy American like Brooke did. Kim had a big German Mercedes on display in her driveway, whereas Brooke had a year-old Ford Taurus parked in hers. An *American* car.

She had been a good student. And she had to admit that Kim was an effective teacher. Unlike Megan, Brooke wasn't preoccupied with how Kim was sourcing her income. She didn't care. It didn't take a PhD in psychology (which Brooke had) to see that Megan was obsessed with instigating Kim's downfall. Brooke found it amusing. She had learned to find the humor in people, even when there was none. She'd spent a year in private practice in Burlington after completing her doctorate at the University of Vermont. A year into listening to the woes of sexual deviants, bored housewives and serial cheaters, she had finally accepted that she was depressed and was prescribed antidepressants. Her career choice had been a mistake. She'd convinced herself she would enjoy it but ended up hating every minute of the endless parade of patients unable to cope with themselves, the world and other people.

Brooke had begun to see holes in the whole *idea* of psychology. The patients who had come into her office were usually smart individuals. And that was where the foundations of psychology became porous. Individuals, with problems exclusive to them, were difficult to treat. Sometimes impossible. She didn't think she'd helped anyone during the twelve months she received patients (the directors of the practice had told her to refer to them as clients. They didn't want their *clients* to get the impression they were sick). She had concluded that her clients would do whatever they felt like doing. That she was merely a receptacle into which they could dispose of the garbage growing a stink in their psyches. That eventually they'd return, looking to rid themselves of a new stink. On and on it would go. A carousal of crazy that had no end; no final result you could point to and say, I solved your problem. There were no solutions.

Brooke had had to cope with the knowledge that she'd wasted the best years of her life on a subject that was like trying to capture a ghost, stuff it in a jar, and study its ways.

She had wasted enough time being a human garbage-disposal unit and returned to Montpelier, able to breathe again. There, she had married Zachary Draper, Jacob Hawkins's farm manager. He ran the day-to-day operations of Hawkins Agri, a network of large farms scattered throughout Vermont.

Unlike Kim, Brooke actually loved *her* husband. There was something *off* between the Loomises. Brooke doubted

Kim had any love for Norman, and she hadn't been the first to question their relationship. Not that there was anything wrong with Norman. Brooke thought he was handsome. There was something essentially decent about him, too. But the fact was, Norman *looked* like an undertaker. Tall, black suit, black shoes, white shirt, black tie. He was in character all the time. And he had a somewhat somber disposition, though that was part of his job; people would balk at a smiling funeral director.

Zack should be home soon. Zack with a *k*, not an *h*. It was one of the few things she disliked about him, although she could live with it. Sometimes he worked after hours to keep the Hawkins empire afloat. Brooke didn't mind. It gave her space to figure out how she was going to proceed.

The plan she and Megan had hatched was simple and therefore likely to succeed. But she'd run into an unexpected pothole: Brooke genuinely liked Norman Loomis.

Nevertheless, she had to find a way to make her own money. It already troubled her that Zack was the sole breadwinner. He didn't complain, of course. He was happy to provide for his wife. Except Brooke wanted to work, craved the independence it would bring. Maybe someday Diane Battle would interview *her*. After all, she was close to being an expert in homemaking. Kim was right about one thing—it was a vocation. A respectable vocation.

There was a knock on her door. Megan was on her doorstep. "Come in," she said. "Where's your car?"

"I parked it down the street a ways. Don't want to feed the gossip mill, do we?"

Brooke shut the door to her small study and showed Megan into the living room. The light was low. Scented candles burned on the end tables sandwiched between the sofa.

"Cozy," Megan said. "Who wouldn't want to come home to this?"

"What can I do for you, Meg? At this time of the night."
Brooke considered offering her something to drink, then
elected not to. Megan had disturbed her train of thought.
She could have phoned her.

"I'm here because I want a progress report," Megan
said. "Is our plan viable?"

"You have a cell phone. I'm just saying, it would've been
easier to call."

"I like to get eyeball to eyeball with folks."

Yeah, I bet you do. "It's day one, but…yes, it can be done."

"Good, good. But there's a problem?"

"Nope, not that I'm aware of."

"Brooke, what is it?"

"I like the guy, that's all."

Megan nodded. "Ah, I see. Well, while you're busy liking
Norman Loomis, I want you to remember you can have
everything the Loomis woman has and more. Seriously, why
should she be successful and not you?"

"So I'm a failure?"

"God, no, not at all. I'm just saying, to use your
expression, you can be even more successful than her. Use
your psychology degree for something useful."

"You think a degree in psychology is useful?"

"Not in the real world, no. But think of the possibilities.
In addition to producing homemaking videos, building your
fan base, you could also have live questions and answers on
social media, sort of an agony-aunt homemaker angle,
helping people with their problems. It's different but it might
appeal to a large audience. Who does the homemaker talk to
all day? Sadly, many don't have anyone to have a
conversation with. You, Brooke, could be their lifeline."

Brooke sat in silence for a moment, wheels turning,
thinking Megan was onto something. Then she said, "You
want something to drink?"

"Chamomile tea. I've had enough excitement for one
day."

FIFTY-THREE

NORMAN WOKE, BLINKING THE GUNK OUT OF HIS EYES. HE turned to his left. Kim was sleeping soundly. He had come home the previous night to find she'd gone to bed early. Norman had microwaved a frozen dinner, and eaten it with no pleasure, alone in the great room. The house, as usual, was impeccable. There had been a strong chemical odor in the air, a sure sign Kim had scrubbed all the floors. And yet Norman had sensed something out of place, a change in the atmosphere.

He had walked through each room of the house. Everything appeared to be in its rightful place. Then he'd stopped in the hallway, at the basement door. He hadn't seen anything unusual at first. He had examined the dark hardwood, then the brass back plate below the door handle. There was a red spot just above the keyhole. Small, round, probably paint. He'd crouched, moved his head closer until his eyeball was barely an inch from the droplet. Norman saw blood often enough to recognize it. But what was it doing on the basement door?

Kim used the basement for sewing. Maybe she had cut herself. She often told him how much she enjoyed it, although Norman tuned out when she discussed the mechanics of embroidery. He tried to remember if Kim had ever shown him examples of her work. Surely she would have asked his opinion on one of her pieces if she loved it as much as she'd claimed.

What are you getting at? She cut a finger, that's all.

With the housework she did, it would be surprising if she didn't cut her hand once in a while.

Norman had decided not to clean the red spot.

A sudden tiredness overcame him; he didn't want to get out of bed. The prospect of facing the day was too much. He was a fraud. Business was dead. He was a funeral director only in name.

Brooke Draper surfaced in his mind. He wondered what her story was. Why had she visited him? Sat with him? Norman's best guess was that she was lonely. Her husband worked a lot, lucky him. But Norman understood loneliness.

It had been a strange encounter. A young woman showing an interest in what most people considered a macabre job. A beautiful woman. Maybe not all young people were hatched from the same shallow egg. Maybe Brooke didn't want to sit in her house all day waiting for her husband to come home. Whatever the case, Norman had felt comfortable in her presence.

Interesting…

Kim touched his face, caressed it. "Morning, Norman."

"Oh, uh, morning sweetheart."

She snuggled close to him, planted her lips on his neck. Norman frowned. She never kissed him in the morning. Why was she in a good mood?

"Norman?"

"Yes?"

"We're going to be all right."

He paused, unsure of how to respond.

"Of course we are," he said.

"I mean it, Norman. I'm sorry I couldn't cook you a meal last night. I was so tired, I had to sleep."

"It's fine. I enjoyed the frozen lasagna." It was a little white lie. Norman thought his conscience would let him off just this once.

"Don't lose faith, Norman. Things will pick up."

Norman kissed her on the forehead and went to the closet. He took his suit off the rail. A label on the coat hanger said *Tuesday*. The other six days of the week were lined up in a neat row. Every suit was the same. He wouldn't have it any other way.

He looked at Kim while he dressed. Her hands were outside the blankets. No blue band aids that he could see. She hadn't cut herself.

On his way to the kitchen he inspected the droplet of blood. It had turned a dark rusty-brown. Definitely blood. But whose was it?

What if it wasn't Kim's? What if was someone else's?

He had to get into the basement. Urgently. Kim was behaving oddly. She was being too nice to him.

His heart was heavy in his chest. He went into the kitchen, opening cabinets. He couldn't find the pills and yanked at his lower lip. He'd forgotten to shower. Why was he sweating?

It wasn't nervousness. It was fear.

"Looking for these?"

Startled, he turned around. Kim was standing in the doorway, holding up a pillbox. She shook it, jostling the little pink pills. "You could've just asked."

His facial muscles went slack.

FIFTY-FOUR

KIM MADE SURE NORMAN TOOK ONLY ONE PILL AND watched him leave for work. His stress levels were elevated today. It was all right, though. If Norman couldn't provide for them, she would. If Norman couldn't secure their future, she would. She had made significant progress in that respect already. But there was always more to do.

Forgoing breakfast, she dressed in sweatpants, sneakers, and a hoodie. Sunglasses sat atop her head. Then she remembered her baseball cap, just in case.

She drove the F150 to Towne Hill Road and parked a comfortable distance on the grassy verge near the Hawkins farm, blinkers winking, creased map on the wheel. Cars passed her, most of them occupied by locals who stared. Kim hated that stare, what she called the shitkicker eyeball. Rural folks were curious types. *No, no, let's not mince words here*, she thought. *They're nosey*. Kim hoped she was doing a passable impression of a lost tourist. The map was an inspired prop. When a vehicle approached, she held it up in front of her and leaned into it. Now, if her luck held, no one would stop and try to help her.

The traffic eventually eased to a trickle. Kim diverted her attention to the farm.

It must kill her not having neighbors to spy on.

The Hawkins house was surrounded on all sides by farmland, mostly corn.

It must be difficult leaving your high-and-mighty mansion to go into town and collect gossip like a squirrel gathers nuts.

That was the problem with the Megan Hawkinses of the world, Kim thought. They had nothing better to do than mind other people's business. Why didn't she just move to Florida, get some sun on those wrinkles? Wasn't there a law that said rich old bats had to fly south into retirement?

She straightened. The maids were leaving for the day. Jacob Hawkins was getting into his car. Kim glanced at her watch.

Clockwork. The Hawkins ran a tight ship.

An hour passed. No one entered or left the house.

Hurry. Do it. Do it before you lose your chance.

Kim ripped the plastic off the biohazard suit. She paused, stared at it.

What's wrong with me? I should've put the bottom half on at home.

She put her distraction, her *mistake*, down to Norman. How she worried about that man. He seemed to be in the grip of constant stress.

Hurry, goddammit. Any delay can put you away.

She kicked off her sneakers. The cab of the truck was spacious enough for her to wriggle her legs into the suit.

Goddamn bitch has me struggling to dress appropriately for a job I didn't want, in my own truck, all because she couldn't keep her nose out of the gossip trough.

Furious, she grunted and cursed, cheeks hot, eyes wide as she forced her arms into the sleeves. By the time she'd pulled the zipper up to her chin she was breathing hard.

Not a single vehicle had passed her as she'd fought her way into the suit, and she took this as a sign. There was a merciful God who wanted her to do it. And she had to do it now. A chance this good was impossible to pass up.

She popped the glove compartment and snatched the binoculars, held them to her eyes. There was no one at the windows and the road was still quiet. Kim put the truck into drive and entered the property at a crawl, heart racing. Smooth asphalt at the side and rear of the house made her smile. Sometimes things just worked out fine.

She got out, leaving the driver's door open, and removed the Walmart bag. Every action she took was quickened by adrenaline. She pulled the hood over her head, put on safety goggles and latex gloves, and walked toward the back door. A garden hose was attached to a spigot on the wall. They probably used it to hose the mud off their rubber boots when they were inspecting the corn, or whatever it was the Hawkins did.

She knocked on the door. Hard.

Kim waited for Megan to answer.

FIFTY-FIVE

MEGAN CAME TO THE DOOR—KIM SAW HER THROUGH THE glass.

"Hurry, ma'am. There's an emergency," Kim said, raising the pitch of her voice.

The door opened.

Megan recognized Kim too late.

Kim grabbed a handful of her blouse and yanked her over the threshold, into the backyard, toward the cornfields. Megan released a cry of surprise. Kim struck her on the side of the head and Megan staggered sideways, almost going to her knees. She looked at Kim, seemingly shocked to see the instrument she'd been assaulted with—a meat tenderizer.

Kim advanced. Megan tried to run but came to a dead stop as Kim caught her by the hair and swung her around. The meat tenderizer bounced off her forehead. Blood flew, skin parted. Eyes wide, mouth open, she stared at Kim.

Kim looked down. Her white suit was spattered with blood.

"You snooty country cunt," Kim said quietly. "Look what you made me do."

The next blow took out one of Megan's eyes. She went down on one knee, a hand raised as though she was making a grotesque proposal. Her face was covered in a sheet of blood.

Kim pulled the plastic bag from her pocket and kicked Megan in the chest. She toppled and lay flat on her back. Kim straddled her, held the plastic Walmart bag over her face, pinned her thrashing arms with her knees.

"What happened?" Kim said, her tone one of casual inquiry. "Did I get too big for my britches?" Kim used all her body weight to bear down on the bag.

After a while, Megan became still. Kim dug her thumbs into Megan's throat, throttling her, just to make sure she was dead.

The heat inside the suit was reaching dangerous levels. It was like a furnace. Her back ached and her arms were stiff. And it wasn't over yet.

You just couldn't mind your business and keep your nose out of mine.

Kim panted.

Even my eyes are sweating.

There was no time to rest though. There was still the small matter of getting the corpse into the bed of the truck.

FIFTY-SIX

THE FEAR OF BEING CAUGHT BUNDLING MEGAN HAWKINS into the F150 made her lightheaded; someone could drive up to the rear of the house just as easily as she had. But the adrenaline coursing through her body was powerful. Kim hauled the torso onto the tailgate, pinned it in place with a trembling hand, and scooped her other arm under the legs. Then she lifted the body into the truck, climbed into the pickup, and dragged the corpse all the way inside. She drew the blue tarp over it, and rolled a spare tire onto one corner to keep it in place. The shovel, spade, and pickax secured the remaining three corners. She had a vision of the tarp fluttering away in the wind, but was confident it would hold. The field was only half a mile away.

There was blood everywhere. Droplets were drying on her goggles. The biohazard suit looked as though someone had dipped a large brush into a tin of red paint and made a throwing motion with it. Kim unzipped it carefully and eased her arms out of the sleeves. She shimmied from side to side, leaned on the cab of the truck, and with her bloodied latex gloves, peeled the legs over her feet. She held it up. It looked like a Jackson Pollock painting. She stuffed the suit, gloves, goggles, and meat tenderizer into the Walmart bag, put it on the passenger seat, and turned on the hose, aiming the nozzle at the darker patches on the asphalt.

She paused, listened to the cars passing on Towne Hill Road.

Get going.

Kim blasted the small pools of blood, then took her finger off the trigger and listened again, attuned to every sound.

What if one of those cars slows down, turns into the driveway?

She was close to panic. She sprayed the rest of the blood as best she could and wiped the trigger and nozzle of the hose with the sleeve of her hoodie. Her clothes were soaked through with her sweat. She palmed it off her face and neck and returned the hose to where she had found it.

After one last look around, she closed the back door. Had she forgotten anything? No, everything seemed fine. She sprinted to the Ford, slammed the door shut, put it in drive, and crawled around to the side of the house. She waited for a lull in traffic—the longest five minutes of her life. When she was confident she could make it to the road without being seen, she stepped on the gas. Stopped at the entrance. Swung her head in both directions. Clear. She pounded the gas again. The tires screeched. She glanced in the rearview. Nothing. And nothing up ahead. Some people had all the luck. She allowed herself a smile.

She pulled into the rutted access road and killed the engine. Towne Hill was far behind her. She was out of sight. A long, shuddering breath escaped her lungs. She hadn't realized she'd been holding it.

Her muscles sang deep with pain. Her lower back promised days of trouble. But if she sat in the truck any longer she might not be able to get out, never mind unload a body and drag it through a field.

Don't think about it. Just do it.

Her bones seemed to creak as she dropped the tailgate, climbed aboard, and rolled Megan's body into the weeds sprouting through the ground below.

She sighed. It had all been so unnecessary, all of this mess. She wouldn't profit from Megan's death. There was nothing in it for her. But...she'd felt something... pleasurable, satisfying as she bludgeoned the woman intent on ruining her life. Kim *had* enjoyed murdering Megan Hawkins. She just couldn't imagine pursuing homicide as a form of recreation. It was hard work. Kim wasn't afraid of manual labor like Hawkins had been. No, it was the lack of control over her environment that made her nervous. In her own home, she had complete control. But not out here. Things could go wrong out here.

That had brought her close to panic at the Hawkinses' house. It was beginning to form in her mind again.

She maneuvered Megan's body onto the tarp. There was only one way to do it, and that was to slide the tarp, with the corpse on it, over the dry mud. The furrows acted like natural tracks. She heaved the tarp further into the field, gasping for air. No one would ever suspect her capable of such a feat. A detective would say it was impossible for a woman of Kim's size and weight to dispose of a body in such a manner. But detectives didn't have to get rid of bodies. The prospect of being caught made your body do things you never believed it could. When every nerve ending blazed with the fear of being discovered, you found the strength.

Megan Hawkins had seen true determination up close before she was beaten to death.

As I promised, bitch.

Her muscles screamed as she wrenched, stopped, and dragged the dead troublemaker. She would need days of bed rest to recover. She wondered if her ligaments had developed micro tears. Pain spiked in her ankles. Both Achilles tendons felt close to snapping.

Who else had Megan poisoned against her? Had she polluted Paige and Brooke's minds with her suspicions? She'd have to keep tabs on them.

Kim was furious with herself for inviting Megan into her club. She hated the woman for forcing her to commit murder in an uncontrolled environment. It was Megan's fault she was dead. She as good as brained *herself* with the meat tenderizer. The fact that Kim had wielded the weapon made no difference.

She fell to her knees and laughed, then sobered suddenly, and looked around.

Face set in a grimace, she continued toward the hole. Just a few more steps.

It wasn't too far now. And she was there.

She wrapped the tarpaulin around Megan and pushed her into the grave. Went back to the truck and returned with a shovel and began filling it in.

She paused, a shovelful of dirt poised over the hole.

The tarp was moving.

Kim blinked, stared. It was probably the material settling.

But it moved again. Up and down, barely noticeable.

She tilted the shovel sideways. Dirt fell on the thick blue plastic. She waited.

Up and down.

Some of the mud spilled off the tarp to the earth on either side of the body.

Dead people don't breathe.

Kim began shoveling faster, dumping heavy clods of mud into the hole.

FIFTY-SEVEN

NORMAN SWEPT THE BROOM ACROSS THE FLOOR OF THE casket room, not really clearing up the dust and dirt, just moving it around. He was distracted. The pill had helped calm him but hadn't dulled the image of the blood on the basement door.

Let's find out what's behind door number one!

Norman laughed. A weak, tired laugh.

"What's so funny?"

Norman wheeled around, startled. Brooke Draper was standing in the doorway, a smile pulling at the corners of her mouth.

"Oh…uh, nothing. Good morning, Mrs. Draper."

"Really, Norman? Brooke, please."

He nodded, looked at the floor, then at the broom in his hand, as though he was unsure how it had gotten there.

"Would you like some coffee?"

"Yes, coffee would be great."

***

Brooke hadn't slept at all. She had stared at the ceiling in the dark, thinking about Megan's plan, Zack with a *k* snoring softly next to her.

It was simple: Megan wanted her to seduce Norman, take a photograph of the golden moment, and post it online. They could blur Brooke's face. Megan's eyes had lit up at the possibilities; she even had a caption in mind for the photo: Respected local mortician takes advantage of young homemaker. The scandal would ruin Kim's ambitions. It would lift the veil on the illusion she had created of the wholesome, hardworking homemaker.

Brooke had actually considered it, and felt ashamed. Yes, she wanted what Kim had. But there was another way to get it.

Brooke liked Norman but didn't know why. In some ways, he reminded her of Zack. There was an essential decency in both men, and she felt it strongly. Her parents hadn't approved of her marriage. As a result, Brooke had cut them off. No one was going to tell her who she could marry, how she should live *her* life. What was she thinking? they'd said. How could she be the wife of a farm laborer?

She had a conscience, even if Megan didn't. Later, she would tell Megan she wasn't going through with the plan. It was devious. Evil, in fact. She wouldn't have any part in it.

Megan had become evasive when Brooke had asked her why she hated Kim so much. But Brooke thought she knew the answer—she was jealous. The simplest explanation was often the correct one. And Brooke admitted—to herself at least—that she was a little jealous of Kim, too. But she'd get over it, eventually.

Megan's poisonous hatred for Kim had surprised Brooke. What was her problem? Every question Brooke had asked her had been met with a politician's greasy answer.

She wasn't worried that her refusal to cooperate would endanger Zack's job. Zack had started out as a farm hand, but Jacob Hawkins had seen greater potential. His faith in her husband had been rewarded. Zack now ran the business. He was efficient, consistently turning a profit for the company. Brooke knew Jacob well. He wouldn't be browbeaten into removing Zack from his post in order to keep the peace with his wife.

They sat at reception, the door wedged open. The sun bleached the outside a dazzling white. Brooke glanced at Norman. He was struggling, that was obvious. The funeral home was quiet. She wondered when Norman's last client had passed through on their way to eternity. And that was the reason Megan had given for her vague suspicions. Where were they getting the money to finance their decadent lifestyle? Norman didn't seem like a big spender. He seemed lost, as though he'd swum too far and was trying to reach land.

Brooke put her cup on the desk. Reached for Norman's hand, and held it.

Norman became rigid, stared straight ahead. If he became too uncomfortable, she would release his hand. Brooke watched him from the corner of her eye, waited for him to pull away, to pretend like it had never happened.

He didn't. They sat that way, holding hands behind the desk, as morning turned to afternoon.

FIFTY-EIGHT

COREY WAS BORED. HE HAD GROWN TIRED OF THE internet, dismayed that some of his so-called friends were still blaming him for Evan's disappearance. He didn't answer any of the accusations. His parents had made it clear that there was no upside in trying to defend himself because the same people who were making up lies about him were incapable of reason.

He needed a distraction, something that would take him out of his own thoughts for a while. He browsed the shelves of the bookcase in the living room while his parents were talking in the kitchen. The kid stuff was easily accessible on the lower shelves; the novels deemed too adult for him—by his mom—were out of his reach higher up. Corey pulled a footstool in front of the bookcase, stood on it, and began to search. There were Tom Clancy and Vince Flynn paperbacks—his dad's—and two by Karin Slaughter, three by Danielle Steele and two by Caroline Kepnes. The title of one caught his eye: *You.* He guessed these belonged to his mother. The paperback was in bad shape, its spine bent and creased, the pages dog-eared, as though mom had read it a hundred times.

He took the book to his room, got into bed, and started reading. When he looked up again it was dark and his father was standing at his bedroom door. Corey didn't even attempt to hide the book. It was too late. And it was unfair. Why did the adults get to read all the good stuff?

"I'm sorry, Dad," he said. "I know Mom doesn't want me reading her books."

He pointed at the paperback. "That book is mine, son." He sat on the edge of the bed and said, "I won't tell your mother. I never saw anything."

"Thanks, Dad."

He mussed his son's hair. "It's probably time for lights out, kiddo."

"Yeah, I'm kinda sleepy."

"You can finish the book tomorrow. Just don't let Mom see it, okay?"

"Okay, Dad."

At the door he hesitated and turned to face Corey. "Son, you know how on TV shows, a parent tells their child they love them, well…your mother and I, we…um, you know?"

"I know, Dad. I really do."

He nodded and closed the door. Corey listened to the soft pad of his feet down the stairs. Soft music drifted up from the kitchen. Corey had been curious about the music his parents sometimes played and *why* they played it. Once he'd peeked to see what was going on. His parents had been dancing together in the kitchen. Corey had found it strange seeing them that way, but they had seemed happy.

He turned off the lights. Looked at the sky through his bedroom window, a big black star-filled sky. He slept.

***

His eyes flew open. The house was silent. He sat up in bed, mouth open, heart racing. His hands felt clammy.

I'm going to check the place out sometime. Have a look-see.

Evan had said those words on the morning they had gone to the park.

I bet they store the bodies round back.

It was just talk. Evan wouldn't have trespassed on the Loomises' property—it would have been dumb. The bodies were kept at the funeral home. Evan could be crazy sometimes, but not *that* crazy.

But what if he'd been serious about going back there? What if he *had* gone back there?

Corey cast his mind back to the day Evan had gone missing. He had been furious about what Evan had said to Rachel. And he'd pedaled away from him outside Main Street Middle School. What if Evan had gone to the Loomises'…then what? What did they do to him? Norman was a little strange, maybe, but not in a bad way. Not in a dangerous way. He couldn't be sure, of course, but Corey tended to trust his instincts. But what if his instincts were faulty?

He considered speaking to Norman. No, that wasn't a great idea. Anyway, what would he say? "Hi, Mr. Loomis. Did you kidnap my friend? If it's not too much trouble, I'd like you to return him to us."

But that was where he'd last seen Evan. Outside the Loomis house. Yes, Evan had been on the same side of the street as the school, but the Loomises lived *across* the road. Corey hadn't mentioned that to the police. But why would he? They knew where the Loomises lived. As far as he knew, the police had questioned everyone on Main Street and had come up empty. They had no suspects. He recalled Mrs. Loomis watching him climb the stairs on his way to the bathroom at the fundraiser, making sure he didn't get lost. Was that why she had been watching him…to make sure he didn't stumble on a secret room, a place where she imprisoned little boys?

Jeez, Cor. Stop it. These were night thoughts. Night thoughts weren't normal thoughts.

He went back to sleep eventually. But Mrs. Loomis followed him into his dreams, watching, making sure he didn't stray, steering him with her eyes, further from her secret.

FIFTY-NINE

HIS DAUGHTER WAS CUTTING HERSELF AGAIN.

Juan listened to his wife, Brigida, chatter down the cell phone, which he held an inch from his ear. He was sitting on the commode, in the restaurant's claustrophobic bathroom, Delia's Delights, on Bleecker Street, his chinos around his ankles. And Brigida was being difficult, blaming him because Abril had sliced her arms. Brigida had rushed her to the hospital for the third time in a year. Abril needed professional help, he told her. What was he supposed to do? He was working.

"You're never home. Your daughter doesn't have her father in her life. She's self-harming because you're never here. She's doing it to get your attention."

Maybe he wasn't sophisticated enough to understand the emotional complexities his daughter was negotiating, the anguish she must be experiencing. All he knew was, he'd built them a house in Tapestry Circle, a wealthy, gated neighborhood in Las Cruces, New Mexico. It wasn't just a monument to the American Dream; it was a home for his family with every possible amenity within easy reach. These were things Juan understood. He could barely believe that his own daughter was willing to bring shame on the family by behaving like a spoilt brat. He'd given Abril everything. She had opportunity. That his daughter had been ungrateful was inconceivable. He hadn't grown up in a house with four bathrooms, five bedrooms, and a walk-in pantry. A walk-in pantry! Whenever he *was* home, he often looked at it in wonder, shelves stocked with food, thinking about where he had come from and where he was now. The anger was a diversion, he realized. Because of course he was worried and scared for Abril. One day, she might cut through the wrong vein, and a hospital visit wouldn't save her. He bounced his fist on his naked knee. It was easier to be angry than afraid. Anger could be worked off. Fear lingered. Disturbed his sleep. And caused severe constipation.

"She needs you, Juan," Brigida said.

"Take her to a therapist. A shrink. Someone."

"That's your answer, is it? Throw money at the problem?"

"Don't speak to me like I'm a donkey. You have no problem accepting the money. You think your diamond collection fell out of the sky?"

"It's not the same thing, Juan. It's our child."

His face was getting warm.

"Abril is on my mind all day, every day. You think I don't know we've got a serious problem with her? I keep telling you but you're too stubborn—"

"You bastard. Don't talk to me like that. I'm not your whore."

He tried a different approach. "Brigida, please take Abril to a doctor. I'll be home soon as I'm done."

"Done with what? Banging your *collection* of whores?"

"What? You're crazy."

"Fuck you, El Chapo wannabe motherfucker!"

She hung up. Juan stared at the phone. His head throbbed. An artery pulsed in his neck. He squeezed the cell in his fist. The plastic creaked. Abril's problem was that she didn't know struggle. Life's gifts were presented to her on a gold platter. If she had been poor, she would...

Stop it.

Anger beat hard in his chest, hot and pressurized. But anger wouldn't help Abril. He'd call Brigida later, when she was calm. They had to check Abril into a facility before she did serious damage. The possibility was horrible. He shivered, shook his head.

He pulled his pants up and fastened the belt. Stared into the empty toilet bowl, dismayed.

Maybe tomorrow?

He flushed, washed his hands in the tiny sink, and returned to his seat by the window.

Miguel was looking at the apartment building on the other side of the street. And at the storefront of Spic N Span Cleaning. He hadn't touched his avocado toast. His coffee must have gone cold by now. Juan had ordered salted caramel cake. He bit a chunk off the large slice but there was no pleasure in it. Every time he talked to Brigida he lost his appetite.

Juan looked around the narrow restaurant, at the arched ceiling. It was like being in a railway tunnel. The tables were round, the walls white, the chairs mismatched—blue, orange, white, of different shapes and sizes. *Why?*

"You rate the décor?" Miguel said, not looking at him.

"Seven out of ten."

"Get used to it. We'll be frequenting this joint until we've got what we came here for."

"Yes, patron."

"I take my eyes off the building, I want yours on it."

"Okay."

*   *   *

Miguel looked at Juan. He'd been in the bathroom a long time. Had he snorted a line or two? Miguel studied his nostrils. They seemed clean but Juan wouldn't be dumb enough to leave traces. There was something different about the younger man. Miguel couldn't figure it out. Who spent a half-hour in a restaurant crapper? Maybe he'd taken drugs and had been trying to straighten himself up before he came back. The penalty for a drug habit was non-negotiable. Juan's fingers danced on his kneecap. Users were fidgety.

"My mother gave me the name Miguel," he said. "I want to be known by my name. No more patron."

"Yes, pat—sure, Miguel, okay."

Miguel turned his head, squinted. An old man was walking toward the apartment building, next to a short-haired blonde.

"That's her," Juan said, a little too loud for comfort.

Miguel glared at him. *Drugs make people unreliable*, he thought, turning his attention back to the woman and the old man. They were chatting, laughing, their arms linked. Having a great old time.

Juan rose from the chair. Miguel held up a hand, motioned for him to sit.

"Not now. Later."

"She's fucking an old man?"

Miguel's patience was frayed. The sooner he was no longer in the company of this vulgar young thug, the better. Juan had tested his tolerance to its limit.

Miguel watched them enter the building. He would take them when they ventured out. Some things were worth waiting for.

SIXTY

MELODY WAS NERVOUS, A CONDITION SHE SELDOM HAD TO deal with. What if Joe's date didn't like her? What if she didn't like Joe's date? She sorted through clothes in the closet, barefoot and impatient. She hadn't been to dinner in a long time. If not for Joe, she would've crashed on the couch in her underwear, watched TV, and eaten a jar of Cheese Balls. But she was curious. Maybe Joe had found someone to spend his life with. She wanted Anna Cassady to be as nice as Joe had claimed she was, hoped the woman hadn't entered his life to take advantage of him. Joe wasn't exactly frail, but he was still an old man in need of company. It was for that reason that Melody no longer spent as much time in Sleepy Hollow. She missed Joe when she was away. Rosa took care of him, brought him anything he needed. He loved Rosa and her too, but she didn't see him often enough.

She pulled a pair of navy jeans and a fuchsia high-neck blouse from a hanger and put them on. *Nothing too fancy. I'm not going on a date with her.*

Melody scanned the shoe rack. And noticed an empty space where her Manolos should have been. She had to retire. The mistakes she had made were too large to ignore. The Shaker job had been messy. Unprofessional. She opted for a pair of smart flat shoes.

As she went to close the closet doors she noticed that the envelope she kept taped underneath the upper shelf had fallen, either because its adhesive had decayed or because of her rough handling of the clothes on the rail. She stooped, picked it up, and shook the photographs loose. They had been taken in Washington, DC. The man in the surveillance photos was Ahmad Shirvani, an alleged high-level Iranian spy.

As a former counterintelligence special agent in the US Army, military occupational specialty code 35L, Melody had followed Shirvani around Washington DC for weeks. She had watched him leave his home in Georgetown every morning and open his coffee shop on Wisconsin Avenue. He appeared to be just an ordinary man going about his business. A family man, with a wife and two children. A young boy and a girl. And that was the point, to blend in as Mr. Ordinary. Not someone who had stolen cyber weapons, who had tortured and murdered an NSA analyst, ransacked his house and escaped with a wealth of intelligence.

She had often shadowed him on foot, her partner Lamar Johnson following her in a sedan with tinted windows. But one night in late November, Shirvani had seen her and run.

As usual, after closing the coffee shop for the day, he had been on his way to collect his car and go home. Melody had caught up to him in the car park. Shirvani had reached into his waistband. Melody couldn't tell for sure, his back had been turned to her. She'd drawn her M11, a Sig Sauer P228, and shot him. Two of the three bullets had been fatal. She had needed to see what he was reaching for so she'd lifted his shoulder and looked underneath. Shirvani had been holding a can of pepper spray. Confused, Melody had wondered if he'd thought she was going to rob him. Why had he thought that? Why had he run?

At the hearing, she learned she had not killed Ahmad Shirvani. She'd shot Abbas Jahandar, an innocent man who was exactly what he appeared to be—a small business owner with a young family. She had been given faulty intelligence, a startling blunder on the part of those she'd trusted and relied on for the smooth running of operations in the field.

Shirvani and Jahandar, it transpired, were not related by blood and had never met, but bore a striking resemblance to each other—same facial features, and Jahandar was only a half-inch taller than Shirvani. And both men had lived on Wisconsin Avenue. What were the odds? Two men, almost mirror images, in the same place, with the same profiles. The circumstances had been exceptional, but Melody could no longer trust the people she worked for. Because of her superiors' mistakes, Shirvani had disappeared. And Melody had resigned.

She had joined the army because there was nothing else for someone like her. No one was going to look out for her, that much had been clear early on. She had to take care of herself. Relatives were unreliable, and friends, though few and far between, were even worse. She had formed a view of herself as adrift but self-reliant, someone who didn't owe anybody anything. Estranged from family and life in general, she'd signed up to be a soldier, rapidly achieving the rank of sergeant. Two years after her promotion, Melody was in Fort Huachuca, Arizona, committed to completing the Counterintelligence Special Agent Course (CISAC). She thought she'd done all right for a nobody from Vinegar Hill.

Now she was seriously considering retiring from her second career as a contract killer. She had enough money to last a lifetime. But what would she do? Put the skills of her first career to use as a private investigator? The idea of tailing cheating spouses and insurance fraudsters didn't appeal. How about missing persons? What if she could help people find lost loved ones? For a small fee, of course. Enough to cover expenses. Melody wasn't seeking redemption. She had no interest in forgiveness. She had killed people for money, and she had been good at it. Until Charles Shaker. That was reason enough to find a new line of work. But she'd lost her edge, her focus. Another lapse and the well of luck might just run dry.

She touched the face of the man in one of the photographs, murmured something, then returned them to the closet. There always had to be a reason—money, lust, or national security. Abbas Jahandar had died for no reason.

Sammy nuzzled her hand, looking at her with wet eyes. She rubbed a hand over his coat. "I won't be long. Bite any intruders for me, okay?"

Sammy licked her hand. She put on her wristwatch, left the apartment, and knocked on Joe's door.

"Come in, come in," he said. He was wearing a navy pinstripe suit and a black fedora with a white band.

"Oh, Joe, you look so cute!" Melody said.

"Jesus, if that's what you think, I'm gonna change."

"No, please don't. It's not often I see a gangster from the forties."

"You make my life a living hell, Melody."

"Say it with the Bogart accent and I'll pay for dinner."

"What did I do to deserve this? I've been a good person. God, why am I being punished?"

Melody embraced him, kissed him on the cheek.

"There's no lipstick on me, is there?" Joe asked. "I don't want my fair lady thinking I'm some kind of philanderer."

"You know I don't wear lipstick. Don't worry, I'll vouch for you, Joe. Are you sure you want me and Rosa to be there?"

"Anna specifically asked me to bring the friend I talk trash about all the time. That would be you. Where *is* Rosa?"

"She's busy at the shop. She might be a little late but she'll be there."

"Business is brisk these days?"

"Yeah. Not sure why, but it has picked up. I blame Rosa."

Joe fidgeted with his red tie. Melody stepped in. "You always pull it too tight," she said. "Hold still."

Joe cooperated while Melody loosened the knot and fixed his collar.

"Better?"

"Yeah. Thanks, Mel."

Melody eyed him closely. He seemed nervous. "Joe, you have to relax. What is it? Date number four?"

"Five."

"Okay, five. Seriously, you look great. Why are you worried?"

"It's nothing."

"Joe, did we just meet for the first time? I know you. Spill it."

"I want her to like you and Rosa. If she doesn't… honestly, I couldn't see her again."

Melody took his hand and led him to the sofa. She sat facing him. "Joe, don't worry. It'll be fine. Take deep breaths and don't anticipate disaster."

"I'm sorry it didn't work out for you and Landon."

"He wasn't right for me, Joe. I'm a simple Brooklyn girl, while he…well, it doesn't matter. We're going to enjoy ourselves, okay?"

He nodded. They stood. "Hug for the road?" Melody asked.

"Your quota for today has been reached, I'm afraid."

"Come here, you old romantic." She hugged him, tried not to squeeze too hard.

"It's not too much, is it? The suit and hat?"

"Of course not." It *would* have been too much if Joe was in his thirties. But when you were a certain age, allowances could be made. Besides, it suited him. He looked distinguished, whereas a younger man would have seemed ridiculous.

"Let's go, Mr. Romance," Melody said. "I'm hungry."

SIXTY-ONE

THEY HAD SPENT ALL DAY IN DELIA'S DELIGHTS. MIGUEL had learned two things. One—toast was meant to be smeared with butter, not avocado. And two—Juan had a problem he couldn't fix. Juan had gone to the bathroom on three occasions, for a half-hour each time. Each time he'd returned, he had seemed highly strung, different. Miguel was convinced he had been snorting cocaine.

Juan sat in the passenger seat, his leg bouncing up and down. His hands were clenched into fists. Miguel turned his eyes on the apartment building; Juan was a distraction he couldn't afford now. Melody Morgan and the old man exited the building, arm in arm. He watched them enter a restaurant on the corner of Bleecker and MacDougal.

"We take them when they come out," he said. Pedestrian traffic would drop off later. It was going to be another snatch and grab. Miguel hated the idea, but Torres had called and insisted he bring them to him. Jennifer Shaker's abduction had gone smoothly, but this was Manhattan and there would be a lot more eyes on them. They would use the ski masks Miguel kept in the glove compartment for just such a contingency. And they had to be quick. The van they were sitting in would need to be buried.

Melody Morgan had no clue as to what she had put them through. But she'd find out soon.

SIXTY-TWO

ROSA MENDES LOCKED THE DOOR BEHIND THE LAST customer of the day and flipped the sign to CLOSED. She added up the receipts. Today, business had been good. And it wasn't just a fluke. She had been busy all week and couldn't wait to tell Melody.

She took her canvas shoulder bag from under the counter, went to the storage room at the back, and changed into a long-sleeve denim dress. She didn't know why Melody was worried about Joe's new friend, Anna. Maybe Melody was being protective. Rosa wasn't keen on admitting a stranger into their circle either, but Joe seemed happier. He had welcomed her into his life and treated her like a treasured family member. If he was happy, then Rosa was happy for him.

She looked at her watch, a gift from Melody. On the surface, Melody seemed cool, unruffled, even icy. But Rosa knew she worried about her and Joe. The watch was a GPS-tracking device, and Melody had made sure Rosa knew how to use it. When Rosa or Melody went to meet a guy, they'd be able to track each other if the date turned out to be dangerous. And Rosa had seen her share of men who saw no shame in beating a woman senseless. She had been lucky to escape with her life. Melody had saved her. The thought crossed her mind at least once every day. Melody didn't go on many dates anymore, as far as she knew. The last relationship she'd had was with Landon Forbes. The guy was a little goofy but not abusive. Melody had probably thought she could do better, and Rosa had agreed.

Now Rosa was beginning to wonder what *better* was supposed to be. She had been to dinner with a nice man a month ago. He'd seemed respectful, had a good job, and had been very polite. But every third word that came out of his mouth was *basically*. Basically this and basically that, to the point where Rosa had begun to eat her dinner faster, drink her beer in long gulps, and make her excuses about needing to leave. A small thing, and yet it had driven her crazy listening to him. When had her tolerance levels dropped? When had she become so picky? The guy might have been amazing, and her refusal to see past his repeated utterance a missed opportunity.

She returned to the front of the shop and paused. There was a hissing sound coming from the shirt press. It was probably an issue with the air lines. She couldn't leave until it was fixed.

She looked at her watch again. She was forty minutes late and didn't want to miss dinner. She sighed, went back to the storage room, and carried her toolbox to the Unipress.

This sucks, she thought, and rolled up her sleeves. She leaned into the machine, feeling for the air lines behind it.

SIXTY-THREE

MELODY WAS RELIEVED, TRUSTED HER FIRST IMPRESSIONS. Anna was a pleasant woman who seemed genuinely fond of Joe. They seemed right for each other. Of course, it was still early days, but she was optimistic.

They talked and laughed constantly, often forgetting Melody was present. Rather than being offended, she found it reassuring. She was content to watch them.

She had gotten some information from Anna before she and Joe had become completely immersed in each other. Anna had retired as a health-center receptionist in the Upper West Side. She'd lived in Waverly Place all her life and walked her dog, Max, a Boston terrier, in Washington Square Park every morning. Melody had asked her if Max had ever had weight problems.

"Oh no," she had said. "He's fit as a fiddle."

Anna had asked about Sammy. Melody had decided not to tell her she'd put Sammy on a diet. She didn't want to seem like a bad mother. Joe—bless him—hadn't mentioned that Melody spoiled Sammy rotten and that the pug was edging toward obesity. But Sammy *had* lost weight. Melody was glad Joe had removed her blinders and allowed her to see the problem.

Anna had also mentioned investing in the stock market. Joe had said something about landing a sugar granny and Anna had slapped him playfully.

They get on so well, Melody thought. She checked her watch and wondered why Rosa hadn't arrived yet. She excused herself, went outside, and dialed Rosa's cell.

"Hi, Mel," Rosa said. "I have a slight hydraulic mishap to fix, but you guys eat up. Don't wait for me. We can go somewhere else later if you want."

"Do you need help?"

"Not at all. I can handle it."

"All right. We'll be leaving here soon, going to Wicked Willy's. Turns out, you're never too old to party."

"I have this image of us escorting two drunken pensioners home in the early hours. I'll be along soon. How is she?"

"She's great. Joe is such a charmer. And he looks well, you know?"

"I've noticed. He has that look, like the cat that's got the cream."

"Or the dog that's got the bone."

Rosa laughed. "You're awful, Mel. *Awful.*"

"If you need my help, call me. I'll run back there and we'll get it fixed. Is it the shirt press?"

"Yeah."

"Goddamn machine. I might just get a new one if it's causing us trouble."

"No need yet. I'll let you know how it goes."

Melody hung up and returned to the busy restaurant, placed her phone on the green-and-white checkered oilcloth. A candle in the middle of the table cast a warm glow on their faces. Joe and Anna were in high spirits.

Joe said, "Are we going to get a cocktail or what?"

"Come on, you old codger. Let's go," Melody said, smiling.

"Yes," Anna said. "Let's go, you old coot!"

Joe clapped a hand to his heart, his face twisted in mock outrage.

"Why, Lord, do I have to suffer this abuse?"

Melody's smile broadened. She hadn't seen Joe this happy in a long, long time.

SIXTY-FOUR

MIGUEL'S MOOD WAS AT BREAKING POINT. HE HAD A powerful urge to strangle Juan. *Both* of his legs were bouncing up and down and his hands fidgeted with the ski mask in his lap. Maybe Juan was nervous about the job. But Miguel suspected otherwise. No one could be *that* worked up over a kidnapping. At least, no one as used to it as Juan.

They were parked at the curb across the street from the restaurant. Melody Morgan emerged, talking on her cell. Juan sat forward. Miguel watched her go back inside. *Who are you?* he thought. His phone buzzed in his pocket. It was Torres.

"Change of plan," he said. "Take them to Sleepy Hollow. I had an associate check property records. She has a house there. I'll be waiting. Get rid of the phones, Miguel. Don't forget."

"I won't." Miguel removed the battery from his cell and told Juan to do the same.

Ten minutes passed. It was full dark. There was a trickle of pedestrians on either side of Bleecker. Not as many as earlier. People were filing into restaurants and bars. Miguel accepted the fact that they would be seen. It wasn't ideal. Vehicles, although not as plentiful as even an hour ago, still cruised by as they waited. He could have snatched Melody Morgan in Vinegar Hill. *Should have*. But Miguel wasn't content with just *her*—he wanted her loved ones, too. She'd be more inclined to cooperate if he were holding a gun to grandpa's temple. Their half a billion dollars was gone. Torres had assured Miguel they might be able to recoup a small fraction of their losses. "Something is better than nothing," he'd said.

Miguel ordered Juan to get in back. "They'll be out any minute. Get ready."

He didn't know when they would come out, but he'd rather have Juan somewhere else. The younger man was like a live wire.

Another ten minutes passed.

Then three people emerged from the restaurant.

Miguel started the engine.

"Go when I say *now*, Juan. Understand?"

"Yeah."

Miguel pulled away from the sidewalk slowly.

Who was the old woman? He hadn't expected a third person. Was she Melody's grandma?

"Juan, there's three people. The old man, Melody Morgan, and an old woman. Got it?"

"Got it."

The party crossed MacDougal Street.

"Masks," Miguel said, pulling the balaclava down over his face.

He stepped on the gas, swung the wheel to his right, and mounted the sidewalk.

"*Now!*"

The side door slid open with such force that it bounced on its tracks, closing halfway. Juan grabbed the old man, jabbed him in the eye with the barrel of his gun, and forced him into the van. Miguel melted onto the sidewalk and rushed Melody. He folded his fingers on her windpipe, walked her to the side of the van, and bundled her inside. Juan waited by the door, gun trained on the van's occupants.

The old woman's eyes were wide and glassy with shock, but she managed to break into a run. Miguel followed her, picked her up off the ground with one arm, and threw her on top of the old man.

He slammed the door shut, sprinted toward the open driver's-side door, and got in. Tires squealed as he tore away from the sidewalk and onto Bleecker.

"Faces down," Juan said. "Do it or I'll kill you." The *screek* of cables ties being cinched around wrists reached Miguel in the driver's seat. What a sound, he thought.

SIXTY-FIVE

ROSA SWITCHED OFF THE LIGHTS, TYPED THE CODE INTO the intruder alarm, and locked the door of Spic N Span. The shirt press would hold for now, but she could see a new Unipress in her future.

She got as far as Percy's Pizza and stopped dead. A van had driven onto the sidewalk. Rosa saw Joe being bundled into it.

Then a masked man seized Melody by the throat. An old woman—Rosa assumed it was Anna—tried to escape. She was cut off by a stocky man. With one arm, he lifted her off the ground. Her legs kicked air. The van drove away at speed.

Rosa shed her paralysis like an old snakeskin. Arms pumping, she raced toward Washington Square Village, handbag bouncing against her hip. She had never run as fast in her life. At times her legs pounded the pavement with such speed she thought she'd fall forward on her face.

It was a straight run to Washington from Bleecker. Rosa's lungs were on fire by the time she reached The Fresh Marketplace with its welcoming red awning. Her heart was in her throat. She bolted for the canopied entrance of Washington Square Village Parking and yanked the zipper's pull tab on her handbag hard, ripping it off. She stared at the broken piece of metal in disbelief.

No! God no!

She urged herself to calm down.

Lightheaded, she eased back the zipper slide until there was enough space to get her shaking hands inside the bag, and pulled. The slide snapped away from the interlocking metal teeth. She fumbled inside, her heart leaping as a finger snagged on a keyring. She got into the car, almost crushing her ankle in the door as she slammed it. She dipped into her bag again and retrieved her iPhone.

She started the engine and brought up the tracking app on her cell.

Nothing.

She backed out, foot heavy on the gas as she headed toward the exit.

Outside, she parked and waited, holding her breath.

Then the tracking symbol appeared.

Her body almost humming with the intensity of her fear, she kept one eye on the road and the other on a little blue icon that told her Melody wasn't too far from her.

Rosa focused, gritted her teeth. Fear had given way to anger. She gripped the wheel and drove through the city lights, toward her friend.

SIXTY-SIX

ALL THREE LAY FACE DOWN ON THE VAN'S FLOOR. JOE WAS on her left, Anna on her right. Melody turned her head to Anna. The older woman was whimpering, muttering something that sounded like *I'm just a receptionist, I'm just a receptionist.*

"Shh," Melody whispered. "Take deep breaths. We're going to be okay."

Anna's eyes were shut tight, as though she was unable or unwilling to accept her present reality.

"Anna, sweetie, look at me," Melody said. "Please, look at me." Anna opened her eyes. "You've got to be quiet. Deep breaths, but you have to stop." Melody hated herself for making the demand but was afraid that if Anna kept talking, the masked man somewhere behind them would resort to violence.

Anna nodded, became silent. Melody offered her a weak smile.

She turned to Joe. One of his eyes was badly swollen and the flesh around it had blackened. A rivulet of blood streamed across the bridge of his nose.

"Mel, are you okay?" he asked.

Melody hadn't cried in twenty years, but she was close to it now. Her throat tightened. She took in a lungful of air to take the heat out of her eyes.

"I'm sorry, Joe. I'm so sorry."

"You didn't do anything wrong."

But she had. This wasn't a random kidnapping. They were here for her. Why? It had to be tied somehow to her work. She had killed a lot of people in her second career. Her victims' associates had come for payback. An image of Jennifer Shaker bubbled darkly to the surface of her mind.

"Mel, I don't think we're going to get out of this."

"Joe, not now, please," she said. "I'll find a way."

"I want you to know I love you like you were my own daughter."

Hot tears cascaded from her eyes. "I love you, too," she said.

Joe's own tears swelled in his wounded eye and he winced. Instinctively, Melody reached out to comfort him, forgetting her hands were bound. It was a miracle, the way you could care so deeply about someone that you forgot your own distress, even if it was only for a moment. Some moments felt longer than they actually were.

"I'm just a receptionist," Anna said.

Melody swung her head around. "Anna, I'm begging you, please stop."

"I'm just a receptionist," Anna said again, her voice rising in pitch. "I walk my Max in the mornings. I walk him in the park…I'm just a receptionist."

Melody sensed movement behind her.

"I'm just a receptionist…" Louder and louder, a note of hysteria in her voice.

The air shifted. A presence closed in. Melody felt the ·man's weight through the floor.

"I'm just a receptionist I'm just a receptionist I'm just —"

From the corner of her eye, Melody saw the butt of the gun arcing through the air, sweeping down toward the back of Anna's head. It landed with a stomach-churning *thud*. Anna became still, soundless.

"You sonofabitch," Joe roared. "You bastard! I'll kill you! I'll kill you!"

"You want some, too, old-timer?" That voice, coming from the dark, was laced with menace, murderous. Melody quickly rotated her head to look at Joe.

"Look at me," she said. "You have to look at me, Joe. Please. *Look at me*."

Joe's one good eye found hers and Melody saw recognition in it.

He blinked.

"Joe, do it for me, please. Focus on me. You have to stay quiet."

They looked at each other in the gloom. Melody began to experience an unfamiliar emotion. Simple heartbreak.

She might be able to negotiate with these people. If they kept their identity concealed, she, Joe and Anna had a chance. If the masks came off, they were dead.

SIXTY-SEVEN

ROSA WAS SOMEWHERE NEAR DOBBS FERRY ON I-87 WHEN she began to suspect where the van was headed. She kept her distance. There were three cars in front of her, then the van. She was no longer worried about losing them. Rosa knew the route well. She passed Irvington and Greenburg and her suspicions were confirmed. Somehow the men who had taken Melody knew about her house on Sleepy Hollow Road.

Rosa and Melody had laughed a lot in that house. Rosa had cried a lot, too. Melody had gotten her out of bed in the mornings and put her to work alongside her, growing vegetables. Gradually, Rosa's confidence had grown. She'd come back together, piece by piece. Rosa had drawn from Melody's strength. There was a *sureness* in her friend's demeanor that Rosa aspired to. And Rosa thought she almost had it. Not quite but the circle was closing. She had never had a friend like Melody. People threw the word around too much, until it lost its meaning, its value. A *true* friend was a rare find.

Rosa fell further back as she entered Tarrytown. She had lost sight of the van. Her iPhone told her she was two miles behind them. Her gaze drifted to the fob hanging from the ignition. There was a way in.

SIXTY-EIGHT

THE VAN CAME TO A STOP AND THE ENGINE WAS SWITCHED off. The double doors behind them opened. Anna was carried out first by the man who had rendered her unconscious. Joe was put into a sitting position by another man and ordered to exit under his own power. Melody guessed this man was the driver. He rummaged in her purse. Her heart sank when she saw her keys. He separated the fob from the bunch, showed it to her.

"It opens the gate?" he said.

Melody nodded. He pointed the fob and pushed a button. She knew where she was. They had found her refuge, her hideaway. Another mistake. She should have hidden the ownership of her house. There were ways to do it. What had blunted her skills, made her so reckless?

It was no good now. The cat was out of the bag.

The masked man touched her elbow. Melody flinched. He held up his hands, palms facing her. "I'm going to sit you up. That's all." He gripped her upper arm. "Okay, the last part." He got her into a standing crouch. Melody jumped onto her driveway, fell forward. The man caught her by her shoulders.

There was a large car parked at the entrance to her home with its headlights on and its engine running. Melody couldn't see who was in it. She looked around for Anna. The man who'd hit her was heading into the house, carrying her over his shoulder like a sack of potatoes. Joe seemed frail. His suit was rumpled, and he was looking at the ground, dazed.

The car outside began crawling up the driveway.

Melody turned and saw a man standing beside it, watching. She couldn't make out his features in the dark. Just his beige slacks. Her skin crawled, tightened. He wasn't wearing a mask.

The lights in the hallway came on and they were ushered inside. Anna was unloaded onto a couch and the man went into the kitchen. Melody and Joe stood before the stone fireplace. Joe stared at Anna's limp body. The man returned from the kitchen with three chairs. He arranged them in a row in front of the fireplace so that they faced the couch Anna was lying on. Melody looked for the rise and fall of her chest. Anna was still breathing, but for how much longer?

Another vehicle idled outside, parked close to the front door. The engine was shut off. Melody thought it was the van.

Joe was pushed into a chair and the man told Melody to sit. She complied, terrified he would hurt Joe. The man who had helped her from the van stood in the doorway. Melody turned and saw Joe was being duct-taped to the chair. A strip of tape was placed over his mouth. Then the man came to her and said, "I'm gonna blind you if you try anything. Best behavior?"

Melody nodded. The man had done this before.

By the time he was finished, escape was impossible.

He lifted Anna off the couch and sat her in the chair. The man who had been standing in the doorway held her up while the other one fastened her to the chair. A strip of tape was also slapped across her mouth. Anna's eyes fluttered.

225

"My name is Miguel Cabrera. We only need *you* to talk," he said, and pulled the balaclava off his head. They were going to die.

"And this is Juan Sanchez." Juan rolled up his mask and tucked it into his waistband.

Melody couldn't believe it; the bastard was grinning.

"What do you want?" Melody asked.

"A portion of what we're owed." The voice belonged to the man in the beige trousers. He came into the room, a laptop under his arm, and scanned the room—the wood-paneled walls, the ceiling-high shelves full of books that had actually been read rather than serving as mere decoration. He shook his head with seemingly genuine regret. "I'm Ricardo Torres."

The name wasn't familiar. He sat on the couch, in the same spot Anna had been moments ago.

"My partner and I," Torres said, "Mr. Cabrera, head the Los Mochis cartel. Have you heard of it?"

Melody shook her head.

"Good, good. I'll get straight to the point. You killed our banker. We lost five hundred and three million dollars."

Joe jerked in his chair, turned to look at Melody. She couldn't meet his eyes, afraid of what she might see. Disapproval? Horror? Disgust? Was he waiting for her to deny it, hoping she'd say they had the wrong person? That there had been a mistake?

Melody remained silent. They knew. *How* did they know? Jennifer Shaker.

"I didn't know he was your banker," Melody said. Joe moaned. "It was just another job."

Torres regarded her with a mixture of surprise, respect, and understanding, as if he'd expected her to disclaim responsibility.

"I won't be able to recoup *all* of our money," Torres said, opening the lid on the laptop. "But as I said, a portion of it will suffice. Your money, Ms. Morgan." Torres had the air of a refined gentleman. He spoke to her in a respectful tone, bordering on admiration. He didn't fit her image of a cartel boss. He wore a knitted cardigan over a crisp white shirt and a colorful tie. And, of course, the beige pants.

"To be clear," Torres continued, "I want you to transfer your money into one of our bank accounts. It won't cover our losses. But I'll sleep well at night knowing we got *something* for our trouble."

Juan took the gun from his waistband.

"Is Jennifer Shaker dead?" Melody asked.

"She is deceased, yes."

"Good."

"You didn't like her?" Miguel asked.

"No. Did you?"

Torres pressed a button on the laptop and it hummed. He tapped the keys, then glanced at Melody. "It's time to make the transfer. Passwords and account numbers, when you're ready."

"I can't do that, Mr. Torres," she said. Anna groaned beside her. Melody checked her condition. Her eyes were open, and there was awareness in them.

Torres sighed, shook his head in abject disappointment. He reclined in the couch, laptop balanced on his knees.

Juan took a single step forward, leveled the gun at Anna's head, and squeezed the trigger. The left side of her head exploded. Blood, bone and brain matter drenched Melody's face, hair, and clothes. Joe rocked in his chair, almost toppling it. He struggled uselessly, a muffled, strangled scream rising in his throat. Melody thought she'd hear those terrible sounds for eternity.

Her ears were still ringing from the blast when Miguel moved in behind Juan and pointed his gun at Juan's head. Another report reverberated in the room. The picture window rattled. Juan crumpled. Miguel met Melody's gaze. Now she was scared.

"He was a drug addict," Miguel said, as though Melody cared for an explanation.

"We don't approve of having addicts in our ranks," Torres said. He tapped the lid of the laptop with his middle finger. "Passwords and account details."

SIXTY-NINE

THE MORE ROSA CONSIDERED HOW TO BEST APPROACH THE house, the more she was persuaded by the simple option. If one of those goons was monitoring the cameras, she'd be seen. It was a chance she was willing to take. She walked right up to the gate, and in the instant it took to press a button on the fob she heard the gunshot. She ran to the rear, keeping her finger outside the trigger guard of her Smith & Wesson M&P 9.

Melody had taught her how to use a gun. Once a month, they went to a rifle and pistol range in Yonkers. Melody had told Rosa she had to learn how to defend herself. The police wouldn't protect her, Melody had said; they showed up *after* you were dead. On her first day using the gun, Rosa had gotten off to a less than promising start, aiming low, shooting the ground instead of the target. Melody had stepped in, told her to stay calm, line up her shot, and remember to breathe. It had taken a lot of trial and error, but with several trips to the range behind her, Rosa had become quite the marksman. Her breakthrough had come when she realized the gun wasn't going to harm her if she used it correctly. She had stopped squeezing her eyes shut and flinching as she fired a round.

Rosa kept the gun in the trunk of her car. She'd never had to use it to protect herself but looked forward to their monthly outings on the range. Afterwards, they would eat in a restaurant, catching up and indulging in casual gossip.

Rosa was glad she'd learned to use that gun, though her stomach tightened at the prospect of putting her training into action. She couldn't call the police. In Melody's eyes, it would be unforgivable. She had told Rosa directly—*don't ever call the police, for any reason, even if my life is in danger.* Rosa hadn't questioned her further, believing she might not like the answers. It was the look in Melody's eyes that had given her pause—cold, black, unwavering conviction. *Don't ever call the police.* Rosa wasn't going to lose her only friend.

She passed the back door and another shot shattered the stillness.

She squatted, crab-walked under the picture window. The bulb from the living room threw a square of yellow light onto the garden. Rosa inched her head above the sill. A man lay on the floor on his side. A woman was slumped sideways in a chair, her head leaking blood. Rosa's breath stopped. Melody and Joe were taped to chairs. Melody was saying something to a man sitting on the sofa, a computer on his knees, looking from her to the screen, then writing down what she said. Apparently finished, he closed the computer.

There was another man, this one standing. He moved toward Joe, gun at his side.

SEVENTY

"THE TRANSFER IS COMPLETE," TORRES SAID. "YOU HAVE been a very busy woman."

Melody hung her head. All of her money was gone. Miguel had promised to spare Joe's life if she cooperated. She doubted him, but there was a chance, however small, that he was being truthful. She still couldn't bring herself to look at Joe. She was ashamed of what she had put him through. Her work had brought these men into her home, destroyed the life of an innocent woman. She was sorry, but she couldn't tell Joe. It would have sounded hollow. A woman he would probably have shared his life with was sitting beside her, half her skull missing.

Because of Melody.

"I'm curious. How many people did you kill?" Torres asked.

"You got what you wanted," Melody said.

"Indeed. Sixteen million dollars doesn't begin to mitigate my damages, but I'll take it. The good news is, I'm going to let you live. The bad news...well, I have to take the most obviously precious thing from you."

Miguel walked toward Joe.

"No!" Melody said. The pleading tone in her voice disgusted her. "Please no! Don't hurt him. *Please! DON'T HURT HIM!*"

Joe writhed in the chair, breathing hard. He was trying to speak. "I stuh wuv yuh."

Miguel raised the gun.

"NOOOO! STOP! PLEASE!"

The explosion buffeted her hair. Melody screamed.

SEVENTY-ONE

ROSA TURNED THE KEY AND EASED THE BOLT BACK SLOWLY, careful not to let the door snap open; the sound would be heard in the living room. Two against one—she didn't fancy those odds.

Then there were the hinges. If she pushed the door fast, they wouldn't creak. Her heart pounded against her ribs, and the saliva dried in her mouth. She recited a prayer in her mind. Another problem—the roller shade inside the door, pulled halfway down the window. She stared at the fat plastic bead on the end of the pull cord. She'd need to catch the bead before it swung back and hit the window, announcing her presence.

The door inside the kitchen, the one that led to the living room, was ajar.

Handle pointed at the ground, shoulder against the door, Rosa took a deep breath and braced herself.

One. Two. Three…

She pushed. A high-pitched ringing filled her head. She sidestepped around the door to catch the pull cord. Her fingers snagged the middle of it but the bead kept going. It stopped less than a half-inch from the glass.

And the hinges hadn't creaked.

Her hands shook and her heart seemed to pound too loud in her chest.

Taking the weight out of each step, Rosa edged toward the door, sipping the air, muscles in her abdomen seized tight.

Someone was talking.

Rosa reached for the gun in her pocket, squeezed the handgrip.

She peered through the crack in the door. Both men were still standing. One had a gun. He had tucked it into his waistband after he'd shot Joe.

A tremor wound its way through her entire body. There wasn't much time left. She was terrified, but if she didn't move now, her fear would only increase and she'd be unable to help her friend.

She took aim through the gap between the door and frame, tried desperately to relax her shoulders. She stared down the line of the barrel, found her target. *Center mass*, she could hear Melody saying. *Two quick rounds and they all fall down. And breathe. Don't forget to breathe.*

She took a deep breath. Held it, released it. She wasn't trembling as badly anymore.

The man who had killed Joe saw her.

Rosa let off three rounds then pushed the door wide. It hit the wall and bounced. She ran into the living room.

The man she'd shot was on the ground.

The other one turned to her. Rosa couldn't deny it—she felt pleasure seeing the shock on his face.

"Who are you?"

The question momentarily confused her.

"The dry cleaner," she said, and emptied five rounds into him. He fell back onto the sofa and landed on top of the computer.

Rosa continued firing, adrenaline coursing through her.

She forced her finger off the trigger. Checked that the man she had shot first was no longer a threat. Two dark patches had formed in the middle of his chest. The third round was embedded in the wall. He stared, sightless, at the ceiling.

The gun fell from her hand. She saw Joe, tilted forward in the chair. Gone.

Melody stared at Rosa, stunned.

Rosa went to the kitchen and returned with scissors. She carefully cut through the duct tape.

"I'm so glad to see you, Rosa."

Tears welled in Rosa's eyes and she hugged Melody, kissed her on the cheek. "I thought I'd lost you," she said.

Rosa helped Melody to stand, began pulling the tape from her clothes and peeling it off where it had stuck to her skin.

Melody touched Rosa's face, as though making sure she was real, then embraced her and sobbed quietly.

Rosa closed her eyes, relieved and close to exhaustion. She couldn't face Joe yet. Joe, a man she had trusted with her life. Her friend. Always ready to give advice when she'd asked for it. He had respected her.

After a while, Melody reached for Rosa's hand. And together, they looked at Joe. They held onto each other for a long time.

SEVENTY-TWO

NORMAN WAS PRETENDING TO BE ASLEEP. KIM STIRRED beside him. She slid carefully out of bed, then showered and dressed. He didn't get up until he heard her car pulling into Main Street. Kim did the grocery shopping on Sundays, even if the pantry and refrigerator were full. He went to the closet, put on sweatpants and a pair of Nikes he had worn once. He closed the doors and paused, staring at his reflection in the mirror, fascinated. Without his suit, he looked like a different man. Younger. Or maybe it was an illusion brought on by the good-as-new trainers with their energetic, youthful colors.

Norman was taking the day off. He hadn't slept well, even though he'd taken a pill before going to bed. He couldn't stop thinking about Brooke Draper, couldn't shake the memory of her holding his hand. Why was this attractive woman drawn to him? She had come to see him every day during the past week. They hadn't talked much; she'd just sat with him, looking outside, holding his hand behind the desk. He figured she was lonely and recognized a kindred spirit. Yesterday, Brooke had caressed his hand. Norman had tried to focus on something, anything, to distract him but his body had responded. It had been an involuntary response. He was weakening, didn't know how much longer he could resist.

But I did, he thought with some pride. *I did stop myself.*

It was good to be wanted. Still, he loved his wife, despite their problems. He'd made a promise to Kim when they had gotten married. Did he have the strength to keep his marriage vows unbroken? That was the question on his mind as he entered the kitchen and began his search underneath the sink.

Last night, he had spied on Kim. He wasn't proud of it. In fact, he was ashamed. But he wanted to know what was in the basement. Then he could move on with his life.

He got on his knees and shoved aside cleaning products. It was here…somewhere. He found the small unpainted pine box and opened it. There it was—the key to the basement door. His heart felt bloated in his chest as it pumped harder and faster, and his stomach fluttered. He was ten years old again, hand inside the cookie tin, fingertips on the crumbly homemade chocolate-chip cookie. Then Elaine, his "mother," had appeared as though she had been waiting for the opportunity, wooden spoon raised. Before Norman could apologize, she'd struck him on the mouth with the heavy spoon, splitting his lower lip in two places. *Do you know what self-control is, Norman? Do you? It means not taking what you want and learning to live with it*, she'd screamed as the blood dripped from his chin onto the floor. *Look at the mess you've made.*

"I'm sorry," Norman said into the empty kitchen.

What would Kim do to him if she caught him with his hand in the cookie tin? She hadn't hit him since he'd initially refused to harvest organs from the dead. That had been three years ago. Kim had slapped him with eye-watering force, demanding he participate, promising to become even more disappointed in him if he didn't agree to it.

She won't find out, he thought, walking into the hall.

The key fit the lock perfectly.

What would he see in the basement? He hoped his suspicions were wrong. He knew Kim was capable of questionable behavior, but murder was a step too far. Wasn't it?

She wouldn't do it. It was unthinkable.

He turned the key. At last, his paranoia would be revealed as unwarranted and irrational.

***

At the Walmart Supercenter in Berlin, Kim loaded the bags into the trunk of her car and returned the cart. She passed JC Penney on her way down Berlin Mall Road, hooked a left onto Fisher, and continued toward Paine Turnpike. She was looking forward to making Norman a large breakfast—eggs, bacon and sausage. It wasn't the healthiest way to start anyone's day, but Kim thought he deserved a treat. And she could use the protein to help repair her damaged muscles. The anti-inflammatory drugs were working, but she still had some stiffness and a deep ache between her shoulders and in her legs from moving Megan Hawkins's body. The day after she had buried Megan, she'd woken in serious pain. Norman had been nervous and concerned, fussing over her. He'd insisted she remain in bed. She had watched him come and go, bringing her medicine and food. Returning for the plates and cutlery when she'd finished eating. She realized two things that day: one, she was still attracted to her husband, and two, she had discovered the reason why. Norman was unaware of how handsome he was.

***

The steps leading down to the basement were covered in soft rubber, silencing his footfalls as he descended to the bottom of the stairs. He looked around, as though seeing it for the first time. In a way, he was. It was unrecognizable. The floor was covered in white tiles and sloped gently in the middle toward a drainage system. The muscles in his face slackened. He gasped.

***

Kim's cell phone rang. She stopped on Main Street in front of the Lost Nation Theater.

It was Ray Porter.

"Hello, Ray."

"Kim, the last job went well…"

"I sense a *but* in there somewhere, Ray."

"You have to speed up the process. Adult female next, Kim. Understand? The initial order stands. Adult female, Kim. It's urgent."

***

A surgical table stood in the center of the basement. It had been used. The metal was streaked where it had been wiped down with detergent. A portable heart-perfusion machine stood near the wall, and beside it, a kidney and liver transporter sat atop a stainless-steel table. Norman looked higher; dirty windows looked onto the back garden.

Please, no, Kim. Please don't let it be true.

But the evidence was here. He was standing in a crime scene.

Now he knew where Evan Fairbanks had spent his final moments.

***

Kim slotted the car into the driveway and popped the trunk. She carried two of the heaviest bags to the front door.

***

Norman lifted the grate away from the drain. Underneath the stench of stagnant water lay another odor. Norman recognized it instantly. Blood. Some of it had clotted on the sides of the semicircular drain, a plastic pipe cut in half lengthwise.

***

Kim used her foot to push open the door. She looked down the hallway and froze.

***

Norman examined the newly installed shelves and cabinets. They were crammed full of medical supplies. Kim had built her own private operating theater, right under his nose. She must have had people come in and build it for her while he was at work.

Ray Porter. His fingers were all over this place.

Norman felt faint. He was living with a child-killer. He went to the broom closet. On the floor lay a long cable tie that had been cut, as though it had been used to secure something. Or someone. He backed out of the closet, bumped into the operating table, and winced. It was difficult to breathe. There was no air in the basement.

Behind him, a voice said, "Good morning, Norman."

SEVENTY-THREE

JIM BAYLISS LOWERED HIS NEWSPAPER. COREY WAS PUSHING his breakfast around his plate, in a state of deep distraction. Lillian threw a worried glance at her husband. Streaks of redness ran through Corey's eyes, and dark shadows lay like black mold beneath them. He wasn't sleeping, that much was obvious. Jim hadn't expected Corey to forget about Evan though. But he had seemed less grief-stricken over the past few days. Not happy, and not exactly depressed either. He had read a book, possibly the most reassuring event to occur since Evan's disappearance. That he'd had the focus to read was a positive sign, Jim reasoned. Proof Corey was healing.

Then he'd changed. It was sudden, forcing Jim to consider his options. Allow his son to work through the darkness alone, or send him to a grief counselor? It was wrong for a child to dwell on death, and Jim made a silent promise to lead his son to some kind of peace.

He wasn't sleeping well, either. Lillian lay awake beside him most nights, too. They didn't talk, but he felt her wakefulness in the absence of her regular breathing.

"You don't like your food?" Lillian asked.

The sadness in her voice alarmed Jim. His throat tightened and he almost reached for her arm, to tell her it was okay. But Corey's head snapped up. He seemed confused.

"Huh?"

"Your food, Cor," Lillian said. "Does it taste all right?"

"Oh, sure, Mom. It's great. Um…can I go to my room?"

"Of course. Let me know if you're hungry. I'll cook something nice."

Jim watched Corey leave the table and listened for the sound of his bedroom door closing.

"What are we going to do?" Lillian said.

"We're going to contact a psychologist."

"You think that'll work?"

"I'm out of ideas. But he needs help, Lillian."

She nodded. "Okay, I'll search online for someone… they still haven't caught the guy."

Jim had let his attention drift. "What?" he asked.

"The guy who took the Fairbanks kid."

"Oh."

The fact that the kidnapper hadn't been arrested weighed on Montpelier. As long as the perpetrator remained at large, the stain on the town's consciousness was only absorbed deeper.

Jim placed his hand on his wife's arm. "It's going to be all right."

But the dark was sometimes more powerful than the light.

It's going to be all right. Those words would haunt Jim Bayliss.

***

The food had been fine; Corey just couldn't taste it. The skeletal thought growing in his mind had invaded his dreams, taken on the flesh of obsession.

Corey brought the flashlight he'd found in the garage out from underneath his pillows.

Mrs. Loomis had taken his friend. Somehow she'd kidnapped Evan and kept him in her basement.

He couldn't tell his parents; they already thought he was crazy. They looked at him as though he was a piece of delicate glass developing a crack and they couldn't prevent it. They wouldn't believe him, anyway. Corey hardly believed it himself. At least if he went and had a look in the basement and didn't see anything suspicious he could forget about it. It might lighten his mood, make him feel a little less sad. But if he didn't check, he would have a lot of sleepless nights ahead of him.

Something else was tearing him from peaceful slumber—guilt.

He had to search the Loomises' basement. It wouldn't go away. He couldn't rid himself of the notion that he had been responsible for Evan's abduction.

Corey went to the window, turned his head far to his left. The Loomises' roof was visible between gaps in the trees.

Tonight. I'll do it tonight.

He recalled the day of the fundraiser. The way Mrs. Loomis had followed him to the stairs, making sure he found the bathroom. Now he saw her in a new, sinister light. She was being vigilant, steering him away from the basement. Watching him.

He would wait until the early hours. His parents would never know he had been outside.

He'd be back in bed before anyone knew he had even gone.

SEVENTY-FOUR

LENA FAIRBANKS WAS IN A HOSPITAL. SHE HAD NO MEMORY of how she'd gotten there. And someone was following her. She fled down the doughnut-shaped corridor, passing windowless rooms with empty beds, and wondered why there were no nurses, doctors, or patients. Medical equipment beeped and chirped, though none of it was attached to the sick. She paused to catch her breath, doubled over, hand planted on the cold wall, and noticed she was wearing a hospital johnny and a pair of slippers that appeared to have been woven from briars. Her pale feet were bleeding, torn by thorns that scratched her flesh and punctured the prominent dark-blue veins.

Her breathing slowed. She turned, swiveling her head beneath the arm still holding onto the wall. Bloody footprints were stamped on the floor like melted red candlewax. There were separate trails, as though she had been covering the same ground over and over. But there was no way out—no exit signs, no doors leading to fresh air and natural light.

The stench of the infirm was overwhelming, a kind of back-of-the-throat phlegmy odor that brought to mind images of finality, a black door that opened onto memories of her own bitter sickness.

Lena wasn't worried about dying. But she was terrified of being caught.

The pale fluorescents flickered. A shadow fell on the floor at a bend in the corridor.

Her lips trembled.

Wetness trickled down her thigh, spilling onto her feet, which had become white hot with pain.

Water slapped the floor between her legs. The sound was canceled out by a labored gasp, as though someone were struggling to breathe.

Her son rounded the bend, his torso hollowed out like a canoe. His broken ribs had been bent outward. The bones in his back sandwiched blackened intercostal muscle. He had no heart, no lungs, and no kidneys. His intestines remained. They spilled from his midsection in glistening ropes. As he moved toward her, a squeaking sound filled the hall. She stared, horrified, realizing the sound was coming from his wet guts that slithered behind him, like the tentacles of a jellyfish.

Evan opened his arms.

Mom, I need a hug. It's dark in here. I need a hug, Mom, I can't feel my heartbeat. Please...

Lena ran, giving voice to a wavering groan. Evan pursued her. He was right behind her. She could smell him—rotting flesh and fresh soil.

I can't feel my heart, Mom...I just want a hug.

Lena glanced over her shoulder. Evan had stopped. He stood in the wake of her bloody trail, breathing hard, even though he didn't have lungs. Still, his dirty white ribs moved up and down as if he *could.*

I'm sorry, Evan. I should've taken care of you. I'm sorry I was a bad mother.

He appeared in front of her, his face so close she could smell his breath. It was like meat that had been left out to thaw for too long.

Lena screamed.

I just want a hug, Mom, please…

***

Lena awoke, and rolled on the couch thrashing and screaming, clawing at the air. A booming sound came from somewhere. She opened her rheumy eyes, picked up a capless bottle of vodka that was sticking into her ribs, and flung her arm toward the floor, steadying it into an upright position. There was a small measure of clear liquid at the bottom. The booming turned into a persistent banging.

She rubbed her eyes and the living room took shape around her. She was free of the nightmare.

Someone was at the door.

"Lena, let me in. You're late again."

That voice was familiar. Slowly, she extracted herself from the couch and staggered to the window. It was Pete Dewsbury, the landlord.

"Lena, I know you've been having a bad time of it, but I need the rent."

Lena had the money; she just had no intention of spending it on rent. She sat in the La-Z-Boy, her head in her hands. Pete would leave, eventually.

As he continued knocking, Lena reflected on the worst part of waking—shame. Full, relentless shame. But now there was something else, a cold truth that swelled in her with each passing day—she had made a terrible mistake.

SEVENTY-FIVE

NORMAN STARED WIDE-EYED AT KIM. HIS MOUTH MOVED as though in the process of forming speech. Thoughts of formulating an explanation disappeared when Kim slapped him on the face. The impact forced his head sideways and shook his gaunt frame. He tasted blood.

An odd stillness had descended on his wife. Norman didn't like it one bit. He was scared. The woman standing before him was different, a stranger. Not the woman he knew and loved. Fire burned in her eyes.

"How dare you invade my private space," she said. The cold, detached tone in her voice worried Norman more than the heat of her stare.

Blood dripped onto his chin. "I'm sorry…Kim, what did you do? Please tell me it's not true."

"What you see is what you get, Norman."

"You killed that poor boy. Oh my God, Kim. You really did do it."

Her face twisted into a grimace. "You simpering idiot. Do you know who's keeping the creditors from the door, Norman? Do you? I had to take the boy's organs. I'm securing our financial future. What have you done, hmm? There is one breadwinner in this house, and that's me. Loomis Memorial is dead. You just haven't accepted the fact yet. But make no mistake, Norman. *You. Will. Not. Stand. In.*

My. Way. I have made us some serious money. You won't ruin it for me, or my sister."

"What does she have to do with this?"

"Never mind. That boy's—"

"Evan."

"—life was hell on earth, living with an alcoholic mother. She's the criminal, not me."

"I'm calling the police," Norman said, and went toward the stairs.

He paused but didn't turn to face her.

"You know it's also a crime to harvest organs from the dead without the proper consent and protocol. You're going to spend the rest of your life in prison because you're weak, Norman. I didn't tell you *because you're weak.* I gave you those pills because you don't have the mental strength to live in this world. I tried to take care of you. You disappoint me, Norman."

Norman laughed. An awful, alien chuckle bereft of humor.

"You disappoint me, too," he said. "You murdered a child. That's the line. You crossed it. Let's see how weak I am. I'll accept the punishment I deserve. I belong in prison for what I've done. I can't—*I won't*—let you get away with killing a child."

He began to climb the steps and was halfway out of the basement when two words stopped him dead in his tracks.

"I'm pregnant," Kim said.

SEVENTY-SIX

COREY CHECKED THE TIME. IT WAS 3 A.M. HIS PARENTS HAD been in bed for four hours and the house was quiet. He put on his jeans, dropped his folding knife into a back pocket, and pulled on a hoodie. He had passed the Loomis mansion earlier in the day on his bicycle, reconnoitering possible obstacles. There had been none, although deep down he'd hoped to find a reason not to do it.

He had been convinced he'd seen a person watching him from a window on the upper floor. But he had dismissed it as interplay between light and shadow. Corey didn't like the idea of trespassing and had promised himself he would be careful not to cause any damage. If he arrived at the basement window and found it locked, he wouldn't force it.

Flashlight in hand, he opened the door in small increments. It seemed to take forever to create a gap wide enough to squeeze through. Then, he had to get past his parents' bedroom. He held his breath and placed the edge of his heel down first. He rolled it forward then repeated the process with his other foot, walking in a kind of half-crouch. He felt distinctly criminal, like he was in the process of burglarizing the house. And what he planned to do was criminal. On the TV cop shows, they called it breaking and entering. Corey had no intention of breaking anything; he just wanted to look around, satisfy himself that he was being dumb, and move on.

He was on the landing. Now all he had to do was make it downstairs without waking the house. The stairs creaked in places, and Corey considered every step. He didn't usually hold onto the banister, but he wasn't leaving anything to chance. It would anchor him in case he needed to pull himself back.

He had reached the last stair when his father coughed above him. He froze, considered abandoning the plan, and shook his head. No. He had come this far. He just hoped dad wouldn't poke his head into his bedroom to check on him as he often had since Evan had been missing.

Another thought got him moving: Sometimes his dad took a pee in the middle of the night, laying the blame squarely on his prostate. Mom would insist there was nothing wrong with his prostate and that it was all in his mind.

Corey unlocked the front door, muscles tensed, heart racing. He needed to hurry. He stood on the doorstep and allowed himself to breathe for a moment before taking his bike from the side of the house and wheeling it onto Main Street. The Loomis house was only fifty or so yards away, but he was taking his bicycle in case he had to leave quickly.

He kept his speed low, listened to the night as he pedaled. It was silent. If he saw headlights he'd hide…swing his legs over the bar and run with the bike toward a tree, or hunker down behind a car in a driveway. But there were no vehicles on the road. At this early hour, he'd be surprised to see anybody.

If Jim discovered he had left in the middle of the night, Corey knew what his punishment would be: grounded for a month and no more reading novels from high up on the bookshelf. Being grounded didn't worry him, but it would truly suck if he couldn't read any grownup books.

Should he have called Rachel, told her what he was doing, where he was going? After all, she was the only friend he had, the only *real* friend, anyway. But what would he have said? That was the problem. *She'd* probably say he was crazy. Well, perhaps she wouldn't say it, but she might *think* it. And he didn't want to lose her respect. He recalled the day he'd handed out the flyers to people, and Rachel had helped. Afterwards, they'd eaten in Subway. Rachel had made him laugh. He couldn't even remember the joke, but she had made him forget for a moment that he was desperate to find Evan and apologize for leaving him outside the school. For getting it wrong. And he *knew* Evan. He would have apologized to Rachel. It just sometimes took him longer to say sorry.

Corey applied the brakes, stopped in the exact spot where he'd last seen Evan, outside Main Street Middle School. In the soft amber glow of the streetlights, a slow mist descended, coating the ground in an opaque film. It was easy to imagine he was the last person on earth, that the buildings all around him were empty, abandoned. He looked at the Loomis residence, at its dark windows, comforted by its aura of stillness. Everyone was sleeping.

He crossed the road, wheeled his bicycle up the driveway, and followed the paved path to the rear of the large house.

***

Norman lay face down on the table, one hand dangling at his side, almost touching the kitchen floor. He was snoring. Kim had crushed two sleeping pills into his peppermint tea. She had insisted he drink it. It would calm him, she had promised. A desperate measure, but Kim needed time to think. What had made Norman so brazen? She knew he was capable of uncharacteristic behavior. She'd seen it before, in the early stages of their courtship. They had been about to leave for a date and he'd pushed her foster father down the steps of the front porch after he'd commented that Kim was "dressed like a slut." Kim had been proud of Norman, especially since she never saw either of her foster parents again. Norman had insisted she move in with him, and Kim had accepted. She had immediately recognized his need to protect her dignity.

Perhaps his current disappointing behavior had been instigated by someone else. It was a sad turn of events. Now he was a threat to her, and she'd have to watch him.

"I'm sorry it had to come to this, Norman," she said, and placed a blanket over his shoulders.

She went to her bedroom, the problem her husband posed weighing heavy on her as she climbed into bed. How long before Norman's conscience overwhelmed his better judgment and he went to the police? Telling him she was pregnant had subdued him for now, though whether his dream of becoming a father was stronger than his desire to report her for killing a child remained to be seen. Her sister would know what to do.

She glanced at the table next to her. In the dark, she saw the sloping outline of the Chamberlain base station. Its light was on, its antenna upright. The motion sensor was in the basement, the weak link in their home security. A determined burglar could get inside by forcing the window. Kim wasn't going to be surprised by an intruder. Norman had said it wasn't necessary, but if it allowed her to sleep well, she didn't care what anyone said.

***

Corey couldn't quite believe what he was seeing—the latch was broken. It wasn't going to be as difficult as he'd thought. He slid the window open as far as it would go and shone the beam of his flashlight into the inky darkness. There were objects in the basement that seemed out of place. He looked at his wristwatch. Five minutes to look around and he'd leave.

He focused the beam onto a table below the window. That was his way in and out.

He sat on the grass and rocked forward, using his arms to propel him. His legs were inside the window. He paused, heart lurching madly in his chest. He had the peculiar sensation of feeding himself to a strange and terrible beast. It was though he wasn't going into the basement, but being consumed by it.

Stop being a baby. It's only five minutes. Not a lot can go wrong in five minutes. His instincts screamed at him to leave but he ignored his gut and levered his body through the window with aching arms. Air shuddered from his lungs as his feet touched the table. He took the flashlight out of his waistband, got into a sitting position on the table, and pushed himself onto the floor.

The base station buzzed. Kim's eyes flew open. Somebody was in the basement.

***

Corey focused the beam in the center of the room. It looked like some kind of medical table. There was a strong chemical odor that lingered in his sinuses. He hated it when his mother used bleach in the bathroom. The smell clung to his nose and throat, and took an age to disappear.

There was a machine next to it. Corey had no clue what it was. He pointed the light at his wristwatch. He had been here just over two minutes. He scanned the tables and shelves. Mostly medical equipment. He steadied the beam on a scalpel set, then lowered it to the shelf below and paused, a slight tremor in his hand. It was a saw, one he hadn't seen before, and his dad had plenty of saws.

***

Kim went downstairs and into the kitchen, her nightgown knotted tightly around her waist. She took a large carving knife from its wooden block and her key from its new hiding place in a cinnamon jar halfway beneath the spice. She stood in the dark by the basement door and listened. She turned the handle, easing it wide. The door didn't creak. No self-respecting homemaker allowed the doors in her house to creak. It was sloppy, slovenly…yes, that was the word—*slovenly*.

Like a feather coming to rest on a body of water, Kim moved her foot silently onto the first step. Then the second, third…She slowed her breathing. Saw the beam of light below, flitting from place to place.

***

Corey sensed a change in the atmosphere, dismissed it as his imagination playing tricks on him, and continued his inspection of the medical supplies. There were bottles and cans of chemicals emblazoned with garish warning labels. A black skull glowered on the side of a glass jar. What were the Loomises doing with all this stuff? Neither were doctors. He shone the flashlight into a corner and found a huge light attached to an articulated arm, the kind he'd seen on TV medical dramas his mother was fond of watching but his father found objectionable for some reason.

Kim was on the last step.

Corey pointed the flashlight at a door. A closet, he guessed.

Kim watched him open the door, and moved forward over the cold tiles.

***

Corey saw the cut cable ties on the floor of the closet. *What the hell?* The beam of his flashlight illuminated red stains along the wall. *Paint? Or something else?*

He closed the door. He had to get out, had to tell someone even if it got him into trouble. If the basement was an operating theater, then what were they operating on? Or who? The thought made his skin crawl. Whatever this was, it was wrong.

He swept the beam around the basement one final time, and became completely rooted to the spot. His hands trembled, his eyes became huge, and an involuntary sound issued from his constricted throat.

"Huuuuuuunhh."

Mrs. Loomis was standing at the bottom of the stairs. Light flickered on the blade of her knife as the flashlight shook in his trembling hand.

Corey broke into a lunging run.

The tops of his thighs struck the steel table.

He clambered on top of it.

Dropped the flashlight. It clattered on the tiles.

He got to his feet, launched himself through the open window, mad, merciless terror pounding in his chest. "Huuuuuuuuhh." It was as though he had been winded. His arms and legs scrabbled for purchase but his body was failing him. He couldn't understand why; he should have been outside already.

Then he felt his hoodie being pulled and he was hauled back into the basement.

His feet lifted off the table and he was airborne.

It was so dark he didn't see the clinical white tiles rushing toward his head.

SEVENTY-SEVEN

MELODY HAD DUG TWO SEPARATE HOLES, ONE NEAR THE house and the other far into the garden, near the treeline, where the bodies of the three intruders lay, wrapped in black refuse sacks, awaiting burial. She stank, and tears leaked from her eyes in a steady stream. Blood had dried in her hair and diesel fumes from the JCB mini excavator had bonded to her skin and clothes.

Rosa was in the house, cleaning the blood off the walls. Her questions could wait, and no doubt she had a lot of them.

Joe and Anna lay side by side on the patio, wrapped in bedsheets. Melody had apologized to their bloody corpses as she cut them out of the tape that bound them to their chairs. Melody and Rosa hadn't spoken since then.

Melody jumped down from the cab of the JCB and used her foot to push the men's bodies into the hole. Loose earth followed in their wake, rustling their plastic burial shrouds.

She backfilled the grave, eager to finish the job and help Rosa clean up her mess.

And it was *her* mess.

***

Rosa dipped the blood-soaked sponge into the bucket of soapy water beside her, squeezed, and scrubbed. It was as if she were on autopilot, that the gravity of what had occurred hadn't yet sunk in. Would she go into shock? She didn't know. Her heart was still racing, and adrenaline coursed through her body. She worked hard and fast, giving the cleaning her full attention.

She stood and wrung the saturated sponge into the dark water, then glanced out and saw Melody spit into the hole. She wondered who her friend really was; it was almost as if she was meeting Melody Morgan for the first time.

She went into the garden and handed Melody a pair of heavy-duty work gloves. Together, they carried Joe's body to the edge of the hole, tied two lengths of rope around his legs and the upper half of his torso. Melody stood at one end of the grave and Rosa at the other. Melody nodded, and they lifted the body over the opening and lowered it gently to the bottom, feeding the rope out, hand over hand. They repeated the process for Anna, laying her beside Joe.

Rosa whispered a prayer, hands clasped in front of her, and Melody listened in silence.

Melody brought the excavator to the graveside, averting her wet eyes as she pushed the mound of soil into the hole.

Rosa watched the white sheets disappear as the earth closed around the bodies, wiping her eyes absently, her lips moving as she continued to pray.

Melody shut the engine off and they returned to the house and resumed the cleanup. There were no words. Rosa didn't know what she would have said even if she'd wanted to talk at that moment.

They returned to the garden and burned the used rags, sponges, and paper towels in an old iron planting trough Melody had brought from the garage. Then they showered. Melody had insisted Rosa go ahead of her.

***

Melody stood in the shower, rinsing the dirt and blood from her hair and skin. It was pure heaven, just for a moment.

They carried their soiled clothes to the trough, burned them, and returned to the living room. Melody twisted the cap off a bottle of whiskey that had been gathering dust in her kitchen for at least a decade and poured them both a generous measure.

Melody expected Rosa to bombard her with questions, but she didn't. She sat on an armchair by the bookshelves, in silence, staring into her glass. Ten minutes ticked by on the clock above the living-room doorway.

Rosa gulped the whiskey, grimaced.

Melody held up the bottle, offering her more, but Rosa shook her head.

"I was going to lie to you," Melody said.

"About what?"

"All this."

"Why?"

"Because you're all I have left and I don't want to lose you...I guess I should just tell you what happened."

She paused, pressing her thumb into the decorative ridges of the tumbler as she considered how to proceed.

Rosa waited. She seemed nervous, too.

"I'm a contract killer." Melody searched Rosa's expression for a reaction. Rosa sat up straight in the armchair. And that was it. No shock, no getting up to leave. "Rosa, please talk to me."

"I suspected you were involved in something illegal. Spic N Span was failing as a business a few years ago. I know—I run the shop. I wondered where you were getting the money to keep it afloat."

"You turned the business around, made it work."

"Yes, but when you went out in the van, to visit a customer, you never brought me invoices, never spoke about the work you did. I didn't ask you what you were doing because I knew that whatever it was…" Rosa shrugged. "Why, Mel? Why kill for a living?"

"It's a job, Rosa. I'm good at it, or at least I was, until I made a mess of the Shaker contract." She told Rosa about Charles Shaker. "There was no way I could have known Shaker was a cartel banker. Obviously, I wouldn't have done it if…if…" She wiped her face with the back of her hand, looked at the floor and shook her head. "I'm so sorry, Rosa. You deserve to know the truth. I was afraid to tell you… before. You have no idea how much you mean to me."

Rosa got up and went to her, kissed her on her damp cheek and returned to the armchair.

"What do we do now?"

"I don't know," Melody said. "They took Joe…they took all my money. I was going to retire, set us up in a new business."

"I'll tell you what I'm going to do," Rosa said. "I'm going to go through this house in the morning, make sure it's properly clean. Then I'm going back to open the shop, feed Sammy, and get on with life, because there's no alternative."

"Thanks."

"For what?"

"For saving my life."

"We're good at *that*. We take care of each other."

Melody managed a weak smile. "Rosa, I need to know we're okay."

"Of course we are. Those men I shot…they deserved to die, Mel. I was worried you were going to say you are a drug-dealer. The people you killed…that's between you and God."

SEVENTY-EIGHT

JIM'S INTERNET SEARCH HAD YIELDED ONE PROMISING prospect: Dr. Steven Anders, a child psychiatrist in Burlington. He wouldn't force Corey to talk to Anders. Instead, he'd persuade him, bribe him if he had to. Jim was old-fashioned, and he knew it. He didn't believe in talking to strangers about problems. But this wasn't for him; it was for his son.

"What if Cor doesn't want to talk to this guy?"

Lillian was spreading butter on her toast. "We'll cross that bridge, hon. He'll listen to you. You know how he's always trying to impress you."

"Yeah, I should let him know he doesn't need my approval, he already has it."

Lillian squeezed his hand. "You're a great dad."

Jim frowned playfully. "Am I a great husband?"

Lillian tapped her lip with her index finger, giving the question due consideration, trying hard not to smile. "Great is a strong word."

"*You!*" He leapt out of his chair and tickled her.

She squealed and said breathlessly, "Okay, I give up. You're a great husband, too. *I'm gonna pee. Stop!*"

He went back to his chair. "That's what I thought you said."

Lillian giggled. "Oh my," she said. "I feel like such a teenager."

"Not bad…for a Tuesday."

Lillian waggled her eyebrows at him. "Hey, great husband, wanna fool around?"

"That's all I am to you, isn't it? A piece of meat?" he said, adding an extra layer of mock outrage. "Why can't you love me for my personality?"

"You got a problem with that…great husband? It's a great piece of meat, too."

They both began to howl.

"Ahhh," Jim said, "I think I'll withhold my meat till I get some respect around here!"

Lillian pressed her hands to her cheeks. "You would hoard your meat and not share it with me?"

They laughed, tears streaming down their faces.

"Oh my God," Lillian said. "We're a couple of goofballs."

"I bet Corey's awake now. I'll go and check on him."

His son was late coming down for breakfast. Maybe he hadn't slept well, but he'd have trouble sleeping again tonight if he didn't get up.

Jim knocked on Corey's bedroom door and opened it. The bed was empty.

"Corey?" He went into the room, looked around. He wasn't here. He checked the bathroom. He wasn't in there, either.

"Corey?" he called, raising his voice.

"Jim, what's wrong?"

"Corey?"

SEVENTY-NINE

NORMAN LIFTED HIS HEAD OFF THE TABLE AND WINCED AT the stiffness in his neck. He placed a hand on his nape and massaged it. Why had he slept in the kitchen? Then he saw the empty cup Kim had brought him last night. She had drugged him. There was no other explanation. Pins and needles hummed a soundless tune in his left arm. Had he slept on it? It was comforting, in a way, to distract himself with insignificant questions. The larger questions were too difficult.

Was he willing to ignore the fact that his wife was a murderer so they could be parents to their unborn child? How could he sleep in the same bed as a woman responsible for such a heinous crime? What would happen to their child if he and Kim went to prison? Because Norman had no doubt Kim would take him down with her if he went to the police.

It was a dream come true. He had wanted to be a father since he was twenty years old. Now he had the chance. But his wife was a child-killer. The scale of the problem dwarfed his ability to even attempt a solution. It was overwhelming.

Perversely, he was grateful for the artificial fatigue induced by the drugs with which Kim had spiked his tea. Fully sober, Norman wasn't confident he would be able to fend off a panic attack.

He sat up, swaying, and touched the indentation on his forehead from the table. There was a blanket around his shoulders.

"How're you feeling, Norman?"

Startled, he blinked away the cloudiness that had blurred his vision. Kim was standing at the end of the table, hands behind her back. Her red dress was loose in the front. Norman usually helped her with the zipper.

"What did you do to me?" he said, his voice thick and low.

"It was for your own good, Norman. I'm not going to lie to you. I had to give you a little helping hand so you could rest."

"You drugged me."

"Norman, that's so melodramatic. I *assisted* you is all I did. You know how stressed out you can get…we need to talk, and we need to do it right now."

Norman didn't like her tone, or the lilting note of menace so poorly concealed behind each word. Perhaps she wanted him to hear the threat in her voice. Controlling him was her number one priority, and he knew it.

I'm not going to lie to you.

Norman had been sitting next to Kim when the FBI agents had questioned her in their great room, over peppermint tea. And Kim had lied to their faces with such casual abandon that he had believed her, as had the feds. There was no way you could *not* believe her—that was how convincing she'd been. Both investigators had left, an air of we've-just-wasted-our-time-this-woman-couldn't-possibly-know-what-happened-to-Evan-Fairbanks clearly evident between them.

So why wouldn't she lie to him? Was she lying about being pregnant? That was the question hanging high in his mind, glowing in bright neon.

"Do you have any proof?" he asked.

"What?"

"Proof we're having a baby?"

The corners of her mouth rose…a slow-motion curl of the lips, as though she had been expecting him to ask her that very question. One hand emerged from behind her back. She tossed the white object onto the table and it twisted toward him. Clearblue was written on the inside of it. At first, Norman didn't know what it was. One end was shaped like a duck's bill. There was a window in the device, displaying the word *Pregnant*. Proof.

"Now can we get past this, Norman?" she asked. "Aren't you happy you're going to be a daddy?"

"You killed a child, Kim. Nothing's going to make that okay."

"I need to know where we stand. Last night you were going to turn me in to the cops. What now, Norman? Do you still want to see me go to prison?"

Norman stared at the pregnancy test…the way he stared at an eye-watering gas bill he'd received in the mail when he was young and broke. Hoping his eyes were deceiving him, playing tricks on him. Hoping the numbers would change. But they didn't. The word remained the same, mocking him with its stubborn existence.

"Boy or girl, Norman, you get to choose the name."

He glanced up at her. And for a split second, he forgot the evil his wife had perpetrated. It was a moment of awe, a sliver of happiness unlike anything he'd ever experienced. He could give his daughter or son a name. Hope flared briefly, then guttered and died. Kim was a monster. What would stop her from using their child for spare parts? And yet his resolve was slipping. Weakness and self-loathing—deep-seated, familiar and comfortable—had replaced any notion of seeking justice for Evan Fairbanks.

He looked directly at Kim and said, "I'm not going to tell anyone." *Yet*, he almost added.

"The police?"

"No, I won't be going to the police."

***

Behind her back, Kim tucked the carving knife back into her panties and moved it out of sight toward her hip. She walked toward Norman, turned, and said, "Be a dear and zip me up."

EIGHTY

THE RATIONAL PART OF JIM SAID THAT COREY HAD GONE out for some reason and would return soon for breakfast. But the other part of him, the part that *knows*, told him something was wrong, that his son was in danger.

He had looked in the backyard and the garage. Corey's bicycle was missing. A low flutter of panic had set into his gut as he searched. Lillian was inside, calling Corey's friends' parents.

He went into the garage again, and this time took a more measured approach. When he'd checked it earlier, his eyes had been everywhere at once. Now, he scanned the tool-laden shelves and the worktops. Every item had its place. Hammers, wrenches and saws hung from nails along the wall. One of the nails was missing something—a flashlight. Jim ran a scenario through his mind and reached a dead-end. Why had Corey left his bed in the middle of the night, and taken his bicycle and a flashlight? To search for Evan? It seemed unlikely, but Corey was suffering, possibly unstable. He hadn't been sleeping. Jim didn't know the true extent of Corey's psychological state. And that scared and saddened him.

He had struggled to talk to Corey, found it harder than it should have been. Maybe it was his upbringing. His own father wasn't a talker. Gordon Bayliss gave the impression he was the strong silent type but the reality was that he simply didn't have anything interesting to say. Nothing to contribute except a grunt here and there. Perhaps it had influenced the way Jim interacted with Corey. The thought appalled him. He was doing his best…

What if he'd inadvertently fed Corey's obsession by searching for Evan in Hubbard Park instead of telling him the awful truth, that his friend was dead? If abducted kids weren't found early, it was unlikely they ever would be. Evan was *somewhere*. The police just hadn't discovered his body yet.

Jim walked to the end of his driveway, his heart's heavy sickening beat thumping in his head. The tendons in his neck stood out, stretching the skin tight. He looked in both directions. A car blew past, the driver waved, but Jim didn't see it. He went back to the house, fingers of dread unfurling in his stomach.

Lillian stood in the hall, eyes wet. Jim felt he had no choice but to rein in his rising panic. Not to show his fear. She was already scared. He didn't want to scare her any more than she already was.

"Jim, no one has seen him."

"What about his friend, that girl, Rachel."

"Rachel Holmes?"

"Yes. Call her parents. He probably went to see her." Her distress cleared like a black cloud passing over the face of the sun. Hope softened her brow. He saw his wife as a younger woman, back when she'd had a perm and he sported an ill-judged mullet. He had bought a thrift-store suit and her secondhand wedding dress had come from borrowed money. It was heartbreaking to see her pick up the phone now, her fear revealing the age in her face.

"I'm going to drive around, look for him," he said, forcing an even tone. "I'll bring my cell. Call me if you hear anything."

She nodded and dialed.

He paused at the door and looked at Lillian. Wanted to tell her they'd find him. That Corey had wandered off because he was in a bad place and needed some space to take his mind off things.

But the part of him that *knows* held him back.

EIGHTY-ONE

CONSCIOUSNESS SEEPED IN AND BLED OUT OF HIM IN WAVES. He couldn't tether his mind. Every time he reached, it got away from him. Remnants of thoughts and memories ebbed and flowed, and he saw himself on a dark shore, trying uselessly to seize the receding tide as it shrank from him. He stared at his hands, at the black water streaked with silver running through his fingers.

Where am I?

Pain blanketed his fragmented thoughts. A swollen, ugly throbbing in the center of his brain made him groan. He tried to put his hands to his face, to compress the brutal torment making his skull feel twice its size. But his arms wouldn't obey.

He was almost fully awake but Corey wished he were back on that dark shore. He was in agony.

He kicked his legs.

Thank God, they still work.

But they were bound, as were his hands. He remembered Mrs. Loomis coming for him in the dark, pulling him off the table. That was where the memory faded. His face felt wet in places, itchy. Whatever was on his forehead had dried to a stiff crust. He figured he had hit his head on the floor; it was the only thing that made sense.

She had locked him in the closet. That was where he was now. There was tape on his mouth. He poked his tongue past his lips and the tip stuck to the adhesive. He reeled it in, and his thoughts turned to escape. He had to get out of here. Despite the pain pulsating behind his eyes, Corey tried to recall what he'd seen in the basement: medical equipment, mainly, but there had also been medical textbooks on transplantation, a whole stack of them. He remembered the operating table, the scalpels. It wasn't difficult to put the pieces of the puzzle together. Mrs. Loomis had killed Evan and taken his organs. Evan had trespassed just as he had. Was she going to cut *him* open and take his organs?

The tape over his eyes had been put on in a hurry, crimping the soft skin around the area. Corey tried to recall if he'd ever seen darkness as total, as fathomless. And maybe his memory was fuzzy because he couldn't remember.

Had Evan lain on the same floor, in the same spot where he was now? Had he been as scared as Corey? None of this would have happened if he'd just stayed with Evan, talked him out of going onto the Loomis property. He had searched for Evan in his nightmares, and in the daylight with his father. It was crazy to think Evan had been locked in the Loomises' basement the whole time.

Corey had known all along that something wasn't right with Mrs. Loomis but he'd blocked out the memory of Evan telling him he wanted to check the mansion for corpses—his first real experience of denial. It seemed absurd, anyway. Mrs. Loomis was friendly. A respected person in the community, although Corey had noticed she was more popular with the men than the women, who appeared to only see her from the corners of their eyes.

He focused once more on his tied hands and feet, and panicked, thrashing around on the hard floor, a piercing cry of terror dampened by the tape over his mouth. He was going to die here. Mrs. Loomis had butchered his friend and she was going to slice him open, too. The veins in his neck and head bulged against his skin as he pleaded for help, scared by the sound of his own voice because it didn't belong here, down in the dark. Then dad appeared in his mind, sitting forward with his elbows planted on his knees, just as Corey was about to take a history test at school. *Listen, son, we all get nervous, even oldies like me. But when you go into the examination, keep in mind a simple rule—if you panic, you fail. Use your nerves. They'll keep you alert. Just don't let them get the better of you. Focus on the problem and always read the question. Twice if you have to. Whatever you do, don't panic.* Corey had remained calm during the exam. When he'd gotten home, he had told his dad he had answered most of the questions correctly. *Most is all you need*, Jim had said, mussing his hair with his big hand. Corey would never forget his father's smile or his quick wink that day. It was as though they had taken on the world together and won. As though they had secret knowledge, and it was just between them.

He cried quiet, hot tears. He missed his parents. And if he wanted to see them again, he would have to escape.

If you panic, you fail.
Always read the question.
Twice if you have to.

EIGHTY-TWO

Jim KEPT REACHING FOR THE CELL PHONE ON THE EMPTY seat beside him as he crawled along State Street, then putting his hand on the wheel, gripping it until his knuckles turned white. He cruised by the two-story cruciform State House constructed from gray Barre granite, a picture of grandeur with its Doric portico and gilded dome, the sun bleaching the gold paint. He scanned the wide lawn, glanced at the mound of trees that rose up from Hubbard Park behind the State House.

Hubbard Park. It was as good a place as any to start.

Corey had gotten it into his head that Evan would be there, and he and Jim had searched the park. Maybe Corey had gone back to look again.

Jim could imagine his conversation with the police when he called and told them his son was missing—*He probably wandered off and he'll be back soon. You know how kids are.* Or *He's only been gone a few hours; he hasn't been missing long enough.* And Jim would tell them that he knew his son, that his behavior was out of character. Jim was past the point of caring what the police thought. Finding Corey was all that mattered.

He picked up speed, turned left at the end of State Street, onto Main, then left again toward Spring Street, where Corey had crossed the bridge over the Winooski River with Evan on the day he had been abducted.

Jim had sat and listened to Corey recount that day to the police. He had been proud of his son for doing his best, for not changing his story because what he was saying was true. Not that he'd actually told Corey he was proud of him, he realized with dismay. And the worst thing was, he didn't know why. It was a simple sentence, easy to string together—*Corey, I'm proud of you, son*. How difficult was *that*? If he found him—w*hen* he found him—Jim would stop treating some words as though they were scarce and had to be rationed.

Foot heavy on the gas, Jim swung the car right into the Old Shelter parking lot. There were people everywhere. Of course there were. It was warm and the sun was shining.

He put his phone in his shirt pocket and moved through the crowd, keeping his gaze low. Then he saw Corey. He was standing at a wooden picnic table, the same one where they had eaten their sandwiches the day they'd searched for Evan.

He leapt forward, put his hand on his shoulder. The kid turned. It wasn't Corey.

Jim's heart sank and his fear grew.

The boy's mother appeared, glared at him over her shoulder as she led her son away from him, as though he was a predator. Jim held up a hand in apology and walked toward the trees, and deeper into the woods.

He was at least a mile in when his composure broke.

"Corey!" he called. "Corey, it's your dad. You're not in trouble. Just come home."

His heart thudded in his chest, pumping a cocktail of abject fear and desperation around his body. He dialed home. Lillian answered on the first ring.

"Lillian, tell me something," he said.

She was sobbing softly.

"I called Rachel's parents. They haven't seen him. Rachel hasn't either…Jim, what're we going to do?"

"I'm on my way home. Call the police."

EIGHTY-THREE

KIM HAD LEARNED MANY USEFUL TIPS FROM *GOOD Housekeeping*, the magazine and the website. One of those tips was a relaxation technique that was supposed to calm anxiety. Kim tried her own variation. She inhaled, held the air for ten seconds, exhaled, and counted twenty seconds in her head before inhaling again. She repeated the process several times and found it highly effective.

She looked beyond the parking lot, at the cars passing on Fisher Road, allowing her mind to go blank.

She checked her MAC foundation in the rearview mirror; it was flawless—satin finish, sheer coverage, because that was all Kim Loomis needed. She pushed the door of the Maybach wide with the toe of her Walter Steiger filo shoes, her favorite classic-red glossy pumps. She stood beside the Mercedes for a moment, adjusted her sleeveless black Armani dress—V neckline, full skirt, the kind of outfit you'd wear to a formal occasion or a fancy dinner party. She slung her Birkin over a well-moisturized shoulder and walked toward the doors that led inside the Vermont Psychiatric Care Hospital, hips swaying, head high.

The sun was warm on her back as she strutted across the lot. She felt many eyes on her as people either entered or left the building. A pleasant shiver rippled through her, as though her pores were absorbing the stares, drinking them in. Kim knew what they were thinking: *Who does she think she is?*

Kim Loomis, that's who.

She spoke to the receptionist and waited in the lobby, sitting on one of the two blue sofas facing a coffee table, looking out through the glass wall, into the courtyard, where patients were enjoying the sunshine.

A member of staff appeared around a corner, tailed by Kim's twin sister. The nurse nodded at Kim and she followed them down a hall to an empty visiting room: beige floor, broken at the corners by blue paint, and tables and chairs. The nurse closed the door behind her.

Her sister sat, hands folded, regarding Kim calmly. They were identical twins but Kim noticed her sister had become more like her since the last time they had met face to face.

Kara had been an inpatient in Vermont State Hospital in Waterbury. Kim's confinement there had been brief but even her lawyer, a ruthless attack dog, had been unable to get Kara released. Then tropical storm Irene blew through and flooded it. It was the final straw for the place Kim knew as the Vermont State Asylum for the Insane. The hospital had been closed, and Kara was now a resident in this new, modern building.

Kara was trim, her arms toned, her stomach flat. In Waterbury, she'd let herself get plump in the face. But there was a gym here and Kara had been using it. She looked healthy, strong. Her black hair shone.

Kim sat and said, "Good to see you, Kara. How are you?"

"Counting the days, Kim. I'll be out soon. You know what that means?"

Kim nodded, her gaze drifting downward.

"Don't nod at me," Kara said. "Tell me what it means."

"The money is in your account. Everything you need is waiting for you when you come home."

Kara leaned back in the chair, and Kim got an eyeful of the flat stomach underneath her tight pink shirt. *She must be doing crunches every day.* Kim wasn't exactly loose around the middle, either, but she decided to increase the number of crunches she did during her workout to avoid unwanted slippage.

"You didn't come here to stare at my rock-hard abs," Kara said. "So what do you want?"

Kim straightened in the chair and said, voice low, "Norman knows."

Kara folded her arms across her chest. "That's your problem."

"No, Kara, that's *our* problem."

"He hasn't gone to the police?"

"Not yet, but he will. I told him I was pregnant."

"Did he buy it?"

"Not at first, only after I faked the test."

Kara pulled her chair closer to the table, leaned forward. Kim mirrored her movements.

"You know what you have to do," Kara whispered.

"Don't say it, Kara. There's a solution to this. I just haven't seen it yet."

"You have to kill Norman, sis. How many times have I told you? He's weak."

"No, he isn't…I mean, he lets his conscience rule his behavior. It's a character flaw, that's all."

"You have to do it, Kim. You owe me."

"Haven't I always taken care of you? Just because I don't visit you often, doesn't mean I don't love you. We talk on the phone a lot, don't we? You don't know how hard it is for me, seeing you in a place like this."

Kara leaned farther across the table. "I get it. You need to keep the gossip decibel level to a minimum. But I've spent almost fifteen years of my life incarcerated because of you. Locked in one hell hole after another. No matter what you say or do, *you still owe me.*"

276

And she did, Kim knew. However she spun it in her mind, it came down to the same thing—if Kara hadn't taken the blame, Kim would be on the other side of the table.

Chandler Road, West Berlin, 2003

It was Christmas Day. Both teenagers had torn open their presents hours ago. Kara had feigned delight at a sweater, and Kim had pretended the dozen or so pairs of socks were just what she'd wanted, which was a pair of red pumps, just like Dorothy in the *Wizard of Oz*.

Bill Peil, their new foster father, had been drinking steadily all day. His wife, Joanne, had been knitting a sweater for herself since after breakfast. The clicking sound of the needles was maddening, but Kim and Kara had woken up on many Christmases with no presents waiting for them under the tree. Their current home wasn't perfect. It was isolated, in a wooded area of Montpelier. There were trees blocking whatever view there was at the back and the front of the gray clapboard house with the flaking paint. It was as though they were in the wilderness. If something went wrong, if someone had an accident, no one would save them because they were too far from civilization. Cars seldom passed on the road outside. But it was better than nothing. They weren't wanted by anyone, including the Peils, who were happy to take the check the state sent them and leave all that parenting stuff to the do-gooders in Montpelier with their fancy education and meaningless diplomas hanging from walls that no one cared about, least of all decent working folks like the Peils.

Kim was nervous. The house was warm and Kara was wearing shorts. Bill was staring at her legs, his eyes on her as she twirled her hair and watched TV. Kim was near the living-room window, thinking of the future, wishing she was eighteen instead of fifteen. Being older meant freedom. Freedom from the Bill Peils of the world. She hated these people, not only because she suspected Bill was a pervert, but because she had to rely on them. Relying on other people for her wellbeing, to supply her and Kara with food and shelter, was becoming intolerable.

It happened fast. One moment Bill was slurping his whiskey, the next he launched himself from his armchair and punched Kara in the face, striking her in the eye. She tumbled off the chair, screaming. He corralled her into a corner and kicked her. Each blow was followed by screams of pain and terror. Kim tried to distract him by throwing a whiskey bottle at him. She aimed it at his head. It missed, smashing on the wall and leaking down the flowery wallpaper like weeping rust. He grabbed her by the hair, backhanded her. She fell, dazed.

"Stop!" Kim shouted. "Please stop. You're killing her!"

Joanne sat in her rocking chair, still knitting, as though everything was fine. The needles clicked and clacked. Kim stared at her, mouth agape.

As suddenly as it had begun, it ended, and Bill left the room. Kim didn't dare breathe until she heard him climbing the stairs.

She crawled to the corner where Kara cowered, hair in knots, face bloody, careful to avoid the shards of glass from the broken bottle.

She brushed Kara's tangled hair aside to get a clear view of the damage. There were cuts below her swollen eyes and the skin on one cheekbone had been split. Bruises bloomed on her chin and forehead. Later, Kara would develop two black eyes, the right so severely injured she wouldn't be able to see out of it for two days.

Kim got Kara on her feet, walked her toward the stairs, and their bedroom. Joanne didn't look at them as they hobbled past her. She was still knitting. Kim was afraid Bill would come back, that this time he wouldn't stop. She needed to get her sister in bed before more pain set in.

As she closed the bedroom door, and pushed the dresser in front of it, Kim had already made up her mind—Bill Peil was going to pay for what he had done to Kara.

***

It was four in the morning. Kim went downstairs and out to the barn at the rear of the house, what Bill called the garage, but it was too big to be one, Kim thought. She needed only three things—baling wire (or farming wire, as Bill called it), a canister of gasoline, and matches. She checked the scarred worktables, the lopsided shelves, and the bed of Bill's rickety old Ford F100 pickup and found two of those items. The matches she retrieved from a cupboard in the kitchen.

She was grateful to Bill for keeping the gas canister full. It was done out of habit. On one of his rare sober days, he'd explained it to her—that his daddy had taught him to keep the gas can full because you never knew when you'd need it in a hurry. Never knew when you would run dry on the road.

And who'd want that, Kim thought as she unwound the baling wire from its spool outside the Peils' bedroom door. She wrapped it around the doorknob, tightening it as she went. There was no way she could risk it coming loose. Index fingers inside the spool, she walked backward, unrolling the wire as she went, and twisted it around the doorknob of the bathroom door. She tested the tension by plucking it like a guitar string. It released a dull twang.

Kim crouched beside the red plastic canister, pulled the retractable nozzle free, and poured a gallon or so of gasoline through the small gap underneath the bedroom door. The fumes burned her eyes and made her gag. Then she hurried down the hall to wake Kara.

"What's going on?" Kara said.

Kim got her arms under Kara, as though she was lifting a baby. They stared at each other in the dimness.

"Don't ask questions," Kim said. "Stay close to me."

Kim picked up the gas can by her foster parents' bedroom door and doused the carpet as she backed toward the stairs. By the time she had reached the doorstep, there was only a small amount of gas left. She thought she had done enough. She struck a match, handed the can to Kara, and told her to get out onto the lawn. Kim dropped the match and the gas ignited with a *whompf.*

Flames raced up the stairs and along the hallway to the bedroom. Bill and Joanne Peil screamed. Kim retreated to the lawn and stood next to Kara. They watched as the Peils flailed in their room, beating at the flames crawling up their bodies, Joanne a stumbling conflagration. Her nightdress had combusted and her mouth was wide and black.

Kara took a step backward when Bill tossed a bedside lamp at the window, shattering the glass. He climbed over the jagged teeth jutting from the frame but lost his grip and fell headfirst to the ground. The snap of his neck echoed in the still night. His socks and underpants were on fire. His white vest was blackened, falling apart, shedding cinders as it smoldered. Joanne's screams became howls of agony, then moans of resignation. She disappeared from view.

Kim heard a sloshing sound and turned. Kara was soaking her hands in the remaining gasoline.

"What're you doing?"

"They'll never believe us, Kim. We have no money, no property. We're bad kids. Orphans. I'm doing this for us."

"No, you can't. Stop it." Kim moved to grab the gas can out of her hand. Kara backed away from her, holding her hand up, palm out.

"Please, Kim. Let me do this. I can say it was self-defense—"

"It was self-defense."

"Please listen. I'll say I was defending myself. Look at my face, at my body." Kara lifted her shirt and Kim winced. Lumps, welts and bruises covered her abdomen. Her features appeared deformed after Bill's vicious beating. "He nearly killed me, Kim. Please, just let me do this. You have a better chance of making a success for yourself. You can share it with me. But you are not going to prison. You're smarter than me. You can be successful for both of us."

"I'm not smarter—"

"Kim, *listen*. They are going to crucify you if you tell them you burned a God-fearing country boy and his loyal psycho wife, no matter what he did to me. Don't you understand?"

EIGHTY-FOUR

KIM ARRIVED HOME, RAGE THREATENING TO DISMANTLE her serenity. Her lower lip quivered and her eyes watered with the sheer force of it. Fury, black and irresistible, punctured her dignified calm, cracking the wall she'd built around herself.

Did Norman think he wouldn't be punished? Did he—?

Then she saw the police cars further along Main Street. Some were cruisers, others unmarked sedans. She counted six vehicles. Kim wasn't surprised, and she would have to get rid of the boy, but there was so much to do. Norman was taking up a lot of space in her thoughts, far more than he deserved. He had betrayed her trust, and for that—

There was another car parked near Loomis Memorial. Kim recognized the Ford Taurus instantly. It belonged to Brooke Draper.

Kim exited the car and dropped to her haunches as a woman emerged from the funeral home. She peered through the glass, watched Brooke get into the Taurus and drive off.

Now what would Brooke want with Norman? Why was she visiting her husband at his workplace?

Kim made some peppermint tea but it didn't restore her calm as she'd hoped. Her mind felt lopsided, see-sawing chaotically, throwing her off balance and allowing paranoia to take hold. How was she going to convince Norman not to talk to the police? She was sick of tiptoeing around the issue. She had to make him see sense. Kim would not be a prisoner to fear. She didn't want to hurt him, but he had to learn a lesson. He had to understand who was in charge.

Her cell vibrated on the table and she answered it.

"Hello, Ray," she said.

"Are you all right?"

"What do you mean?"

"You sound a little…*off.*"

"What do you want, Ray?"

"I want you to fulfill your contract with me, Kim, that's what I want."

"I have a male, young like the last one—"

"Not yet. I told you, Kim. Adult female. Just keep him fresh for now."

"Ray, it's available *right now*, do you hear me?"

"I hear you but I have an urgent case and it's not what I require at the moment. We've discussed this. Are you sure you're okay?"

"Don't concern yourself with my wellbeing, Ray. I'll fill the order."

Kim opened a deep drawer, the one where she stored large kitchen utensils, and extracted a wooden rolling pin.

Norman would be home soon. Kim looked forward to it. There could be no doubt about who was in control.

***

Two hours later, Norman unlocked the front door and tossed his keys into the bowl on the narrow hallway table, another antique Kim had picked up for a 'bargain'.

In the great room, he called for her. "Kim? Are you home?"

He didn't hear the soft whisper of her rubber-soled tennis shoes as she crept up behind him.

An explosion went off inside his head.

At first, everything was white. Then black.

EIGHTY-FIVE

MY SON IS MISSING. THE THOUGHT HAD OCCURRED TO HIM several times that day, but when he saw the police cars it gained weight, added layers of reality, of *thereness*, amplifying the peculiar sense that this was happening to someone else. He held Lillian close, and there must have been at least a dozen pairs of eyes on him. Some police officers were in uniform, others in civilian clothes.

A woman, late thirties, wearing a navy suit, approached him and he held up a hand to ward her off. He was worried Lillian would fall down if she didn't sit. He guided her to the couch, asked her if she wanted a drink. She shook her head.

The woman was back. "Sir?"

Jim turned from his wife, from the awful shell-shocked expression on her pale face, away from her wet, red-rimmed eyes.

"I'm Detective Sergeant Gwen Rohm, Major Crimes Unit. I need to ask you some questions. Time is important in these matters, sir."

Jim glanced at Lillian. She was looking around at all these strangers in her home, standing around as though they were attending an exhibition, fascinated by the artwork on display.

"It's crowded in here," Jim said, and Detective Rohm ordered everyone out, except a stringy young man with a thin face and untidy brown curls, wearing a suit that was a size too big for him. He sat uncomfortably on the couch opposite Jim. Probably Rohm's partner, although he looked more like an app developer than a detective.

The uniforms shuffled into the hall and Rohm closed the door behind them. She sat and said, "When did you last see your son, Mr. Bayliss?"

Was this the same question she had asked Lena Fairbanks when her son had gone missing? The police had stopped calling on Lena after a while. It was only a matter of time before they stopped coming to his house.

Jim explained how he believed that Corey had left the house and gone in search of Evan Fairbanks.

"In the middle of the night?" Rohm said.

"He was obsessed. His friend was missing and he believed he was still out there." Jim told her about their search of Hubbard Park, that he'd only done it to make Corey feel better. How he had thought it had worked, but he'd been wrong, that Corey had become broody in the past few days and Jim had considered seeking the help of a therapist. "I didn't get the chance to see if he'd agree to it," he said.

Rohm looked at her hands.

Jim was startled by Lillian's voice beside him, hoarse and raw. "Will you find my son? Please find him and bring him home to us."

The young man leaned forward. "We can't promise anything," he said. It was the correct response, just not the most sensitive one.

"We'll do our best," Rohm said quickly.

The living-room door opened and a rotund man in his fifties entered. The two detectives stood. He ignored them and went directly to Jim Bayliss, offering his hand. Jim shook it.

"I'm Detective Lieutenant Ray Porter. I'm sorry for your situation, Mr. Bayliss, but I promise you, we're here to help."

Rohm looked at her hands again, her mouth forming a grimace.

EIGHTY-SIX

THE PAIN IN NORMAN'S HEAD JOLTED HIM AWAKE. BLACK dots danced across his vision. He groaned, on the verge of passing out again. He became aware of his perilous situation in installments. First, the cable ties binding his wrists to the arms of a dining chair. Second, his ankles strapped to the chair's legs. And, finally, his nakedness. It was worse than being held prisoner in his own house. If he'd at least been wearing underpants, the intensity of his humiliation would have been manageable. But he hadn't got a stitch on. He fought the waves of nausea rolling in his gut as he averted his gaze from his bare flesh.

He lifted his head as high as he dared. His neck was stiff and hot fingers of pain tickled the center of his brain. On the table before him, mash potato and peas steamed.

Kim sat at the other end of the table, eating dinner, a steaming gravy boat next to her plate, staring at him the way a spouse will when they believe themselves to be morally superior.

"Your dinner is getting cold, Norman…eat."

How was he supposed to eat when his hands were tied? And there was no knife or fork for him to use.

"You don't get gravy tonight, Norman. You don't get pork chops either. Gravy and pork chops are for people who behave. For those who mind their business, Norman. Who don't go snooping into other people's shit." It was the curse word that scared him. Kim didn't use foul language, and *never* at the dinner table. He could be in serious danger.

"This is how the world ends, Norman—when people let their consciences overrule common sense. All I did was adapt to our personal economic difficulties, used my American-made initiative to earn us a substantial living. You think the world cares about us, Norman? Don't you get it, Norman? We're on our own."

She was saying his name a lot, and that meant she was close to losing control. Norman's lower lip trembled. He was desperate to pull on it, to stop her seeing him like this, helpless and afraid. His hands twitched. Oh, how he needed to stop the tremor in his lip.

"In case you missed it, Norman, you're being punished for betraying my trust."

"Kim," he said, his voice thick, "I need my clothes. It's cold."

"Eat your peas, Norman."

"Please, Kim, let—"

"*EAT YOUR FUCKING PEAS!*" Kim stood. The large carving knife in her hand gleamed dull amber from the wall-mounted lights turned low.

Norman lowered his head to the plate and sucked the peas into his mouth. He needed to be careful. If the tiny green balls went down the wrong way, he could suffocate, and he didn't trust Kim to administer the Heimlich maneuver. He hoovered one pea at a time, glancing at Kim, relieved she was sinking back into her seat, though slowly.

"The worst thing is," she said, "I actually *do* love you, Norman. I'm doing this for you. For your own good."

***

And she was. Because if she couldn't be sure Norman wouldn't talk to the police, she was going to take Kara's advice and kill him. He didn't know how lucky he was. He should be thanking her. She ached to ask him why Brooke had been visiting him at Loomis Memorial, but she was saving that little slut for another day. She'd ask *her* why. Up close.

And she *did* love Norman. There were many reasons she had devoted her life to him. Norman didn't know what Facebook or Tinder or Twitter were. He didn't moisturize. He kept his problems to himself. He didn't hover in front of a mirror. He didn't put Brylcreem in his hair and spike it. He didn't care about celebrity or homemaking. He didn't understand Bluetooth. The internet was a mystery he had no desire to investigate. He didn't care about all the things *she* cared about. Kim Loomis had no need to share her obsessions with anyone. He was the last of a dying breed, a real man who planted small squares of paper over his shaving cuts. Norman was *rare*. And he *could* be brave, she knew. But while they might have been admirable qualities, if Norman decided to dust off his courage and test drive it by going to the police, it was all over.

But surely he must know she'd take him down with her.

What if that didn't matter to him? What if he had negotiated his way past caring about the consequences?

"Eat your mash, Norman," she said. "There's no butter in it. Bad husbands don't get butter…or gravy. Eat."

***

Norman looked at Kim, focused on her face. He had feared his wife before, but now he was terrified. The mask she usually wore of wholesome goodness had slipped, and Norman was staring at a monster. She was dangerous, homicidal, probably wondering if she couldn't save herself a lot of trouble by killing him already.

And so he complied because he wanted to live. To die, with no clothes on, tied to a chair, was unthinkable. The humiliation of being forced to feed like an animal was bad enough, but the shame of being naked was worse. He might still be able to do some good, to atone for his crimes. Perhaps even put an end to Kim's murder spree. How many people had she dissected in the basement? How many children had she butchered, removing their organs and selling them to Ray Porter? Given the right opportunity, Norman would see to it that Ray Porter ended his days in a cold cell.

He pressed his face into the lukewarm mash potato, biting off chunks and sucking them into his mouth.

Kim was speaking, and Norman realized he had underestimated her by a huge margin.

"I'm going to cut you free, Norman. We are going to continue as normal. I'm going to chair meetings of the Homemakers Association of Vermont, which, due to interesting circumstances, has been reduced to three members, including me. You, Norman, are going to be on your best behavior. I mean, you're going to be the attentive, respectful husband in company I know you're capable of being…*Respectful*, Norman. Remember that word. It's a perfectly good word…on the other hand, if you give me any trouble, I will abort our child—*your* son or daughter."

She had him.

Spuds—butterless—fell from his chin as he stared, mouth wide.

"You wouldn't," Norman said.

Kim smiled. "You *know* I would. I am giving you my personal guarantee, *sweetheart*, that I will leave for an abortion clinic if I even suspect you might go to the police. This is my solemn promise, Norman. Bet against it and see who wins."

He was afraid of her, mad at her, repulsed by her, and yet she wasn't ruling out the possibility of winning him over again. The enormity of her self-belief astounded him.

She put her knife and fork on her empty plate, the finest Noritake bone china.

"Dinner's finished," she said, the newfound pertness in her voice sudden, startling. She was the perfect homemaker again. Not the murderess that had extracted obedience from him in cold, calm, icy tones.

And Norman *would* obey, or she'd destroy his unborn child. She had meant it.

Kim walked toward him, knife at her side.

"Oh, don't worry. I'm not going to hurt you. I *love* you, Norman."

He *had* loved her, too. Tears welled in his eyes as he remembered those early days of falling in love with Kim, when every day had felt like a gift, and the world was right side up. He hated cheese-dipped phrases like *head over heels* and *floating on air* and *love conquers all* and *we are soulmates* and *our love is special* …but yes, all of those.

Tears streamed down his face, tears of horror and dismay: he *still* loved Kim.

EIGHTY-SEVEN

THE THOUGHT HAD TAKEN ROOT IN HER MIND AND GROWN too big to ignore: Lena Fairbanks had kidnapped Corey.

Lillian Bayliss gulped her fourth shot of whiskey and rocked back and forth on the edge of the sofa. She had turned the lights off when Jim had gone to bed, as though unwilling to spotlight her loss, to illuminate the empty space Corey had once occupied—the armchair he sat on to watch his shows, his PlayStation by the TV. It hurt her just to see those things, Corey's things.

After the police had left, the full weight of her loss had broken through her shock. The amputation had felt real. A part of her was gone, probably forever. She had screamed, pulling her hair and collapsing on the floor. Jim had comforted her. He had gotten on his knees and caressed her hair. She had been sorry she'd lost control, because then Jim had panicked too. Whenever she was troubled, Jim was troubled. When she was sad, Jim was sad. They hadn't been able to look directly at one another, each sensing the depth of despair they knew was lying in wait, a clear window on how much their lives had changed.

But still she had screamed until her voice was nothing more than a hitching moan. And then a strange calm had enveloped her, as though all her valves had blown, all the hysteria exhausted.

She poured herself another shot and downed it. Lena had come to her house, accusing her of abducting Evan. What if she really believed that and she was seeking revenge? What if Lena had Corey locked away somewhere? It didn't seem far-fetched. Every scenario, every possibility, however baseless and wild, was viable. When a loved one was missing, you didn't' rule out anything. The absurd lost its luster, and the mind opened itself to a million valid possibilities.

Lena was past caring about life, so why should she care what happened to Corey? Had she kidnapped him to teach her a lesson? Lillian was going to ask Lena that very question.

She put the tumbler on the coffee table and left the house, not looking for her shoes. She didn't care. Speaking to Lena was urgent; it couldn't wait for her to find footwear.

The night was blanched by the moon, but the road ahead was black.

Her lips moved, softly singing "Twinkle, Twinkle, Little Star." It had been Corey's favorite lullaby when he was small. "…how I wonder what you are. Up above the world so high, like a diamond in the sky…"

EIGHTY-EIGHT

JIM WAS AWAKE. SLEEP WAS SOMETHING OTHER PEOPLE DID, and it would be that way for a long time. He lay in bed, resting his tired, sore body. Adrenaline had surged in his muscles until it felt like he had suffered an all-over cramp. He knew he shouldn't leave Lillian alone in the living room, and planned to get up soon, go to her, put his arm around her waist and tell her it was going to be all right. But the rational part of his mind was working overtime, the maddening voice of reason that told him the nightmare was fresh and would ripen soon, get soft with rot, begin to smell and...

He clapped his hands to his face, applying pressure to his head, as though in an effort to drive out the horrifying images crafted by his mind's own cruel hand. His son would have had time to be scared, to realize that his life in danger, for the fear to mushroom into full terror, the kind that locked up your throat and drew water from your eyes. He *felt* it.

Jim had built a bond with Corey during the past few weeks. He had wanted to know who his son was, and he thought he'd made progress. He had promised he would spend more time with Corey, as soon as he had this thing or that thing finished. As soon as he was done with the job at hand, he'd make things right. But it had been easy to take him for granted because he was there. *He was always there.* And then he wasn't.

And you can't make things right when they're gone.

Gone?

He sat up at the sound of the front door closing. Made his way in the dark to the window. Lillian was walking fast down the driveway, turning right down Main Street, past the trees that lined the road.

Jim hurried to the side of the bed, put his pants on, heart high and heavy in his chest.

He slipped into his shoes, leaving the laces untied, and raced downstairs.

EIGHTY-NINE

LENA WAS AFRAID TO SLEEP. EVAN WOULD VISIT HER. HE was getting closer with each nightmare. He was going to reach out and touch her with his cold, withered hands. Even comatose from too much alcohol, he came to her, hand outstretched, the flesh falling in rags off the bone, pointing at her. Accusing her.

Lena wasn't drunk, yet. She'd had only two small measures of vodka. To calm her nerves. Her sober moments were haunted by two people she wished she had loved better: Evan and Travis. She knew the exact moment her life had taken a downhill turn. It was the day Travis had left the house and never returned. There had been no clue, no indication that he would run out on them. But run he had, all the way to Concord, North Carolina, where he'd managed to find employment with the United States Postal Service.

Lena had spent months looking for him, and for an explanation. She had used the last of her money to hire a private investigator, figuring the least she could do was sue him for support. But Travis had been in no mood to explain himself. She had approached him on McCachern Boulevard after his shift had ended, and Travis had literally fled from her, sprinting to his car, driving like a maniac to get away.

Her hired gumshoe had told her what turned out to be the most disturbing piece of information—Travis wasn't seeing another woman. The PI had been adamant. Which meant Travis had left Lena *because* of Lena and not for someone else.

She never got to sue Travis for child support. That day, he had quit his job and North Carolina, and she'd had no money left to find out where he had gone.

She had spent months combing her memories for any hint that Travis had been unhappy, and found none. He had been loving, had treated her well, taken care of her. Travis was a gentleman. He had left their home on Main Street, kissed her as he always did on the cheek, said he loved her and would be back soon. Then he was gone for good.

There were no answers, but Lena's mind had a way of formulating ones she didn't want to hear. Travis had realized he was too good for her and walked out on her to live a great life. Or he'd gotten tired of her, or her looks were fading, or he just couldn't stand her anymore. It was all noise. Her mind didn't even have the decency to feed her these thoughts in the early hours, instead choosing to bombard her at two in the afternoon.

Every afternoon.

Alcohol helped dull the answers she'd stopped asking for. But they came, anyway.

Travis hadn't wanted children but Lena had forgotten to take her pill one too many times and fallen pregnant. She'd thought Travis had come around to the idea of having kids. He'd seemed happy when she had announced they were pregnant. He had been a good father, too.

Her mind was always ready with an explanation—maybe she was so superficial that she couldn't dig beneath the surface and see people for who they really are.

Lena felt as though she had been tricked. But perhaps Travis had felt the same way.

Her resentment toward Evan had rankled to the point that she had admitted she hated her son. Hated his existence, the *fact* of him. Yes, it was pathetic and awful to build your life around a man, to stake your emotional health on his presence in your life. She *knew* this, and yet it hadn't changed the way she'd felt in the slightest. Her hatred of Evan had real venom, and she had used alcohol to prevent the poison from spreading. Sober, she had been inclined to backhand him. Drunk, she'd fought the violence welling up in her. So she drank, for Evan's sake. *For his own good.*

Now, with all the lights on, afraid of her dreams, of the dark, reduced to a child again, Lena wished she had been kinder. It had the texture of a selfish wish—if she had been nicer to Evan when he was here then maybe he wouldn't haunt her sleep. It wasn't Evan's fault he had been born. She didn't absolve him of blame, though. He had been a walking reminder of her loss, of what could have been. If Evan hadn't kicked and screamed his way into the world, Travis would still be here, starting the day by telling her he loved her, returning home later in the day with warm croissants and coffee…

There was a knock on the door, at first hesitant, then persistent.

She staggered to her feet, more intoxicated than she'd thought. She held onto the La-Z-Boy for support and brushed aside the yellowed curtain.

"Lena Fairbanks, you get your ass out here."

What in God's name?

Lena recognized Lillian Bayliss but not the situation. Her shoeless neighbor's presence at her home was a sign that the woman was in danger. Maybe Jim had beaten her. Chased her from their house, finally sick of her superior attitude. The thought fattened into hope, and Lena answered the door.

"Where's my son?"

Lena stared at Lillian, confused.

"Where's my son, you drunk whore?"

The confusion evaporated and Lena tried to slam the door. Lillian caught it with her foot and rushed her, closing her hands around Lena's neck and digging her fingers deep into the soft flesh.

"No! Stop, Lillian. Stop!"

It was a male voice. Lena didn't have time to look for its owner. She stumbled backward, Lillian on top of her. Something was sticking into her back. It had the shape of a vodka bottle.

"Where's my boy?"

The lights dimmed and somewhere in the distance she heard heavy footsteps on the floor. Seconds later she was gasping for air, clutching her throat. Jim Bayliss held his wife in a bear hug. Lillian's hair clung to her face in damp streaks.

***

Jim was appalled. That Evan had had to cross this junk-strewn floor, to inhale the stench, was unbearable, a crime. He had a new understanding of why Evan had often gotten himself into trouble, and felt sorry for him. The woman on the dirty floor, staring up at them wide-eyed and drunk, was responsible for his bad behavior. Evan had never had a chance.

He walked Lillian to the doorstep, a heavy hand on her shuddering shoulders. At the end of the driveway, he scooped her into his arms and carried her home.

She burrowed her face into his neck and wept.

***

Lena watched them leave.

Where's my boy? she'd said.

Her skin crawled and she shivered.

Corey was missing, too.

NINETY

KIM WAS HAVING A RACHAEL RAY DINNER PARTY, EVEN though her personal hero was the ex-convict and lifestyle guru, Martha Stewart. As she positioned the platters and plates on the table in the great room, she wished America's domestic goddess had played to her strengths and avoided becoming involved in insider trading since she clearly wasn't any good at it and had been caught. But Martha had bounced back, and Kim admired her for it. When she was financially secure—she was close—Kim would achieve similar heights.

Brooke and Paige applauded the arrival of the food, sweet sausage and broccoli rabe meatballs, prepared following Rachael Ray's recipe. Kim analyzed the strength of each woman's loud praise: Paige had clapped enthusiastically, with a shrill screech, eyes big. Brooke's effort had been half-hearted, less noisy, obligatory.

It was funny in a pathetic way, Kim mused, how people like Brooke Draper really thought you were stupid. That you didn't know they were trying to emulate and surpass your ambitions, that they were jealous of your—admittedly— moderate success. Kim knew about Brooke's website, *True American Homemaker*, and the people she followed on Instagram. Brooke's heroes were trendier, younger than Martha Stewart. People like Sarah Michelle Geller and Reese

Witherspoon and Shay Mitchell. Brooke was deluded; she thought Kim was oblivious, and that was fine—for now. But Brooke didn't have a fraction of the subscribers to her YouTube channel. The number of Brooke's followers on Twitter and Instagram were paltry compared to Kim's. People had to believe in your message, and Kim believed in hers completely. That was something Brooke didn't understand. You had to be genuine. A real person. Brooke's mistake was thinking she could fake it.

Brooke's heroes were all talented, but what was Brooke's talent? Visiting a married man while he tried to work? *Her* man. Kim didn't see the alleged virtue in patience, but she needed to be patient—*for now*. It was a practical means to discovering what this *younger* woman wanted with *her* husband.

There was more applause as Kim returned to the great room with a fennel-stuffed roast chicken.

"It looks so good," Brooke said. "You're going to hate me, Kim. It's just that I'm going vegan. I've overdosed lately on gluten and dairy. I should've told you."

Kim stared at her in disbelief, the words echoing in her mind, churning the pit of her stomach. *I'm going vegan...*as if it distinguished her from everyone else *going vegan* when in fact it was some fad she'd quit in a few weeks. Brooke wasn't a real vegan; she was doing this to irritate Kim. *I've overdosed on gluten and dairy*, essential foodstuffs she was excluding from her diet because it was a *thing*. And here Brooke was in Kim's great room, announcing proudly that she had OD'd on gluten, a protein Kim knew was harmless to the majority of the population except those suffering from Celiac disease, people forced to forgo gluten for *actual* health reasons and who often had to pay more for gluten-free food. Worst of all, she was chewing on a piece of pumpernickel bread that *contained* gluten as she'd said those words. Those awful, ugly words. *I've overdosed on gluten and dairy*. She wasn't even lactose-intolerant.

I should've told you.

Yes, Kim thought, you should have.

Her smile underwent the facial equivalent of rigor mortis, then loosened and was back to full beam.

"It's no problem at all," she said. "We must respect those who have specific dietary needs. I'll whip something up in the kitchen." Kim had never felt as close to vomiting into her own mouth as she did then. Brooke was a *fake*. And Kim knew more about the fake in her great room than Brooke realized. There was a sliver of nobility in failing at a creative or sporting effort, but to fail as a shrink? How did Brooke Draper leverage herself out of bed in the morning? How was it even *possible* to fail as a shrink?

Kim pondered that question as she tapped up another Rachael Ray recipe on her iPad. Unlike Brooke, Rachael was helpful, providing her with a vegan recipe for pumpkin pie and pumpkin soup. She didn't have the ingredients available for any other dish. Well, what did the woman expect on short notice?

Kim had noticed Paige's discomfort when Brooke had said she was *going vegan*. Paige would never make a fuss; she wouldn't alter the menu. She wondered if her husband had overcome his addiction to internet porn. She'd ask later. Kim didn't want to hand Brooke a juicy morsel of gossip. She wasn't thrown off balance often, but she was surprised by how much she *liked* Paige, despite her tendency to inflate what were really small problems.

This was going to be tough, she thought as she ladled pumpkin soup into a bowl.

***

Norman had been downgraded to a guest bedroom. Kim didn't want to sleep next to a man who had so easily betrayed her. Norman needed to *think* about the situation he had caused. Kim would be ready to receive his thoughts when he was ready to arrange them into some kind of order.

The longer he waited to contact the police, the harder it became to make the move. And he knew he should talk to the police. He couldn't, though. As much as he felt the need to do the right thing, Kim had been sincere in her threat to abort his child. He was beginning to appreciate the complexity of the problem he faced. He hated himself for still being in love with Kim. There must be something seriously wrong in his mind to love a woman responsible for such horrific crimes. How could he love a woman who had perpetrated the most brutal murder of a young boy? And yet he was *still* here, watching a twenty-inch TV set, digesting two Xanax pills.

The local news came on, and Norman sat up. His mouth ran dry and his skin shrank tight. The anchor's words were like miniature ice picks in his pores: *another missing boy*. That was all Norman heard, and it changed everything.

***

"It's delicious!" Paige said, fawning over the food, chewing heartily.

"Thank you, Paige," Kim said. "I'm glad you're enjoying it."

She was always watching, even when she gave the impression her attention was elsewhere. Paige was seeking her approval. Her eyes had brightened when Kim had thanked her. Good. And Kim would feed her need to be liked. After all, Paige was about to give her something *she* really needed. Paige just didn't know it yet. Feeding these two women was the least she could do. Depending on opportunity, it would likely be their last meal. Still, Kim was aware of the potential pitfalls, not least Norman's presence. Yes, she had banished him to a remote corner of the house, but it wasn't far enough. Perhaps tomorrow would be a better day, a day for new opportunities.

Then Brooke cooled the warmth of Paige's praise by asking, "Does anyone know where Megan is?"

Kim didn't hesitate. "I invited her. I left a message on her answering machine." And she had, just before she had prepared dinner, before she'd served Norman a Hungry-Man fried chicken frozen meal. She had suspended his privileges until further notice. Or until Norman quit being a baby about events. Home-cooked would return when Norman learned to behave.

"I've been calling her all day and I get her voicemail," Brooke said.

"She's probably busy," Kim said. "You know how business women are—busy most of the time."

Of course Brooke didn't know how successful business women were, but Kim wasn't going to miss a chance to rub Brooke's nose in her own lack of success.

Brooke said, "How's Norman?"

Oh, you bitch.

"He's fine. Norman is thinking." *Norman is thinking* was a phrase she had borrowed from Norman's foster father, who had said it in such a way as to suggest that Norman was engaging in an exotic and strange act, bordering on snobbish, and would soon snap out of it.

***

Brooke was making an effort—a *supreme* effort—to win friends and followers online. Progress was slow. It was frustrating, especially since she knew she was just as good as, if not better than Kim at homemaking, lifestyle, and fashion. Maybe she was suffering from information bloat. Her mind felt fatter, overloaded.

She was on the internet constantly, looking for new and improved ways to compete. She couldn't understand Kim's popularity. Her videos received thousands of views daily. What galled her most was that Kim appealed to a young audience, even though she worshipped Martha Stewart, who was old, and whose portrait hung above the fireplace in Kim's great room. Maybe it wasn't even a question of age. Maybe Kim and Martha Stewart were perfect examples of talent triumphing over ability. Ability faded, but talent had longevity, which was probably the reason Martha Stewart was still on top.

Maybe Brooke was just one of those people who had to be content with ability.

She spooned the hot pumpkin soup into her mouth and swallowed hard. Kim was even talented in the kitchen. Brooke couldn't ignore the larger truth anymore—Kim Loomis was more attractive than her, sexier, stunning in fact. Her skin was flawless. *Flawless.* She was tall, model material. Brooke wasn't lacking in the looks department, but she was only *sort of* attractive. And *sort of* was never good enough.

Brooke ate her soup and eyeballed the thought clawing its way center stage in her mind: she hated Kim, hated her beautiful face and her toned body that defied all reasonable expectations of how a woman should look, hated her perfect pumpkin soup, hated the ease with which Kim executed *everything.*

It was poisonous, the psychology major in her thought, to view people in this way. It was how obsession began. As a client, what advice would she give herself? That internet silence was required for perhaps a month. That she must focus on her goals, make them clearer.

Except sometimes your own best advice just wasn't good enough because it didn't change how you felt.

She felt isolated, boxed in, trapped. She had sensed the same about Norman. He barely spoke, he didn't need to— his back was against the wall and he wouldn't say why.

The first time she had met him, she knew she'd found a kindred spirit. Earlier, at Loomis Memorial, he had held her hand, his grip firmer than usual. He was responding to her in a different way.

She had watched the way Kim treated him, especially at the fundraiser for the poor Fairbanks kid. He was her man-servant. It was obvious Kim was in charge.

Kim didn't deserve Norman. Brooke didn't deserve Zack either. He'd be happier without her. She would be happier with Norman. She had accepted Kim's invitation only because she'd hoped to see Norman, even if it was just a glimpse. Brooke hadn't come here to be served perfect food by Kim, whose vintage apron had a bright-yellow bow tied on its front and lemons on its ruffles, an apron that had been in the kitchen and yet was still somehow spotless.

Kim continued to bring food, not a hair out of place. When Brooke cooked, she got hot and sweaty and her hair frizzed.

And Norman hadn't made an appearance. He was somewhere in this loveless mansion, *thinking*.

"This is *marvelous*," Paige said, and Brooke sighed inwardly. Poor dumb Paige.

"I'll be taking in new members of the Homemakers Association of Vermont soon," Kim said. "It's best to expand the circle of knowledge."

"That's great," Paige said a little too loudly. "Maybe Diane Battle can interview you again when you really get up and running."

"I was thinking maybe Gayle King could do the interview next time."

Now that *was* belief, Brooke thought, or arrogance; she couldn't decide which.

Paige actually clapped, bounced in her chair, her excitement brimming. A noise escaped her that sounded suspiciously like *squeee*.

Brooke was sick in her heart. She should leave, she knew, but she couldn't, any more than she could turn away from watching a car accident unfold.

"When *we* get up and running, Paige," Kim said. "There is no *I* in homemaking."

Brooke gaped at her, wondering whether she was joking. She *had* to be. But Kim's face didn't betray any hint of humor.

Oh my God, she believes her bullshit. She honest to God believes it.

Maybe that was the secret. You had to believe. Maybe that was Brooke's problem—she didn't believe her own lies. Maybe self-delusion paved the road to success. Maybe.

There is no I *in homemaking.* Not even a sly wink, a glint in her eye, or a subtle upward turn of her lips, her perfect lips.

***

Norman stuffed his clothes into a suitcase and flushed the little pink Xanax pills down the toilet. He left the empty bottle on the sink, a signal to Kim that he was free. All he had to do was escape unnoticed, go to the police, and they could arrest her in time to save his child. He glanced at the TV, at Corey Bayliss's parents, flanked by police officers and FBI agents, pleading for their son's abductor not to harm Corey—he was a good boy; he wanted to be a scientist when he grew up.

One missing kid was unlucky, perhaps even random, an outlier. Two was no accident. Two got noticed. Had Kim killed Corey already? Probably. Kim was a risk-taker but even she had limits. Keeping the boy alive was a risk too far. She wanted organs and she'd take them. She had murdered two children that he was aware of. What if the number was higher? What if she had traveled further, kidnapped more children?

Norman paused, stared at his bulging suitcase. He had no choice but to confess to *his* crimes. There was no justification for what he'd done, in his eyes or those of the law. The only difference between his crime and Kim's was that he had stolen from people who were already dead. Norman had been wrong, but he wasn't a killer. He couldn't imagine the horror Evan Fairbanks had suffered. *And* Kim had organized a fundraiser for the boy she had murdered.

It was difficult to process. Norman didn't crave the limelight the way Kim did. When he confessed, Norman would be the most famous person in Vermont, possibly America, forever tainted by the unspeakable murders committed by his wife. They would say he had conspired with Kim, that he'd known about the abductions. They would condemn him for not turning her in sooner. And because he was a tall, gaunt *mortician*, the press would crucify him. If a man couldn't be trusted to treat the dead with dignity, what must he think of the living? His picture would be plastered on the front page of every newspaper. His remorse would make no difference. Remorse wouldn't cut any ice with the jury that would surely convict him.

The nature of the murders was undeniably horrifying, but so was the prospect of unwanted fame. He had kept his head down and worked hard for most of his life. He hadn't complained or interfered in other people's business. And now he would be fed to the lions—the public. And what would happen to his unborn child? They would take his baby into the system, the same foster-care maze that he'd found his way out of, in the end.

He lost the strength in his legs and sat on the end of the bed.

He thought about the torment Jim and Lillian Bayliss were going through second by second. And for the first time in his adult life, he cried quietly. The Baylisses' pain was beyond cruel. He couldn't help feeling responsible, for contributing in some way, however small, to Corey's death.

Was this delayed shock? Whatever the case, Norman felt it wasn't too late to do the right thing. There could be no forgiveness. He didn't deserve it from anyone, least of all himself. He had to suffer, he knew that now.

Sadness overcame him in the form of *nostalgia*, a reminder of what was no longer available. His marriage to Kim hadn't been all bad. They'd had good times, they had laughed. Thousands of moments he wouldn't trade for freedom passed through his mind—Kim touching his hand across a table at a restaurant, smiling at him, *seeing* him. Caressing his face before he went to sleep at night; the *love* in her touch. The many times they had stayed up into the early hours discussing their misadventures as orphans; the game they had invented called My Foster Family is Worse Than Yours. The cakes she had baked for him; how she had been poised for his reaction, excited to discover whether he liked the consistency and the taste and whether they were too sugary. Not sweet, *sugary*. The fact that she had been interested in his opinion. The way she'd leant toward him, anticipating his answer to whatever question she'd asked, eyes wide, giving him her full attention.

His mind went dark. Kim was standing in the basement, slapping him in the face.

He was strapped into a chair, naked.

He was eating his peas.

He had mash potato on his nose.

He had promised her he'd behave.

He was sorry.

***

Paige excused herself from the table and went to the bathroom. Kim's instincts were sharp, highly attuned to Brooke's changing perception of her. Brooke wasn't buying into Kim anymore, that much she could see. That was all right. Kim didn't need her approval; she just had to appeal to Brooke's self-importance to slot the final piece of her plan into place. It was visible in every tweet, in her Facebook posts and on her Instagram—all of which Kim had read and analyzed. Brooke was one of those people who, in her pursuit of happiness, had neglected to add several ingredients that made her ideal state possible—she had no self-respect.

Kim had been embarrassed for her when Brooke had tried and failed to get Reese Witherspoon to follow her on Twitter. Instead of letting it go, Brooke, reeking of desperation, had asked again and again, openly. And she had been denied with the absence of a reply from the star. Self-respect was essential to achieving happiness. So was being comfortable with the fact that she wasn't extraordinary. That was her main problem: Brooke was ordinary and couldn't cope with it; she felt she was entitled to *more*. Most people were ordinary and led good, happy lives, but Brooke would always be unhappy. Because of *more*.

The countless hours Kim had spent on the internet getting to know Brooke had been a worthwhile investment, for she had discovered something else that had amused her—Brooke hated ambition in other women. It was sad, somehow, *so* sad that, in person, Brooke didn't reveal much about herself. She was sitting at Kim's dining table fermenting an air of mystery when every sentence and photograph she had published to her social media accounts told anyone interested enough to look exactly who she was. Tragic, Kim thought, *so* sad.

"You know," Kim said, "there's more to homemaking than scrubbing floors."

"Yeah?" Brooke produced a smile that belonged on a rubber Halloween mask.

"It's simple, really. It's about *feeling* good. That's all it is, but it's important. It's about dressing well, enjoying your achievements. By the way, small successes are *still* successes. I remember my first attempt at making banana bread and using Norman as a guinea pig. He only grimaced, but he did *not* vomit. I was so proud. The second attempt was a big improvement. It's about getting better, Brooke. Feeling good and getting better. Taking pride in your appearance—"

"I take pride in my appearance."

Of course she did. She wore too much makeup because she had watched too many YouTube videos of young women who thought it acceptable to paint themselves up like sex dolls.

"Oh, I know. You really do look great," Kim lied, and happily, too.

"What are you saying?"

"That it's okay *not* to wear sweatpants while vacuuming. I sometimes wear my Steigers when I get the Dyson out. Norman likes to watch me rolling it across the floor. I think it arouses him." Kim fixed her gaze on Brooke, searching for a reaction. But Brooke dropped her head, stared at her empty plate.

Was that out of shame or embarrassment? Kim hoped it was both.

Paige returned to the great room, Kim's copy of *InStyle* magazine in her hand. Nicole Kidman was on the cover, as well as a quote from the actress: "Good love can heal so many things." Yes, Kim thought, wise words, but bad love can scar many good things.

The atmosphere in her home had turned, like milk that had been left out too long and spoiled.

"Can I borrow this?" Paige asked, "I mean, if you're finished with it. I'll bring it right back."

"Sure you can," Kim said. Of course she'd bring it right back.

Brooke made her excuses and left, thanking Kim for the *wonderful* dinner.

She needs a role, Kim thought as she stood on the doorstep, waving, smiling. *And I might just have the ticket.*

"I have to go, too," Paige said, and Kim realized that Paige would stay indefinitely if she could. She wasn't in a hurry to leave. "I have to check on the kids."

"You're welcome anytime, you know that Paige."

"I do. Thanks, Kim."

"For what?"

"For being *you*."

Oh God, Kim thought, and bile rose in her chest. *For being* you.

"How's Isaac?"

"Oh, he's fine," Paige said. "He learned his lesson. I think he has more respect for me now. It's not easy being married to a pornography addict."

"I'm sure it must be difficult."

"It is, but you know what? A little understanding goes a long way. I'm learning something, too. Isaac is close to being cured. Addiction is so *awful*, Kim."

"Yes, but he's back on the right path."

"We do need to help our husbands *find* the right path, don't we, Kim?"

Kim nodded, and Paige thanked her for the magazine—again. She honked as she pulled onto Main and Kim waved, went into the kitchen and began peeling and chopping carrots into sticks.

She carried the carrot sticks upstairs, balancing the knife on the plate. Norman sometimes cut his food into smaller pieces. Kim didn't understand why, but no one was perfect.

The right path. Norman was on punishment, but Kim was worried he was malnourished. She wasn't going to feed him meat yet. A generous slab of protein awaited him when he found the right path.

She turned the handle and elbowed the door open.

"Norman, I brought you a little snack."

Norman was wheeling a suitcase toward the door. He stopped dead, mouth wide, staring at her. The fear in his eyes was unmistakable. She could read him like an open book; he hadn't expected her to be kind and bring him a snack.

"Norman, where are you going?"

"I have to leave. The Bayliss kid…what did you do, Kim? Can't you see what you're doing is wrong?"

Kim picked up the knife from the plate, drew back, and launched the plate at Norman. He ducked, and it smashed against the wall behind him, scattering carrot sticks all over the floor.

Norman started toward her.

Kim lifted her dress and held the knife to her stomach, the blade slick with carrot juice.

"Don't come any closer or I'll cut your child out of me."

Norman paused. Took another step forward.

Kim pressed the knife into her gut.

"I'm warning you, Norman."

She slid the knife in a horizontal line over the area above her belly button. Norman stared, dumbstruck, as blood trickled down her abdomen and onto her underwear.

"You're going to do as I say," she said. "Follow me to our bedroom. Any funny business, you'll never be a father. Do you hear me, Norman?"

He seemed hypnotized.

"Do you hear me, Norman?"

He blinked and met her gaze. "Yes."

Kim backed down the hallway. Norman followed. His reflexes were intact, but if he lunged at her she was confident she could react in time.

In the bedroom, she reached behind her, hand probing the drawer in the bedside table.

Then she brought the revolver from behind her back and pointed it at Norman's head.

"I'll kill you if you don't do what I say. I won't like it, but I swear I'll do it."

She dropped the knife on the floor and reached behind her again, this time throwing a blister pack at his feet.

"Pick it up."

Norman stooped, read the label. Sleeping pills. He saw himself strapped to a chair, naked.

"Pop two of them. Do it, Norman."

He squeezed two pills from the pack, put them in his mouth, and dry swallowed.

"Open wide, Norman. Lift your tongue. Good. Now get on the chaise."

Slowly, hands raised, he lay down on the chaise longue. Kim sat on the bed. Norman stared at the gun, seemingly mesmerized by the dark hollow of its barrel. Kim held it steady.

"You, of all the people in the world, should understand, Norman. You're an orphan, too. I spent half my life wondering where the next roof over my head was coming from. You know what it's like to be at the mercy of the system, to bow your head for other people and let them know how grateful you are for taking you in because no one else wants you. It made an impression on me, Norman. Remember those times, when you're taking food from someone else's fridge and it feels like you're stealing? Sure you do. Even though you know your foster family is getting paid by the state to feed you, it still feels like stealing. Do you know how scared I was all those years? It left its mark on me. It's worse than simple fear, though, isn't it? It's terror. The way you mind your manners, the way you tip-toe around, the way you stay in your room because you don't want to be in anyone's way. Not knowing if this is your last day with shelter, food, and warmth. You, Norman, know how it was, the awkwardness of it all. Saying thank you a million times a day, like a good orphan. But it was seldom ever *No, thank you*, was it? You were so intent on people liking you, and it was bad manners to say no. No money, no property equals no prospects. America, Norman. I'm telling you this because I want you to understand the terror I felt for years. What it does to a person when they're in constant fear of being homeless."

Norman was drowsy. The pills were pulling him into artificial sleep.

"It wasn't easy for me, either," he said.

"You're a man, Norman. It's *always* easier for you."

"What if it isn't?"

"What do you mean?"

"We're all human. Do you think I feel fear less than you? Hurt less than you?"

Kim felt caustic tears welling in her eyes.

"Confess, Kim. Those boys…it wasn't supposed to be this way."

"Most of all, I want you to know something, Norman. Whatever happens, just know that I am not lying when I say this—I love you. There were occasions when I could've conducted myself better, done things differently. But I never stopped loving you. Sounds cheesy, yes, but it *is* true, Norman. I love you. I know what other people say about us. They don't think you're good enough for me. They say a woman like me has no business loving a man like you. An outcast, the weird outsider. But I'll see those fuckers in hell, make no mistake on that score. Even though I've seen bad times, I've never begged another human being for anything. I'm *begging* you now, Norman, please reconsider. *Please.* Let's work this out."

Norman dried the wetness in his eyes with a long index finger. "Kim, I can't. I wish it didn't trouble me as much as it does. I have to go to the police…I can't live with it. They were children, Kim. How could you do it?"

"Norman, those kids helped a lot of other kids live. Do you know how many lives they saved by donating their organs?"

"That's the problem, Kim, don't you see it? You donated their organs *for* them, against their will."

"I'm calling it a stalemate for the moment, Norman, but we'll talk later. Stand."

He stood, shakily. His head drooped.

"Downstairs, to the kitchen."

They made their way downstairs and Kim instructed Norman to wheel the chair out of the pantry at the rear of the kitchen, the one she used for the high shelves.

Norman brought the chair to the kitchen table and sat. His eyes were heavy and rolled in his head as he tried to look at her.

"It's time to rest, Norman. You'll feel better about things later."

He looked at her as if he doubted it. And he was right, too.

***

Norman woke in the pantry, his wrists and legs cable-tied to the chair. He looked down, and was relieved to find he wasn't naked. He rocked the chair forward but it wouldn't move. He twisted sideways, trying to see the wheels. Wooden wedges normally used to keep doors open had been placed underneath.

He called for Kim until he was hoarse from screaming her name. But she didn't answer him. She had left him here to starve, to die among the spices and dried goods.

NINETY-ONE

IN A FIT OF ANGER, LENA HAD ALMOST CALLED THE POLICE to come and arrest Lillian Bayliss for barging into her home and making a respectable effort of strangling her. But she didn't want a visit from the police. They hadn't been a welcome presence when they were questioning her about Evan's disappearance and the next time the police came to her door, they would be taking her in. After what she had done, talking to cops was too risky. She was guilty, and if she believed the news, the FBI were involved and *fully committed* to tracking down the person responsible for kidnapping Evan Fairbanks and Corey Bayliss. The feds were *pursuing several leads*. It was a matter of when, not if, they came for her.

She had watched the news conference. Jim had had to hold his wife up, literally. Lillian had been distraught. Still, Lena doubted Lillian was having the same kind of nightmares she had to kick, scream, and claw her way out of every night. Lillian didn't have her rotting son chasing her along a never-ending hospital corridor, pleading for just *one hug*. Lillian didn't feel the bony tips of her son's fingers touching her hair as she ran. Lillian hadn't neglected her son.

Lena couldn't outrun Evan. Every night he got closer, shedding dark flesh from his bones, and when at last he wasn't weighed down by muscle and skin, he'd catch her, all the lifeless flesh left in his wake along the endless corridor.

The expression she had seen on Jim Bayliss's face as he surveyed the mess that was her living room haunted her. Lena was ashamed. And it was shame that prompted her to start a cleanup. She'd filled five Hefty trash bags with empty bottles and food packaging, wondering if Pete Dewsbury would forgive her for the stains on the floor and the unpaid rent. He had been good to her. He wasn't the complaining type. If something needed fixing, he got on with the job. Broken washing machine? *No problem, I'll get you a new one.* That was Pete. Lena was surprised he hadn't started eviction proceedings. She wouldn't blame him if he did. She had nine hundred and sixty dollars remaining in her wallet. It wouldn't compensate Pete, but it might take the sting out of his losses a little.

The walnut coffee table was actually a nice one, now that she had cleared the junk off it and wiped it with a cloth. In the hall, she rummaged in Evan's book bag and took a pen and a notepad back to the living room. She sat on the La-Z-Boy and began to write. Her note finished, she ripped the sheet from the pad and taped it to her chest.

She brought her last bottle of premium vodka from the kitchen and lined up three shot glasses. Her hands weren't shaking yet, and the next phase of her life demanded a steady hand.

She drank for three hours and was grateful for the absence of bad thoughts and disturbing images.

That's what it'll be like. No more nightmares.

She unlocked the front door, went upstairs to the bathroom, and removed the belt from the bathrobe hanging on the door. Concentrating hard, she tied it around the banister, then her neck. She climbed over the banister and let her body fall.

The breath was ripped from her and her eyes bulged. The belt tightened. It was supposed to be quicker than this.

She heard a rustling sound beneath her. Evan was looking inside his book bag.

Where's my notepad?

He was waiting for her. Lena had changed her mind. She didn't want to be with Evan in death. She fumbled for the balusters behind her but her hand flew to the noose squeezing her neck. She thrashed and kicked at the empty air, the way she had in her nightmares.

Mom, where's my notepad? You can't touch my stuff. I'll get in trouble if my notepad is lost.

Frantic, she yanked at the belt, swayed from side to side, a tragic human pendulum.

WHERE'S MY NOTEPAD?

Lena screamed. There was no sound. Evan floated in front of her face, the skin peeling from his nose. His eyeless sockets were tunnels into eternity.

His dead face remained as the dark closed around her, hovering, a wheeze on its breath. Was it Evan? Had it ever been Evan? Had her mind turned against her so completely?

Yes, it is Evan. I've been waiting a long time.

NINETY-TWO

THE AUTHORITIES WERE DRAGGING THE WINOOSKI RIVER for Corey's body. Rohm had called to inform Jim of the operation, although she had been more sensitive in her phrasing. But what other reason was there for dragging a river? A search party made up of volunteers and police officers were combing Montpelier's largest wooded area, Hubbard Park. Jim wanted to join the search, to help in any way he could. But Lillian wasn't coping well.

He'd called in Murray Cummings, the family doctor, and he had prescribed her something to help her relax. The bedside cabinet was cluttered with pill bottles and Lillian was resting at last. Jim had sat in a chair against the wall all night, watching her sleep. If she woke, he wanted to be there to reassure her. He couldn't go to bed; it felt wrong to sleep when your son was missing. It felt wrong to eat, to live.

The press conference had been the most draining experience of his life, and the washed-out feeling lingered. Sitting before the media, their cameras clicking and flashing had made it real. *This is happening*. It was probably the reason Lillian had lost control.

Early-morning light filtered through the drapes and Jim asked God, the Universe, and anyone else who would listen to keep his son safe. In his mind, he was having a conversation with Corey. They were discussing science,

Corey's favorite subject. Corey was eating breakfast and Jim was reading the newspaper, which in reality lay folded and unread on the kitchen table because there was something wrong with reading a newspaper when your son was missing.

Jim sipped his orange juice and felt as though he was experiencing what Corey had described as time dilation. "Dad, if you were traveling at light speed, time wouldn't slow down for *you*. You'd perceive time ticking away as normal. But you'd observe time slowing for all other objects you're moving relative to." Jim had stared at him, proud and baffled. "Where did you learn that? At school?"

"No, some books I'm reading."

"Well, good…uh…good, Cor." Because he hadn't known what to say. His son was smarter than he had been at twelve. And Jim was grateful for it, secretly glad that Corey was interested in science, because jobs for someone with a degree in the humanities didn't pay well. But he'd kept it to himself, hadn't wanted to sound like a parent.

"What other interesting facts are rattling around that brain of yours?" he'd asked.

"The DNA in every nucleus in your body is six feet long."

For the first time since Corey had gone missing, Jim managed to smile.

Then the doorbell rang, and he opened his eyes.

Lillian stirred. He tiptoed out of the bedroom. Rachel Holmes was standing on the doorstep, holding a foil-covered casserole dish.

"Good morning, Mr. Bayliss. My mom wanted you to have this."

Rachel's parents were parked on the road. They waved at him. Jim returned the gesture, though it was a feeble effort, and wondered why people kept their distance when something terrible happened, why they didn't want to talk to you.

"Thanks, Rachel," he said. "It's very kind of you."

"Mr. Bayliss, I haven't given up hope that Corey will come home."

He was alarmed by the sudden sting of tears in his eyes. He took a deep breath and managed to smile.

"I just came by because he was good to me."

Jim was on the verge of losing control; if he said anything it would tip him over the edge. He nodded and looked at the ground instead, looking up only when she walked back down the driveway. Then the media arrived. The news vans parked along Main Street, satellite dishes pointing at the sky. Jim shut the door and locked it.

NINETY-THREE

KIM DIDN'T USE THE LAPTOP OFTEN BUT SHE NEEDED IT now. She connected to a VPN, opened the Tor browser, and began her trek through the dark web. She had been here before, even meeting one of her neighbors, a surprise for both of them. A dozen clicks on as many websites later and she was bored. But she persevered; she had no choice. Or at least the choice she did have carried many risks; the consequences could be severe.

She entered a website, read as fast as her eyes could move across the screen, and clicked on a link. It redirected her to a sparse webpage—nothing but an email address. She memorized it and created a new Gmail account under a false name. She had already purchased a burner phone for just such an eventuality, and typed in the number at the end of the email.

She closed the lid and stared at the laptop for a moment, then walked to the great room and looked out the window, eager for the arrival of her visitor.

Norman had stopped shouting. Although the pantry was well insulated, she had heard a faint commotion coming from the rear of the kitchen in the initial stages of his confinement. But it wasn't loud enough to alert anyone to his captivity. He was probably sleeping now. If only he knew how much it broke her heart to treat him this way. Maybe he wouldn't think she was capable of heartbreak, but warm blood coursed through her veins just as it did in his. She could have left him in the kitchen overnight and wheeled him to the pantry when she woke up this morning. But she couldn't look at him, at the heat of his moral outrage. She had never believed Norman would agree with her, but she was saddened that he had been prepared to turn her in to the police.

What difference did it make, anyway? Donating organs from the living or the dead? She was *helping* people.

She made two cups of peppermint tea and placed each cup carefully on the kitchen table. She went to a window in the great room again, and saw her visitor walking up the driveway. Kim waited for the knock and swung open the door.

"Hello, Brooke," she said. "So good to see you. Thanks for coming."

Brooke followed her into the kitchen and Kim gestured for her to take a seat.

Kim sat and watched Brooke reach for the cup. She had called Brooke earlier and told her she was going to make her treasurer of the Homemakers Association of Vermont.

"What does the position entail?" Brooke asked.

Straight down to business. Good, now drink up.

"It's an exciting opportunity," Kim said. "There are literally dozens of applications to join our little club. But I won't charge a fee for membership. The association is all about informing homemakers and, I hope, having a good time, too. But we *will* accept donations. I would really appreciate it if you would take on the role of managing the money and our presence on Pinterest. I'll assist you, of course. You know more about social media than me. With your knowledge and charisma, we can make an impact."

Was it too much? Had she spread the butter on this slice of bread too thick?

Brooke seemed pleased and Kim relaxed. *I knew I could appeal to your ego.*

"Your talents could be used more," Kim said, and Brooke drank her tea. "Really, I'd be a fool not to put your gifts to good use."

Careful.

"You actually have that many applications to join?" Brooke asked, and sipped her tea.

"The truth is, Brooke, I have *hundreds* of applications. It's one of the reasons I asked you over. I don't think I can narrow the list down to a manageable number of members, so I was wondering if you'd help me decide. We can go through the applications together."

"Sure, I'd be happy to." The tea had cooled, and Brooke swallowed the rest of it.

The right moment to ask the Main Question had arrived. Brooke's eyes clouded over, became distant. She swayed on the chair.

"What's...*wuh*?"

"Are you fucking my husband?" Kim said quickly.

"*Wuh*?"

Kim stood and went to the cabinet beneath the sink. She pulled on a pair of yellow rubber gloves that reached almost to her elbows and shook loose a plastic carrier bag from the pile she had stuffed in a corner.

Brooke attempted to stand, one hand on the seat of the chair and the other on the table, but slumped into the backrest. She tried again but flopped, a heap of loose flesh. It was as though she had no bones.

Kim stood behind her, shaking the bag. It caught air and puffed out. She placed it over Brooke's head and pulled backward. Brooke clawed at the rubber gloves. Then, in a burst of strength that surprised Kim, she was on her feet, bag still wrapped around her head and bolted toward the kitchen doorway. She struck the doorframe head first and bounced. The blow sent her reeling backward, arms flailing, and she collapsed onto the tiles.

Someone was calling Kim's name. It was low, muffled. Norman.

Kim knelt beside Brooke and removed the bag from her head. She pressed her fingers into the side of her neck, checking for a pulse. It was weak but regular.

She opened the pantry door. Norman's face was sweaty, frantic.

"What's all the noise for?"

"Let me out of here, Kim."

"Okay," she said, and wheeled him to the kitchen.

Pleasure shivered through her at the sound of Norman's sudden intake of breath when he saw Brooke lying on the floor.

"What did you do?"

Kim stepped around the chair and looked down at him. "Do you think I'm an idiot, Norman? I know she's been visiting you at the funeral home."

Norman's eyes darted left and right as though searching for an explanation, a way to slither out of *being caught.*

"Is she alive?"

"She's breathing. Don't change the subject, Norman. It's insulting…for a man of your dignity, for a man of your moral superiority."

"Let her go, Kim, please."

"Did she suck your cock?"

Norman's mouth moved.

Kim grinned. "She didn't, huh? Well, more fool you."

"*Stop it!* It wasn't what you think."

"Then what was it, Norman? I'm all ears."

His mouth moved again, making wordless sounds.

"That's a shame, Norman. I honestly thought I knew you, but I was wrong. If you had to cheat on me, couldn't you have chosen someone less objectionable?"

Norman gaped at her.

"No? It's been good chatting to you, Norman. Don't worry, I'll fix you some breakfast. I wouldn't let you starve. I'm not an animal."

She wheeled him back into the pantry, parked the chair underneath the bare lightbulb, and turned to leave.

"Kim?"

"Yes, Norman."

"Did you ever meet someone?" he said, "and have a visceral reaction to them? Like your instincts are fired up, like you're tuned *into* that person right from the get-go?"

"Yeah, so?"

"When we meet new people, we either like them or we don't. Without talking to them, without knowing anything about them. Sometimes we just don't like someone but we don't know why. We get what you might call a bad vibe—"

"Your point, Norman?"

"My point is—and I can't believe I'm only seeing it now; I'm just not smart enough—but you set off a flare in other people. There's something not quite right with you. Something off. Some people get it instantly; for others it takes time. But one way or another, they *see* you, Kim. You can get rid of me, go on with your life, but you'll never be the star you think you should be. Because eventually, people *see* you. It took me years to see the real you. There were signs but you were good at hiding in plain sight. Maybe I'm a fool, but if you think Oprah is going to have you as a guest on one of her shows, you're wrong. You send up flares, Kim, and people who are smarter than me will see them."

Kim stared at him, then closed the door and locked it. She went to Brooke, lifted her legs wheelbarrow-style, and moved her toward the basement.

NINETY-FOUR

BROOKE WAS PARALYZED. SHE STARED UP AT BRIGHT LIGHTS, her eyes tracing their source to an articulated arm. A pumping hiss came from somewhere, and a machine bleeped close to her head. Air was being forced into her lungs. A mask was clamped over her mouth and nose. Her head was raised, and her eyes rolled downward to see what was causing her paralysis. She gasped. The bleeping became urgent, quicker. Her chest was a grotesque mouth with tubes snaking in and out. Confused, she blinked, stared, blinked again. Her sternum had been cut and was now held open by a steel device. She could see her own heart pumping fast.

The surgeon approached her, pointed at the device, and said, "It's a Finochietto retractor, or as I prefer to call it, a rib spreader." It was Kim, dressed in surgical scrubs, wearing a face shield with a clear visor, similar to a welding mask.

"I have most of the equipment I need for the procedure," she continued. "Not quite up to the standards of an OR, but adequate. It gets the job done."

Brooke tried to speak.

Kim pulled the mask past Brooke's chin and said, "I'm listening." She tilted her head sideways, pointing her ear at Brooke. "Don't want to talk, huh? Well, Brooke, let me give you a rundown of events so far. I drugged you, as if you hadn't figured that out. Then I tried to render you unconscious. You gave me a scare when you made a run for it but, as luck would have it, you headbutted the doorframe and knocked yourself out. Let me assure you, your heart will be preserved for transplantation in the finest equipment money can buy. You see that machine by the wall?" Kim pointed with her gloved hand.

Brooke's eyes remained frozen on Kim.

"That's a portable heart-perfusion machine. When I remove your heart, it will keep the organ in transplantable condition. Neat, huh? Cold ischemic storage will be obsolete soon. Norman and I used it for storing harvested body parts from newly deceased cadavers. Technology, Brooke. It really is amazing...Oh, you didn't know Norman was capable of stealing from the dead? He did, Brooke, and I helped. That's the man you love. You stole Norman's heart, now I'm taking yours. A heart for a heart."

Despite the drugs in her body, Brooke was terrified. The heart rate monitor was bleeping rapidly. She saw Kim through an icy prism of tears.

"You know, I'm going to be so busy in the next few hours, but I'll try to wake you the moment the operation is done and your heart is in the perfusion machine. I want to show it to you. Unfortunately, I don't have a replacement heart to give you. But, Brooke, you are saving the lives of many people."

"Please..." Brooke's voice was a whisper.

"Oh, Brooke, it'll be fine. I studied transplant surgery for months. Do you know how many YouTube videos I watched? A lot, Brooke. Medical textbooks, the works. You know why? Because I'm prepared to sacrifice to get where I need to go. If only Norman had showed the same commitment. Anyway, I have to excise a lot of organs today. Paige is up next. Although I promise to be gentler with her. She won't know what's happening. I don't want her to be afraid. But I *do* want you to know what's happening to you."

Tears rolled down the sides of Brooke's head and dripped onto the metal table.

Kim's cell phone vibrated. "Excuse me a moment. So sorry about the interruption."

***

It was Ray Porter.

"Ray, *what?*"

"How long is it going to take?"

"A few hours." Kim heard a jingling, trilling sound in the background. "Ray, are you gambling again? Tut, tut, Ray. Tut, tut."

"Kim, listen. I cannot—*I cannot*—stress this enough. Finish the job, and do it fast. I saw Gwen Rohm parked outside my house yesterday."

"Gwen who?"

"She's one of my detectives."

"Oh. I'll get it done, Ray. Sounds like a problem only you can take care of. I have enough to deal with."

"What?"

"Norman's not on board. I'm afraid our marriage is over."

"As long as you don't do it yourself, Kim. You'll be suspect number one if you do. Don't forget that. Sorry it came to that for Norman."

"So am I, Ray."

"Did you find someone to do it?"

"I did. Waiting for the call."

"Good. How is your supply of acetone?"

"I have buckets of the stuff."

"Walls, ceiling, floors, drains—every single item in the basement, Kim."

"I know the drill."

"Finish with the adults, then the kid. I'll send my people to dismantle and sanitize the equipment when you're ready."

She hung up and adjusted the line in Brooke's arm.

"Please…" Softer, no strength behind it.

"I can't chat now, Brooke. I talk too much, don't you think?"

A liquid flowed into Brooke's arm. Then she was out.

NINETY-FIVE

A PENCIL-THIN BEAM OF LIGHT SEEPED THROUGH THE GAP beneath the door. Corey was glad he was in the dark; danger lay beyond. He had no doubt now—if he was taken into the light beyond the door he would die. He had heard everything Mrs. Loomis had said. She had somebody on the table, and she was taking their heart. Fear and panic twisted in him like barbed wire. But he did not remind Mrs. Loomis of his presence by making a sound. His lips were pressed together in a bloodless slit beneath the duct tape.

Corey had been fascinated by one of the five basic principles of biology—homeostasis, which, according to his teacher, Mr. Davis, could be explained simply as nature in balance. Homeostasis kept the body in balance, but what about the mind? Could you experience so much fear, reach the outer limits of terror, that eventually the mind flatlined and returned to its normal steady state? Corey didn't think so. Especially under these conditions, where he was fighting a constant swell of panic. Was that why Mrs. Loomis was doing such horrible things to people? A loss of homeostasis? Corey knew lots of words, but he didn't know the one that described the absence of homeostasis in the *mind*.

He had to get the tape off his mouth. Not to call for help, but to be able to breathe freely and escape. He had to get back home, so he could talk to dad about homeostasis. He would look away from his newspaper and listen, never asking Corey *why* he was bringing up his science stuff at the breakfast table, no hint of annoyance in his voice. Because dad knew he wasn't being a know-it-all smarty pants, understood that Corey talked about amazing biological processes and mind-blowing physics facts simply for the sake of basking in their wonder, that he was just happy to live in a world where nature was a constant source of *awe*. It *had* to be discussed.

As Mrs. Loomis taunted somebody in her well-lit basement, Corey's thoughts turned to his mother. His eyes stung as though he was in a smoke-filled room. The guilt of leaving his warm bed in the middle of the night bore down on him and he hoped she would forgive him.

He pushed saliva past his lips, swirled it around, wetting the tape. It might loosen the adhesive. He stretched his face, loosened it, and repeated. The sounds of medical equipment bleeping and chirping outside brought back the memory of mom watching her hospital dramas, the ones dad didn't like. It was sad when people were sick, and Corey couldn't understand why anyone would deliberately make themselves sad. He had seen his mother tear up many times while watching her shows.

The drama unfolding in the basement was far more sinister.

He pushed the tape forward with the tip of his tongue. There was some give, but not much. He scraped one end against the rough floor, twisting his head as though he had an itch. How much time did he have left?

Trying to get the tape off his mouth was a welcome distraction from the pins and needles in his feet and hands. His shoulder joints ached, and the muscles in his upper back were stiff. He clenched and unclenched the muscles in his legs and arms to get the blood flowing. If he managed to get free, he would have to move fast. He rolled onto his back and felt something digging into his buttock. His breath caught.

Beyond the door, a saw whirred to life. It hummed, seemed to meet resistance, then hummed again.

His heart was hammering so hard he thought Mrs. Loomis would hear it.

He rolled onto his side and reached for his back pocket.

NINETY-SIX

KIM SHOWERED. DESPITE HAVING COVERED HER ENTIRE body with protective clothing, organic matter slid off her body in a foam of suds, landing in the shower tray. She had shampooed her hair twice already and groaned at the thought of doing it again. The groan was born more of disappointment than the idea of spending another thirty minutes in the shower. She had wanted to keep Brooke alive with the cardiopulmonary bypass pump, so she could wake her and show Brooke her heart in the perfusion machine, like a Rolex in a display case, only more valuable. But Ray Porter had forced her to cancel her plan. And he had been right to. The boy was probably dehydrated by now, and if his organs became damaged Porter wouldn't accept them. And there would be no payment.

Kim dried off, poured acetone around the shower stall and down the drain.

Disappointed or not, Kim was pleased with the job she had done so far. She'd never have to read a tweet by Brooke again, contaminated as they often were with insincere words like *lifehack* and *empowering*.

There was no time to pick an outfit. In the bedroom, she pulled on sweatpants and a hoodie and ran downstairs, Gwen Rohm on her mind. If Rohm was a problem for

Porter, she was problem for Kim. There was so much still to do.

Kim dialed Paige, and fed her the same story she had Brooke: would she be interested in being treasurer of the Homemakers Association of Vermont and could she come by to discuss it?

"Huh?" Paige said. "I thought you wanted Brooke for the position."

Shit.

"She called you?" Kim asked.

"Oh, sure. Brooke just needed my opinion. I told her I'd jump at the chance. Is everything okay, Kim?"

Kim snatched blindly at the assortment of lies colliding in her mind.

"She couldn't do it, Paige," she said. "With all the work involved, she didn't think she could commit the time to it… Can you come by? It won't take long."

"Okay," she said, and Kim detected a note of eagerness in her tone, "but it might take an hour or more. I have to find someone to watch the boys while I'm out."

"Thanks, Paige. I don't deserve a friend as good as you."

Paige giggled. "You're so kind, Kim. See you soon."

Kim hung up and went to the kitchen, poured Cheerios into a bowl, doused them in milk, and wheeled Norman to the table.

She loaded the spoon and brought it to his mouth, looking at his face for the first time. It was flushed and damp, almost maroon. His eyes were red-rimmed, confused, as though he'd stumbled out of a car fire.

"I'm busy today, Norman, so please, eat. I may not be able to feed you for the rest of the day, so this is it."

Norman complied, opened his mouth. Kim spooned the cereal in, the way a mother would feed her baby. Norman chewed. There was no relish in it.

"What did you do to her?" he asked, his voice cracking.

"Tell me what you two were up to at the funeral home, and I'll tell you *exactly* what I did to your little slut."

"It wasn't like that."

"Then what was it like, Norman? She wasn't visiting you to talk about the weather."

"I can't explain it."

"Why don't you give it a try?" she said, milk dripping from the shaking spoon onto his lap. A Cheerio tumbled over the lip of the spoon like a miniature life buoy and landed on his crotch. "There's one last chance for you to confess, Norman. No? Well, eat then."

Norman closed his mouth against the spoon, but she jabbed it at his lips, rattling it on his teeth. Norman gave in, blood dripping down his chin, turning pink as it mixed with the milk that slopped out of his mouth.

"It's funny," she said, waving the spoon at him. The bowl was empty save for a small amount of wheat-flecked milk. "It's as though you're not convinced that I love you. Yes, Norman, I'll admit I treated you badly on occasion. I hold my hands up to it."

Norman flinched as milk droplets speckled his face.

"I keep repeating myself, Norman, but I see I can't persuade you anymore. I can't get it through your skull." She tapped his forehead with the wet spoon the same way she cracked the top of her boiled eggs.

Norman shifted, shrank from her.

"Those things you said to me earlier hurt my feelings, Norman. It's like you think I'm an empty shell. Do you know how hurtful your words were? *Do you?* Why wouldn't Oprah want to interview me? *Why not me?*"

The doorbell rang.

Norman's pupils dilated and his mouth stretched open wide.

NINETY-SEVEN

KIM CAUGHT NORMAN'S SHOUT FOR HELP BEFORE HE could give full voice to it. She clamped her hand over his mouth, mashed his bloody lips into his teeth, swung the chair around and rushed him toward the pantry. The wheels squeaked as she pushed him to a corner. She grabbed the strapping tape from her pocket, the kind used by physiotherapists. His head thrashed from side to side as he tried to avoid it, his screams for help filling the stifling pantry.

She fumbled on the shelf for a weapon, picked up a jar of Mt. Olive pickled hamburger dill chips, and drew back, intending to brain him into compliance. Norman shrank from her.

"Stop!" he said. "Okay. I'll cooperate." He became still, apparently accepting that his chance for escape had gone.

Kim put the pickles back on the shelf and used her teeth to bite strips of strapping tape off the roll, plastering them onto Norman's mouth as though it were a wound.

She was hot and sweaty when she emerged from the pantry. She combed her hair with her fingers, took two deep breaths, and strode down the hall. In the foyer, she summoned a smile and opened the door.

Paige smiled back at her, but it faltered. "Kim, what happened to you?"

"Oh, it's nothing," she said. "Come on in. I'll tell you about it."

Paige handed her the *InStyle* magazine she had borrowed, and Kim put it on the table. She showed Paige to the same chair Brooke Draper had sat on not long before.

"I'm coming down with something, Paige. A cold, or flu—I just pray it's a cold."

Paige placed a hand on Kim's forehead. "You're burning up. You should be in bed, Kim."

"Oh, I'll be fine. We homemakers are tough. I'll make us some tea."

"No you will *not*, Kim. I'll get the tea. Peppermint?"

"Paige, really, I can—"

"Nope, I'll do it…what happened here?" Paige had seen the milk drops on the floor.

"I'm so clumsy, Paige. Let me get a rag and clean that."

Paige led Kim to the table as though she was an invalid and said, "You sit. I'll take care of the spill. I know all about spills, especially with my two little demons at home. You don't look well, Kim. You shouldn't be on your feet."

This wasn't going the way she had intended. Kim liked Paige and didn't want her to suffer. Unlike Brooke, who had *craved* suffering in one form or another. But Paige had left her with no choice.

Paige hunkered on the floor, cleaning up the spilled milk. Then she rinsed the cloth in the sink and prepared the tea.

Kim knew she had to do it quickly. The more Paige talked the more difficult it would be to…Kim was furious. Megan Hawkins should have been sitting across the table from her now, tea steaming beside her, but Ray Porter had forbidden it—too old, he'd said. Her organs weren't in prime condition. *Too much wear and tear, blah blah blah.* Porter could get on her nerves but he was the one paying her. And Brooke and Paige would make Kim a millionaire. The boy would be a nice bonus.

Paige cupped her hands around the mug, warming her palms, and Kim said, "You know, Paige, you're one of the finest people I've ever met." And it was true.

Paige beamed at her.

Sadness, so unexpected that it startled her, tugged at the center of her chest.

Don't delay. Do it now. NOW.

Kim stood up fast, went to the sink behind Paige and turned on the tap, filled a glass. She glanced over her shoulder. Paige was facing the kitchen doorway.

"Thanks, Kim. Ditto. Truth is, you're my idol."

Heartbreaking.

Kim glanced over her shoulder again and saw her chance. Paige was sitting straight, still cupping the mug, her neck exposed. Kim sidestepped directly behind her, curled her arm around her neck, and squeezed. Paige stiffened, tried to stand. Kim held her in the chokehold. Paige bucked, kicked at the air underneath the table.

"Shh," Kim said. "Go to sleep."

Paige reached out, wildly fumbling for something. It was the mug of tea. She threw the hot liquid over her shoulder, scalding half of Kim's face. Kim screamed, fell back against the sink. Then Paige was out of the chair, running down the hall. Kim bolted after her. Paige turned the handle and pulled open the door. Kim ran at it full tilt, lifted off the ground, leg in the air, and kicked it shut. She grabbed a handful of Paige's hair, swung her around in an effort to unbalance her. It worked, and Paige stumbled, face down on the floor. Kim climbed on top of her, brought her arm around her neck again, and choked her with all her strength. Paige's body went limp and Kim ran back into the kitchen, turned on the tap, and held her face under the cold water, the tips of her hair trailing in the sink.

She patted her face dry with paper towels and ran upstairs. She yanked open the medicine cabinet, tore apart the Medi-First box, and quickly applied the burn cream. The left side of her face was red from forehead to jawline, and her affected eye wept. The lidocaine in the cream would relieve the pain for now.

Kim returned to the foyer, checked Paige's pulse. It was there, but for how much longer?

She towed Paige by her ankles toward the basement door, lay her down gently, then hooked her forearms under her armpits. Her breath came in ragged bursts as she carried Paige down the stairs, flaccid feet thudding on each step.

Kim wasn't angry with Paige. In fact, her admiration for the younger woman had swelled into respect. She had fought well. She was a warrior. Despite scaring Kim half to death with her near escape, Kim wouldn't make her suffer. Paige would be unaware of her own death; it was the least Kim could do.

Her face stung though, and the skin seemed to be tightening. Paige might have disfigured her.

She brushed Paige's hair away from her face, and said, "I take no pleasure in this, Paige. Believe me. It's not like Brooke."

She called Ray Porter.

"Listen, Ray, send two of your guys to pick up two vehicles. One is parked in my driveway, the other is across the road from the funeral home. I'll leave the keys in the flowerpot on the doorstep."

"What's wrong with you, you sound like you've been jogging."

"I'm working. Goddammit, Ray. Do as I ask. And I need proper burn cream. Can you get me some?"

"One of my guys will drop it through the mail slot. Are you all right?"

"I was scalded, one side of my face."

"Jesus, Kim, what's going on?"

"It's under control, I promise. Just do those things, Ray, and I'll call you later to make the pickup. I'm sure you'll be pleased with what I have."

"Okay, done. Hang tight."

Hang tight? What an asshole.

Kim sat on the end of the operating table for five minutes to get her heart rate under control. Then she went upstairs, found Paige's car keys in her handbag, took Brooke's keys from the cabinet over the sink, and went to the front door. She cracked it, peeked through. There was no one around. One hand on the doorframe, she lunged forward, tossed the keys into the flowerpot, and reeled herself back inside.

Christ, what a day. A woman's work was never done.

NINETY-EIGHT

MELODY ROLLED THE FRAYED TENNIS BALL TOWARD THE wall, and Sammy chased it. Not at a run, more like a casual trot. Sammy was taking his time. He brought it back to her and dropped it next to her hand, panting. She rolled the ball again, looked at the untouched glass of whiskey sitting next to her on the floor and the letter in her hand.

She hadn't left her apartment on Bleecker for three days. The walk to her door had been the hardest because she'd had to pass Joe's apartment.

"Come on, Sammy. Take a break." Sammy rested his head on her thigh, constantly glancing at her, as though sensing something was wrong. She read the letter again.

Mel:

I have to leave for a while. Don't worry about me. It's too much to deal with. I thought I'd be okay with your work, but I'm not. You don't have to worry that I'll go to the police. I'd never do that. I'll come back home sometime, I just don't know when.

Love,
Rosa.

She felt foolish for thinking that any sane person would have accepted the fact that she was a killer for hire. The letter had been the incentive she needed to sit the exam for a private-investigator license. A new career that might help her win back Rosa as a friend. Her current job was hazardous, she had always known it. But the Charles Shaker contract had been cursed. It had cost her everything. That she hadn't known Shaker was the cartel's banker made no difference. All the money she had worked for was gone, and she still needed to work. She picked up the glass of whiskey and poured it down the sink. Sammy had followed her, eyeing her cautiously.

She checked her inbox, picked up her cell phone, and dialed the number given at the end of the email.

"Hello?"

"You want to meet?"

"I'm in Vermont. Where are you?"

"Somewhere. Let's meet halfway. There's a restaurant in Turners Falls, Massachusetts, called the Great Falls Harvest. Tomorrow, 1 p.m.?"

"I'll be there." Melody hung up, caressed Sammy's head. She'd seen dozens of movies where the trope was *one last job*. And it never went well. But that was Hollywood, and this was life.

NINETY-NINE

It was ten after three in the morning. Ray Porter called to let Kim know he was outside. She told him to pull the van round back, where they could load it in private. They carried the ice coolers one at a time, careful to preserve the integrity of the organs inside. Each cooler was placed on the bed of the van gently, the way you would lay down a newborn baby. The final two containers were heavier, large-capacity black plastic boxes. They didn't need to be careful with these. Ray took one handle, Kim the other. They were sweating by the time the van was fully loaded.

Ray wiped the perspiration off his forehead with a paper towel, reached inside his pocket, and brought out two large brown envelopes. He handed them to Kim. She left them unopened on the table.

"You want to count it?" Ray asked.

"You wouldn't stiff me."

Ray ignored that, and said, "The boy next."

"Norman next," Kim said. "He knows too much."

"You have a plan?"

"I do have a plan, Ray." But she wasn't going to tell him what it was.

"All right. You've done an excellent job so far, so I'll trust you. But feed and water the kid or he'll die of dehydration and starvation. His body will start consuming itself, and we don't want to compromise the quality of his organs."

It made sense. Kim nodded. "Okay, I'll do it. Are the vehicles taken care of?"

"I had my people excavate a large hole on the farm. They pushed that backhoe to its limit, but they're gone for good, Kim. Don't worry."

"And the detective you mentioned, Rohm? Sounds to me like an urgent matter that needs your attention."

"She didn't follow me here if that's what you're worried about."

"So she *is* a problem, Ray?"

"I'll deal with her. Just remember, don't get rid of Norman yourself otherwise all the strings I can pull won't do you any good. Understand?"

"Goodnight, Ray." She closed the door behind him and looked in the refrigerator. There was a bottle of Evian and some meat. Kim made a ham and mayonnaise sandwich.

***

The knife was so close, yet it might as well have been on Mars. Corey couldn't reach it. His stomach growled miserably, and his headache had returned. His energy reserves were depleted, and there had been a worrying development—he was losing the *will* to reach. He hadn't given up, he was just weak, his mind like a thick soup.

Someone was coming down the steps. Corey paused, listened. Footsteps approached the door. He lay still.

The door squeaked on its hinges. Hands grabbed his shoulders and he was lifted to a sitting position. The knife in his pocket dug into his buttock. He made no sound, not even when the tape was ripped off his mouth.

"Don't scream or I'll hurt you," Mrs. Loomis said. Corey remembered her voice; he would never forget it.

He gave her a slight nod.

"I'm going to feed you a ham sandwich. Then I'm going to give you water. Okay?"

He nodded again.

"Open wide." Corey took a bite of the sandwich. It was overwhelming. He hadn't tasted anything this delicious in his life. Fireworks went off in his mouth, in his mind. He chewed rapidly. His body hummed with a need so great that he almost choked.

"Careful, take it easy."

His stomach made pinging noises between chewing. How could eating a sandwich be this wonderful? How could—?

And then there was none left. A bottle was at his lips and he was drinking water. Mrs. Loomis let him rest after he'd drunk a third of it.

"Ready to go again?"

He was. She held the bottle to his mouth and he drank. He was in severe pain, parts of his body were numb, but an important thing had happened—his will to reach for the knife was back.

***

Kim put the duct tape back on Corey's mouth and went to the kitchen. She grabbed a rolling pin from the drawer where she kept her baking utensils and took it to the bedroom. She stripped off her clothes and stood before the full-length mirror in her underwear. Gripping the rolling pin until her knuckles turned white, she sucked in a breath and struck her stomach with it as she exhaled. She refused to pause for even a moment; she might change her mind and not go through with it. She struck her abdomen again and again. Then moaning, and in dreadful pain, she beat her thighs with the heavy wooden pin, dropping it on the floor only when she could take no more. Finally, she unsnapped her bra and began twisting and pinching the soft flesh of her breasts.

She examined her shuddering body in the mirror.

It was all about persuasion, she thought. You had to persuade your audience.

She'd have an audience of one soon, and she intended to convince her.

Welts and lumps rose on her breasts, abdomen and thighs. In a few hours, the bruises would blossom darkly, and if her plan was going to succeed, Norman wouldn't be a problem anymore.

Hands shaking, she fumbled for her cell phone in the pile of clothes on the floor, and called Ray Porter.

"Don't you sleep?" he said.

"Ray, I need a favor."

ONE HUNDRED

THE DRAPES WERE DRAWN, BUT JIM COULD FEEL THEM OUT there, on his lawn, eager for a story. They had knocked on his door, *hammered* on it. And now Lillian was awake upstairs, still in bed, crying. He had tried to console her, but she'd asked him to leave. She wanted to be alone.

Console her.

Her sobs were those of grief. Of hope lost. She had given up on the idea that Corey was alive. Jim had, too. It was that part of him, the part of him that threw reality into sharp relief, the part that *knows*, and it told him calmly that Corey was dead. Lillian hadn't wanted his consolation because there was none to be given. Jim understood. Holding his wife wouldn't bring their son home. Telling her everything was going to be all right would be an obvious lie. Jim didn't think anything would be all right for the rest of their lives. Even though Lillian didn't want his comfort, the urge was there to go upstairs, lay a hand on her shoulder, and say nothing.

The TV was off and he supposed it would remain off indefinitely. He had watched the local news earlier and regretted it. Some pundits were speculating that a serial killer was stalking and abducting children in the Montpelier area, and that it would happen again. People had been approached on the streets by reporters. Each interviewee had lamented bygone days when children had been able to roam unsupervised. *This type of thing never happens in Montpelier*, they'd said. *It must be an outsider*, they'd said. *No one is going to risk their child being abducted by a predator, so playtime is strictly monitored*, the reporter had said.

Jim was hungry but he had never felt less like eating in his life. Taking that first bite of food would feel wrong. But he had to do it. He had to be able to take care of Lillian, who was still refusing to eat.

He listened to his wife sob and the sound wrenched at the center of him. His heart ached, because she was trying to control it, trying not to cry too loudly.

ONE HUNDRED AND ONE

MELODY DROVE BACK AND FORTH ON AVENUE A SEVERAL times, searching for the restaurant in Turners Falls. The fully crowned trees on the sidewalks and the sun rising over the brick buildings obscured her view. She shaded her eyes with one hand. Her temper began to fray. Why were there so many goddamn trees in what appeared to be a business district? But she found the Great Falls Harvest and parked in one of the diagonal spaces in front.

A man sat in his car in the space next to hers. He looked up from his cell phone and she held up a hand. He waved back. Turners Falls and its residents seemed nice, and Melody felt a little foolish for having almost lost control. Perhaps she was just nervous. Meeting a client was never dull. Or maybe it was caution; she had to be careful. The thought hovered nearby, a beacon in the black, a warning bobbing on the surface. Close behind was an image of Jennifer Shaker. There had been no excuse—she'd known exactly who her client was, and it had been a mistake to get involved with her. Melody was glad the woman was dead. Another shameless human the world wouldn't miss, who was aware of her motives and could still look at herself in the mirror and respect the person looking back at her.

She was angry but this wasn't the time or place. She needed to focus. Forget Jennifer Shaker and the rage warming her blood. There would be plenty of time for regret. Now, Melody needed to work.

She entered the restaurant. There were a few lunchtime customers, men and women dressed in suits. She looked for a lone diner and found her. The woman was sitting in a corner booth: red table, black seats, photographs of flowers hanging on a butterscotch-yellow wall, light fixture overhead.

"Kim?"

"You must be Valerie." Kim stood and shook her hand.

Melody sat, immediately picking up the aura of vulnerability Kim Loomis carried around like a poison. A box sat in the middle of the table with *Cindy's Cakes & More* written on the side. The box didn't contain cakes. So far, Kim had done well.

A server handed them a menu but they both asked for coffee. "We'll order later," Kim said.

"Are we agreed on the price?" Melody asked as the server left.

"Half a million dollars? Yes, if that's what it takes."

"It is."

The server returned with their coffee. Melody barely noticed. She was watching Kim.

"How are you going to kill him?" Kim said when the server was out of earshot.

Melody stared at her, at her floral pattern dress that buttoned at the front, the whole way to the hem. She let the question hang in the air.

"Meet me in the restroom in one minute," Melody said, standing.

"Wait, we need to discuss—"

"One minute," Melody said, and walked away.

In the restroom, she checked the stalls. They were empty. She kept one eye on her wristwatch. Every second felt like three. There was no window she could escape out of. None she would fit through, anyway.

The door opened. It was Kim.

"Did I say some—?"

"Unbutton your dress."

"What?"

"Do it or I swear I'll kill you and take my chances. *Do it now*."

Kim undid the top buttons.

"Keep going till I say stop…Faster."

Melody pulled open Kim's dress and recoiled. "What the—?" Black and yellow bruises covered her breasts and abdomen. Kim hoisted the hem high on her thighs.

"Oh my God," Melody whispered, her eyes running across the red lumps and contused flesh.

"Norman," Kim said, "the man I hired you to get rid of. He did this."

"Listen to me, Kim. We need to be quick. I have to check you for electronic devices."

Kim held her arms outward as though she were going through airport security. Melody patted her down lightly. She was clean.

"Let's go back," Melody said. "Someone might come in."

They returned to the table. Melody's mind was racing. It was as though a camera was flashing rapidly within her, snapping her anger and deep sadness. In that moment Melody decided this would be her last job as a contract killer. She would take the money then find another career. Her final contract was worthwhile. She had to help Kim Loomis. And she'd enjoy shooting the sonofabitch who had beaten her. It wasn't a bad note to end on.

"He's going to kill me," Kim said. "I can feel it."

"Don't worry," Melody said. "He's your husband?"

"Yes."

"What did he use? His fists?"

"A rolling pin."

Melody reached across the table and held Kim's hand. Cruelty stirred an elemental thirst for vengeance in her. Her ex-boyfriend, Landon Forbes, had been an asshole in suspenders pretending to be somebody he wasn't, with shitty taste in music, but he had never been cruel. She hadn't met an abusive man before, but she was looking forward to meeting Norman Loomis.

Tears shimmered in Kim's eyes. "I tried my best to make the coffee the way he wanted. I cleaned the house as best I could, made his dinner taste the way it should, but it's never good enough. He's going to kill me one of these days, so please, please do it for me."

Melody didn't need a reason to kill a person, except money. But this was a bonus.

"I do a lot of stuff on the internet about lifestyle and homemaking," Kim continued. "Norman doesn't approve. I'm not doing anything wrong, just trying to guide the next generation of America's homemakers."

Melody didn't get it. The last thing on earth she wanted was to be a homemaker. But some people did. "You mean YouTube videos?"

"I do a lot of those. I help as many women on Pinterest as I can by answering their questions, too. It can get busy."

"It pays well?"

"Yes. In the real world, I'm a mortician."

Melody liked Kim. They could easily have been friends, but it wouldn't be possible. When the deal was done, that was it. They wouldn't meet again. A wave of blackness swept through her. She missed Rosa, hoped her friend would come home.

"Okay, we have a few things to talk about before I leave," Melody said. "Access. How do I get in?"

"I'll leave the back door open."

"When do you want it done?"

"Tomorrow night, at 2 a.m."

"I know what you're going to say, but I have to say it— once it's done, you can't take it back. Are you absolutely sure you want this?"

"It's me or him. It has to be him." She meant it, too; Melody had glimpsed a fleeting hardness in her gaze.

"Do you have any jewelry in the house you wouldn't mind me stealing?"

"I'm sorry, what?"

"The number-one suspect is always the spouse. I can make it look like a burglary. If you have jewelry, quality stuff, especially if it's insured and holds no sentimental value, taking it could help you. I won't sell or pawn it. I'll dispose of it."

"I keep my jewelry in a box on my vanity table in the bedroom."

"Now I have to bring up the ugly subject: money. It's half up front, cash, the other half in bitcoin once it's over." Melody handed Kim several folded sheets of paper. "Just follow the instructions. Get rid of any phones you use to contact me. Only disposable phones allowed. Agreed?"

"Yes." Kim handed Melody a single sheet of paper with an address and cell phone number on it.

"I really wish you the best of luck, Kim."

They shook hands, and Melody headed toward the exit, the cake box tucked under her arm.

ONE HUNDRED AND TWO

KARA LOOMIS WAS GOING HOME. HER LEVEL 1 INVOLUNTARY detention expired in a few hours. Of course, they didn't call it detention or imprisonment; the word they used was *admission*, as though she had been *allowed* into the Vermont Psychiatric Care Hospital. The psychiatrist assigned to her was preparing her release papers. The second they were in her hand, she would be out the door. She had done everything right—modified her behavior, taken her medication, and told the psychiatrist exactly what he wanted to hear, all while he'd stared at her chest and said *hmm* as he'd fidgeted with his poorly knotted tie.

Her detention hadn't been terrible. The staff were decent, some even restoring her faith in human kindness. They were genuine, for the most part, and wanted to help.

Her clothes were spread on the neatly made bed, her only suitcase open beside them. Kim knew her size and had bought every item of clothing she owned, most of it from Forever 21. Kara had tried on some of the dresses to see whether they were appropriate for her environment. She wouldn't wear anything that would draw attention to her, anything controversial. Outside, life would be different, but in the psych unit she needed to keep a low profile, stick to her plan. Which is why she hadn't chosen the crushed-velvet cami dress, the corduroy zip-front jumpsuit, or the off-the-shoulder mini skater dress. There was a time and place, and the clock was ticking.

She finished packing and sat on the bed, hands folded primly in her lap, looking at visitors and patients passing in the hall through the open door. A few familiar faces waved at her and said hi. And Kara did her part—she waved and said hi back.

***

Kim was exhausted, yet fully alert. She couldn't remember the last time she had slept, and it didn't matter, especially when you were in the zone, when you were *doing it*. There was no feeling like it. She'd had days when she had made two videos, uploaded them to YouTube, responded to comments, pushed Send on fifty tweets, updated her Facebook status, posted images and advice on Pinterest, cleaned the house—*every single room*—paid bills, made dinner, and done other assorted chores, because the *feeling* was there, the sensation of *doing it*.

Kara was coming home and Kim wanted that homecoming to be perfect. She had arrived back from Massachusetts excited, and checked on Norman. His head had been bowed, and he'd seemed unexcited by her presence. She had shrugged, gone to the garage, hopped in the F150, and driven to Vermont Psychiatric Care Hospital.

She would give Kara the keys. The F150 was a gift, and she hoped her sister would appreciate it. The space she had parked in on her previous visit was available and she slotted the truck into it. Those things happened when you were *doing it*—everything seemed to be available, even something as mundane as a parking space.

Her cell phone vibrated on the dash.

"Ray, what do you have?"

"I ran the tag you gave me through the DMV. It belongs to Valerie Price."

"An alias?"

"It's possible. If she's cyber-savvy, she could have any number of stolen identities. I did a little more digging around property records. There's an apartment on Bleecker Street in New York in the name Melody Morgan, if that means anything."

"Could be someone else."

"Well, think about it. How often do you hear the name Melody?"

"So you're saying Melody Morgan is her real name, and Valerie Price is an alias?"

"In my opinion, they are one and the same. You want the address?"

"Hold on a second." Kim popped the glove compartment, tore the bottom half off a utility bill—paid in full—and dug a pen out of the clutter. "I'm listening, Ray."

She wrote down the address. She'd give it to Kara. Everyone needed an insurance policy.

ONE HUNDRED AND THREE

IT WAS 1 A.M. MELODY CRUISED ALONG MAIN STREET IN Montpelier. She hadn't met a single vehicle. She glanced at the address Kim had given her, saw the brick structure of the middle school ahead, and slowed. The house across from it was green, just as Kim had described. The driveway was clear. Melody continued on Main Street and crossed the bridge over the Winooski River onto Northfield Street. The woods became dense and dark on either side of her.

Beside the Econo Lodge on Northfield stood a derelict restaurant with a large paved area she guessed had probably been the restaurant's parking lot. She stopped the van close to the side of the abandoned building and next to an embankment, visible only from vehicles traveling toward Main. Trees on the embankment obscured the view of anyone watching from their window in the Econo Lodge. But the road was quiet. So far, anyway.

She opened the glove compartment and screwed a silencer onto the barrel of her gun and placed it in her customized shoulder holster underneath her jacket. From the jacket's inside pocket she pulled out a photograph. Her, Joe, and Rosa smiling, their arms around each other's shoulders. For security reasons, she never stored photographs on her phone. Instead, she used a digital camera and printed the images. Kept things simple.

Two of the finest people she'd ever met were in that photo. One was dead and the other had left. It was her fault. Though she'd had no way of knowing about Charles Shaker's involvement with a cartel, it didn't ease her guilt. It had been a bad job. And hadn't she known that one day it would be her turn to spin the wheel of fortune and find that her luck had run out?

This time she was helping someone. Melody had researched Kim Loomis online. Kim had a promising career in front of her if only she could get rid of the human battering ram that was her husband. Melody looked forward to making that happen. It was ten after one and she was wired with anticipation.

***

Kim brought Norman out of the pantry and into the kitchen. He was weak, probably close to heat exhaustion. His face was pale and slick, and he stared at the floor, body trembling. Kim sat at the table. She was angry, furious even. But she could not kill him. It had nothing to do with being suspect number one when Norman turned up missing. She *did* love him. Norman Faulkner had taken her name when they had gotten married. He had loved her, and because of that she *could not* be responsible for his death. Poisoning him would have been relatively quick and painless. But she would have known she'd done it. No, she didn't need Norman's death on *her* hands, on *her* conscience. Better to get a stranger to do it.

Kara was coming home tomorrow. Kim was hopeful for the future. Once this *awful* episode in her life was over, she'd begin putting her dreams at the center of her world again.

She placed her cell phone on the table. She'd make the call soon.

"Norman? Look at me, Norman."

Norman raised his head as though he was floating in thick syrup.

"I have a confession to make."

She had his attention.

"I'm not pregnant. The test I showed you was a prank kit, the kind you can buy from a joke shop, a novelty store. The internet...some of the products you can find...well, I wanted to be honest with you in your final moments."

Norman's eyes widened like a frightened horse's, and his complexion darkened. A guttural scream erupted from his throat but was dampened by the strapping tape over his mouth. He contorted and rocked on the chair as though he was being electrocuted.

Her face was as still as lake water on a windless day. "I had to be honest with you, Norman," she said, as the volume of his wretched struggle grew louder. "I figured I'd be the better person. You weren't honest about why Brooke was visiting you. So, I'm taking the higher ground by confessing. I was lying, but the truth has set me free. You made me do it, Norman. You made me lie to you."

She picked up the phone and dialed.

***

Melody was cocooned in the silence of the night, lost in her thoughts of how she hadn't taken the time to grieve, to process everything that had happened.

Her phone vibrated. It was Kim Loomis, and she sounded frantic.

"Hey, wow, slow down," Melody said. "What's wrong?"

"Norman attacked me for no reason I had to drug him so I could tie him up so he can't beat me anymore oh my God I think he cracked my ribs I got him into a chair he's in the kitchen he's tied up oh my God I need you to do it now please Valerie please *oh my God* ..."

Kim's distress jolted Melody into action. "I'm coming right now," she said, her voice cold, dangerous. "I'll take care of him."

She started the engine.

ONE HUNDRED AND FOUR

COREY HAD RECOVERED FROM THE NEAR INTOXICATING effects of being fed and rehydrated. With that first mouthful of bread he'd realized he had been literally starving. He couldn't remember if he'd been aware of it before Mrs. Loomis had come into the room. And he was injured, he knew, just not how badly.

The calories he'd consumed enabled him to try harder. He bent his body backward as far as it would go and pushed some more. His fingers touched the lip of his pocket, then wriggled into it, the tips sensing the knife, as though it was giving off static. Almost there. The pain only made him increase his efforts. He faced it, looked it in the eye, and dared it to stop him now.

Just a little further.

A bit more...

There. He snagged the handle, squeezed it between his index and middle fingers. He held his breath and leaned forward. Felt the knife rise out of his pocket. It slipped from his fingers and hit the floor. He slithered like a sidewinder toward the sound, hands touching the cool ground, probing, like a catfish's whiskers exploring its murky fathoms for food and danger. For obstacles.

There was a brief but sublime moment when he touched the knife and there was no pain. He didn't pause to enjoy it, but focused. He held the knife in one hand and tried to open the blade with his thumb and forefinger. It was awkward, and he had to pause to still the tremor in his hands.

Keep calm. You can do it. Deep breath, hold, let it go.

His thumbnail slotted into a groove on the blade and he pulled it all the way out. It locked in place with a dull click. Corey wouldn't have traded that sound for any other in the world.

He took his time to maneuver the blade carefully into the correct position under the cable tie. If he panicked, he might cut himself.

A strange calm engulfed him. He held his excitement in check.

Even though he could *feel* the blade cutting through his bonds.

***

Melody swung the van into Kim Loomis's driveway, drove past the side of the house, and parked in the backyard. She wriggled her hands into a pair of latex gloves, then got out fast, and gently pressed the door shut.

Kim had said she'd leave the back door open, and Melody was about to find out if she had remembered this important task while being terrorized by her husband. She turned the handle and pushed. Moonlight filled the kitchen in a pale whitewash. Kim had followed her instructions: turn off all lights.

She brought the gun out of its holster, and pointed it at the man in the chair, his face in shadow, the rest of him bleached in the ghost light. He was murmuring something. Melody raised the gun, aimed at his chest, and fired twice. He slumped forward, head lolling before his chin came to rest on his chest.

She went to him, held two fingers to his neck.

Norman Loomis was dead.

She went upstairs, holstering the gun. She wondered where Kim was, hoped she was all right. At least Norman's campaign of cruelty had come to an end.

The master bedroom was exactly where Kim had said it would be—first door on the left in the upper hallway. Melody emptied the jewelry box.

**

Kim heard Melody coming up the stairs. She hid behind the open door of the room next to the master bedroom, a carving knife held at chest level. Her plan was simple yet elegant. She would stab Melody, then tell the police she had broken into their home, tied Norman up, and tortured him and *her*. Kim's bruises were ripe, angry and painful. Red lumps had sprouted on her legs and torso. Melody had scalded Kim with boiled water, putting them through hours of agony before stealing Kim's jewelry. The reporters would tell the story of how local personality Kim Loomis had fended off a home invader and saved her own life, despite being beaten unconscious several times, even though, sadly, she hadn't been able to save her husband.

But before she called the police—distressed, incoherent, traumatized—she would harvest the boy's organs and dismantle the lab. With Ray's assistance, it shouldn't take long.

Kim rounded the door and stalked toward her bedroom, soundless as a cat. She peered around the doorframe, and saw Melody stuffing her jewelry into her pockets.

She started forward then froze. The Chamberlain base units light on her bedside table pulsated. She sprinted to the stairs, faster than she had ever moved in her life and fled into the great room, heart pumping, blood sloshing in her ears. She listened in the dark as Melody went out the back door, then hurried to the basement.

***

The knife was cutting air. The plastic cable tie had snapped apart. His hands were free. Rather than jubilation, Corey experienced a strange sense of disbelief. It didn't last long. His joints screamed like rusted hinges but he leaned forward in the dark and sawed at the tie around his ankles. He severed it in seconds, tore the tape from his eyes and mouth, gasping as his skin protested. He crawled to the door, fumbled for the handle and grasped it. Pain washed over him as he stood, white dots exploding across his vision. He took in a blessed lungful of air and turned the handle. It opened. Tears stung the skin on his face.

He stepped into the basement, relieved to see moonlight shining through the window. His vision swam in and out of focus but he put one foot into the path of lunar light and followed it to the table beneath the window. It was a graceless, uncoordinated climb. Pain lanced through him with blinding agony and the fear that his freedom was only temporary. He clamped a hand over his mouth to hold the scream inside.

He needed to hoist himself through that window. But it was impossible.

Impossible.

He was furious with himself for even thinking that way. Corey didn't believe in *impossible*, so what had changed?

He composed himself.

I'm going home.

He stood, paused to let the pain subside, reached for the window.

The basement door opened.

Someone was coming down the stairs.

***

Melody was on her way to her van when she saw the boy's face at the basement window. He was knocking hard on the glass and calling for help. She moved closer. A woman's face flashed behind the boy, caught in a moonbeam. Kim Loomis.

Their eyes met.

Kim pried the boy away from the window as Melody sprinted back inside the house. She yanked open the basement door. Kim's arm was around the boy's chest, two steps from the top. There was a knife in her other hand.

Melody's leg kicked forward. The heel of one of her Doc Martens crunched into Kim's nose. Blood squirted and her head jerked backward. Kim lost her balance and tumbled down the stairs, taking the boy with her.

Melody's legs pumped down toward Kim's prone body. She launched a kick into her ribs. Kim screamed and scrambled to her feet, waving the knife in Melody's face. The boy lay still on the ground.

Melody reached inside her jacket and Kim charged. The knife sliced toward her in an overhand arc, blade glinting. She feinted left, clamped a hand around Kim's wrist, and jabbed her with two quick punches. The blows stunned Kim. The knife clattered to the floor. Kim collapsed and Melody fell on her, gouging her eyes with her thumbs. She grabbed Kim's hair and slammed her head repeatedly into the tiles, cracking her skull, not stopping until the back of her head had become a soggy mess. Breathing hard, she checked for a pulse. There was none.

She went to the boy. He was moaning. Melody scooped him into her arms and carried him out of the basement, laid him on the ground outside. She shook him, patted his face.

"Hey, kid, wake up."

His eyes fluttered open. Melody gathered him into her arms, hugged him. "Kim's dead, kid. You don't have to be afraid."

He cried and thanked her in a hoarse whisper.

"It's okay," she said. "You're going home. Do you know how long you were in there?"

"No. She killed my friend, and some other people."

"What's your name?"

"Corey."

"Corey, listen. Do you know where you live?"

"I live on this street. It's not far."

"Can you walk?"

"I'll try."

She took both of his hands and pulled him to his feet.

"When we get to the road, point out your house, okay?"

"Okay. Thank you. Really, thank you for not leaving me."

They walked slowly down the driveway, hand in hand. She had to get out of there, should already have been far away by now. But she couldn't leave him.

The road was deserted. Fifty or so yards along it, they stopped. Corey pointed. "That's my house," he said, wincing with the effort.

"Corey, I need a favor. You can't tell anyone you saw me, okay?"

"Why? You saved me."

"Please, Corey. It's all I ask. I'm no one's hero. You never saw me."

He nodded. "Okay," he said. "If that's what you want."

"What are you going to tell the police?"

"Whatever I want. Can't remember much, you know?"

Melody liked the kid instantly. Someone was definitely missing this one.

"Mrs. Loomis. She took people's organs."

"I saw the little lab she had down there," Melody said, "and the medical manuals."

Melody was officially retired. No more hits. She had to find Rosa.

"Go on, Corey," she said. "Go home."

Melody walked fast toward the Loomis house. She looked back. Corey was watching her, a smile on his lips, his hand raised in a salute.

He limped across the lawn, to the place that feels like nowhere else on earth.

Home.

ONE HUNDRED AND FIVE

KARA PULLED THE FORD OVER ON MAIN STREET, STOPPING well short of the police cordon around Loomis Hall. She'd never seen so many police vehicles, except in movies. She turned up the volume on the radio, listened as the newsreader said, "Kim Loomis, a suspect in a spate of murders, was found dead…Raymond Porter, a lieutenant in the Major Crimes Unit, was arrested this morning as part of an ongoing investigation into the trafficking of human organs for transplantation…"

She picked up the paper Kim had given her and read the name and address, executed a three-point turn and drove away.

**

Pete Dewsbury knocked on Lena Fairbanks' door, rattling it in its frame. His other hand held an eviction notice. He had been patient to a fault but Lena had to leave, no matter how much he sympathized with her recent loss. Pete knew how hard it was to be a tenant. He had rented enough apartments and houses in his time to know the sense of insecurity that living in someone else's house brought on. This house was his retirement plan, and it hadn't worked out. He was selling it. He'd had enough of being a landlord. Which was saying something. Not much fazed Pete Dewsbury. He was a former marine, four tours of Iraq and three in Afghanistan under his belt. But renting to Lena Fairbanks had pushed him to the brink.

"Lena, goddammit. Open up."

He twisted the doorknob and it gave way. She'd left the door unlocked. Great.

"I'm coming in, Lena. Hope you're decent."

The body hanging from the banister was bloated, and his eyes stung from the stench of the foul gases that had accumulated. He moved closer, hand over his mouth and nose. It was Lena. She had probably known this day was coming and decided she'd had enough, too. Pete took no pleasure in evicting her. He was on the hook for the mortgage, and the bank didn't care what the circumstances were; they were only interested in getting paid.

There were two notes taped to her chest. He read one:

> *Hi, Pete. I left some money for you on the table. It's not much, but it's all I have. I'm sorry I caused you any trouble. I haven't been well. I hope you can forgive me. You probably found my body, and I'm sorry for that, too. Yours, Lena.*

Christ, she didn't have to go this far. He would have found a way to help her out somehow. Until he read the second note:

> *My name is Lena Fairbanks. I loved my son but I needed money. I made a deal with the devil. Kim Loomis and I had an agreement. I sold her Evan for ten thousand dollars, and in return she promised he wouldn't suffer. But I see him everywhere. I can't take it. Kim lied. He did suffer. He haunts me. I'm sorry.*